ASHES TO ASHES

Books by Gwen Hunter

The DeLande Saga:
BETRAYAL
FALSE TRUTHS
LAW OF THE WILD

———

Rhea Lynch, MD. Series:
DELAYED DIAGNOSIS
PRESCRIBED DANGER
DEADLY REMEDY
GRAVE CONCERNS

———

Ashlee Chadwick Davenport Novels:
ASHES TO ASHES
SLEEP SOFTLY

———

Stand-alones:
SHADOW VALLEY
BLOODSTONE
BLACKWATER SECRETS
RAPID DESCENT

ASHES TO ASHES

Gwen Hunter

ASHES TO ASHES
ISBN 978-1-933523-17-0

Copyright © 2010 by Gwen Hunter

First USA printing: December 2010

Library of Congress Control Number: 2010941565

Previously published in Great Britain by Hodder & Stoughton. 1996; ISBN: 0340637994

Printed in the United States of America on acid-free paper.

10   9   8   7   6   5   4   3   2   1

To my husband Rod –
For being strong and determined in the face of difficulty,
Moral and upright in the face of adversity.
For never taking the easy way out.
And for knowing that love is more than an emotion, it is a decision.

ACKNOWLEDGMENTS

For help in Real Estate Developments and associated problems, I thank Ralph Norman.

For help in Rescue Squad scenes and proper lingo, thanks go to Kenneth Craig, Ted Bowden, and Shane Stuart, and Amanda Philbeck. For periodontal disease information, thanks to Dr. Cody Fishburne. For help in veterinary scenes and information, thanks to Dr. Michael Ferguson and Dr. Eric Setzer.

For help with horses, I thank Mike and Pam Hege, and Kathern Hege. For info about turkey-shoots, thanks go to Richard Copeland. For help with A-flats, thank you to Sheldon Timmerman.

I thank Bob Prater, my dad, for answering a thousand questions at the drop of a hat.

For colloquial "cuss" words, I thank Joe and Pat Gentry, Chris Cogburn, Betty Cryer, and my Maw-Maw, now deceased, Gladys Bass Hennigan.

For reading and re-reading this book and for all the helpful suggestions, I thank my mother, Joyce Wright.

ASHES TO ASHES

PROLOGUE

I invited death into my home.

Oh, I never thought about it in exactly those terms, with exactly those words, but that's what I did. I issued a formal invitation, then stood back and waited for death to move in, make himself at home, put up his feet and stay. Like a guest who quietly takes over, surrounding your life with his own until he belongs there as much as you, and asking him to leave is impossible.

I did that with death. All unknowing and innocent, all guileless and full of kind intentions. And I paid the price.

There is a price for everything. Jack taught me that. In his insistent, determined, and deliberate way, my husband taught me everything about life—and by his death, started me on the journey into the past, his past, searching for meaning amidst lies and deceit and ruin.

The end of the journey was the same as the beginning. Death. Just death. Death of dreams. Death of illusion. Death of truth as I had known it.

And the curious antithesis of death. Resurrection. A new beginning. Whether I wanted it or not.

CHAPTER ONE

Jack died in late spring, when the wisteria and dogwoods no longer have blooms. When the jonquils and daffodils and early blooming irises hang, wrinkled and brown, on their stiff green stems. When the heat is bearable by day and the night breezes are enough to cool the house. When blankets are kept handy for the occasional dip in temperature that makes the gooseflesh rise by morning. Brisk. That's what they call the time of year he left me.

It was quick. He didn't suffer. Dr. Hoffman told me that in the ER, where I stood afterward, shivering and blank-eyed and bewildered. He didn't suffer. He just . . . went. A single, massive, intracranial bleed.

He was dead when the EMTs arrived. They knew it. I could see it on their faces. A major artery had burst in his head, and he had fractured his skull when he fell. Jack was dead when he hit the floor. The blood from Jack's ears and nose and mouth proved it. The bloody tears that seeped down his blue face confirmed it. But I was doing CPR when the medics arrived, his blood all over my mouth. Ground into my hands. And they had no choice but to continue.

We compressed his chest. We breathed for him. All the way to the hospital emergency room where I worked as a nurse, I gave feverish orders in the back of the ambulance. Administered drugs. Shocked him over and over again.

The EMTs, out of sympathy for me and respect for the dead, permitted my futile attempts. A paramedic or a stranger might have gone by the official protocol and forced me to ride up front, following a standardized outline, a formalized list of priorities. But I knew these guys. Had worked with them for years in the emergency room and in the field at accident scenes and drownings, crisis situations handled by the county's volunteer Rescue Squad.

So, out of pity, and out of custom, they let me run the code. For all the dark and lonely miles of narrow farm country roads, they let me do what I could to save a life already bequeathed to the hand of God.

By the time we arrived I had Jack intubated with a long, firm plastic tube in his lungs, an IV in his right arm running LR—lactated ringers—and another in his left running normal saline. I never checked his pupils beyond that first time. Fixed and dilated. A certain sign of brain death. But I couldn't let him go. Not then, when I still believed in the man I thought him to be.

And now it was weeks later, the funeral long past. The cut flowers in their plastic urns had curled and withered, the grave where they buried Jack was no longer a fresh red scar in the green sward of cemetery lawn. The condolence calls and visits by the church members had slowed. My Nana no longer came every morning and every night to sit with me while I cried, and . . . the sun still rose in the mornings and I was still alive. And alone. The Jack I thought I knew still hadn't come home to fill the empty place at the table. To curl around me at night spoon fashion, sharing business concerns and tidbits of his day. To make me laugh and feel safe.

I knew he never would.

I had been trying for the last week to find the strength to begin my life again, to pick up the shattered pieces and start over. To leave the safe confines of my home and blink my way into the bright glare of the world, like a bear emerging from hibernation at the end of a too-long winter.

I had called Lynnie Bee, my supervisor, and requested an end to my leave of absence. But now that it was the day for me to return to work, to walk back into the same room where Jack had died, I found myself retreating, longing to crawl beneath the covers and hide just one more day.

I couldn't. I knew that. But the tears had started the moment I opened my eyes, and I had accomplished nothing, though I had been awake since long before dawn.

I was standing in my closet, choosing a uniform from among my scant supply of "skinny clothes" in preparation for my first day back on the job, when I heard the first, faint jingle of the phone. It was followed by the even fainter, dull voice of the personal line's answering machine.

I seldom answered the phone anymore; even more seldom did I listen to my messages. I just didn't have the energy to deal with the world, now that Jack was gone. But for some reason, just this once, I stepped out of my room and listened.

The amorphous, asexual, computer-generated voice spoke its generic message and sounded its banal tone. I listened as the man on the other end changed my life—again—forever.

"Jack. It's Bill. Pick up the phone."

The voice was gruff, brusque, the words commanding. Moving slowly, my bare feet on the satiny, hardwood floor, I stepped down the hallway toward the small table holding the phone and answering machine.

"Jack, damn it, pick up the phone. I know this is your private number. I paid plenty for the listing." There was a short pause, as if Bill expected Jack to answer. "If you want to play hardball, you picked the wrong man. I have contacts you don't know about."

Again there was a short pause and I stopped before the old machine, chilled by the air conditioner blowing icy air beneath my T-shirt. I crossed my arms and shivered slightly.

"It's been six weeks, damn it. You said you only needed four. I've been more than fair."

I trembled with uncertainty and the cold, lifting my right hand. It hovered over the receiver, pale and thin.

"You promised me restitution, you thieving bastard. I've got a kid in med school," he added. "And if he doesn't hear from me soon, he'll have to drop out."

I rested my hand on the cool plastic of the phone. The air conditioning went off, leaving the house still and icy. Jasmine, my daughter, had been adjusting the thermostat again. She and Jack liked it cold in the house. Too cold for my comfort.

"You son-of-a-bitch! If you're trying to get out of compensating me for damages then you've got a bigger fight on your hands than you ever bargained for." The pause was even longer this time, and when he spoke again, his voice was lower, a coarse growl. "It's been six weeks, damn you," he repeated. "If you don't pick up this phone, I'll see you in Columbia, in front of a judge. I'll ruin you, you sanctimonious son-of-a—"

The machine clicked off in mid curse. The silence of the house wrapped around me, a cloak of loneliness and solitude. The cold gripped me, and raising my left hand, I adjusted the thermostat up five degrees into a more temperate zone. My heart seemed to slow, the hallway wavering around me as shadows moved and shifted. I licked my lips, salty with old tears.

I looked again at the phone, my skin white against the maroon plastic. Dark red . . . one of Jack's colors. Power colors, he called them. Parts of the message came suddenly clear, as if my mind dilated, focusing on the words. Depraved words, words of a madman.

Six weeks? Jack had only been dead that long. How had . . . Bill, was it? . . . gotten the personal line's number? It was listed in my name. *Six weeks?* And then other parts of the one-sided conversation began to penetrate the haze in which I had wrapped myself.

Restitution? Jack had never cheated anyone in his life. Jack had been a saint. Tears spilled over and traced fresh tracks down my chapped face.

Turning, I moved down the hallway, the house still dark in the gray, post-dawn light. In the stillness of the empty house, I stepped into Jack's office, my toes sinking into the rich pile of deep red carpet. Intended originally as a study, the office was L-shaped, built on to the front and side of the house. Jack had added onto it over the years, enlarging the space to include a small conference room, a secretary's office, and a fireproof storage room built like a vault, keeping plans and financial records safe. Inside the small room was an old-fashioned black bank safe from the forties where Jack kept important papers. He liked— had liked—old technology, like the answering machine, his ancient adding machine, and the safe.

Although the day-to-day business of DavInc, as Jack called his myriad real estate development companies, took place on the jobsites in various developments, the paperwork had been generated here. The brainstorming, deal making, problem solving, and long-range planning transpired here, and the legal papers were here, locked in the safe. I opened the blinds. A rosy glow brightened the rooms.

Hunting prints hung on the paneled walls, dogs and turkeys and bucks, a seascape with sea oats waving in an invisible breeze. Photos of Jas and me. The head of the twelve-point buck I had killed took center stage of one whole wall, surrounded by dozens of Jack's kills from over the years. None was larger than mine, a fact Jack had boasted of to his men friends without mentioning the circumstances of the accidental kill. Awards, diplomas, and maps dotted the other walls. Photos of past developments, slick advertising shots, were framed and hung between.

Upholstered, low-backed chairs squatted in the reception area, leather-covered chairs everywhere else. The dark carpet was still marked with Jack's footprints. His gun cabinet stood by the door to the hallway, solid and dark and ugly, filled with the handguns and antique weapons he collected. I hated having guns in the house. Jack and I had argued about their presence for years, one of the few subjects over which we ever disagreed.

Dust lay like a fine gauze veil over everything. The room smelled musty. The business answering machine blinked a steady red rhythm. I stood over it, alien-looking in the dim light. The house was hushed around me, as if it too were curious about the machine's recordings.

I pressed PLAY.

And listened to Peter Howell's voice as he told Jack he would be in late to work in the morning. He had called at ten-fifteen P.M. the night Jack died. At that exact moment, I had been standing in a corner of the Cardiac Room in the ER, watching a first response team cut away the rest of Jack's clothes as they worked to revive him. Watching Jack's feet turn blue.

Tears were trailing steadily down my face; I wiped them with shaking fingers. The next six messages were shocked calls from Jack's subcontractors, two clients calling with condolences, and Esther, Jack's secretary.

And then the infamous Bill. This was a calmer Bill, his voice sounding only slightly concerned, telling Jack he appreciated the meeting on Tuesday afternoon, and the calls Jack had made to Paul Wilkes, the North Carolina governor. And he looked forward to a "resolution of the situation." All in all, it wasn't a very helpful message.

There were over three dozen messages covering the following weeks, weeks I had ignored the office, the development out at Davenport Hills, the business entirely. Without thinking, I picked up the pad and pen beside the phone and began making notes, just as I would have if Jack had been here. At some point, my tears dried.

Between messages, I jotted notes in the margins, small things that needed attention, possible solutions to the site problems mentioned, though often as not, Peter Howell would leave a second message with the solution he had worked out. However, Peter himself had a problem that I should have handled weeks ago. Payments on short-term operating costs out at the development were seriously overdue. Work on roads and housing construction had been about to shut down just two weeks after Jack died.

I sniffed. Jack didn't believe in power of attorney for employees. He signed each check drawn on almost every account, overseeing all areas of DavInc. No bit of minutia escaped his notice. Jack had been a control freak, an A type personality, obsessive-compulsive about every aspect of his life. Yet, he had the charisma to pull it off without becoming an ogre.

Even when bulldozing his way through a business meeting, forcing other, powerful men to bow to his will and preferences, he was so charming that they went away happy, convinced that Jack was a brilliant businessman who had their interests at heart. Jack always got his way.

I smiled as I wrote up the next message, a petty complaint from some rich, whining housewife that her kitchen floor was coming up beneath the refrigerator and that her house stank. It sounded like she had a leak. A bad one apparently. I made a note to have Peter get the plumbing contractor back over there, pronto.

Yes, Jack had always gotten his way. My Jack, who could handle anything. I looked at my ring, the two-carat diamond he had insisted I wear the night we went to tell my parents I was pregnant and that we were getting married in two weeks.

Even then he had been certain of success. Success in winning me.

I was nineteen, and halfway through nursing school at Presbyterian Hospital, while Jack was nearly thirty-four and never married. I had pursued him recklessly and seduced him with all the intensity of my innocent teenaged heart. He was far too old for me and guilty of disgracing the child of his business partner . . . but he was rich. And that, after all, was what mattered to my mother. The money overrode the shame. The money overrode everything. Jack had known that. And Jack had won, then as always.

He had swept me up from my dorm and carried me to his car, much to the amusement of my friends hanging out the windows. And though he hadn't called in over two days prior to that, and though I had been both frantic with worry and furious with him, and though I had determined to ignore him completely when he did finally call, I wrapped my arms around his neck and held on.

"I wanted to wait till you were out of school, but since I can't stand it when we aren't together, and since we managed to get you pregnant with my son and heir, I decided it needed to be now." He dumped me into the front seat and ran to the driver's side, gunned the motor and took off down the road. He proposed as he drove, a reckless grin on his face, the wind tearing through his hair.

"Marry me. And wear this." He tossed me a velvet ring box. "I haven't had it sized yet, so don't lose it."

"Marry you? I haven't heard from you in two days. I thought you were dumping me," I wailed. "Why haven't you called? Or come by?"

Jack looked at me a moment before snapping his eyes back to the road. There was a devilish glint in his eyes. "I had to buy the ring. And get the preacher. And make the honeymoon plans. I've been busy. What do you think about Italy? I've never been there. Do you have a passport? And by the way, if it isn't a son, don't worry about it. We can always do that next time."

I had laughed then, through my tears, and placed the ring on my finger. Jack had taken care of everything from then on. My parents, my future, my very life. And now he was gone.

Bill's voice on the machine forced me back to the present. My smile slipped away. "It's been four weeks and two days, Jack. Call me." He hung up. I had never heard anyone order Jack around. US senators were polite to Jack. Bankers were polite to Jack. Even my mother was polite to Jack, and my mother . . . well . . . was my mother.

Then Peter Howell again. He sounded desperate, needing checks written, or access to the accounts. I stood there, in my T-shirt and bare feet, ashamed. I looked at Esther's desk. It was locked, the checkbooks in the side drawer. The message was two weeks old. Why hadn't someone come to the house? They all knew where I was.

Bret McDermott had left a message just after Peter's. Bret, DavInc's banker, was a local boy made good. Starting out as a teller in the Dawkins County Savings and Loan, he had moved up fast through promotions and mergers. Now, he held a vice-presidency in the prestigious First America Bank, working in the bank's Charlotte headquarters some thirty-five miles away.

Bret had solved Peter's dilemma, transferring funds from DavInc's line of credit into Peter's petty cash account. Bret could do that without Jack's signature, although the petty cash account had never been intended to handle such large sums of money. It was a financial loophole Jack would have closed had he spotted it, and it was a smart move on Bret's part.

I hadn't known Bret and Peter were acquainted. Interesting. I'd have to tell Jac— The thought cut off, mid-conception.

"Jack, it's been five weeks. I have bills and problems of my own. My lawyers are getting antsy and want to hear from you. Don't make me take this to court. I don't want the legal fees, and I don't really want to see you ruined. Call me." Bill hung up.

"Court?" I murmured to the quiet office. It was the same thing he had said earlier, about seeing Jack in Columbia, in front of a judge. Only Federal Criminal Court and large Civil Court cases met in the state capitol.

The next three messages were from Bill, each one more vituperative and angry than the last. But not once did he explain the nature of the problem. Jack had known what was going on. Jack had been handling . . . something.

I looked around the dusty office. It offered no clues.

The last message from Bill was left the night before. It was similar to the threat I had heard on the personal line only an hour past.

"Jack. This's Bill. When you cheat a man, you have two options. One is to make restitution. The other is to go to court and be exposed as the thieving bastard you are. Either way, I'll get what's mine." His voice sounded slurred, as if he had stopped off at the local bar before placing the call. "And if the courts wont handle it, I'll handle it myself. Just you and me." The phone went dead, the little red light no longer blinking up at me. I opened the door of the machine and removed the incoming digital message card and replaced it with a spare from the drawer beneath.

"Court." Jack would never cheat anyone. He had been a deacon in the First Baptist Church of Dorsey City. Jack was a trustee. A member of the County Council. Jack had a reputation as an honest man. Jack was gone.

The tremor was back in my fingers.

I walked down the hallway, into the master suite, yanked on a pair of old jeans and sneakers. Changed T-shirts. Pulled a nurse's scrub suit from the closet at random and tossed it on the chair beside the unmade bed. It no longer seemed important what I would wear back to work this afternoon. Any old thing would do.

Upstairs, it was silent, Jasmine already at the barn, helping Jimmy Ray feed the horses—if he bothered to show up for work, that is. Jimmy Ray, a twenty-year-old, high school dropout, helped out at the farm whenever he was sober, which was less and less often these days. Even he seemed to fall apart after Jack died. After checking to see that Jimmy's battered old truck was indeed parked out back, I returned to the office and flipped on an overhead light. Where to start?

Esther, Jack's secretary, had once kept the office up to date and organized, but I didn't want to call her. Not about this. Not until I knew what was going on.

There were two sets of file cabinets in Jack's fireproof room. One set housed old business. The other cabinet held newer stuff. And this definitely was a new problem.

The top two drawers were for Davenport Hills, the most ambitious real estate project Jack had ever undertaken. It was so huge, it would one day be a town, just off I-77, between Charlotte, North Carolina and Columbia, South Carolina. It involved hundreds of acres and millions of dollars. And I knew it was beyond me the moment I started on the files.

Contracts full of legal mumbo-jumbo, I set on the worktable in the conference room. Computer printouts of overhead costs went nearby. The list of investors in the project I studied, recognizing a few names. There was no Bill. No William either. Setting the list of investors aside, I plowed through the file cabinet, not recognizing half of the contents. Until I found a file of letters from the investors. They were careful letters, offering support and help, but which actually said little of substance; the only thing they had in common was Davenport Hills and some problem. It had to be a major problem, to have the investors all tiptoeing around it.

Jack had never mentioned a problem of any great importance to me. But then, Jack had never mentioned a Bill to me either. Bill who?

At the back of the file, I found a letter written by Jack. It was a memo, the kind of thing he would compose before giving his notes to Esther to key in and revise. Unfinished, unsigned, undated, it was handwritten in Jack's careful script on company letterhead, the errors scratched out with neat x's the way Jack always did.

I wanted no part of this. You gave me your solemn assurance that no one would be hurt, and now the inspector is dead. It should have been a paper problem, not something that needed your special talents and connections. xxxx It shouldn't have required such extreme measures to clear the way for use of the land. Because of your incompetence, the entire project is in danger. But be aware, xxxx I have managed to retain the evidence. All of it. If this comes to light, you will take the lion's share of responsibility, and criminal consequences will fall on you and your man. I will not go to jail for murder.

I sat down slowly on the leather chair. It sighed beneath me, a melancholy sound, half grief, half shock. A numb heat flushed through me and was gone. Placing the file on the table, I went through the investors' letters again. Surprisingly, some were from Senator Vance Waldrop, a democrat from South Carolina. Reading them carefully, I tried to fit the word "murder" in place of "problem", tried to read between the lines. But nothing fit. Nothing made sense.

Shaking, though no longer from the cold, I gathered up the file and the list of investors and went to Jack's desk. I sat in Jack's chair, the file with his letter on top, open before me on the desk. Dust motes wafted in the pinkish, early light from the windows.

I read the letter again, carefully, hoping for some other interpretation. Hoping for something to wipe away the meaning of the last word. Murder. The words were the same the second time I read them. And the third. I looked away from Jack's writing, my eyes unfocused in the dim room. After a long moment, I paged through the files, studying each piece of paper for . . . something. I wasn't certain what.

The financing for the development was provided half by private investors, half by First America Bank through Bret McDermott. The individual investors comprised a small list put together by Jack:

Virginia Reaburn Waldrop (Wife of Senator Vance Waldrop. Vance was a flamboyant elected official of the old style, dealing in good-ol-boy, homegrown rhetoric and convenient politics. I didn't like Vance, but Jack had liked his influence in government circles.)

Taylor, Inc. (A rival investment company whose appearance on the list was surprising.)

S&B Investments, Inc. (A company put together by the husband of an old school friend, Monica Beck. S&B had invested with Jack for years.)

Caldwell and Caldwell, Inc. (My parent's company.)

Hamilton Holdings (My Nana's company.)

MJM Investments

Enterprise Investments

Carolina First, Inc.

All companies I didn't recognize. And no "Bill".

And then there was Bret McDermott.

I had a feeling it wasn't exactly ethical for Bret to have a finger in the pie as an individual as well as a banking big-wig, but then ethics were bent so often in this business that if you could actually see them, they would all look like pretzels. Jack's words. I smiled at the memory. Jack, of course, was above such bending. *Wasn't he?* A small voice at the back of my mind whispered the question. My smile faltered.

Tilting the desk lamp, I reached beneath it and removed the key that opened Jack's desk. A singularly simple hiding place, but then, this part of Dawkins County was practically crime free. Security measures were more trouble than they were worth out here, as Jack had discovered after he had the tamperproof safe installed in the vault room. It had been an expensive lesson.

The center desk drawer opened with a slight click and revealed little of interest. Paper clips, a box of staples, White-Out, several of the fine-tipped pens Jack used, a nail clipper, phone book, small calculator and electronic address book programmed with Jack's subcontractors. There was a leather business card folder, tape, a New Testament, small calendar, checkbook, his cell phone, the battery long dead. Stuff. Nothing helpful. Nothing that said "Murder. Look here."

Jack's briefcase was on top of the desk, the clasps open. I lifted the lid and peered inside. Just the usual jumble of bits of paper, two business checkbooks, pens, several sets of folded houseplans. A miniature road map of Davenport Hills with the velum overlay he had been working on the night he died. A lot of contractors went with CAD, a computerized program for builders and developers, but Jack liked hands-on plans.

This set of papers and vellum contained the solution to a standing-water problem on the newest golf course. A costly problem to correct, but nothing to do with murder. I closed the lid. Opened the bottom side drawer. There were weekly and monthly company record books.

Paperwork for the different corporations. Tax notices. More stuff, but not murder stuff. Closing it, I opened the top drawer.

My eyes settled on the photograph, focused and stayed still. A hot sweat broke out, beading around my chest. I tried to take a breath and couldn't. A suffocating heat cloaked me. Long seconds went by. All I could see was the photograph.

The air conditioning came on, cooling my suddenly hot skin. I blinked. In a stretchy, elastic moment, time dilated and condensed, whorled and steadied. I reached into the drawer and removed the photograph. All of the photographs.

The one on top was a woman. A tall, slender, beautiful woman, stretched out on beach sand in the sun, her skin glistening with oil. Her dark hair was braided and curled around to lie between her naked breasts.

It was Robyn. Jack's former secretary. My best friend.

I forced a breath into my lungs. The air made a tortured sound. The second photograph was more revealing. Robyn, naked, playing in the surf, on some deserted beach, long ago. I studied it, not thinking, not feeling. Just seeing. I scanned slowly through the rest of the shots, feeling breathless . . . fouled.

There were perhaps sixty photographs, most of them of Robyn in various stages of undress. In some of them, she was with Jack. These photos were tilted or slightly out of focus, as if they had been taken on a timer. Jack and Robyn were making love.

I felt nothing. A curious, sterile, lack of feeling. Slowly, I went back through the photos, studying each one carefully. Memorizing the play of light on Robyn's skin. Seeing for the first time what her face looked like in passion. Learning all over again what Jack's face looked like when he was aroused.

When I had searched each face, each expression, when I had examined each photo with painstaking deliberation, I stacked them carefully against the desk top. Aligning the edges, my fingers moving in the strange light like a card sharp at a dusty poker table.

When they were perfectly stacked, I stood, and carrying the files and the photos, I left the office, shutting off the lights. Closing the door. In the kitchen, I chose a plastic grocery bag the cleaning crew had folded and put in the recycling basket beneath the sink. Inside, I placed the photos, the file of letters, the list of investors, and the murder letter. I tied the handles and hid the bag in my bedroom closet beneath my winter boots.

I didn't stop to think about my mother, who would have done the same thing to block out an unpleasantness. I didn't consider that I was hiding from a truth I needed to face. My only consideration was Jasmine. That she not discover any of this. That she never know about her father and his affair.

Firmly, I closed the closet doors, my palms flat on the painted raised panels. They made a solid sound, final and hollow.

A light tap sounded on the bedroom door. Jas' knock. Three beats, a pause, and three beats. Before I could answer, she entered. Jas was taller than I, slender, and bronzed by the sun, but she looked older than I remembered from just weeks ago. Somber. Her face was marked with grief and drawn tight with tears; my heart turned over at the sight.

We had grieved together for the first few days after Jack died, leaning on one another, crying and comforting one another. But since then, Jas had stayed apart from me, mourning in solitude with only the horses for comfort—Jack's horses, the huge, black Friesian work horses my husband had bred. It was a habit she acquired as a child, withdrawing from people, clinging to horses when life went wrong. This time, solitude had not been good for my baby.

"Mom?" Tentative tones, so unlike my usually decisive, strong-willed child. "Mama?"

My hands were still on the closet doors, and Jas didn't immediately see me. Her large brown eyes took in the unmade bed, sheets soiled, unchanged since before the funeral. Jack's dirty jeans piled on the floor, his shoes beside the bed, one on its side, unmoved since he died. There was a layer of dust over everything. She grimaced.

I almost smiled, but my skin felt stiff, frozen by old tears into a chapped mask. Jas was neatness personified. She and Jack had regularly straightened up the house between visits by the cleaning crew. I never had.

"Looks like a museum," she muttered.

I did smile then, and my face didn't crack. The motion just pulled unused muscles against my skin. "Yes, it does," I agreed. Jas jumped. "Want to help me clean it up?"

She stared at me, my ratty hair pulled back into a ponytail, my tear-chapped skin and out-of-date clothes. I thought she might comment on my appearance. Instead, a peculiar expression crossed her face, a look heavy with shades of emotion. Tenderness. Fear. Determination—as if she had reached a decision and was here to follow through with it. And then the emotions vanished, and only tears remained, misery swimming in her eyes.

She shrugged and whispered, "I miss Daddy," wretched and fighting tears I hadn't seen in days. "And I'm worried . . ." she took a deep breath, ". . . about you."

I suddenly recognized the extra burden I had placed on my child when I allowed her to grieve alone. Perhaps it was her nature to turn to horses instead of people, but Jas needed my comfort, whether she knew it or not. My child needed security and stability, not the worry of whether I would survive Jack's death.

Holding out my arms, I reached for my baby girl. My nearly grown, only child. I held her as she cried, my own eyes dry and hot, our arms around each other for comfort, Jasmine's tears falling into my tangled hair from her greater height. The tears fell for only a short time, as if she had used up all the heavy grieving. As if she needed only this small moment in my arms to find a reassurance she had lost. Afterward, we simply stood there, silent, sharing our warmth.

When we stepped apart, Jas was smiling, a smudge I hadn't noticed before smeared across her cheek. "Daddy would have really hated this mess, you know."

I frowned, looking at the room. "Are you volunteering to help?"

"Sure. And we can go to Miccah's for lunch. And then we can buy groceries." Her eyebrows went up, making the point that the kitchen pantry was empty. Jas sounded like her old self again, resolute and determined, and just a little bit bossy. "And if we have time, we could walk down to Nana's," she added, pointing out that I hadn't been to visit my grandmother in weeks.

She was so resilient in her youth. The world could move beneath her, quaking and heaving, and she would flex and spring with the motion. I felt my own inflexibility keenly, staring up at her. My world had changed around me twice now. Once with Jack's death, and again only minutes past, with proof of his infidelity. A betrayal that had left me feeling seared, like a wound cauterized by brutal surgery. I put that thought aside for later consideration, and smiled again.

"I take it you've made a decision not to hide in the barn anymore?" I teased, moving into the bathroom and facing myself in the mirror. I flinched at the sight. I really was a mess, all puffy and red and hollow-eyed. I focused on her reflection over my shoulder, her clean, soft beauty, skin pink and young.

I took a deep breath. The movement hurt my ribs. I was sore from hours, weeks, of solitary crying. "Miccah's, huh?" It was Jack's favorite restaurant, a dark, rough paneled place with uncomfortable booth seats, cobwebbed lighting fixtures, and delectable food. Left to my own choices, I would never have passed through the door again.

"Yeah. They have a special on shrimp and crab legs." It was my favorite. I used to salivate at just the mention of shrimp and crab. Jas was watching my face in the mirror as she spoke. I was being manipulated.

Sighing, I turned the shower spray to hot and pulled off my T-shirt, tossed it into the laundry bin. The rest of my clothes followed, clothes I had worn as I looked at photographs of Jack and Robyn. I stepped into the shower, feeling dirty and sweat-slick.

Jas had only one parent left. On my own I might have hibernated for months, but for Jasmine's sake, it was time to get on with my life. She might be nearly grown, nearly ready to move ahead with her own life, but for now, Jas needed me. And though she didn't know it, she needed me to clean out Jack's office, deal with the troubling hints of wrongdoing, and destroy the evidence of his long ago affair with Robyn. She needed to *never* know the truth I had discovered.

"How much weight have you lost?" she said over the sound of the water.

I paused, a hand on the liquid soap. "I don't know," I fibbed. I did know. Seventeen pounds. But I wasn't going to admit it. Jas had been trying to feed me for weeks and I had been tossing plates of post-funeral food out to the dogs. "Not enough in my thighs," I added, looking down.

"I can see your bones," she yelled as I closed the door and steam boiled up around me.

I pretended not to hear, burying my head beneath the scalding spray. When I got out of the shower long minutes later, the bed was stripped, the vacuum was roaring and Jack's shoes had been placed neatly in his closet. Another part of him was gone. I waited for the tears, the misery, the pain. But there was nothing except a numb emptiness.

Scrubbing my hair dry with a towel, I pulled out the cosmetics that might help heal my tear-dried skin. Or at least hide the worst of the damage. Fortified with makeup, I entered the closet I had shared with Jack and considered my wardrobe. Especially the "skinny clothes" I had saved from the last time I was this small. They were hopelessly out of style.

CHAPTER TWO

I leaned back, relaxing against the Jeep's padded headrest, and closed my eyes. It had been an easy, quiet night at work, this first night back in the ER since Jack died, due to the rain that fell in a steady sheet for six hours. I had been hoping for a busy evening, wide open, full of traumas and codes, people who needed me. Instead, by the end of my shift, I had helped treat a dozen sickly babies, one bi-lateral pneumonia in a nursing home patient, two headaches, and a drunk who had spent his disability check on several cases of malt liquor instead of his prescription Phenobarbital. He had a bad case of DTs mixed with grand mal seizures. Not a pretty sight. Dawkins County Hospital had several "regulars" who routinely drank away their medication money.

ER nurses and doctors often had a difficult time working with noncompliant patients, and drunks were the worst. Alcoholism was a disease, but compassion was difficult when a man was vomiting, seizing, cursing and kicking, all symptoms he could have avoided had he stayed on the wagon and taken his medicine.

Compassion was the first thing to go in my profession, and I had long ago become cynical about most of the patients who frequented the emergency room. Yet I loved my job, still derived satisfaction from being a nurse, still needed the rush of adrenaline and victory when we brought someone back from the edge of death. It didn't happen often in such a small, rural hospital, but it did happen, and I had missed the excitement, the frenzied tumult of traumas and turmoil.

Then I remembered Jack, his hands and bare feet blue, his face mottled and purpled and crusted over with blood. Tubes hanging from his mouth and arms. His clothes in a heap on the floor, jagged edges where they had been cut away by my friends trying to save his life. And then I remembered the photographs.

I started the motor and the Jeep roared to life before settling into a heavy thrum. It had been Jack's Jeep; now it was mine. Placing my hands where his had rested, I pulled out of the parking lot and left the Dawkins County Hospital behind.

Hospital property was county land, outside of Dorsey City—called DorCity by the locals—and was located near the FHA—the Federal

Housing Authority—the sheriff's department, the county jail, and the highway department, "near" being a relative term in the empty square miles of undeveloped land. There were miles of rolling hills, fields, pasture, and acres of timber and forest between each county building. As the hospital lights faded behind me, I called Jas to tell her I was on my way home. It was an old ritual, begun many years ago when Jack had worried about me traveling alone. The cell phone was for vehicular emergencies. The 9mm locked in the glove box was for trouble.

I had never needed the gun, except for the time I hit a deer with my car near midnight. It totaled my car and left the deer in agony. I'd emptied the ammunition clip into his thrashing form, caught in my headlights. That was the twelve-pointer mounted in Jack's office with a bronze plaque bearing my name and the date of my kill.

I got the answering machine at home, left a short message, and hit the end call button. Jas was still with Topaz, the two girls out cruising. Jas had her own cell and a .32 locked in her glove box, the only legal place to carry a loaded weapon in a car in South Carolina. Jas was a far better shot than I and preferred a smaller weapon. I left a message on her cell too, and dropped the phone in the passenger seat.

Black night swept in as the hospital lights fell behind, and the roar of tires on asphalt was a soothing sound, the headlights reflecting off pools and brightening muddy ditches left by the earlier rain. The Jeep was the only car on the road at half-past eleven.

Dawkins is one of South Carolina's largest counties in terms of square miles; mostly rural, the wide open fields of soy, cotton, corn, and hay flashed by, broken by stands of tall pines in perfect rows, and dark, empty textile mills with cracked concrete parking lots, barred doors, and boarded up or broken windows staring into the night. Cheap foreign textile imports had cost the county thousands of jobs and seriously depleted the tax base back in the seventies, in many ways returning Dawkins to its pre-industrial, agricultural roots.

When foreign imports were mentioned, the state's most vitriolic senator would redden and splutter and offer a practiced speech, often bringing up Dawkins' unemployment rate as a result of international free trade and foreign imports. It was one of many well-rehearsed per-formances that had kept Senator Vance Waldrop in his powerful Washington position for two decades. My husband had contributed to Vance's campaigns for years and referred to the man as a friend.

Vance had come to Jack's funeral, posing with his hand in mine as the local papers snapped his photo for the next edition. I didn't like Vance and resented being used to further his career, but there was little I could do short of making a scene, and I couldn't do that to Jasmine.

The senator had called twice since the funeral to offer his con-dolences. Now I wondered if he had a hidden motive as well. Perhaps Davenport Hills and a problem that included murder? I had let the answering machine in the hallway handle his mournful words, and erased the message as soon as the connection broke. Now I wondered if that had been wise.

The bright red gleam of animal eyes caught the headlights to the right. Too high up for rabbit, possum, stray dog, or cat, the usual road-side victims. I slammed my foot down on the brake pedal. Brakes squealed, tires ground, seeking purchase on the wet asphalt. A doe dashed across the road. I pulled the wheel left. Hard. And said some-thing succinct. A phrase for which my Nana would have washed out my mouth had she heard.

The doe's back hoof was captured in the passenger headlight, up high and flying. Six inches from the glass. And then she was gone. The Jeep rocked to a sliding stop, straddling the center line. Headlights stared into woods that dropped off sharply to the side of the road.

I was breathing hard. Hot sweat prickled beneath my arms. My heart was racing, my body remembering the experience with the twelve-point buck and the accident that had totaled my car.

There was movement in the trees as the doe vanished, leaves and branches waving, tossing large droplets from the recent rain. The fact that Dawkins County had the state's largest number of deer-versus-car accidents for two years running did nothing to ease my fright.

Before I could regain a sense of calm, I pulled back into my lane and continued home, driving slower than usual and watching for the tell-tale red gleam of eyes in the bushes beside the road. Deer wouldn't lie down and sleep in heavy rain, yet they seldom ran in wet weather unless spooked. I watched for packs of wild dogs, or illegal hunters poaching in the off season. Of course, the wind alone could have startled her into my path.

Still agitated, I flipped on the radio hoping for music to settle my mind. Instead, I got Jack's favorite preacher on Jack's favorite radio station, Christian broadcasting out of Asheville.

I turned off the radio.

Slowing, I made a right at Felix's Texaco on to the unmarked road that once had been a part of Ethridge. The township had vanished with the advent of polyester in the sixties. The town's sole employers—the Ethridge family—closed the cotton gin, the depot, the corner store and Ethridge Knits. Soon after, Ethridge itself disappeared from the state maps. All that was left was a Feed and Seed Store, a couple of churches, and the local vet's office.

I took a right on to Mount Zion Church Road, drove beneath I-77 and back into the darkness as rural surroundings again enfolded me. A splatter of rain pounded the windshield. Dawkins County was a pocket of farming and textile communities, only now being introduced into the computer age. Yet, it was only minutes from the symphony, the museums, the design shops—the cultured gentility of southern city life.

Jack moved us here the first year of our marriage, trying to escape the crime and the smog and the noise of city living. We moved away from Charlotte and the social climbing obligations insisted upon by my mama and daddy, back to my family farm, to live just down from my Nana on the several hundred acres of forest, fields and pastures of Chadwick Farms. We moved toward a simpler lifestyle, hoping to find a safer and calmer place to rear our child, a place close to Jack's business, yet green enough to breed the horses he remembered from his childhood, the Friesians once raised by his grandparents in Maine. I'd learned to love his horses. Then he died. Standing in the shadow of the grand old brick church building, listening as clumps of earth thudded onto the steel of his coffin lid, I had buried Jack in the red clay of the First Baptist Church cemetery. Remembering, my hands trembled on the wheel.

Slowing the Jeep further, I negotiated the bridge over Magnet Hole Creek and rounded Trash Pile Curve only a mile from my house. The site was a ninety degree curve in the road that had taken more lives and collected more refuse than any unofficial dump in the county.

A mattress and a load of shingles, remnants of some nearby renovation, partially blocked the left lane. The debris was in a dangerous spot; if a driver was traveling too fast, he might overcompensate and end up in the creek. It wasn't a wide creek, but there were some spots in Magnet Hole Creek deep enough to swallow a car and hide it forever.

I reached for the cell to report the mess when headlights appeared, pulling out of Chadwick Farm Acres, the subdivision near our home. The car was traveling fast. Too fast for Trash Pile Curve. Blinking my lights to warn them of the rubbish as they sped by, I slowed, watching my rearview, dialing the sheriff's department by touch. It was busy. I coasted in the darkness.

The car behind me swerved, its lights leaving a red streak on the night. I opened my mouth to shout a warning, useless in the distance. And then the red tail lights tilted, first to the right. Then down.

"My God." I whispered. In the silence of my car, I watched the lights roll over and over, the headlights illuminating the trunks of trees, green twisted ropes of climbing kudzu, glinting off the rain-swollen, churning water of Magnet Hole Creek. And then there was only darkness.

I closed my mouth, remembering to take a breath. Fumbled for the turn signal in my shock. I whipped the wheel hard left, executing a three point turn.

Somehow I turned the Jeep and dialed 911 at the same time.

"Nine one one. What is the nature of your emergency?"

It was Buzzy, an EMT who moonlighted nights at dispatch. "Buzzy, this is Ashlee Davenport. I'm reporting a single car accident at Trash Pile Curve on road four fifty one. I'm at the location now." I hit the gas pedal and whipped the wheel again. My hands were shaking. "They went off the road."

"How many victims, Ash?"

I slammed on the brakes and pulled off the road, angling my headlights down. "I see one, but the car's upside down. And the creek's up. You better call out the squad," I said, referring to the Rescue Squad. "I'm going down. I'll light flares."

"I'll send the cavalry."

It wasn't exactly the proper response for a dispatch operator, but the analogy was heartwarming, something I desperately needed after my brief glimpse of the body below. It was male, impaled on a broken branch sticking up from the muddy bank of Magnet Hole Creek.

I cut the motor, my feet hitting the pavement before the engine died. With a single flip of a switch, I lit the Jeep's overhead emergency lights, the yellow ones the county permitted on any Rescue Squad vehicle responding to an emergency. The lights Jack had installed the day he bought the Jeep.

In the blinking yellow glow, I opened the back hatch and pulled out six electro-flares. Three of the yellow strobes went in the road behind the Jeep, three in the road on the curve, visible to anyone traveling from I-77.

My heart beat hard and fast as I ran back to the Jeep, the rhythm irregular. I had never responded first to an accident. Not alone. Always before I had been one of several who reached the scene at once. Or I had Jack. He had helped to fund the Rescue Squad and had trained most of the volunteers. He had led the squad in hundreds of dangerous rescues over the years. Jack was everywhere in my life. And nowhere. Except in photographs of an old affair. . . .

"Damn," I whispered to the night and to my dead husband, as I reached for the red emergency supply box in the back of the Jeep. Opening it, I checked my supplies and pulled on heavy blue trauma gloves over my trembling hands.

"Flashlight. Blankets," I counted off. "Backboard," which I leaned against the Jeep for someone else to bring down. "Jacks. Extra flares and batteries. Fire protection gear," which I ignored. I lifted the twenty-two-pound supply box—called a jump kit in squad speak—feeling the strain in my shoulders and back. Jack had always carried it before.

Pausing in the lights of the Jeep, my shadow was thrown in a dozen different directions by the headlights and the flashing emergency lights. I couldn't get a clear picture of the car below me. It was hidden behind a stand of young oaks, green with early summer foliage, tall briars, and splintered driftwood, resting beyond a patch of tangled, leafless honeysuckle and old kudzu curling with fresh green growth. I smelled gasoline. More faintly, wild lilacs. And the stench of dead fish and garbage. Below, someone groaned.

Flicking on the flashlight, I slipped down the muddy incline to the car. There was no clear path. The car had been airborne for part of the way down. Red mud caked on my nursing shoes, squashed up over my ankles and down inside my shoes. Briars grabbed at my scrub suit. I heard a rip over the sound of my breathing and the groans from below.

I should have grabbed the heavy raincoat that was part of the fire protection gear. I would need it in the mud below, but it was too late to go back.

Behind me, a second Jeep roared up and braked to a halt, yellow lights and headlights adding to the glare. I turned and waited an instant as a door slammed and a form moved into the lights.

"That you, Ash?"

"Yeah! Bring the backboard and some rope," I shouted.

"Right behind you!"

Relief sped in my veins and I remembered to take a breath as I slid on down the hill. I had no idea who had joined me so soon, but the rest of the cavalry couldn't be far behind.

In the light of the flash, the body I had first seen looked surreal. A life-sized, mangled toy. A branch had penetrated low in his abdomen, and poked out, slick and red and jagged between his shoulder blades. The smell of feces and the amount of blood let me know that if he wasn't already dead, he soon would be. He wasn't a priority. The woman was.

Her legs were trapped beneath the car. Her upper body protruded. She had a broken left shoulder and multiple compound fractures in her left arm. If she lived, she might lose the arm. She would surely lose the use of it.

Her face was a pulpy mass. Blue eyes watched me intently. Her mouth worked silently, filled with blood and broken teeth.

"Help me. Help me. Help me," she mouthed.

I couldn't believe that she was alive, let alone conscious. Kneeling in the muck beside her, I dropped the jump kit and cleaned out her airway with my fingers. She took a ragged, wet breath.

I had wanted traumas and emergencies and crises, and now I had them. And I wasn't ready. Not for this. In the distance I heard a siren. Then another. The rest of the cavalry had arrived.

I opened her shirt and cut away her bra with shaking fingers. Her chest was livid with bruises and bright with blood. The man from the hill crashed through the underbrush behind me, joined almost instantly by another.

"I'll tie off the car. You help Ash." Welcome words. From above, more headlights illuminated the scene as more vehicles turned off the road and stopped.

On the woman's chest I saw bubbles in the blood, appearing each time she breathed out. A sucking chest wound. Something I could help. Throwing open the jump kit, I ripped open the foil package of a Vaseline gauze dressing. Without touching the sterile gauze or the inner foil, I placed both dressing and foil package over the bubbling wound and pressed gently, leaving a tiny opening for escaping air. Quickly, I added an entire package of 5x9 gauze over the foil and taped it all into place with two-inch-wide clear body tape, careful to leave the tiny space that could prevent the total collapse of her lung.

Sucking chest wounds are caused when some object penetrates the chest cavity and into the lung, creating a hole through which air seeps when the patient breathes. Dangerous, but a manageable wound.

Voices sounded above. Shouts. Suggestions. Conflicting orders and confusion. Help had arrived. *Thank God. Thank God.* The shaking in my hands eased a bit. I pulled out my stethoscope and inserted the ear pieces so I could listen to my patient's chest.

The smell of gas grew stronger, blanking out the sweet smell of wildflowers. The battery of the overturned car spat and spluttered just feet away from my head—the positive battery cable resting against the metal body of the car, a common problem at accident scenes.

Gas and sparks. Lovely. Just *lovely*.

Beneath the bent A-pillars of the windshield was a human foot. Bare. Garish in the uncertain light. I cleared the woman's airway again, followed the foot to the ankle with my eyes and up ripped pants to a knee as I listened to the woman's breathing and heartbeat. Above the knee was a bloodied leg with a bone sticking through skin and fabric at mid-thigh. *Femur bone. Compound fracture.* Blood welled, pulsing slightly from the wound in weak but rhythmic gouts, looking bright but thin in the sharp glare of my flash. A briefcase was open at his side, bloody papers scattered in the mud.

I smelled vomit beneath the sharper scent of gasoline. Gray eyes met mine. Blood ran from his forehead, obscuring his face. He wiped at the trickles running down his right eyebrow.

"Guns and Roses," someone said beside me, using the old band's name as curse words. "How many are there?"

"Three, so far," I said. "We need to get the car off her. Call Medevac and get a chopper here stat."

"Yeah, right. I got this one. You'll have to take the man."

I glanced up quickly. It was Irene Rodgers, on her knees beside me in four inches of mud. She was right. Irene would never fit beneath the car. I was the skinny one on this call. I went back to my patient.

Someone spoke into a radio, relaying the need for a chopper and another wrecker. With the muddy conditions it might take two tow trucks to remove the overturned car, especially if one became mired in the muck.

A second stethoscope searched the woman's chest. Another pair of gloved hands reached for the cervical collar. A third pair steadied the woman's head as the brace went into place. A pen light checked her pupils. An old Leardal—a battery-powered suction machine—came on with the soft sound of air pumped by a plastic piston. A stiff tube cleared the woman's airway better than I had been able to do alone. Hands and helpers. The cavalry had arrived. The woman groaned.

"She's got a sucking chest wound. Pulse one-forty-five and thready. A probable hemo-pneumothorax. Respiration's twenty-four and shallow," I said without looking up. "I haven't checked her blood pressure."

"Got it," a voice said above me. A third body joined me, knees in the mud.

The car was upside down, hood pointed directly at the creek water roiling only feet away. The back part of the roof was crushed down to the seat tops, trapping the woman. The man was lying on the roof at the front of the car, his broken leg beside him. His other foot was over his head, wedged into the dash. The steering column was bent, the wheel pushed up against the dash between us. A woman's shoe was caught in the twisted metal and plastic.

"My wife." The words were whispered, barely audible in the confusion. "My wife." My eyes snapped into the cavity of the car, meeting the gray eyes of the man with the compound fracture. "Is she—" he started.

"I don't know. I wish I could tell you," I lied. I had never learned the art of telling the truth to accident victims. But I wasn't very good at lying either. I changed the subject. "How many people were in the car with you?" I tucked my stethoscope down into my shirt, grabbed a handful of supplies from the jump kit, stuffing pockets. Added a fresh pair of gloves.

"Three of us," he whispered.

"Any children?"

"No." His pants were soaked crimson.

"Are you sure? Tell me how many people were in this car." It might sound cruel to badger the man, but he was shocky. Confused. He might not know what he was saying. I reached for my flash, pulled it close.

"Three," he said.

"Just three? All adults?"

He nodded.

"What's your name?"

"Alan. Alan Mathison."

Other hands were caring for the woman. Still others were positioning cribbing and bringing in the Jaws of Life and the generators: one generator for the jaws, whose massive spreader arms would force apart the mangled metal of the car's body, one generator for the lights. The accident scene began to grow brighter as the squad's oldest generator roared to life.

The first wrecker was sliding down the hill to the creek bottom. I had been working for less than half an hour. If the woman was to live, we had to work faster.

Pushing my flashlight in front of me, I wiggled through the broken side window, across the ruined roof and the mud that had scooped into the car as it slid toward the creek. I was wet to the skin. And if the A-pillars—the front roof support struts—gave way, I'd be crushed.

Moving Alan's bloody hands away, I found the pressure point in his groin and pressed. The bleeding in his thigh wound stopped instantly.

"No pulse down here, Ash. Foot's cold."

I knew what that meant. Alan could lose both his wife and his leg.

Keeping pressure on the man's groin, I checked his pulse, listened to his chest. His heart and lungs were clear. "Respiration's forty-five and shallow," I called back, "pulse one-thirty."

"Got it," a fresh voice answered from the far side of the car. It was Phillip Faulkenberry, Jack's second in command, in charge of the squad now that Jack was gone.

"Sending in a blanket and a cervical collar. All we got's a large. You make the call?"

I couldn't see who I was talking to but the voice was familiar.

"Yeah," I grunted, reaching up for the blanket. My fingers closed on the loose weave of the cloth and I pulled it to me, opening it one-handed, covering Alan as best I could.

"No shit. What happened?"

With those words, I identified the voice I had first heard on the hill above me. Mick Ethridge. One of the Ethridges' of the long departed township, a young, gung-ho kid who started any meaningful conversation with the words, "No shit". He had hardly started to shave and he was up to his elbows in axle grease and mud and Alan's blood that had flowed out of the car and down toward the creek.

I could hear Alan's wife breathing. It was an awful sound, but better than a silence. I struggled with the cervical collar. Managed to get it around Alan's neck. The leg wound started bleeding again as I shifted against his side, but I couldn't help it. There wasn't room for another body inside the car.

"Mattress in the road," I said, grunting with the effort. "They were going too fast to avoid it and make the curve. Lost it."

"This place needs some warning signs."

"Jack asked the county for some last year," Phillip said.

The sound of my husband's name startled me. I searched around in my pockets for the supplies I needed. My hands were shaking again.

"They got put on the county's *wish list*," Irene said, her voice too angry to be merely wry.

I glanced up at Alan; he was out cold. His color was bad, pale and bluish around his lips. His respirations had increased, as had his pulse. He was very shocky. He had lost a lot of blood.

"I need some hands in here," I called up to Phillip. "Somebody has to hold this pressure point. This guy needed an IV yesterday. And he's out. See can someone get a splint on his leg while he's unconscious."

An arm snaked up into the car through the hole where the windshield once rested. Rounded bits of glass rained in upon me. I ignored them.

I guided the hand to the pressure point above Alan's wound. The helper's hands were warm on my icy fingers. A Citadel ring pressed against the blue of the wearer's trauma gloves. Bret McDermott's hand.

For an instant, I remembered the list of investors from Jack's office and the scrap of letter talking about murder. Bret could be involved. . . . My mind clicked back to my patient.

Other hands pulled at Alan's broken leg, positioning it in the stiff splint. Velcro made it snug, and a hand air pump provided padding, supporting the limb.

Although there was help aplenty from beyond the broken out

windows of the crushed car, no one joined me inside. Gas fumes burned
my throat and eyes, bringing tears.

Alan started shaking. Opening his eyes, he gagged and vomited off
to the side, struggled against the cervical collar, his movements further
hampered by the steering wheel over his head.

"What's your wife's name, Alan?"

He licked his lips. The car settled further into the mud. The metal
groaned like a ghost in a nightmare, a long and piercing screech. I pulled
my legs in a bit, but there was nothing I could do to protect myself if the
car's front roof supports gave way. The back supports—the C-pillars, in
squad lingo—were flattened against the car's body.

"Marjorie. My . . . Margie," he added.

"Margie what?"

Alan looked puzzled. "My wife?"

"Right. Her last name. Your last name. What is it, Alan?" I had
asked that one before, but I wanted to assess his mental condition and
repetitive questions were my only tool.

I reached back for the IV set being pushed up the length of my
body and grabbed it. Resting my elbows in a thin layer of mud, I
untangled the IV's plastic line, setting it on the briefcase I had noticed
earlier.

"Alan Mathison. Margie . . . Mathison. My wife. She wants a . . .
divorce," he added, his face devoid of emotion. I didn't respond to his
statement. "She's leaving me for . . . somebody else if I don't. . . ." His
voice trailed off.

"Ash, we're getting cribbing and a couple jacks in place to stabilize
the car. Then we're going to cut away the A-pillars and lift the car off
her." Phillip bent over to speak to me through the passenger side window opening. I nodded my understanding. I had never been inside a car
before as the jaws went to work. But I'd heard about it. I took a deep
breath.

Alan shifted and pushed at the unfamiliar hands, cursing softly
under his breath, though his eyes didn't open. His lips were blue. "She's
going to take everything . . . all the money," he whispered.

"I'm sorry," I said. And I was.

He tried to focus on my face. His eyes settled instead on my
nametag swinging in the light of the flash. He frowned, and then the
frown slipped away.

"Jesus . . . I hurt." It didn't sound like a prayer. Alan was confused
and getting angry. Quick swings of emotion were expected in a trauma
patient, but I had to keep him calm and still. Cooperative. "I hurt."

"Alan, I need you to make a fist." I touched the hand pushing at

McDermott's. "I need to put an IV in. And my friend here's going to hold you still so I don't hurt you. Okay? Alan, do you understand?"

"My wife . . . doesn't want me anymore."

Bret's other hand slipped in beside mine and steadied Alan's against the briefcase in the mud as I tightened a tourniquet around his arm. I swabbed Alan's hand with an alcohol pad. Beside me and to my rear, sledgehammers slammed into the cribbing, driving the blocks of shaped 4x4s into the openings around the roof, supporting the A-pillars. The sounds were like cannons exploding in the confined space. The entire frame of the car sang and vibrated.

Alan had no veins. I milked blood up the arm, trying to restore enough volume to find an IV site. Nothing happened. Alan's arm was a pasty bluish gray.

Saying a quick prayer, I opened a number eighteen Jelco angiocath and picked a spot on his arm almost at random. "Alan, I'm going to stick you with a needle now. Hold still."

"Yeah. Okay. . . ." He licked his lips again. "Water. I want some water. No. Iced tea with lot's of sugar. Get me some tea," he commanded.

I inserted the needle, missing the vein. Pulled back and tried again, repositioning. On the fourth attempt to pierce the vein, I got a slight flashback—a show of blood at the back of the needle letting me know I was in the vein. I removed the steel part of the Jelco, flipped down the plastic security device, and dropped it on Alan's once-white shirt. Starched. Expensive looking. Carefully I pushed the IV's plastic sheath up into his vein. Popping the tourniquet off, I shoved the IV line into place and thumbed the valve wide open on the IV solution. Held it up in the air so gravity would force the fluid into the arm.

"Not bad," Bret McDermott said in his slow, calm way. I grinned over at him, flushed with success. "They teach you that in nursing school?" I laughed, the sound shaky, and taped the IV line and the Jelco to Alan's arm. He was out again. The sledgehammers beat into the body of the car like a giant intent on vehicular vandalism.

Resting the IV bag on the underside of the car seat above me, I checked Alan's pulse once more, using the carotid. It was fluttery and indistinct. About one-sixty. Way too fast. McDermott handed me a blood pressure cuff and helped me get it around Alan's other arm. I couldn't find the pressure. There was no blood pressure at all. I was losing him. I pulled the ear pieces of my stethoscope back out and draped the device over the steering wheel above me.

A second blanket was shoved at me, and then a third. "Cover up Ash. We're ready to cut the A-pillars," McDermott said.

The roar of a second generator followed by the scream of the scissors against metal interrupted my response, putting an end to both conversation and any chance I might listen to Alan's chest. I pulled the blankets over me and over Alan's head. Our faces were inches apart, tented in white cotton and moving shadows and the din of destruction. He licked his lips again, his eyes on me. He smelled of vomit and gasoline.

I needed more room. If the weight on my legs eased a moment, I could pull them into the car, perhaps saving a broken bone or two should the car collapse on me.

Reaching over Alan, in the tent of blankets, I found the briefcase at his side, fumbled it shut, and pushed it toward the broken windshield. Alan grabbed my hand. "No!" he mouthed. His face was twisted in anger. "No."

"Sorry, Alan. I need more room." I pushed again and the briefcase slid through the mud and out of the car, giving me a few inches of leg space. Alan glared. "Sorry," I repeated.

The noise was unbelievable. A raucous, screaming roar of dual generators and the sound of pry bars and hammers forcing cribbing beneath the car.

The A-pillar on the passenger's side gave way. The car above me settled again, resting a bit of weight on my legs. I pulled the blanket off, gestured to McDermott, and pointed to my legs. He yelled something back over his shoulder.

Hands were at my legs almost instantly as someone muscled a stair-step-shaped block of 4x4s in beside me, following it with the jaws. Though the Jaws of Life did the work of forcing apart twisted metal, huge scissors, like deformed, overgrown toenail clippers, did the actual cutting, the short, power driven blades snapping through misshapen metal with ease.

The jaws went to work near my legs, forcing up the top of the car at the passenger's side window through which I had entered. As the car moved, I pulled my body inside, taking up the inches left by Alan's briefcase. The rear roof supports—the C-pillars—were thick, giving way to the scissors with a grinding shriek. The noise of the rescue operation was incredible from inside the car. A ton of bent metal rocked over my head. I was in a cage with a dying man.

McDermott suddenly appeared beneath the white blankets, pulling himself head first into the car, carrying a pry bar. "Want company?" he shouted, grinning at me. I had never been so glad to see a human face. "We're supported. Let's get him stable and get some pants on the girl."

He handed me a second IV kit and bag of fluid. This one was

normal saline; unlike lactated ringers, saline wouldn't help with my patient's blood volume problem, but normal saline was the preferred fluid for giving medications. The doctor in the ER would need it for that purpose. Pumping up the pressure cuff on Alan's arm, Bret pointed to a vein, cleaned it with an alcohol wipe and steadied the flaccid arm.

My hands were shaking so badly I could hardly hold the needle. With no finesse at all, I shoved it beneath Alan's skin, attached the line, and taped off the long plastic tubing as my helper opened the valve. Alan groaned, his voice buried beneath the sound of the jaws.

His gray eyes focused on me. He had nice eyes, clear and bright in a blood smeared face. "Ashlee. Ashlee Davenport," he murmured.

I started, and then remembered the nametag I still wore clipped to my scrub top. I smiled at him and patted his hand. It was even colder than mine. "Right." Alan closed his eyes again, saying my name twice more before he slipped into unconsciousness.

The jaws finally stopped. Silence roared in my ears, the aural echo of dueling steel. Using a pry bar, Bret beat at the dash casing prisoning Alan's foot beneath the bent steering column. The casing, made of high impact plastic, cracked and Alan's bruised foot fell free. McDermott and Mick Ethridge pulled him from the car, hands supporting his back and broken leg.

And then there were helping hands everywhere, offering backboards and listening to Alan's chest and taking his blood pressure, checking his pupils. Out in the road, the chopper from Carolina's Medical Center in Charlotte, the area's closest trauma center, landed in a ring of lights set up by the fire department, guided to the site by GPS.

Bret grabbed me beneath the arms and pulled me through the windshield opening to freedom. The blanket that was still across my body and wrapped beneath my legs protected me from both battery acid and antifreeze dripping from the hood, and the sharp metal and glass below me.

And then I was in open air, breathing in oxygen without fumes, being carried away from my cage by McDermott, held against his chest like a baby. The noise of the crash site decreased as one of the generators went off.

Figures in flight suits slid down the hill, looking capable and proficient and in control. And clean. The squad was ready to lift the body of the car off Margie.

"Jack gave orders you weren't ever to go into a car," Bret said conversationally.

"Jack. . . ." The anger I had been nursing against my dead husband erupted in the aftermath of adrenaline and fear. I struggled to be set down, out of Bret's grip. He resisted. I ground out, "Well Jack's dead and I'm here, and I don't guess it makes too much difference *what* Jack thought, now. Does it?"

Bret grinned again, his teeth shining white in the glare of the emergency lights. "No ma'am, it doesn't. I always thought his orders about you were pretty stupid. You did a great job in there."

I found myself leaning against a tree, dumped there, mud welling around my bottom as my anger dissipated. McDermott brought another blanket and draped it around me. Bret didn't talk much. He didn't need to. Instead, he pulled the trauma gloves off my hands, positioned a flash where it shined on my lap, handed me some report forms and a pen. And a cold Coke.

I usually drank diet, but I didn't argue. I knew I needed the sugar; I was a bit shocky myself. I drank the Coke fast, emptying the can and resting it on the ground beside me.

"Thanks," I said, "for the Coke . . . and the compliment." Bret nodded and left me alone. My hands no longer trembled. I took a deep breath and expelled it. The half smile on my face was a strange sensation. I was calm and drained and oddly peaceful. For the first time since Jack left me, I felt good inside, thanks to Alan Mathison, a deadly car wreck, and Bret McDermott. It was a feeling I didn't bother to analyze. I just sat back, the reports in my lap, and enjoyed the un-expected sense of peace for a moment.

Mosquitoes, attracted by the smell of blood, swarmed in. The fumes had kept them at bay closer to the car. I swatted a few before giving up. I had paperwork to complete.

Before the chopper took off with Margie Mathison, I was finished with the reports. Bret McDermott took them as silently as ever and disappeared, leaving me to watch the organized chaos of the accident scene. The coroner was taking pictures of the body on the branch. It didn't look real in the flashing lights, more like a Halloween prop for the county haunted house. Cops and Highway Patrol Officers wandered around the site, taking notes and talking over the sound of the single generator still chugging away.

An electrical whine started low, almost at the edges of hearing, and raised to a wail. The chopper blades began to turn. A slow thumping sound, like the beat of a heart filled the clearing. An artificial wind roared as the chopper lifted off. Margie went with them, which meant she was still breathing. The chopper didn't take back dead bodies.

A highway patrolman squatted at my side, his boots both shiny and muddy. I knew him too. It seemed a shame, suddenly, but I realized that I knew every person who ever responded to a disaster in Dawkins

County. If I hadn't been so tired, I might have cried. I told my story to the patrol officer, and again to the coroner, gave an official statement, and watched as Alan Mathison was bundled on to a backboard and carried up to the road. I watched the crowd as it thinned. I watched McDermott as he lifted my red emergency supply box and carried it to his truck. I didn't know what he was doing, but I didn't really care.

It occurred to me as I lay against the tree, my bottom cushioned by the cold mud, that I had worked in the hazardous confines of an over-turned car, doing my professional best to save two lives. Alone. Without Jack. It was a curious moment, a peculiar feeling. I tested the fact of my success, mouthing the words, "Solo. Alone." I leaned back, the rough bark rubbing against my hair. I had done it. Without Jack.

As the gawkers and the squad members cleared out, I thought about going home though I couldn't leave just yet. My Jeep was still blocked in and I didn't have the energy to ask anyone to move a car. Not until Jas and Topaz came crashing down the hill did I find the strength to stand.

"Mama!" Jas shouted. "Yo! Where are you, Mama Ash?" Topaz shouted right behind. It came out Mamash. I had been Mamash ever since Topaz could talk. Topaz's mother had been Mama Pearl to my daughter for just as long. It was an unconventional friendship by some standards, Topaz being half black, but Dawkins County had run off the KKK in 1907, and though there was still a great deal of racial prejudice on both sides, mixed race marriages and friendships were curiously common in this neck of the woods. And besides, in the Dawkins County way of the Chadwicks, Topaz was kin.

I levered myself up off the ground and pushed away from the tree, glad of the blanket McDermott had draped around me. It hid both mud and blood. "Over here, girls. I'm fine," I added before they could ask.

"You're a hero for calling in the accident," Topaz said.

"Yeah, Mama. Everybody's talking about how you saw the whole thing and then crawled under a burning car and rescued two people." Jas eyed my clothing for burns, her expression dubious.

My lips curled up. "The car wasn't burning. And I didn't rescue two people. But I did roll around in mud and a little blood for a while. Why aren't you two in bed or at home or something?" I said, to take attention away from myself. I wasn't a hero. It hadn't been that dangerous to crawl under the car. Had it?

"The road was blocked off for the chopper and so we couldn't get home. And then we heard about you and so we waited for the roadblock to clear off and we came down here."

"Well I need a shower." I looked down at my filthy clothes. "In the yard. With the hose pipe." I was a mess. I looked like I had been mud wrestling. Which I had been, sort of. I didn't know if Margie would survive; I thought Alan would, complications notwithstanding.

It was only then that I remembered I hadn't checked him for head wounds. Some hero. Alan could die from the amount of IV fluids pumped into his system if he had a head wound and his brain swelled, but he could have died on the site without the fluids. I shrugged and held my arms out to my girls. Together, we trudged up the hill to our cars.

Bret McDermott watched us from below, a briefcase open by his side, pages scattered in the mud. He waved once to us as we reached the Jeep. I nodded back. And headed the last half mile or so for home, to my empty house and cold, impersonal bed.

An hour later, mud free and sipping a glass of wine, I wandered the house, trying to relax in the aftermath of the rescue. Barefoot on the wooden floor, I roamed from the master suite to the kitchen, back along the hall, past the answering machine with its insistent flashing red light, to the dining room, and the living room Jack and I had used for entertaining. I made my way out to the screened porch, where I finished my wine, sitting in the swing hung from the rafters.

It was two A.M. and the dogs were sleeping beneath the back deck or in the barn, according to their preference. All except Cherry, the pregnant mixed breed terrier who had taken up residence with us since Jack died. She was a sweet dog, abandoned by her previous owners, probably due to her pregnancy. Disturbed from her sleep, she waddled up to me and licked my fingers before she returned to the box Jasmine had cut down to size for her.

Jack had loved dogs, passing that love on to his daughter. Like Cherry, Herman and Hokey had just wandered up, lost and alone, finding a home here on the farm and a love for Jack that bordered on fanaticism. They missed him intensely, hiding out in the barn by night in the hopes that he would appear and give them a treat and a hug. And then there was Big Dog, another stray, but one Jack had trained to be my protector.

My dog. Big Dog was part great Dane, part retriever, and part giant. In color and conformation he was a common enough mongrel for the area, blond, with medium-sized, flopped over ears and a long-haired tail; in size he was something else entirely. Sitting, Big Dog's head came above my waist.

His teeth were enormous wolf-teeth, gleaming yellow-white, looking sharp enough to pierce his careless tongue, a smiling threat. For all his training and ferocious looks, Big Dog was really an old softy, as gentle as a Teddy Bear. I could see him even now, meeting Jack in the drive, happy to have the master of the house returning from the barn late at night after bedding down the Friesians. Everyone had loved Jack. Especially Jas who, like Hokey and Herman, followed Jack everywhere, eyes adoring.

A kind man, was my Jack. A man who knew how to inspire love and confidence from animals and men alike. A man whose eyes crinkled up in ready laughter. *A man who knew about blackmail and conspiracy and murder.* I set down my empty glass and pushed off with my toe, sending the swing swaying. Jack had been a good man. Jack had slept with Robyn.

Robyn who had never married. Who had been in the midst of a long overdue, three-month vacation in Europe, backpacking and biking from country to country when Jack died. We had talked once, long distance from Italy, when she had checked her messages in Atlanta. She had been shocked, weeping, sorry for me. And perhaps for herself.

Jack and Robyn. My swinging stopped. Jack and Robyn and murder. And Bret McDermott beneath the body of the car, helping me save a life. Had he known about the murder? Had he been responsible for the death of the inspector in Jack's letter?

Quietly, I picked up my empty glass and walked inside to listen to the messages on the personal machine. I knew what I would hear. With the volume turned down low, so Jas and Topaz couldn't hear, I hit PLAY. Bill's gruff voice growled into the phone. "Jack. It's Bill. We have to talk. Damn it, don't make me come out there. There's no reason for your wife and kid to know about this. Call me."

Wife and kid. Well, I did know. But Jas never would, not if I could help it. Thoughtfully, I erased the messages so Jas would never hear, turned off the lights and went to bed. Jack and Robyn. Jack and Robyn and murder.

CHAPTER THREE

Though Lynnie Bee, my supervisor at the emergency room, told me I wasn't ready for a full schedule yet, I disagreed, clocked in and worked a split shift, eleven A.M. to eleven P.M. the next three days. Taking more than my fair share of patients, I answered all the in-house codes and buried myself in paperwork.

The night following the accident, Bret McDermott walked into the emergency room still dressed in his banker's black, and asked for the key to my Jeep. He bore only a marginal resemblance to the man who had pulled me to safety the night before. In his usual silent way, McDermott restocked the jump kit, put it back in the Jeep, brought me my keys, and left the ER without waiting for thanks. It was a courtesy, the kind of thing I had come to expect from Bret.

He had always been a quiet, kind man, sweetly attentive. Although I hadn't been able to think about the problems with Jack's business, I couldn't see Bret having anything to do with the investor's letters I had discovered. Bret wouldn't hurt a flea, let alone be involved with murder.

I would have to make some kind of decision about DavInc, Jack's business. I couldn't continue to ignore the office and the answering machines, letting the problems multiply at the development. I couldn't keep my head buried in the sand forever. Yet I couldn't force myself to walk through the door of Jack's office and listen to the machine. Not again.

Instead, I worked long hours, straining my body to carry out the farm chores once shouldered by my husband, followed by long hours at the hospital. I spent my few quiet moments trying not to think about the letter Jack had written, the letter ending with murder.

But, when security ran off someone trying to break into my Jeep one night in the employee parking lot, I realized just how alone I was. *I had to make the decision to call the police or not. I* had to inspect the Jeep for damage. And I had to do it *alone.* Still, I persevered. And as I faced one small challenge at a time, both at home and on the job, I began to feel more alive, more energetic, more like my old self. Maybe in some ways, better. I was alone. I was making it. And next time, I wouldn't leave a pair of good gold hoop earrings on the dash to tempt a criminal. I was learning, finding the courage to face my life. Eventually, I would find the courage to face Jack's.

Mornings, before I went in to work, I cleaned. Not the house, as the cleaning crew took care of that; I had never cared a lick about housework in the first place. Instead, because Jimmy Ray was off on another binge and Jas needed to work the horses, I cleaned the barn. Shoveling manure was mindless drudgery, numbing my thoughts and tiring my body, the steady scrape, lift, toss rhythm totally engrossing.

With Jas leaving for college in the fall, I'd have to hire more help at the barn or make other arrangements for the breeding stock. The Friesian's were Jack's dream, not mine. I couldn't handle the farm alone, so until Jas could decide what she wanted to do about the horses, I would have to make some temporary decisions. Until then, there was work to do.

On the fourth morning after the accident, I was rolling a wheelbarrow full of manure out to the front pasture, stinking of sweat and sunscreen, my hair in a mussed ponytail, my face flushed with exertion. Nana was driving the John Deere across the front twenty acres, dragging a manure spreader to fertilize the ground. I was bringing her raw material when Senator Vance Waldrop pulled up in the yard. He was unaccompanied by his usual retinue, no secretary, no aides, no security personnel. Just good old Vance, driving his wife's old, dark maroon Lincoln, with the tinted windows and the private citizen's license plate.

Vance and I met at the back of the house, the dogs sniffing at the senator's shoes and crotch, barking, or standing back, emitting a low, menacing growl, depending on their level of training or personal inclination. He shooed them and said my name, the word a question, as if he wasn't certain the dirty apparition was really me. I grunted in acknowledgment of his presence, gave Big Dog the hand signal to sit and stay, and kept on with my work. I bore little likeness to the genteel Southern lady my mother had tried so hard to nurture, the one who had graced Jack's side at political and social functions for years. I was surprised the senator even recognized me.

Vance followed in my wake, avoiding the occasional meadow muffin that tumbled from the overloaded wheelbarrow. Big Dog didn't like Vance's attention, but he sat, his eyes on the senator, his tongue lolling comically. Big Dog looked harmless, but I had seen what he could do to an attacker.

Nana nodded to Vance as she drove past, her weathered face stiff with disapproval, her dark blue eyes hidden beneath a wide-brimmed straw hat. Vance nodded back, lifting a hand as Nana turned the big tractor and pulled the manure spreader back toward the road. It was the same thing she had been doing for the last hour, yet somehow, this time, Nana managed to make the turn an insult. She didn't like Vance or his politics and didn't much care who knew it. I hid a smile.

Vance turned back to me, watching as I tipped the wheelbarrow up and made a fresh pile. Seeing him was unsettling. He had never come to the house alone when Jack was alive, and in light of the letters he had written to Jack about problems out at Davenport Hills, his appearance was worrisome.

Senator Vance and Jack had been neck deep in something that neither would have wanted made public. Because I hadn't been back in Jack's office in days, I still didn't know what the problem was. I would find the courage to face the company's problems eventually, but I resented the senator's arrival before I had done so.

Returning the empty wheelbarrow to its upright position, I nodded Vance to the house. "You want some tea, Vance?" Unlike Nana, I couldn't be rude to the man. Jack's presence was still too strong, my mother's training too powerful. And so, frankly, was my own rather morbid curiosity. Perhaps I could learn something from this unexpected visit.

"Thank you, Ashlee, that would be most appreciated." The senator was perspiring, sweat beading in his receding hairline, high on his pink scalp. Silently, we went to the house, the wheelbarrow leading the way, dual wheels squeaking. Vance was deep in thought, his hands clasped behind him, his lips slightly pursed. It was the same expression he wore when pondering a brash reporter's impertinent questions, an expression I had often privately thought looked a bit sneaky, as if he were picking and choosing between lies. Like Nana, I didn't trust the politician.

Neither did Big Dog. He was stiff with displeasure, the ruff standing up on his back, his eyes attached to the soft skin of the senator's neck, where he would like to sink his teeth. I warned him off, but Big Dog only stared harder at the senator, his growl a faint rumble.

I had no idea how I should respond to Vance. A wife has many duties totally separate from the job description of income-bringer—homemaker, hostess, businesswoman, mother, doctor to sick babies, cook, lover, friend. With Jack gone, I suddenly had no clear picture of the role I was to follow with Senator Vance Waldrop.

I wasn't dressed for the role of hostess. I wasn't yet a business-woman ready to deal with Jack's myriad corporations and investments, and certainly none of the other hats I routinely wore would work for Vance. The thought of treating him like a sick child or trying to entice him with lacy night clothes could have made me smile, but didn't.

I had married Jack, an older man, right out of nursing school, becoming a mother within the year. All the roles I played in life had been based on Jack or Jas or the hospital. Predictable. Dependable. Unchanging. That was Ash Davenport—just plain dull.

Now, my life was different. The safe roles that had protected me for so many years were no longer there for me. I was a hostess without a host. A wife without a husband. For the first time, I realized that Ashlee Davenport didn't really exist except as the shadow of her husband, and the thought shocked me. But, I had no time to consider that now. I had time only for the senator and what had brought him to Chadwick Farms and Davenport Downs, the fancy-sounding name Jack had given to his horse-breeding business.

In the kitchen, I removed my leather work gloves and washed my hands before offering fresh brewed tea, ice, and packets of artificial sweetener. As I worked, I tried to decide just how to respond to Vance. Nothing came to mind.

Vance and I sat at the table, sipping and silent. Once, he cleared his throat and opened his mouth before changing his mind and swallowing back his words. It was probably the first time in years the politician had nothing to say. And I said nothing to make it easier on him, concentrating on the tea. It was delicious, but I wished he would get on with whatever he had come to say. Nervous, I tapped my glass, the sound a dull tink-tink-tink.

"Ashlee." His throat was gruff and he cleared it again. "There is no way for me to express the depths of my sorrow for your loss."

I stopped my fidgety tapping. It was verbatim the same phrase he had uttered when the reporters were listening at Jack's funeral, and with his words, I suddenly thought of a way to handle Senator Vance. When in doubt, copy Mama. It would be a coward's move, imitating Mama, but then, I wasn't doing so very well on my own, was I? I smoothed back several loose strands of hair and waited, wondering if I could pull off the impersonation. After all, there was only one Josephine Hamilton Caldwell. Thank God.

"Your Jack was a fine man. The salt of the earth, and we—uh—I will miss him."

I figured he would really miss all the money Jack had poured into his campaigns over the years, but I kept my peace. A breeze blew through the kitchen window, ruffling the short curtain. I said nothing, just gave a vacuous smile and sipped my tea, thinking about Mama and the list of investors and what Vance knew about the letter hinting at murder. Wondering how some other, stronger woman would handle this situation. Wondering what Vance Waldrop was here for.

He took a sip of tea and stole a look at me. The silence seemed to unnerve him, as if he had come prepared for all sorts of emotional responses from grief to misery to hysteria, but my silence was unexpected.

"Ah, well." He drained his glass and set it down on the kitchen table with finality. I knew instantly that the preliminaries were over. I smiled and tilted my head when he spoke, showing how interesting I found him, just like Mama when one of her guests at some boring social function began to pontificate.

"Ashlee, have you considered what you will do about the corporations and Davenport Hills?" Some small voice in the depths of my mind whispered "*ahhhhh.*"

"I realize it is a major undertaking and I worry that the . . . mmm . . . the strain of finishing the development will be too much for your slender shoulders in this, your time of mourning. And I'm not the only one of your husband's friends who has grown concerned. Bret McDermott and I spoke on the phone just this week and he agreed with me that the corporation was a major undertaking for a delicate little lady such as yourself."

I raised my eyelids politely, hiding my pique. The chauvinistic "little lady" comment aside, I didn't particularly like my husband's business partners talking behind my back. Especially when one was a powerful politician and the other held the purse strings. Then again, Bret was supposed to be my friend. I wondered who had initiated the conversation between him and Vance, and just how important the details were. But the senator hadn't slowed.

"I wish to offer the advice and assistance of my staff at any time for anything you might need. I won't allow the widow of a close personal friend to be bowed down under the heavy stresses of . . ." blah, blah, blah.

I searched his words for anything that might be pertinent to the letters and the problems mentioned in them. The senator droned on, using parts of different speeches, by different speech writers he had hired over the years. I bet that if I tried real hard, I could remember where each of the phrases were originally used.

He talked about the South as a growing region of business and commerce, ripe for development. He talked about farming and the virtues of working the land as God had intended. And still there was nothing about problems, or Bill and his messages, or murder.

And then Vance said something that captured my attention. "All those problems out at the development—the permit problems, the paperwork, the water problems, dealing with inspectors and such—well, I wouldn't want you burdened down by them, not now, my dear. And

I'm more than willing to help, my staff and I." Vance patted my hand gently.

I pulled it away and drank my tea, holding the glass in both hands like a child, to hide their trembling. Inspector. He had said inspector. Jack's letter flashed through my mind.

The senator smiled. I wasn't certain it was a pleasant smile. I gulped the rest of my tea, wondering for the first time if I should be afraid.

"Old friends are the best in times like these, Ashlee. You should call on us when trouble finds you. Are there any problems you might want assistance with?"

"No," I said, surprised at the sound of the word. Calm, in control, not shaking as I was inside. "Not that I can think of, Vance." I put the glass on the table and folded my hands in my lap to hide my fear. What did he know? In one sentence he had mentioned problems, developments, inspectors . . . *Just how involved with the murder was he?* A strange disquiet settled on me, thinking what a powerful man might do to hide his involvement in a murder.

"Old friends like Bret, and family members, perhaps even your mother would be willing to help you in this time of difficulty. You should consider contacting them. Perhaps even the Becks could assist you. They all have experience in dealing with life's tragedies."

Tragedies, and my mother? My mind latched on to his words. What did my mama have to do with this? *Caldwell and Caldwell, Inc.*, my mind whispered. Mama and Daddy's company, listed among the investors. I shook my head. And then, almost as an afterthought, I heard the other names. Bret and the Beck's. *Bret.* My fear grew.

Vance lapsed into silence, having said what he came to say. Was it a warning, delivered in the most oblique terms possible? I had no idea what to say in reply.

In a faint panic, I opened my mouth. "More tea?" The persona of my socialite mother took command. I smiled brightly. "Cookies?"

Ignoring his upraised hand, I poured him a second glass of iced tea. "Aunt Mosetta baked a fresh batch this morning." I rose from the table and lifted the cake plate cover, exposing two dozen delicately brown cookies. "Try the oatmeal. They're Aunt Mosetta's best I think. Of course, I must admit, I'm a bit prejudiced. I grew up eating cookies at Aunt Mosetta's and I always thought she cooked the oatmeal just for me." I rambled on, the words ascending from some dark pit of buried memory and unknown evil talent. I stacked cookies on a china plate, acting just like my mother did when she was faced with something unpleasant that couldn't be handled with simple hysterics. Retreating into the formalities of southern graciousness like the senator's "delicate little lady". "She uses South Carolina's own Adluh flour and local honey, and only the freshest homemade butter she purchases from an old friend." My act would have been more appropriate had I been wearing a pink organza tea dress, pearls, and white gloves, instead of dungarees and work boots, but it served well enough. The senator's eyes simply grew bigger and bigger as I rattled on.

"Ashlee—"

"Here you are Senator," I interrupted, putting the small plate in front of him, the cookies arranged just so. "I remember when Jasmine was a little girl, she just loved these cookies. It's in the genes, I always say. Here try one." I smiled sweetly, and pointed to the cookies.

The ruse of cookies and tea wouldn't hold off Vance Waldrop for long, but Mama could always come up with something to keep any unpleasantness at bay. I figured I could, also.

"Ashlee, I'm sure the cookies are wonderful but I'm—"

"Indeed they are. And you should especially try the sugar cookies. I know you always had a soft spot for sugar cookies. I remember hearing you say so at a church bake sale one year." I remembered nothing of the sort, but it seemed like the kind of thing a politician would say.

"Well, yes, but I—"

"And I'll bet you've never tasted anything so wonderful as one of Mosetta's chocolate chip cookies. Do taste one, Senator." And honest to God, I think I simpered. I was overdoing it, making a fool of myself, but I couldn't stop.

He took a breath as if to object, and I smiled even more sweetly, just like Mama does when she wants her way. Dutifully, he took a sugar cookie—his favorite?—and bit into it. And while his mouth was engaged I spoke again.

"Now Senator, you just put any worries about poor little old me right out of your mind." Oh my . . . *poor little old me*? I had my mother down perfect, though I didn't know whether to be proud or ashamed. At least the barrage of words was suppressing my fear. "I'm doing just fine here, and I've made a few decisions about the development. You remember Peter Howell? You met him when Jack took ya'll duck hunting last year."

The senator nodded, his mouth full of sugar cookie. They were all oversized. After raising ten children, Aunt Mosetta didn't know how to cook anything regular sized. Vance washed the cookie down with tea, but before he could reply I took up my prattle, imitating my mother with flighty words and useless gestures.

"Well, anyway, I've decided to put Peter in charge of finishing the development." I had made no such decision, but perhaps my mind had been active on some deeper level, because it was an excellent solution to all the unsolved problems coming over the phone in Jack's office.

"And the CPA will be handling all the money transactions except for the signing of the checks—you know that Jack had a thing about allowing power of attorney."

Again, I had not contacted the CPA, but it was a good idea. "And, Senator . . ."

"Call me Vance, Ash. I—"

"Vance, you kind man, try one of these chocolate chips." I lifted a cookie and carried it to his mouth. He had no choice but to bite.

"I just adore chocolate chip cookies," I continued. "Anyway, you needn't worry about me at all. I'm stronger than I look and I'm sure I'll do just fine with the business. Jack was well insured both professionally and personally," I said, dropping my voice to imply some great and confidential disclosure, "and has provided for my welfare."

I stood and took the senator's hand with my right, picking up three or four cookies with my left. Like any well-bred, southern gentleman, Senator Vance Waldrop stood as well, chewing and swallowing at once. "And I do appreciate you coming to look in on me, Vance. But I assure you I'll be all right." I guided him by the elbow to the door, opened it and stepped out on to the deck as I spoke. The senator followed, scraping chocolate from his dental work with his tongue.

"You and the other investors out at Davenport Hills should be receiving a letter from my business manager by the end of next week concerning target dates and such like." I looked up at him beneath my lashes as I've seen my mama do a thousand times, but he didn't notice my ploy. It seemed a chocolate chip was wedged in a precarious spot in the senator's front teeth.

"And again, I do appreciate your kind visit, but I assure you I'm doing fine. Here, take some of Mosetta's cookies for your trip back to Columbia." I shoved the cookies into Vance's hand and stepped back inside, shutting the door in his face.

My last picture of Senator Vance Waldrop was his open mouth, chocolate stuck between his upper front teeth, a confused look on his face. It was exactly the expression I often wore after dealing with my mother, overwhelmed, nonplused, and completely outmaneuvered.

I laughed softly, resting my head against the jamb, ignoring the tiny jabs of my guilty conscience. I had long ago promised myself that I would never succumb to the wiles and ways of my manipulative mama, but that was before I had to deal with the likes of Vance Waldrop. Considering that Ashlee Davenport didn't have the slightest idea who she was anymore, I thought I had handled the senator quite well.

"Very nice. I had no idea you were so talented. It must be the Hamilton genes. I know no Chadwick could ever pull that load of crap off."

I whirled, dropping back against the jamb, my hands behind my back like a child caught with his hand in the cookie jar. Which I was, sort of. Nana was propped against the hall entry, her arms crossed and a half grin on her face. My Nana was in her seventies, her exact age a well-kept secret. She was stocky, gruff, and weather-beaten, a woman who had run a four hundred acre farm alone and overseen three others for over forty years, since the death of Pap Hamilton. Determined, astute, and competent, she was the most straightforward woman I had ever met. She was also the richest woman in Dawkins County though you would never have guessed by looking at her.

"Nana. You 'bout scared me out of my skin," I said, sinking further against the wall. I noticed for the first time that the John Deere was silent, and wondered just how long she had been listening.

Nana's eyebrows went up and one corner of her mouth went down in an expression that said, "Try that one elsewhere, my girl." Apparently she had been there awhile.

I grinned, feeling flushed with success. It was my first foray into the world Jack had bestowed upon me, and I had survived. "Personally, I thought I caught your daughter to a 'T'. I especially like the part where I shoved a chocolate chip cookie into his mouth."

"Played hell with his dentures. I was watching from the hall."

"Yes. Well. I never realized the . . . the . . . power my mother wielded with her little-girl-lost-please-let-me-serve-you routine. Well," I amended, "I knew it kept me in line, but I never knew just how successfully it could work on the public." I pushed away from the door jamb and walked to the kitchen, washing my hands at the sink and pouring Nana a glass of tea. My grandmother didn't move to take it, retaining her position against the hall entry, a speculative look in her eyes. The silence in the room was uncomfortable and just a bit disapproving.

I could see Jack's golf bag in silhouette beside her, the club heads rounded shadows. I'd have to move it eventually. There were a lot of things I'd have to do eventually.

Nana hated Mama's "dithering" as she called it, yet instead of commenting again on the little act she had witnessed, she said simply, "You're a lot stronger than your mama. Stronger and brighter and more capable. I don't think you'll have to hide behind her image for very long."

While I was trying to digest that, Nana turned the topic away from me. "You want to tell me why a United States Senator would fly down from Washington, drive across state in his wife's private car, without his 'yes' men and visit with my granddaughter?" It wasn't exactly a question, it was more in the nature of a demand.

I put her glass on the table near Vance's empty, filled my own again and took my place at the table. In the background, I heard the senator drive away in his wife's Lincoln, the dogs barking in a desultory fashion. Sighing, I covered my face, trying to organize my thoughts. Tears of frustration and confusion filled my eyes. I bit my lip and waited them out. After a moment, I was able to speak in a normal voice. "Nana," I took a breath and uncovered my eyes, focusing on the calm face of the woman I admired most in the whole world. "I think Jack was involved in something he shouldn't have been." Her eyes didn't change, yet I felt myself flush, and looked away. I picked up my sweating glass and put it down again in a different spot, making the edges of the water rings touch just barely.

"I think he did something—or maybe many somethings—that were unethical. And, well, illegal." I paused. "And dangerous." I thought of Robyn and the pictures I had found, knowing I could have added sinful, evil, and adulterous. Instead I said, "And it's even possible there was a . . ." my thoughts veered away from the word murder. ". . . death involved. Somehow."

Nana said nothing, but I could feel her watching me, her eyes sharp and loving all at once, just like when I was a child and had something to confess. Like the time I stole Wallace's clothes while he was skinny dipping in the back forty's pond. Or the time I hid a king snake in Mama's bed just minutes before she was to arrive for a summertime visit. No one could not say something like my Nana. Her silences were more powerful than words.

"And Senator Vance is involved in it up to his armpits."

Nana snorted and I relaxed suddenly, grinning, making a third water ring. The chair legs scraped as Nana sat, and I watched as she drained her tea glass, placing it squarely back into the water ring it had made. A psychologist might have thought there was something significant about the placement of our water rings.

"Always was a sneaky old toad," she said, and poured herself a second glass of tea. A silence played itself out between us as Nana ordered her thoughts. She was a methodical woman and I was accustomed to her long pauses. Dealing with Nana had taught me the virtue of patience, but her insights had always been worth the wait.

"When Pap died," she said, "Joanetta Chadwick came to me and claimed that Wallace had been fathered by Pap. I didn't want to believe her, but it made so much sense I couldn't help but." Nana looked at me across the table, her eyes matter-of-fact and steady. "I found check stubs where Pap had been supporting her and the boy for years. And so I took responsibility for my husband's light-of-love and his illegitimate child. Sent 'em both to school, gave 'em a place to live, though there's those who laughed at me for it. And some white bigots criticized me for it."

I made another water ring on the table. There were four of them now, all touching. I understood where Nana was going with the story of Wallace and his African American mother, and yet I waited. Listening.

"The point, my child, is that no man is perfect. Given the opportunity, seven out of ten would break every one of the ten commandments without blinking if they thought they could get away with it. Some get caught. Or they die early and their families get left to clean up the mess.

"Jack was no better and no worse than any other man. He was a rich man, with a rich man's opportunities and a rich man's temptations. But in his own way, he loved you and Jas. Whatever you discover as you go along, remember that much." I thought of the pictures of Jack and Robyn in his desk drawer, and wondered if Nana had known or guessed about the affair.

"Now. If there are any illegalities involved with Jack's problems, you'll need help dealing with them. Wallace's half-brother Macon has both the time and the resources, and he has no financial involvement in any of Jack's developments so he'll be totally impartial, unlike that self serving little weasel Rolland Randall the Third." The way Nana said it, the name sounded slimy. Rolland was Jack's attorney, a very wealthy Charlotte lawyer. A man with his fingers in everyone's pie. A man who knew everyone and everything and made a fortune bending his knowledge to self-serving ends. The kind of man Nana hated on sight and let him know it, much in the same way she had let Vance Waldrop know her opinion of his politics and ethics.

I smiled slightly and bit into a chocolate chip cookie. The chips were gooey and sweet. With my mouth full, and managing to sound innocent, I said, "And while I'm at it, I'll be redirecting the family fortunes, sending both financial and moral support back to the Chadwicks."

Nana looked at me hard. "Macon may not be as close as Wallace, but he's still a Chadwick. And the Chadwicks stick together. Period."

I took another bite and said meekly, "Yes, ma'am." Nana nodded and pushed away from the table. Moments later the John Deere roared to life, leaving me in silence.

Family. Black, white, male, female, right or wrong, good or bad, the Chadwicks had stuck together for two hundred, forty years, sharing land, food, fortunes, and opportunity. And ever since Growling Jim Chadwick married his half-black cousin and former slave just after the Civil War ended, they had openly shared genetic heritage. The marriage ended eight years later with the threats of the KKK and the burning of a particularly fine cross on Growling Jim's front lawn.

Jim Chadwick left his wife and their six children, deeding them two hundred acres of the county's best bottom land and married a more socially acceptable white woman in Dorsey City. Shortly thereafter, the KKK came under attack, with the so-called secret society members returning from raids to find their barns torched and their livestock run off, their homes burned and their children without a roof over their heads.

Before Growling Jim died in 1923, he had run the last known KKK member out of the county, fathered four children on his new wife, two more on his former wife, and enriched the coffers of both families considerably. For some reason, Jim was always the first to know when a KKK member was ready to sell out and move on. He would appear, cash in hand, to buy the drastically devalued farm, often while smoke was still curling up from the charred timbers of the family home. Growling Jim Chadwick was no saint, but he believed in family and justice.

I had grown up knowing my black cousins, swimming in the same ponds each summer while the city pools were still segregated. Together we built snowmen in winter when school was out, sharing books and toys and play time. I had always known the story of Joanetta and Pap and Wallace, but considered it for the first time from the vantage of a widow left to deal with problems. I wasn't sure I would have had the courage to do what Nana had done and welcome my husband's child and lover into the embrace of family. I wasn't sure I was strong enough to do the right thing in the face of public censure and gossip.

I had grown up with Wallace, my half-black second cousin . . . or was it third? As a child I had admired the bronzed young man, looking up to his greater intellect and admiring his perfect features, while simultaneously pulling practical jokes on him at every opportunity. Now, Wallace Chadwick, MD was the second in command in the emergency room and acting Chief of Staff of Dawkins County Hospital. Most weeks, the family tradition continued as the two branches worked together to save lives.

The family tradition continued in other ways as well. Nana and Aunt Mosetta, Jonetta's mother, now lived together in the big, remodeled Chadwick farmhouse half a mile away, ruling the multiracial family with two pairs of iron hands in matching velvet gloves. Wallace's daughter and mine were best friends, Topaz and Jasmine, inseparable since they were children. All because Nana had been a strong woman. Which I wasn't, Nana's declarations notwithstanding.

Putting the glasses in the dishwasher, I looked up the number for Chadwick, Gaston and Chadwick, Attorneys at Law, and dialed it before I had time to reconsider. Half an hour later, I had a new lawyer who was willing to see me through probate and oversee the paperwork involved in restructuring the corporations now that Jack was no longer around to run them, or handle a sale should I decide I didn't want to be a businesswoman. He would even handle the appointment of Peter Howell to the position of overall supervisor out at Davenport Hills.

And he agreed to handle any improprieties he might uncover in Jack's office. Such a kind word, improprieties. I was grateful to Macon for choosing it. He had a gentle, deep voice, one I instantly trusted. The relief to be doing something about the problems I had uncovered in Jack's office was intense and fulfilling. A sweet satisfaction. It felt good to make a decision.

Maybe this was what had seen Nana through all the gossip and innuendoes so many years ago. This kind of satisfaction. As she had always maintained, there was something healing in dealing with family. Something uplifting, like being wrapped in a warm, protective blanket and held out of harm's way. By the time I hung up the phone I was calmer than I had been at any time since Jack died. My last recollection of Macon was of a boy with big greenish eyes and short-cropped hair, standing hip-deep in the back pond where the farm kids cavorted on hot summer days. He was all grown up now, yet I knew that Macon Chadwick would help me, and the thought of a Chadwick in that position was deeply reassuring, even though he was a Chadwick I hadn't seen in years.

Carrying the newfound sense of calm with me, I returned to the fields. There was still a good bit of manure to be wheeled out to the front pasture. Hard work. Work that would keep my mind and body busy and tired.

A letter came in the mail before I left for work at eleven, no return address, unsigned. The grammar was perfect, the tone educated and menacing, the message succinct and to the point.

You have the samples, the reports, the permits, the files, the evidence. Safeguard them.
Protect them from exposure. You are vulnerable, Ashlee Davenport.

Take great care.

What file? What permits?

Someone somewhere was trying to get a reaction out of me. *Bill?* Had he mailed this? *Or was it Vance? Or Bret?*

"*Damn you,*" I whispered to Jack. Just *damn* you. Furious, I tore the letter to shreds and threw it in the dumpster beside the back door. My hands still shook and I had to force my feet to move slowly as I re-entered the house.

CHAPTER FOUR

By nine-fifteen that night, we had seen forty-seven patients in the emergency room, responding to everything from terminal cancer patients and accident victims with major traumas, to headaches, minor cuts, and GOMERS. GOMERS—from Get Out of My ER—were patients endured by every emergency room in the country. They were people complaining of pain of unknown origin, mental patients with problems too minor to merit the attention of the state mental hospital, hypochondriacs, the lonely, and those seeking attention not given in their everyday lives, and drug addicts looking for a free hit.

We had also seen a dozen regulars, patients with chronic health problems so severe that they made the ER their second home. Patients we knew by name as well as disease or condition.

Mattie Lou White was a regular with diabetes and high blood pressure who, two or three times a year, refused to take her medication. She wasn't exactly noncompliant, she was simply healed by every passing tent revivalist. Each time a man of God laid on the Hands of Healing, Mattie Lou flushed her medications into the county sewer system.

This time her blood sugar was over nine hundred, about nine times above the medically acceptable norm, and her blood pressure was two-forty over one-thirty-five. Stroke territory. She was admitted to the Intensive Care Unit. Again. And because Mattie Lou didn't have private health insurance, the government would pay the price of her faith. As usual.

Ronellen Williams came in with a migraine, her face puffy and tear stained, sporting a black eye and multiple abrasions. Her husband, crude, insolent and hostile as usual, sat by her bed as she was seen. He'd kill her one of these days. We had all told her so, but she loved him and wouldn't even consider legal help. She had migraines every time he beat her, depending on the hospital for compassion and tenderness.

Olajawan Thomas, a three year old black child with sickle cell, was carried through the doors in a crisis. Curled into a fetal position, he was moaning softly as his joints swelled and stiffened and his abnormally shaped red cells sliced into his joints and internal organs with brutal efficiency. Olajawan's mother knew her son didn't have long to live unless a new medication or treatment was discovered soon. We did what we could for the boy, and gave his mother the compassion she needed to make it through another day of watching her only child slowly die.

A seventeen year old came in with a fork stuck in his thigh. It quivered when he walked, pulling the denim of his jeans tight. Food still graced the tines, rice and English peas. At least it was a balanced diet.

Three fourteen year old boys with the clap tried to get treatment, hoping for an end to their misery. All three were sent home without medication. In South Carolina, a fourteen year old can't be seen by a doctor without his parent's consent unless it is an emergency. And the clap isn't an emergency, although it may feel like it.

A cardiac patient took up an hour. He was a triple bypass with angina—pain with no apparent physiological cause.

And then there were the bloody patients. A shooting victim was still in surgery having his spleen removed and his intestines temporarily rerouted. People in Dawkins County had yet to understand that the human digestive tract was never designed to withstand the effects of double-ought buckshot delivered from two feet away. They kept having to learn the lesson over and over again, and the latest one would be lucky to survive. The victim's family was out in the waiting room, drunk on beer hidden in a cooler in their car and plotting vengeance on the assailant.

An accident victim spent hours up in X-ray having his bones zapped before a surgeon could sew up his buttocks. According to his story, he had two beers—two quart sized beers at least, judging from his blood alcohol level—and then decided to test his coordination and balance by standing on the open tailgate of his best friend's old Chevy truck. At seventy miles an hour. Once on his feet, he failed his own test and slipped from the relative safety of the truck bed to the asphalt. The landing tore a hole the size of a man's fist in the patient's backside, a fact the EMTs had a few tension relieving laughs over once they got the bleeding stopped.

One of the Dover boys came in with his scalp all cut up. The cuts were almost perfectly circular, the diameter of a beer bottle bottom. Bo Dover had neglected to display the proper amount of jealousy when his girlfriend of the moment stopped to talk to a good-looking stranger at the neighborhood bar and back-room poker joint. She had banged an empty against the wall, knocking out the bottom, and stabbed his head repeatedly with the broken end.

When Bo came to, lying in a pool of sticky blood, he got up, walked down the street to the pay phone and called an ambulance. Then he returned to the site of the attack and lay back down in the blood to await help, pretending to be unconscious. All within the sight of witnesses. Bo wasn't real bright, even before his girlfriend rattled his brains.

Wallace Chadwick, MD, finished suturing up the last patient at about the same time that I finished giving a shot to a four year old with an earache, and JoEllen, the only other RN on duty, finished with a twelve year old girl. JoEllen's patient was a sexually active child with abdominal pain who turned out to be pregnant. As a group, the patients gathered at the desk to sign the medical forms. The mother of the four year old was relieved, while the mother of the twelve year old was furious, stalking through the automatic doors as if the emergency room personnel were personally responsible for the fetus growing in her daughter's belly.

Moving slowly, Wallace, JoEllen and I gathered at the desk, watching the last three patients and their families depart, sharing the sudden silence and the sense of space in the vacated rooms. Wallace shook his head. "I need coffee," he said wearily, resting his elbows on the desk and his head on his arms. "I need coffee bad."

JoEllen grimaced and glanced at the clock. "The last time I saw a bathroom was six hours ago. If I don't go soon we're going to need an ark." Neither of them moved.

There was nothing I wanted except for my feet to stop throbbing. The pain radiated up my legs and nestled into the small of my back. Acetaminophen would have been nice, but like my friends, I was content to let the desk hold up my weight, relishing the moment of inactivity and quiet. Forty-seven patients in ten hours was an unbelievable horde in an ER as small as this one.

From down the hall came a steady soft squeaking, the sound growing progressively louder. "If that's another patient, I'll strangle him myself," JoEllen said.

"I'll help," I murmured. "You want to use gauze, an ace bandage, or your bare hands?"

"An ace would be nice. I don't want to damage my nails."

Wallace made a breathy, laughing sound into the cavern of his arms. "And I'll pronounce him. All for one and one for all. We can share a prison cell."

Tricia, the nursing supervisor, who certainly had better things to do this time of night, came around the corner from X-ray, pushing a lightweight utility cart. In a hospital the size of Dawkins County—one hundred twenty beds plus outpatient and same day surgery facilities—the shift nursing supervisor was often only a highly educated, glorified, gofer, referee, and receptionist. Her position was largely administrative, even on weekends and night shifts, a job that meant settling disputes between exhausted doctors and equally tired nurses, investigating employee accidents and filling out incident reports, listening to dissatisfied patients, and making repeated trips to the pharmacy for narcotics and antibiotics, trips to linen for sheets and towels, and trips to general supply for fluids and nursing supplies. And that was just for starters. But tonight, the supply cart she pushed wasn't laden with linens or replacement IV fluids or any of the other usual paraphernalia. It was, however, overflowing with at least three dozen long stemmed red roses in a cut crystal vase. The roses waved delicately with the forward motion of the cart.

To the left of Tricia was a patient on crutches. A man, about six feet two inches tall and very slender, wearing a pair of paisley silk pajamas and a navy silk robe. The clothes were surprising; most patients who could afford it went to Charlotte or Columbia when health problems forced them to a hospital. However, seeing Tricia with a man was not surprising at all.

JoEllen snorted delicately, sharing that thought. Tricia, who was single but still looking, was smiling broadly, her brows arched almost up into her artfully highlighted hair. "Look-y whaaaat I got," she sang, her voice echoing teasingly down the hallway.

"I don't know what you had to do to get them, but it couldn't have been legal," JoEllen said, glancing from the roses to the man hobbling beside the supply cart.

"Don't let my wife see all that," Wallace said, pushing away from the desk and stepping into the break room. "She might start getting ideas. Coffee fresh?"

No one answered. The squeaky cart came to a stop at the desk and the man, pale and wan, stopped beside it, transferring the crutches to one hand. He was good-looking, though too pale to be healthy, and was somewhere in his forties—that wonderful age for a man when he has all the wisdom and discipline and culture of an older man, but still with the looks and power of a younger man. Too bad women don't have a stage of life like that.

"Actually," Tricia said, lifting the heavy vase and placing it on the desk with a soft thud, "I've just been enjoying them all evening waiting for things to slow down in here. I was afraid I'd have to take them home, ya'll have been so busy." She didn't sound as if that would have been so great a burden, and smiled back at the man beside her. It was the flirtatious smile she used on any available male in visual range, not the professional smile she used on fractious patients.

I glanced at the man to gauge his response to Tricia's words, but there wasn't one. He was looking at me. A sober, steady gaze that brought a sudden flush to my cheeks just as Tricia finished up her little speech with the words, "Unfortunately, the roses aren't for me. They're for Ashlee."

JoEllen's mouth dropped open. Wallace, listening from the break room, laughed softly. He always did have a wicked sense of humor. I said nothing. I was looking into the quiet gray eyes of the blond man at the desk. He had a healing laceration above one pale brow and a small scabbed-over abrasion on his jaw. He was balanced on one leg as if the other pained him.

"Alan Mathison," I said softly.

"Ashlee Davenport," he said in the same tone. We both smiled, a bit uncertainly.

"The guy from the wreck?" JoEllen blurted out. "The one whose wife—" she stopped, embarrassed. I had seldom seen JoEllen make a blunder with a patient. It must have been the roses. The scent of the magnificent blooms was filling up the ER, erasing the smell of old blood, unwashed bodies, and disinfectant.

"I'm sorry about Margie," I said. Alan's wife had died shortly after she arrived at Carolina's Medical Center, her internal injuries too severe to survive. "I lost my husband last month and I know—" I stopped and swallowed down the words I had been about to say. *I know what?* The scenes from a dozen photographs flashed through my mind. Jack and Robyn. . . . After a moment I continued. "I know how hard it is."

JoEllen and Tricia stepped away, joining Wallace in the break room. I could hear him making coffee, and Wallace always made it too strong. Their departure gave us a semblance of privacy, though I'm sure they could hear every word.

Alan's eyes never left mine. I had never seen eyes like his. They were hypnotic, compelling. As if he was searching for some hidden truth deep inside of me. And they were strangely ambivalent eyes, as if he didn't want to be here with me. As if seeing me made something in his life more difficult than it already was. Or perhaps more real.

"I don't remember much about that night," he said finally. "I don't remember much about the next few days as a matter of fact. But I remember Ashlee Davenport, who climbed into the car with me and who tried to keep Margie—" The words stopped abruptly and he cleared his throat, looking away. His eyes reddened, though they stayed dry. An awkward silence settled between us. After a moment Alan said. "I know you did all you could for her." I nodded. "And Jim, my assistant. Was he. . . ?"

Jim. The body hanging on a branch over Magnet Hole Creek. The stench of feces, and the slick red glint of blood in the glare of my flash. "He was gone when I arrived." Only a little white lie. Did Alan notice? Emergency workers save the savable before we work on the bodies with little or no chance of survival. Jim, even if still alive when I arrived, was not among the lucky ones. It wasn't the kind of thing I could say to a patient.

"At any rate," Alan said with a wobbly smile, "I wanted you to have a small token of my appreciation." He had a refined smile, chiseled lips. Aristocratic. Mama would have approved.

I looked at the roses and lifted a hand to touch a bloom. It was feathery soft, like velvet brought to life. I didn't know what to say. I had never been sent flowers by a patient before, although it wasn't uncommon for the entire emergency department to receive a bouquet in appreciation for some heroic effort.

And Jack had never been the cut flowers type. He said he hated seeing them turn brown and die. On special occasions, he sent perfume or jewelry or gift certificates to Macy's in Charlotte. Never cut flowers.

Awkwardly, I lowered my hand and nodded. Realizing that was a far from adequate response, I said, "Thank you. They're beautiful. I've never seen so many roses in one place before." Suddenly my eyes filled with tears I couldn't control. I had seen dozens of roses at Jack's funeral. White roses for death. And as if proving Jack's complaint, I had watched them crinkle, turn brown and die in the days following his funeral. Angrily, I caught a tear on the back of my hand. I didn't *want* to mourn Jack. Not now. "I'm sorry, I don't know what came over me," I said, laughing shakily. I could hear the falsehood in my tone, and the anger, smothered beneath. The lies were catching up with me, building one atop the other in a rickety pyramid.

Alan glanced away again, that ambivalent look back in his eyes. I knew I had made him uncomfortable, and I was ashamed. He had offered a lovely gift and I had been less than enthusiastic in accepting it. I didn't know how to remedy the situation. "Well," he said. "I'd better get back to bed. The surgeon said I could go home tomorrow if I still looked good. I don't want him to change his mind." His smile faltered with exhaustion, and I offered him a wheelchair, which he refused, shaking his head. "Exercise. Doctor's orders. I'm just glad I didn't live fifty years ago before a break like mine could be pinned and braced instead of put in plaster," he said, gesturing to his leg. "Look Ma. No cast."

I smiled at the weak joke. "Don't overdo. It was a nasty break."

He tucked the padded crutch supports beneath his arms and headed up the hall, his gait the unsteady amble of someone new to crutches and pain. "Alan," I called. He stopped and glanced back.

"Thank you for the roses. They really are beautiful."

"Thank you for saving my life. I understand I would have bled to death if you hadn't been there. Doctor Hoffman said I have about six pints of other people's blood floating inside me as it is." His smile faded. "Hope they were all healthy."

"Me too." It was a common worry among blood recipients; even with science's most advanced testing procedures, hepatitis and AIDS were still the rare deadly results of transfusions. I was reminded of the carnival barker's chant at the county fair over in Ford County when I was a child, "Ya' pays ya' money and ya' takes ya' chances." But then, all life was like that. One big gamble. Alan disappeared around the corner, passing X-ray on the way back to his room.

"He wasn't well enough to make his wife's funeral," JoEllen said beside me. "I heard that her parents flew into Charlotte, made the arrangements, cleaned out her trust fund and bank accounts, buried her, and flew home." She shook her head slowly. "They didn't even bother to call Alan while they were in Charlotte. Bad blood between her parents and her husband.

"I heard they decided Margie married beneath her when she married him. Mr. and Mrs. Moneybags never did accept him."

JoEllen knew all of the hospital gossip. She was a regular receiving station, and the phrase "I heard" was her most overused favorite. I didn't know how JoEllen had garnered her information, but I had little doubt of its accuracy. JoEllen had impeccable sources.

"Did they charge him for the accident?" I asked.

"Police came down to question him several times, but I haven't heard about formal charges. Nothing in the paper about it though, so I guess not. Maybe the other guy was driving."

I nodded. Even though Alan's foot had been forced beneath the dash near the steering wheel, that didn't mean he had been driving. The occupants of the car had been thrown around violently; they might have been sitting anywhere. The night I hit the twelve point buck I ended up under the dash on the passenger side of the car. I'd worn seat belts religiously ever since.

The scent of coffee mingled with the scent of expensive roses. I looked up at the bouquet. It was huge, and I had no idea how I would get the thing home.

"Pull up the Jeep and I'll help you put them in," Wallace said from behind me, making me jump. "We can drain out most of the water and wedge them in place."

Wallace was always sneaking up behind me. He always pleaded innocence, but I knew he enjoyed scaring me out of my skin.

Retaliation, perhaps, for the years of practical jokes I had pulled on him every summer for most of my life. He had never forgiven me for the time I stole his clothes and made him walk bare-bottomed back from the pond to the house. His revenge had been swift and complete. He had taped a conversation between a boyfriend and me and given it to Monica Schoenfuss . . . who had played it all over school for days. I had been mortified. According to Nana, Wallace had been justified. He never let me forget it.

The roses were easier to transport than I expected, arriving home with only a rare bruised petal. However, the ribbing I received from Topaz and Jas made me wish I had tossed them on Trash Pile Curve on the way home. It would have been a suitable memorial to Margie.

"Mamash got a boyfriend," Topaz sang as I struggled to get the flowers out of the jeep. I was working in the glare of the security spotlight out back, hunched over in the harsh shadows.

"Oh Mama, shame on you," Jas said laughing. But it was a strange laugh, a strained tone, and I paused in my efforts with the roses, identifying the sound in my daughter's voice. It was the uncertain sound of a child who isn't really sure she gets the joke, and who hopes it isn't on her. Grunting, I lifted the flowers, keeping my back to them, trying to decide how I would respond to the words and the tone. I kicked the door shut with the rubber sole of my nurse's shoe.

"Umhum. Mamash be a fine lookin' woman, Jasmine Davenport," Topaz said in her best street talk. "You bes' be prepared to fend off all the available men in Dawkins County, 'cause they be knockin' at yo' door sooner than you think. In fact, we bes' be thinkin' a plan to keep her virtue safe, like actin' as chaperones." Topaz was the only teenage rapper I knew who would use the words virtue and chaperone in the same sentence and still make it sound like street talk. The girl was talented. I grunted again, not bothering to respond. My virtue was safer than a nun's.

"All the broke, available men, you mean," Jas said, her tone still odd. And then she added, trying to sound offhand, "Would you believe, Jasper Jenkins asked me if I thought he should wait another month before he called my mother for a date."

I stopped and turned, standing in the shadows, the roses heavy in my arms, impeding my view of the two girls. It was clear that Jas had spoken to Topaz, not to me, yet it was also clear that I was supposed to respond to the statement, not my daughter's friend. Jasper Jenkins? Jasper was a plumbing contractor with legal problems. He did some work for DorCity back in '92 and a year later a cement truck fell through the street, breaking open a water main and depriving the city of water for two days. He declared bankruptcy to handle the legal repercussions, but the judge ruling on his case lived in the city and had done without a bath for the two days the city had no water. He had tied up the case for some time just to spite Jasper. "He didn't," I said.

Jas' eyes, always so much sharper than mine, settled on me in the darkness, picking out my face between the bobbing blooms, her features troubled. "Yes, ma'am. He did." The sound I had been trying to identify beneath Jasmine's light tone was suppressed misery, resting beneath her words. And I understood. Jasmine was afraid. She had suffered a catastrophic loss not fair in the life of one so young. And she wanted assurance that her mother wasn't going to make matters worse. She reached around me in the ensuing silence and opened the back door. Dull light washed the ground at our feet and brightened Jas' face. She didn't meet my eyes.

"Well. I hope you informed him that I have no intention of dating anyone, now or in the future. One husband in a lifetime is a gracious plenty," I said.

Jas raised her eyes from the roses pulling on my arms and met mine, covering the distance of our disparate heights, covering the distance in our perceptions of the future and our fears of the present. She sucked in her breath. Her eyes widened, and she put out her hand, touching mine. It was one of those mystical, almost religious moments of mother-daughter intimacy, where information and understanding are passed back and forth, seemingly at a glance. But just in case I was misreading the moment, I repeated myself. "I will not be dating, Jas. Feel free to quote me." Jas nodded, her face both relieved and sur-prisingly guilty. I went on inside the house, feeling the tension in my arms and in the air outside.

As the door swung to behind me, I heard Topaz snort. It wasn't a ladylike snort but a full blown, two nostril snort of disgust. "That was a low blow, girl. I mean it, that was a major league cheap shot. You can't make your mama promise to stay single for the rest of her life. She a young woman—" The door closed on the rest of her tirade. From the kitchen I could hear angry tones as the girls' disagreement degenerated into heated dispute.

Silently I placed the crystal vase in the sink and added water. The vase wasn't one of the cheap pressed glass vases used by florists to hold bouquets. It was real crystal, the Waterford sticker discernible on the bottom. I placed it on the breakfast table in the bright, overhead light. The scent of roses had already filled the room. By morning it would have spilled out into the rest of the house, filling the air. The smell would be the first thing I noticed when I woke.

My hands trembled, the reaction as startling as the quarrel outside. Paz and Jas never argued. They were like bookends, a balanced pair, uniformly harmonious in all things. The best of best friends. But then, nothing in life was the same anymore. The girls voices rang out in final insult, accusation and retaliation shouted at the same instant. A car door slammed, tires crunched on the drive. Topaz's little Mazda roared off. Moments later, the lights in the barn came on as Jas turned to her horses for comfort. As usual. When she got over the spat, she would come to me, I hoped. But what would I say to her?

My uncertainty surprised me almost as much as the argument had. How would I respond when my daughter came inside? Lie? Claim that I liked being alone? That I enjoyed the heartache, the silent house, the empty bed? I had no desire for another man. Not on any level. Yet, it was also true that I had never been alone. I had moved from my mother's house straight into Jack's. I had never been a solitary being, detached from a family group, independent, isolated, or lonely. I hated being a widow.

A radio came on in the barn, the distant strains of Elvis singing about blue suede shoes. Once again, my daughter had gone to her horses and the solitude of the barn, leaving me when grief, anger, and guilt overwhelmed her. Instead of crying on my shoulder as she did in the early days after Jack died, Jas went to Mabel, burrowing up under the old mare's mane, crying on the muscular shoulder of the barn's oldest, and only pregnant, occupant.

Not knowing what else to do in the aftermath of Jack's funeral, I had followed Jas the first few times she disappeared into the barn. Moving stealthily in the darkness, I had watched to be certain that my daughter would be safe with her sorrow. Tonight, again. I let her go. Wasn't that what the pop psychologists said? To let a child have privacy, her own space, to grow through pain in her own way? I could only hope that should she need me, she would come to me. And she knew I was here for her—didn't she?—ready and waiting whenever she needed to talk.

I showered and climbed into bed. It was after two A.M. when I heard Jas open the back door and tiptoe up the back stairs to her rooms. Guilty but not sure why, I turned into my pillow and waited for sleep, eyes gritty and burning in the night.

I woke from an uneasy sleep at six A.M., the sound of the phone in

Jack's office jangling me from unclear dreams. Bleary-eyed, I reached over to nudge Jack awake. The mattress was cold, the sheets taut, as if never slept upon. I jerked fully awake, stifling a cry.

Jack was dead.

Fists clenched, I bolted from the bed and stopped, my motion arrested like a stop-action sequence in a motion picture. Slowly I turned back, curled my toes into the carpet, and stared at the barren place where Jack used to lie. The phone rang again, the tinny sound of a distant demand. Barefoot, an old tee shirt scanty coverage, I whirled for the office. The answering machine picked up on the fourth ring. I stood in the darkened doorway and listened.

"You've reached Davenport Developments. At the sound of the tone, please leave your name and number, and someone will get right back to you." Jack's voice, steady and sure and in control. And dead. So very dead.

A small sound escaped my lips. I stumbled and stopped, my palms against the door jamb separating Jack's office from the rest of the house.

The tone sounded, an A flat note. Plaintive.

"Jack, you pick up this damn phone. You can't hide behind a machine forever." Bill paused, as if waiting for Jack to answer. He had called on the office phone. As if what he had to say wasn't for every ear. "Jack, if you want to face this in front of a jury down in Columbia you go ahead and keep ignoring me." Another pause. "Jack, you pick up this phone!" he shouted. "Jack!" His words changed with his anger, a frustrated, out of control fury that escalated as he swore. "My family is suffering, you S.O.B. And nobody hurts my family. An eye for an eye, Jack. You hurt what's mine and I'll hurt what's yours—" The phone beeped in the middle of the threat, cutting off the words of a madman.

I pressed my face against my left fist, bruising the tender flesh of my lips and cheek. *"I'll hurt what's yours."* Had Bill just threatened me? Threatened Jasmine? I took a deep breath. *What had Jack been involved in?*

Macon. The name whispered at the edges of my mind, the syllables a balm and deliverance to my shattered emotions. Macon would be here today at eight A.M. to take over all my burdens. To provide me with answers and solutions and explanations. Macon Chadwick, attorney at law, would handle this for me. But did attorney-client privilege extend to the dead?

Moving slowly, as if I were in deep water, I pushed myself away from Jack's office and half turned. Jas stood behind me, the heat of her body like a furnace. So close I wavered to keep from falling into her. We seized each other's arms to keep from colliding and did a clumsy little dance to regain balance. She smelled of horses, as if she had been to the barn before dawn. Or had never changed from the night before. I knew instantly that she had heard.

My eyes traveled up and met hers, tousled hair above, dark rings a mask below, the crusty residue of tears and sleep in the faint lines. Lines my daughter was far too young to have, pressed into her skin by grief. Her lips parted. "Mama?" The word vibrated with confusion, her voice clotted with sleep. She blinked and opened her eyes wide, cracking the salty silt. "He said—"

"It's okay, Jasmine." I pushed her from the office opening. "You know how people are when they lose money. He's all bluster and sweat. And besides, I've hired a Chadwick to handle things from now on. You remember Macon? Wallace's little brother? He'll be here at eight."

I maneuvered her toward the kitchen, intending to distract her with food as I had for many years. "And part of his job is to find out what those phone calls are about." As soon as the words left my mouth I knew I had blundered.

"Phone calls? There've been more of them?" With her greater strength and height, Jasmine brought our kitchenward momentum to a halt. "Mama, are you hiding something from me? Are we in some kind of trouble?"

We. With that single word my heart clenched and opened, like a fist grasping at nothing. A strange heat filled me and was gone. *We.* Lifting a hand, I brushed her hair away from her face. We. The word of inclusion. Of family. Jack and I had been a "we", however false. Then Jack and Jas and I. Now, after so many years as a threesome, my family had changed back to a twosome. And soon Jas would reduce the numbers again, going to Clemson where she would begin the years of study that would take her toward her goal of being a large animal veterinarian. At some point, Jas would meet a boy and start a family of her own. A new "we" that wouldn't include me.

I smiled up at my daughter—so much taller and more beautiful than I had ever been—and moistened a fingertip to rub at the salt on her cheek. She had likely cried herself to sleep. Her skin was the skin of a young woman, not a child, an adult expression regarded me out of her dark eyes. Child-woman. Woman-child. How should I relate to this near adult? I decided to tell my baby the truth. Or at least a version of the truth. "Sit down, Jas."

"Mother," she said, in that warning, irritated tone teenage girls use when they think they are about to be manipulated.

"No really. Sit down and let me fix us some breakfast. And while I'm doing that I'll. . . ." I faltered, turning away, focusing on the roses Alan had given me. I breathed in their heady, sweet scent, noticing for the first time that, as I had predicted, the fragrance had filled the house. I had been breathing their perfume even in my sleep. What would I say to my daughter? What illusions about her father would I destroy? "Eggs?" I asked briskly.

"You know I don't eat eggs." In that tone again. I was making a mess of this.

"Oh. Right. Nonfat, unflavored yogurt and that too-sweet, blueberry cereal you like."

"Are you stalling?" Jas demanded.

"Absolutely."

Jas laughed, a high, tinkling sound that I loved. Sitting at the table, she leaned her chair back on two legs and propped her bare feet in my chair. "So I should just wait and let you figure out how much of the truth you want your little girl to know," she said, her voice amused.

Little girl? This was no little girl staring up at me, her head angled back on a long stalk of neck, her body slightly arched in startling and unexpected sensuality. This was no child. Where had my daughter gone? My little girl? I turned away from her bright, perceptive gaze.

"Something like that," I admitted. "Although it's more like I'm trying to decide exactly how much I really know." The truth of my statement startled me. What precisely did I know? What verifiable *facts* did I have? Only an angry man's incoherent accusation and a few, possibly unrelated, pieces of paper in Jack's office. And that fragment of a handwritten note penned in Jack's neat lettering. *Murder. . . .* But hints were not the same thing as proof, my mind insisted. And just because Senator Waldrop had dropped by for no reason didn't mean anything was illegal. Perhaps I had been tormenting myself needlessly over nothing. Nothing at all. That rationalization made the partial lie I was about to tell easier on my conscience.

Moving about the kitchen with effortless familiarity, I spooned a half cup of plain yogurt into a bowl, setting both bowl and the cereal Jas loved on the table. She dropped her feet out of my chair and sat up straight.

"Jazzy Baby," I paused. *Jazzy Baby. Her childhood nickname.* I started with it again. "Jazzy Baby, I think your father had a bad business deal he was trying to clean up in the last weeks before he died." I opened an English muffin and popped both halves into the toaster, setting a sterling spreading knife and cream cheese on the table. "I think Senator Waldrop was involved in whatever it is, and because I've been too upset to worry about business since your father died, I let the situation go unresolved. In fact, I've let the entire business go too long and the problems are piling up." The muffin popped up from the toaster and I spread cream cheese on thickly. I had always loved cream cheese, the rich white taste of it on my tongue. "Anyway," I said, taking a bite, "I hired Macon to take a look at things and help me clear up the outstanding company debts and make decisions. It'll take a good year to finish up Davenport Hills, and—"

"I know," Jas interrupted. "I never trusted RailRoad the Third either." RailRoad was Jasmine's pet name for Rolland, chosen because he could railroad anyone into anything. She stirred blueberry cereal into the yogurt, making a white and purple slimy mess.

Jas loved the mixture, but it looked vile and I couldn't watch her eat it. Instead, I concentrated on the muffin. "Well, it's not that I don't trust him—"

"Puh-lese. The man's so smooth, he's greasy. This is good," she added, the words making their way past the mouthful of yogurt and cereal. "You really should try it."

"No thank you," I said delicately.

"I don't get it. You can drain a peri-rectal abscess and play in blood and human excrement all day long, but you can't watch me eat breakfast."

"I couldn't watch someone *eat* the contents of a peri-rectal abscess either. And speaking of peri-rectal abscesses, you know your father hated it when you called Rolland 'RailRoad'."

Jas grinned at me unrepentantly and deliberately stuffed a spoonful of her breakfast into her mouth before speaking again. We had taught her better. I distinctly remember teaching her it was impolite to talk with her mouth full. "You gonna sell the company?"

It unnerved me that Jas had considered the possibility, but her face was unconcerned, more involved with chewing cereal than in my response. "It's a possibility," I said cautiously.

"I think you should. You never liked all that stuff, so why burden yourself with it. On the other hand, you could sell the major part of the company and still keep an interest, kind of like a silent partner. We got any tea?"

"Silent partner?" I put my muffin down, two bites missing from the edge. I had never thought about the possibility of keeping part of the company but giving up the responsibility. I was staggered that Jas had come up with the idea. "That's a thought. In fact, it's a good thought."

"Yeah, Paz thought you should offer it to old RailRoad, but I thought you should keep it in the family. You know, sell it to one of the Chadwicks."

"The Davenport Hills investors might have a say in my selling, but I like the idea. I like it a lot." *Unless the investors were involved in a plot to kill a man, which would make any thoughts I had about the development a moot point anyway.*

Jas scraped the bowl clean, her eyes on the motion of her spoon. It was a crisp sound, a click and scrape that echoed slightly in the silent house. She was concentrating too hard on her empty bowl, the click of her spoon filling the void where words should go. And her eyes didn't meet mine. "Did you get things straightened out with Topaz yet?"

"I knew you were going to bring that up."

I raised my brows, feeling like Nana when someone said something she thought was dumb. "You think I should ignore the fact that you and your best friend had a huge, screaming fight out in the yard last night? Over the idea of me dating?" Jas kept her eyes on the empty bowl and still spoon. "Jasmine, look at me," I said gently. She raised her eyes slowly, unwillingly, a frown on her face and a stubborn tilt to her jaw. *God, she was beautiful.*

"I have no desire for another man. Your father was the most wonderful, important man in my life. He was my partner and my friend." The words sounded stilted and thick, shouldering their way past the lump in my throat as I spoke what had once been the truth. Tears welled and started to fall from my eyes, making slow tracks down my face. I swallowed, but it didn't help. And there were tears in Jasmine's eyes as well.

"I have no interest in testing the waters for another man. Dating has no attraction for me. But I also don't like the idea of being lonely. When you go to school, I'll be alone in this big house, rattling around with no one to talk to, share with, or love." Elephant tears spilled from Jas' eyes and ran down her face, dissolving the salt in the cracks and corners. She sniffed and wiped her cheeks. I let my tears fall untouched. "So I'm not going to promise that I won't make new friends some day. And I'm not going to promise that all the friends I make will be female. But please understand. . . ." I paused and wiped my face, realizing that this was my first cry in days. I had counted them once, adding up the totals when I went to bed. My record was twenty seven—almost nonstop tears. Now, it felt strange to be crying again. My T-shirt was damp where the tears had fallen. "Please understand that I have no intention of dating or seeing anyone without us talking first. Our grief is a . . . a shared grief. And we have to get through this together. You and me." Jas buried her face in my lap, sobbing. Through my own tears, I hadn't even seen her move from her chair. With damp hands, I stroked back her hair, loving the silky length of it. It seemed to glisten with golden highlights, the way it had when she was a child and still blonde.

"I couldn't replace Jack, sweetheart. I wouldn't even want to try.

Don't worry about that." And then I simply had no more voice to speak as we sat, mother and child, and cried, silently. Long minutes later we both sniffed and the moment was broken. "And now you go on upstairs and shower and change clothes and call Topaz and make up. You hear?"

"Yes ma'am."

"And be figuring out who we need to hire to help out around here. The farm is too much for the two of us and a drunken stable hand. If you intend to keep the horses, we'll need to hire a trainer and a handyman." I decided I might as well lay out all the cards and let Jas pick up the ones she wanted. My baby wasn't a child anymore.

"Yes ma'am," she said again. She wiped her face on her T-shirt, stretching the neck out and up over her nose. From inside the shirt she said, "I have a few contacts, people I can call to see who might be available, who might want to relocate." She spoke through the wet cloth, hiding the bottom part of her face. "And for a handyman, let's get Aunt Mosetta to send a couple of Chadwicks over to help out this summer. We can look for someone permanent come fall."

"Alright," I said, hiding my reluctance. "I owe Nana and Aunt Mosetta a visit; I'll go by and get her to send me some of her brood." I hadn't visited Nana since before Jack died, breaking a practice of years standing. Weather and my work schedule permitting, each evening after dinner Jack and I had routinely made the short trek to the old Chadwick farmhouse where my Nana and Aunt Mosetta lived, to visit and swap news and gossip. It was time to renew some old habits, even if I did have to go alone. It was also time for Jas to renew old habits. "And speaking of Aunt Mosetta's brood, what about Topaz?"

"Oh Jeez." Jas dropped the T-shirt. It was stretched to the shape of her fist, and settled slowly against her breastbone. "I guess I was a real idiot." I said nothing. "I shouldn't have yelled at her huh?"

"Yelling seldom accomplishes anything productive," I agreed. Jas looked so forlorn sitting on the kitchen floor beside me, her head framed by the spray of roses. Nose swollen, eyelids puffy and damp, and still a bit of sleep salt around them, she looked for a moment like the little girl she had once been. After a moment, I added, "But then again, apologizing helps to build character. Or so my mother always told me."

"Mama Caldwell wouldn't know that. She's never apologized for anything in her life."

"Jas!"

"It's true. Daddy always said so."

I ignored her comment, concentrating on the subject at hand. "Do you owe Topaz an apology?"

Jas opened her mouth and closed it with a snap. I could see her toying with the idea of saying no, the thoughts bounding around like bunnies behind her eyes. "If I said Paz owes me a bigger apology than I owe her, you wouldn't fall for that would you?"

" 'Fraid not."

Jas sighed, one of those theatrical heaving sighs that played so well on the silver screen back in the fifties. "You're going to end up just as opinionated and stubborn as Nana when you're old, you know that?"

"Thank you. I choose to take that as a compliment."

Delivering another melodramatic sigh, Jas got up from her place at my feet and moved to the back stairs. Her pace picked up as she reached the top, and I figured she had either gathered her courage to call Topaz, or she had caught a glimpse of herself in the mirror.

Jack and I had built the house with plans to have four children, two boys and two girls. My inability to carry another child to term had left Jas with no siblings, and three rooms and two full baths to call her own. The fourth upstairs room was used for storing luggage, the nine foot tall Christmas tree that graced the two-story entry hall for one month out of the year, and what Jack had referred to as "stuff": miscellaneous papers, photos, art works we had grown tired of, an old rocking chair with a busted out bottom, Jas' old toys, my old Barbie collection. Lots of stuff.

I could hear Jas moving overhead, muffled thumps, a blare of music. Then silence, as I assumed she dialed Topaz's number.

The storage room. As usual, every thought brought me back to Jack. We had vowed to clean out the fourth bedroom this summer, disposing of the mounds of accumulated and unused possessions. Now I would have to tackle the job alone. Propping my head on the kitchen table, I cried silent tears of mingled sorrow and self-pity, tears which burned and left my throat aching. I allowed myself ten minutes of selfish release. The scent of roses, so strong I could taste it on my tongue, and the sunlight brightening my kitchen pulled me back to the present. Drying my face on my T-shirt, much as my daughter had dried her own, I stood and took the remainder of my muffin back to the master suite. A master suite without a master. God, I hated being a widow.

CHAPTER FIVE

Macon pulled up in front of Jack's office at precisely eight A.M., parking a brand new, four-wheel-drive Jeep at an angle to the office door. The price sticker was still on the Jeep's window. I hoped he hadn't run right out and bought the new toy as soon as we concluded our phone conversation the day before.

The truck was bright teal green with an iridescent glow to the shiny finish; rubber strips ran down the sides and oversized wheels anchored the vehicle. The stereo system would have delighted a half-deaf teenager, blasting a Black Sabbath '70s hit through the open window. Not a very lawyerly vehicle. But then, Macon Chadwick wasn't a very lawyerly-looking man.

Crisp new jeans, a madras plaid shirt with the sleeves rolled up to the elbows and leather Docksiders completed his wardrobe. Only the leather-bound briefcase marked him as a professional. With a jaunty step he came to the doorway where I waited.

There was a shock of delayed recognition as Macon took my hand. The greenish brown eyes and dark-skinned face I remembered from my childhood melded into a man I had seen recently. At Jack's funeral.

"Ashlee. You're looking lovely as ever."

I managed a smile, realizing suddenly that this was going to be a lot harder than I'd expected. Especially with what I had discovered this morning when I returned to the office after breakfast. Macon tightened his grip, his gaze direct. "We'll get through this, Ash." His full lips lifted slightly higher on one side in a charming, asymmetrical smile that exposed even, white teeth. "We Chadwicks stick together." I laughed then, a strangled sound and squeezed the hand that held mine. He had a nice handshake, a good grip, firm and sure, as if nothing in the world would ever shock or startle Macon Chadwick. I held on to that thought as I dropped the hand and guided him into the depths of Davenport, Inc.

Switching on lights as I went, I opened the blinds, exposing the havoc and disorder of the office. Macon stopped, staring at the mess, his brows raised. I gestured to the room and tried for another smile. "Jack's office." File drawers were hanging open, papers were scattered on the tables, the floor, the desk tops. Fingerprints marred the dusty surfaces. Only a few were mine. "It wasn't this way the other day. I suppose Jas might have been in here, but I can't imagine her leaving it like this. My daughter is neatness personified." I laced my fingers together and squeezed. It was a helpless, nervous gesture, but I couldn't seem to stop myself.

Macon set down his books and briefcase on the floor in a rare clear spot. Turning on lamps with the tips of his fingers, he moved slowly through the office, stooped, studied the disarray and the fingerprints in the dust.

After a long moment, he said, "Humm."

"Is that a professional 'humm' or a general, run-of-the-mill 'humm'?" I asked.

"Professional. There are very few prints in the finger marks. At least two people ransacked this place, and one didn't wear gloves."

"I'm pretty sure that was me," I whispered.

"Have you called the police?"

"No. And neither will you." My voice sounded weak and vulnerable, not the strong, determined tone I'd intended. I swallowed. "Nothing's missing. Not the TV, not the guns, not the computers. And according to Jack, there's no way in to the safe." My voice sounded better, but still not firm and in control. I needed to work on that. "I have no intention of telling the local sheriff's office about Jack's problems. Or this." I handed Macon Jack's handwritten letter, the letter about murder. He held it without opening the envelope, his eyes on me. I was sure he was seeing more than I wanted him to. "Besides, with no prints, what can police do?" It wasn't so much a question, as a challenge. And my voice sounded stubborn, which was better than whiny.

"I don't like this, Ash. I don't know what problems you have with Jack's company or his estate, but—"

"Lot's. Lot's of problems. You want to back out?"

Macon sighed, sounding exasperated. "No. Show me what you have."

I explained about the strange, threatening letter I had destroyed. About the phone calls from Bill, saved on the digital memory in the drawer beneath the answering machine. And I pointed to the letter he still held. As I spoke, Macon watched me, his lips tight and obstinate. I took a deep breath, proud that I still sounded forceful. Hoping it would be enough. My hands were white where I had squeezed the blood out of the flesh. "You're going to need some help. I gave Esther two months off with pay when Jack died, but she says she's just sitting around getting fat and annoying Sherman's—that's her husband; he's retired. She'll be here at eight-thirty and if you need anything Esther can help you. She's been with Jack for years." That stopped me.

Esther had been with Jack ever since Robyn quit and moved to Atlanta to take a job with the Coca-Cola company. Robyn who had betrayed me. Slept with Jack. But I didn't say that. Not yet. Perhaps never. Not unless Macon uncovered something I had missed in my last minute search of Jack's desk. It was the one damning piece of evidence I had left out of my narrative.

I had gathered several more pictures of Robyn and Jack from my husband's desk, all the matchbooks from places he had never taken me, all the love letters and dried four leaf clovers I never knew he collected. Gathered them up, all the memorabilia left over from the affair and added them to the bulging grocery bag, returning it to my closet like the dirty little secret it was. I would destroy them later, when Jas wasn't likely to catch me. I pointed to a place on the floor. "Here's the papers that have piled up in the last week or so, the company records, the list of investors from the Davenport Hills project, and—" The phone rang, the shrill, electronically generated, digitized bell interrupting my words like an omen. I jumped, my bravado slipping from me like fleas from a dead rat.

Jack's voice answered. The voice of a powerful man, secure in himself, strong, confident, forceful. Sounding so alive. I clenched my jaw. And then that voice, that hateful angry voice that had woken me so early. "Jack, damn you!"

Macon's eyes moved from the machine to my face and back, yet he made no move to pick up and halt the fierce attack. How could he? He had no more idea what the man was ranting about than I. Less in fact. I sat down quickly and re-gripped my hands. As before, Bill grew increasingly angry, his language coarse and foul. And threatening.

"And I'll see to it you never do business anywhere else again. I'll destroy you and everything you have. Everything you love—" The final tone sounded, cutting off the barrage. A measure of calm descended on the dusty office.

Macon's brows were raised, waiting. I opened my mouth and said the words I had planned ever since Jas and I collided in the hall. "I don't want my husband's reputation ruined, Macon. If he was guilty of something unethical or even illegal, I want it kept quiet. For Jasmine. I have assets both real and liquid, and if you discover that Jack was involved in something criminal, then I want to buy off the man. Settle with him." I stared at my hands, my grip painful. "You need to read that letter." I jutted my chin to the envelope in his hands. He opened the flap and pulled out the single sheet. "It looks like a portion of a handwritten first draft. I don't know who the recipient was. I don't even know if Bill, the man on the phone just now, and this letter are related, or if there was more than one problem."

My hands were no longer trembling or white. Just turning this problem over to Macon was easing the strain, diluting the fear. I was breathing almost normally. I could do this. I could make the necessary decisions to protect my daughter from her father's misdeeds and infidelity. *I have come a long way from the grieving widow who thought her husband was a saint.* I put that thought aside along with all the others I wasn't ready to face. "If I read the letter right, Jack's improprieties went way beyond simple financial transgressions," I said.

Macon unfolded the single page. He scanned the note, looking older and wiser than his young years. He had passed the bar only recently, yet, standing in the unused office, Macon looked like the Rock of Gibraltar to me. As if he could handle anything. I hoped he could.

I had always detested the kind of person who could read a passage once and recall it word for word years later. It wasn't a talent I shared. In school, I made good grades by hard study, not by natural ability. But this one time was different. This one time, I could remember each word of the letter. Each error scratched out with neat little x's. And that damning last word. Murder.

Macon folded the single page, reinserting it into the envelope. "This isn't good, Ashlee. It hints of blackmail and somebody being killed. If Jack was involved in a murder, there isn't much I can do to prevent the truth from coming out."

I didn't want Jas to suffer. If her father was involved in something illegal, I didn't want Jas to discover it. I didn't want her relationship with Jack to be tarnished when he wasn't here to defend himself. I shook my head and turned away.

"On the other hand," Macon said gently, "you and Jasmine are free from culpability. You shouldn't have to worry about the law coming to look for you. And Chadwick connections can protect you from the worst of any fallout. I'll be here to help you handle anything that comes from this Ashlee. You won't be alone."

"I know," I said around the pain in my throat. "A copy of the will is in the stack of papers and the rundown of insurance benefits we received. Macon, I don't care how you handle this problem, whatever it is," I took a deep breath and finished fiercely, "but protect my daughter."

Macon smiled. "I'll do my best, Ashlee, but even with Esther I'll need help. From others in the company, from the CPA firm who handles the general business, from the firm retained to handle the legal business of the corporations. And from you."

My heart sank.

"And we aren't talking about uncomplicated results here. No quick solutions or easy answers. With an estate the size of Jack's, we're talking months. At least."

"Just don't bankrupt me," I said. "I saw the new truck."

Macon laughed, exposing more teeth on the left than on the right in that lopsided smile. More than anything, it was an indicator of Chadwick genes. Many of my cousins had that bent and charming smile. "I bought the truck last Thursday, long before you called me."

"Good."

"I bill only for the hours worked, which is one reason why I'm not in some fancy New York law firm making two hundred thou a year. And I give a family discount. Once I get a good grip on the situation here, and on your personal finances, I should be able to offer you a general idea of the length of time you'll need me. I promise to leave your finances intact. Mama Moses would skin me alive if I took advantage of a Chadwick."

Macon wasn't bragging about the New York law firm. I had heard the glowing reports of the Chadwick's newest success story. He had been courted by some of the nation's best and most prestigious, but he had come home to practice law and eventually go into politics, a far easier goal to reach in the backwoods of Dawkins County than in New York. Macon Chadwick's dreams weren't limited by the apparent step back he took by coming home. I wondered how he would feel when he discovered that Senator Waldrop was involved in Jack's business problems.

And as far as his Mama Moses was concerned, she would just as likely take a hickory stick to me as to Macon if there was trouble. Aunt Mosetta and Mama Moses were one and the same. Together she and my Nana ruled the Chadwick clan, overseeing the physical, emotional, and financial health of the multi-generational, multiracial family. Although I had seldom seen Aunt Mosetta resort to violence, I wouldn't want to be on the receiving end of her sharp tongue. I had seen her deliver a metaphorical flaying more than once, and it wasn't pretty.

A knock at the door alerted us to Esther's arrival, and the tone of the conversation changed to introductions and business. Esther was short, slender, and fiftyish—though she didn't admit to anything over forty. She wore her blond hair ear-length, permed and perfectly coiffed, taking off every other Thursday afternoon to have her roots bleached and her acrylic nails touched up. She tended toward a brightly colored wardrobe and had a strong mill-town accent, her speech liberally laced with country homilies and unexpected mill-town maxims.

Today, Esther was wearing red. Red lipstick, red nail polish, red dress with shiny brass buttons, and red shoes. On some women, the reds might have looked gaudy; Esther looked perfect. Seeing them together, the young, trendy Chadwick lawyer and Jack's vivid, astute secretary, the pain I carried lightened. The load I had carried alone was now shared by three.

I sat in Jack's chair, pulled my knees up and circled them with my arms while Macon and Esther got acquainted in typical southern fashion with comments like, "That means I went to school with your uncle . . ." and "Your daddy worked with my second cousin in high school . . ." They placed one another in Dawkins County's pecking order for the last two generations. I realized I had a smile on my face, and that the pressure between my shoulder blades was gone. This seemed to be working out just fine. I should have done it weeks ago.

Once introductions were over, Esther placed her red leather purse on her desk, her hands on her hips, and surveyed the office with pursed, crimson lips. Speculatively, her eyes turned to me. I grinned, knowing what she was thinking. My reputation as a less than tidy woman was well known. "I didn't do it, Esther."

"Well, who did? It wasn't like this when I left, and you can't tell me that Jasmine Davenport did this."

"It looks like the place has been searched, Esther," Macon said.

"For what?"

"That's what Ashlee wants us to discover. Apparently Jack was having some problems with the business before he died. Possibly serious problems," Macon said. Esther cocked her head. "Ash, would you replay the last message on the answering machine?"

Unwinding myself from Jack's chair, I crossed the room, hit PLAY, and turned to watch Esther. Bill's voice shouted into the office, cursing and threatening. Esther's bleached brows lifted. Her expressions were mobile and eloquent as a monologue. Esther could lie with a poker face when she put her mind to it, but when unguarded she gave everything away, even when she claimed she had nothing to say. When Bill's message ran out, I hit the STOP button. "You know him? I've got a number of messages from him," I said, moving back across the room.

"Bill McKelvey," Esther said. More of the weight lifted from me. Bill had a last name. I didn't know why that should seem so important to me, but it did.

"Jack and Rolland have been tryin' to work out a settlement plan with the man since Christmas."

"Rolland?" Macon asked.

"Rolland Randall the Third. Jack's and DavInc's lawyer, and a sleazier character you never laid eyes on, honey. But then, until I set eyes on you, I never met a lawyer I liked," Esther said as she stepped out of her heels and walked to the filing cabinets. "I've got a file on McKelvey if I can find it in all this mess." Esther had always worked barefoot except when Jack had someone important in the office, and Esther was the sole arbiter of importance. Meaning she went shoeless except when an investor was present. Jack had always been amused at her habit. She went directly to the cabinet storing old business and, almost immediately, returned with a file. Competent Esther at her best. "McKelvey owned the old Peterson Plantation and the two adjoinin' farms that became Davenport Hills. Part of the deal that let Jack develop it went bad."

Esther opened out the file on Jack's desk, the cleanest surface in the office. She glanced at me. "The problem was difficult, but not insurmountable. I'm familiar with the particulars." Esther used the word "problem" like the letters from Senator Waldrop. The problem wasn't some great evil or some private sin. It was a business deal gone wrong, just as I told Jasmine. Hearing the words stripped the mystery and the melodrama from my worries. *But what about the letter and the murder?* I ignored the small voice. Esther and Macon could solve it, whatever it was. Anxiety was worthless in the face of such quick and easy answers.

"The payment for the Peterson Plantation was an equal value exchange involving cash payments spread out over the last ten years, and a piece of land in downtown Charlotte. Only, the land was tainted."

"Tainted how?" Macon asked.

"Chemical contamination. When McKelvey's crew started to dig a foundation last fall, they discovered a World War Two era dump about twelve feet down. Brought McKelvey's commercial development to a halt. And because it looked like an expensive cleanup—we're talkin' millions here honey—he lost his financing. His partners tucked tail and ran."

"Millions?" I asked. Esther nodded. Millions gave immense power back to the word problem. No wonder the senator and investors had tiptoed around it in their letters. *Millions?* I didn't have millions.

"World War Two?" Macon asked. "Like an army dump or something?"

"No one's sure. Rolland was still chasing the paper trail of the land owners and tenants when Jack passed on. But first indicators are yes, an armed forces dump. Which is good, because the government would be responsible for the cleanup."

"And if the government isn't responsible . . ." Macon prompted.

Esther shrugged and looked for a place to sit. Her own desk was visible through the open door to the reception area, but the chaos of littered papers was much worse there. She finally pulled a chair up to Jack's desk and sat, her crimson painted toes rooting around in the darker red of the carpet. "In that case," she said, "McKelvey's on his own. Unless he can prove intent to defraud on Jack's part, or prove that Jack knew about the dump before he sold the land, or prove some other wrong doin' on Jack's part, there's little he can do but accept the loss."

"Could he prove Jack knew about the dump?" Macon asked. A lawyer's question. Not "Did Jack know?" but "Could he prove it?"

"I don't think, so, honey," Esther said. Esther called everyone honey. Even Jack. Even the meanest, toughest, dirtiest, drunkest sub-contractor in the business. It had always been, "Take off your dirty workboots, honey, if you come into my office. I ain't your mother." Or, "Listen here, honey. I said Jack ain't here, and that means he ain't here. So mind your manners or I'll call your wife and tell her how you're actin'." And as strange as it seemed, the combination of endearment and tough talk from so petite a woman always worked. "Rolland didn't think so either," she continued. "But a lawsuit would tie up the last phase of Davenport Hills in court, maybe for years, so to avoid that, Jack was willin' to help out McKelvey. Jack had been talkin' about putting together some investors to replace the ones McKelvey lost, and he talked to people in the North Carolina state capital and up in Washington about expeditin' the cleanup."

"Maybe Bill couldn't *prove* Jack knew about the dump before he sold the land. But *did Jack know about it?*" I asked.

Esther didn't respond to my question, and the words hung on the air like a faint, foul scent. Like something rotten in the office, waiting to be discovered and tossed out. Esther pursed her lips again, her eyes on Macon. "Probably," she said finally. I nodded, no longer surprised that my saint-of-a-husband was guilty of dirty dealing. Suppressing my dismay was another matter, but I had a feeling I would get used to that in the next few days. All that I knew of Jack had been a lie. My whole life with him had been a lie. Jack himself had been a lie.

I looked away for a moment, focusing on an English countryside painting. Beside it was the tiny fireproof room hiding the safe. The ones who trashed the office had left the door cracked. To cover my thoughts, I stood and walked to the room. Like Esther, my toes were bare in the carpet, but mine were unmanicured. I dialed up the random numbers Jack had programmed into the safe when he bought it so long ago. The tumblers clicked softly, and the heavy door swung open.

Inside, nothing was disturbed. The yearly record books for the corporations were still there, neatly stored in their navy binders. The most expensive gun in Jack's gun collection was there. Land deeds, records of various deals and settlements, legal papers. The two-foot-tall metal soil sample canisters which had been there for as long as I could remember still stood casually against the back wall. Even my wedding license was there. All untouched. Whoever had ransacked the office hadn't been able to open the safe.

Jack had chosen this particular safe—used—because it was so secure. An article in the Charlotte Observer had once recounted the tale of determined thieves who had knocked down the wall of a local business with a bulldozer. Lifting the safe with the front-end loader, they had dropped it repeatedly to the parking lot. All they succeeded in cracking was the concrete. In desperation, they had placed the safe on train tracks running behind the business. A train had pushed the safe along the tracks for four miles before the rattled engineer had been able to stop. The safe was still sealed. Jack had bought the same brand, same model, same year.

My jewelry, most of the expensive collection once belonging to Jack's mother, was still in their velvet boxes. I opened one and tilted the ruby and diamonds to the light. They gleamed and sparkled, but the settings of the choker and earrings were too heavy for my short stature. On impulse, I pulled off my diamond engagement ring and its matching wedding band. The stone was brilliant, still beautiful even after all these years. I tucked the two rings into the corner of the velvet box with the ruby and diamond set. Propping open the safe door, I walked back to Macon and Esther. They were talking softly, their heads together. Both looked up when I returned.

"Macon, you better keep Nana and Aunt Mosetta updated on whatever you find. One of the companies that financed Davenport Hills was Hamilton Holdings, Nana's company. And Aunt Mosetta is a shareholder in Hamilton, isn't she?" He nodded. "My guess is that Jack hadn't gotten around to telling them about the problems, so I want them apprised of the situation. And any of the other investors who need to be informed—" I stopped. *Was I going to tell them that the man they trusted may have been a crook?*

"We'll need to send out a great deal of paperwork in the next few weeks, Ash. I'll handle it. And I'll take special care with Hamilton Holdings. Is there anything else we need to know today, Esther? Any problem Jack was working on that might impact Ashlee and Jasmine?"

"Honey, this business is nothin' but problems, day in and day out. And with me bein' gone so long, there's no tellin's what's took root and bloomed up ugly."

"I've listened to all the messages and made some notes and

suggestions. I put the pad on your desk chair, and the full message disc is in the drawer where the spare usually stays."

"I'll get right to it, and soon's I have all that handled, I'll start in on this mess. See can I find what's missin' and what's not. You leave it to me, honey. Me and this good lookin' Chadwick kin o' yours will have this place cleaned up and runnin' like a well oiled machine by sundown or later, which ever comes last." It was a typically Esther twist on the old saying, and I grinned when, without missing a beat she turned to Macon. "You married, honey? Cause there's a new librarian down to the DorCity branch, and she's pretty as a picture. Sexy as hell, but don't tell Sherman I said so. He hates it when I cuss." With Esther settled in and already working at her second profession—matchmaking—I left to get ready for work. I had a long day ahead.

It was a wild night in the emergency room, a night full of drunken teenagers, wreck victims, DOAs, cops, and distraught families. It was the kind of night emergency room personnel truly hate, where police clash with both accident victims and disbelieving, abusive families. Parents who claim that their son would never drink and drive, never buy liquor with a fake ID, never, ever try to outrun the cops in the family Ford, and surely never, pray God *never*, crash and kill his best friend. Never. Not *their* kid. All protestations delivered with alcohol scented breath and liquor reddened eyes and a gentle sway not induced by grief or rage. The police confrontations routinely took place in the hallway, in front of the nurse's station, in front of witnesses so no one could claim that local LEOS—law enforcement officials—did or said anything untoward or brutal. Even when a rare parent struck out in rage. It was the kind of night when nothing we do is ever enough. Where the trauma center's chopper arrives too late, leaving us with damaged bodies and no medical recourse at all.

It was the kind of night where the waiting room fills up with teenage classmates, alerted by cell phones' early warning system. Rowdy and teary by turns, trying to get a glimpse of the injured or the body, they displayed that sense of duty and curiosity, prescient and persistent, that seems to be a congenital trait among the young. It was the kind of night that left a sad, sour taste at the back of my throat, a grim, acerbic flavor that no amount of cola or coffee could wash away.

The coroner's working conditions were even worse than ours. He took the parents of the deceased to the morgue's waiting room, where, with a compassionate voice, and sympathetic words, and carefully phrased euphemisms, he gently destroyed their lives.

Like I said. A hellish night. Long, hot, and emotionally devastating.

At ten-thirty the crowd finally thinned out, leaving us the cleanup, the paperwork, and the emotional letdown of failure. I stripped down a bloody stretcher, catching up the bits of brains that the coroner had missed. Gathered up the paper and plastic trauma suits, gloves and PPE—personal protective equipment—left by the doctors and emergency personnel. Discarded IV lines, a half empty bag of blood, the caps, bits of foil, and trash that always accumulate in emergencies. Around me, the housekeeping crew washed down the floor and blood splattered walls with diluted bleach. Death is always much more messy than the way it's portrayed on television.

The Soiled Utility Room looked like a charnel house. There was a sink full of bloody water soaking contaminated surgical instruments. Two, hundred-gallon, heavy-duty plastic drums overflowed with bloody sheets, like a staged scene at a Halloween carnival. Someone had left a pair of Nike's in the corner, the laces bloody. There was blood everywhere, and I dropped more bloody sheets on one pile, closed up the drum and wrapped my arms around myself, needing some nameless something that simply wasn't there for me. I dropped my head against the wall in the cramped space, my eyes dry but closed in pain. The Soiled Utility Room was always hot, summer and winter, for no reason I ever understood. It was a pressurized heat that blasted out into the hallway each time the door was opened. A heat that closed out the rest of the world.

On nights like this, when I would come home so drained and worn, Jack had always been there. He had pulled my dirty work shoes from my feet, undressed me, and climbed into the shower with me, knowing without words that it had been bad. Really bad. And that I needed him. He had smiled that seductive smile, soaped me down, rubbed my shoulders, and made gentle love to me. Tonight when I got home he wouldn't be there. All that would be there were the memories and, resting in the bottom of my closet, the photographs that branded them a lie.

The door opened silently behind me, given away by the small whoosh of depressurized air as the heat escaped, the sudden influx of noise and unintelligible voices. Releasing a pent up breath, I dropped my arms, plastered my professional smile on my face, and started to turn. Someone gripped my wrist and jerked me back. Tightened. My hand shot through with pain and went numb. Before I could think, before I could cry out, I was immobilized.

Cold, sharp metal pressed into my neck. Hot breath against my head. A foul smell enveloped me, the smell of death. The smell of rotting corpses. I tried to turn my head away and my arm protested. *Rotten meat. . . . And he was tall.* Outrageous thoughts. *He had a knife.*

"Ashlee Davenport. They know you got the file. And them permits. They know you hid 'em somewhere. Long as you don't use 'em, long as you don't ask no questions or cause no problems, you'll be safe. Understand?" He leaned into me, pressing me against the wall. *He was aroused. He was enjoying this.* "I get to take care o' you if you forget." The hand twisting my wrist lifted, sending a searing pain up my arm. The knife lowered and gently touched my breast. He laughed. "I'd enjoy every minute of it, but I don't think you would. So remember, keep your mouth shut, or you're all mine." His tone was almost caressingly gentle, the scent of rotting meat strong enough to choke a mule. "Oh. And they tol' me to tell you. That McKelvey shit? That ain't nothin' to the trouble you'll be in if you mess with *them.*"

He whirled me and shoved, a hand between my shoulder blades, snapping back my head. I stumbled. Landed on the Nike's, bruising my knee on the cabinet. I caught myself one handed; the hand he had twisted was useless. Panicked, I pushed upright. Whirled. The door was closing. I gagged, tasting coffee and pimento cheese, my supper of hours past. Smelling the scent he had brought with him.

After a long moment, when nothing happened, I reached for the door. For safety. Pulled it open, feeling the whoosh of hot air escaping. The hallway was empty. Only the thudding of my heart and the tingling of my hand convinced me he'd been real. I took a breath, and my ribs hurt.

JoEllen glanced up at me as she passed and flashed a distracted smile. "Got a stabbing and a beating coming in from the Bunny Club, Ash. ETOH and fighting mad. A real prize. Thanks for getting Trauma Two cleaned up so fast."

I blinked. "What? Oh. Yeah. Trauma Two." She smiled a tight little smile, walked behind the nurse's desk, and picked up the phone to alert the doctor in the call room. All normal, all routine. Didn't I look different? Or had it all been a waking nightmare, born of imagination and the stress of the last weeks? But my wrist ached and my chest was bruised and . . . and . . . the smell. He smelled of rotten meat. *Like a walking corpse,* my mind whispered.

The doors to the ambulance ramp opened, buzzed electronically from the outside, and in came the two emergencies. Holding my injured arm against my body, I directed the first stretcher to the Trauma Two bed, with its fresh sheets and no brains littering the pillow, the blood mopped up. Behind them came Bret McDermott with the second stretcher. He nodded, flashing a white smile. Medic crews and the

Rescue Squad had both responded to the call—perhaps a fire and accident. *But Bret.* . . . Was it just coincidence that he was here? At this particular moment? I shivered and wrapped my arms around myself, searching for comfort in the only place left to me. I nodded back and licked lips which were dry and rough. I asked, "Did . . . did you see a man come out of here?" I gestured at the Soiled Utility door, and then pointed to the ramp and the outside exit where the emergency vehicles sat, doors thrown wide.

Bret looked over his shoulder, then down the intersecting hallways, and shook his head. "No ma'am. You want this guy in here?" he nodded to the Trauma Room.

"Yes." Bret pushed the gurney into the Trauma Room, still talking, but all I heard were the words, "*That McKelvey ain't shit . . .*" And, "*. . . permits.*" What permits? What had he meant? Esther's words came back to me then, spoken in her slow mill-town manner. *Honey, this business ain't nothin' but problems . . . No tellin's what's took root and bloomed up ugly.*" What had Jack done? What problems had he left? I shivered, standing there in the doorway, hot air blowing around me.

"Ash, this monitor's not working," Bret called.

Monitor? I shook myself alert and stepped into the Trauma Room. The heart monitor was stubborn, a piece of equipment needing to be replaced in next year's budget. I turned it off and on several times. Finally resorted to rapping it smartly with my open palm. The monitor came on.

"Got a problem? Ask the lady with the solution," Bret said.

I jerked my head, staring at him. *Problem* . . . I backed slowly away. Bret smiled. Bret, who was an investor in Davenport Hills. Who might know about problems that involved murder. Who might be more than he seemed . . .

At the end of the long and grueling day, when my feet ached and my legs throbbed and my stomach felt like a smoldering fire ready to erupt, I called my supervisor and asked Lynnie Bee for a few more weeks off. She agreed with no hesitation, even though filling in for absentees is expensive. Her haste in accepting made me wonder if my problems had made me less effective on the job. I should have cared enough to ask, but I didn't. Instead, I clocked out and slipped from the hospital to my car with no farewells to anyone. I drove home through the night with only the sound of the tires to keep me company. I started shaking as the Jeep barreled through the night, my breath coming in gasps and sobs, half fear, half disbelief. And everywhere, I smelled the smell of death. I *knew that smell.* It was the scent of rotting flesh, distinctive and sharp. What *was* the man who had threatened me? My mind filled with images, vile and rotting, the walking dead out of a cheap B-Grade movie. But I wasn't a teenager watching a low-budget film, I was an experienced medical professional. And I knew that smell. My hands gripped the wheel.

And suddenly it was there before me, as if I saw it in a textbook. The scent of periodontal disease. A particularly bad case. I laughed, the sound hollow and coarse. *The man's gums were rotting. That's all.* . . . I drove on, trying to calm my childhood fears, trying to convince myself of the diagnosis. Trying to swallow past the dryness that claimed my throat.

It had rained again while I worked, one of the violent storms so common to the Southeast. Now, the world was still, windless, and suddenly chilled, as a front moved down from Canada, dropping temperatures and taking us back nearly to winter. Big, silent drops gathered at the tips of young leaves and fell, to splat against the windshield. Wisps of fog rose from the warm ground, formed tendrils, coalesced, thickened. Driving became hazardous.

I slowed the Jeep, the tires humming wetly on the pavement, the headlights a white blur on the fog. I passed a dead skunk, its white/black coat washed by rain, its stench strong. Road kill. I pitied the driver who had hit the animal; he would carry the musk scent on the underside of his car for weeks before it finally faded.

I laughed then, the sound wild and shaky. The unbalanced laughter of the not-quite-sane.

I had been attacked tonight. *Threatened.* Pressing the gas pedal, I increased speed, though the curves and hills made speed dangerous, especially with the fog. *The man had threatened me* . . . I should have left the hospital immediately. I should have called the police. I should have—

The tires went silent on the wet road, the Jeep sliding into a bank of fog. *Hydroplaning* . . . I pumped the brakes, turned into the skid. They caught; the Jeep rocked to a halt. Spinning the wheel, I gunned the motor and pulled back into my lane, my breath too fast, my hands tingling with hyperventilation and fear.

Cornering the turn at Magnet Hole Creek, the curve where Alan and Margie and Jim had lost control and crashed, a spray of water shot from beneath the Jeep, like the spray made by a water skier on the lake. The road was inches deep in running water from the overflowing creek. Fog wrapped around me. Forced to slow even more, I made the turn into Chadwick Farm Acres, Jack's first development in South Carolina after we were married. He had turned one hundred acres of the Old

Chadwick Farm, Nana's farm, into upper-middle income housing. Nana had contributed the land, taking her payment in long term dividends, one of the business decisions that had made her richer. I laughed again, clenching the steering wheel. Now he was about to ruin us all. *Jack.* . . .

Still moving too fast for conditions, I swept though the development and on down Chadwick Farm Road. The houses disappeared. Trees, cadaverous and pale, hung over the road, dropping rain like tears. Darkness, made nearly gelatinous by the mist, closed in around the Jeep. My drive was suddenly *there*. I slammed on brakes, my tires an anguished whine. The lights picking out— "No," I whispered.

Across my dented mailbox was a cat. Demented teenage boys sometimes tortured cats. Rarely, teenage girls would injure one. But they seldom arranged them so decoratively. The cat was on her back, hips splayed open and tied into place. Her intestines, pulled from the abdominal cavity, were braided down the simple pole to the ground. There was amazingly little blood.

"Oh my God," I said, into the silence. My eyes were glued to the sight illuminated by the headlights. The car idled in the middle of the road, thick strands of fog drifting past in an inconstant breeze.

I leaned forward and right, pulling the cell phone from the glovebox. I dialed 911.

"Nine one one. What is the nature of your emergency?"

The words jerked me up from the dark, immobile place I had fled to in my mind. "I . . . have a cat . . . a case of animal cruelty . . . to report," I said, my lips numb and moving in slow motion, like the fog that slid past my car. Hiding the cat. Revealing the cat. Hiding it again. I described the cat, gave my address and directions to my house, and was promised a deputy would be here soon. After I pressed the power button, I sat numb, staring at the disemboweled cat. And then I remembered. I hadn't called Jas on the way home, breaking our long-standing rule. Lost in the scent of rotting meat, I had forgotten.

Jas . . . Dropping the phone, I floored the truck. Tires ground on the wet asphalt and sprayed gravel as I completed the turn. The ground was nearly dry here, the storms missing the farm or passing through here first on the way to town.

The drive was nearly a quarter mile long, a twisting snake of a lane with pasture and fields to either side. Young green leaves and wild cedars lining the white wooden fence hid the open spaces just beyond. The house blinked into sight, alternately revealed and obscured by the fog, the trees, and the glaring headlights. I fought the wheel as the spin pulled at the Jeep.

I took the right fork, the quickest way to the barn, passing the two-horse trailer, the six-horse trailer, and the dual wheel Ford truck that pulled them both. The hay barn, nearly empty now, in the early summer, sped by in a flash of headlights. The tractor shed, with the John Deere and the bush-hog and the manure spreader and the plow. The carriage shed, all locked and bolted. If Jas was here, she would be at the barn.

The tires spun out, the Jeep rocking sideways. I fought the vehicle to a standstill and exploded out the door, grabbing the 9mm out of the glove-box as I moved. The pain in my ribs and wrist was forgotten. I left the car behind, wanting surprise and needing the silence. The car was still running, the motor a civilized hum in the quiet, a way out in a hurry, if I needed it.

Fog—damp and chill—and blackness enveloped me. My breath was a billowing cloud in the sudden cold. Rushing through the darkness, I raced toward the barn. No security lights showed through the thin-leafed trees. Only blackness ahead and silence behind; the hum of the Jeep had been swallowed by the night. Fog wrapped around me, a specter of disembodied hands, grasping and groping, wet and slimy cold.

My nursing shoes were never made for running on gravel. I stepped wrong, my ankle twisting a spiraling agony as I fought for balance.

A faint light poked through the dark. The barn was gently lit from within, yellow brightness spilling out from open stall half-doors. Jas never left the lights on when she left the farm. She was here. Some-where. I limped, wet and bruised, through the open, heavy, four-foot wooden front door. Just inside, I stopped, holding the 9mm in both hands, the barrel pointing to the ground. Training remembered from lessons Jack had forced on me during a major rabies epidemic.

The barn was a small affair, with four stalls, a tack room, and a wide area near the big front doors for grooming and saddling a mount. Horses stomped, snorted, and made the less appealing noises of four footed creatures everywhere. The sound of my breath was loud, hoarse. I fought to control it, to breathe silently. Standing inside the barn, the pain in my ribs and wrist from the attack in the Soiled Utility Room returned, blending with the pain from my near fall. I had some bruised ribs, perhaps a sprained ankle. I didn't care.

The barn seemed empty, yet it was the place Jas went since Jack died, talking to Mabel, pouring her heart out, too young to realize that grief shared with humans was grief diminished.

I slipped from the doorway to Mabel's stall. The big, pregnant Friesian raised her head and snorted. Stomped with displeasure, her massive left hoof thumping into the hard ground beneath the thick bed of hay. It was past Mabel's bedtime and she wanted the light off so she could rest. Mabel was crotchety when pregnant. Her stall was otherwise empty.

I checked each of the other stalls. No Jas. The three other mares and their foals were unharmed, though stomping and uneasy. Perhaps the cat was killed close by and feline screams had frightened them. Yet the light was on. *Where was Jas?* I shivered again with cold and shock.

Gripping my 9mm, I stepped from the barn. My hands were slick on the pearl-handled grip—the gift from Jack on our second anniversary, before he understood that I hated guns. I was still breathing hard.

The lights of the Jeep flickered up the lane as patchy fog wisped thicker and thinner before them. Listening carefully, I could barely make out the engine's hum. And then I heard it. The silence. Thick and lifeless and cold as the fog itself. Unnatural. Cloaking me in clammy terror. *The dogs. Where are the dogs?*

Thumbing off the safety, I left the circle of light, moving silently along the path toward the house. The security lights were off, wrapping the house in blackness, the security lights that came on automatically at dusk unless I flipped a control switch. And I hadn't.

The silence was ominous. A complete absence of sound, more insulating than the fog which touched my face in lifeless tendrils. *No dogs.*

"Big Dog?" I called softly. The words vanished in the white. The moon broke through, high and cold, turning the world around me blacker than velvet, overlaid with the grayish white of gauze.

No dogs. No answering whine of delight. No security lights. A whiff of air touched me. Something dead. . . . I looked into the fog, straining to find the scent. *Yes. There it was.* I gripped the gun in sweating palms. *He was here. The madman with a knife . . .*

My feet slipped. I stopped. My heart was racing, an uneven cadence against my ribcage. I ached, bruised ribs a slow, constricting suffocation. *Sticky.* My feet were in something . . . sticky.

I knew before I bent down. . . . Before I touched the sticky stuff with my fingertips. Blood. Tacky. Hours old. "Jasmine?" I whispered. "Jas. . . ?"

The moon above pierced through, higher up and brighter than before, a sterile ancient brilliance, turning the blood at my feet, on my hand, into a glistening blackness. As if the night itself had dribbled down, puddled and congealed.

A dog, his fur dark and mottled, slept a foot away. Slept, eyes open and drying, in dreams from which he'd never awake. Hokey or Herman. Mangled. His back broken. The scent of death, fresh and damp, wafted from him. Similar to the scent of my attacker.

"Jasmine?" I called, moving in the dark. Bile rose again as my feet slipped in the blood.

A few feet away was Herman. I was sure this time because Herman's chest and abdomen were white, and there was enough light to identify him. Herman was belly up, his head twisted to one side. I bent over him. I had seen enough shotgun wounds to recognize this one. It was about three inches in diameter. Close range.

The clinical part of me had clicked on at the sight of the body, the analytical and unemotional part of every nurse. The part that looks at blood and death and suffering everyday without flinching. The part that seems callous and unfeeling, in part because it is. In an instant I became the medical professional who had pressed her bare hands against a child's thigh to stop its lifeblood pumping away. Who had covered the naked bodies of infants and grandmothers when they breathed their last. I was icy cold. Shaking. My hands tingled from fear-induced hyperventilation, but my mind was clear and functioning.

And suddenly I was angry. So angry the trembling in my hands became the shaking of rage, filled with a desire to fire the gun I held. I wanted to aim and fire and— I knew what I ought to do. I ought to wait on the sheriff's deputy who was undoubtedly on the way. I wouldn't.

I no longer considered the possibility that the cat at the drive was put there by kids. I knew that the man had done this long before he visited me in the emergency room. It was a warning, like the letter I had thrown away. Like the telephone messages I had feared. McKelvey? He had claimed to be far worse than McKelvey. *How had he known about McKelvey?*

The anger blazed up, a feverish rage. He *dared to* threaten what was mine!

I laid my hand on Herman's chest. He was cold and stiff. No heart beat in his chest cavity. I backtracked and checked Hokey. Also definitely dead. Raising up, I wiped my sweaty, bloody hands on the uniform at my waist and stepped into the fog. Moving toward the house on the stone path, my footsteps were muffled by the blood caked to the bottoms of my shoes. I was glad I hadn't thought to bring the flashlight in the Jeep or the one in the barn. The one used by the vet when he did minor surgery. If the killer of my dogs was nearby, he couldn't spot me in the darkness. I no longer called out for Jasmine.

The deck and screened porch were suddenly before me, sturdy structures in the wispy fog. Moving right, I searched for a car in the drive. Except for my Volvo, unmoved in weeks, it was empty. I bit my lip, keeping in the sound of my relief. Jas wasn't here. It wasn't she who had left the lights burning in the barn. *It wasn't Jas.*

Turning back to the house, I watched for an attacker who might be waiting in the white shadows for me to finish in the barn and move noisily for the door. But there was nothing there. No lights. No one I could see. Only silence and stillness. The absence of life.

Bending in the shrubbery by the back door, I found the spare key beneath an azalea, pushing through the damp soil with quick stabbing motions until I touched the cold brass. Moving bent over to keep my shadow from showing inside, I cleaned the key off and unlocked the door. If I had activated the old alarm system, would the dogs still be alive? I had never turned it on, not in all the years we had lived here. I wasn't sure I knew how. After all, we were safe, here on Chadwick Farms, at the end of Chadwick Farm Acres. Nothing ever happened out here, so far from the city life Jack and I had fled.

Slipping out of my shoes, I moved into the house and closed the door behind me. The air was still inside, the way a house feels when no one has been in it for hours. If anyone had been inside, it was long ago. From room to room, upstairs and back down, I moved in my sock-covered feet, the 9mm close in front of me, held steady in both hands. Checking each room, each closet, taking special care in Jasmine's quarters, even looking into the attic. No one was here. Nothing was missing. Nothing appeared to have been moved. Jasmine hadn't been here in hours.

Returning to the back door, I slid my feet into my cold, damp shoes and looked into the darkness. By the back door was a slim pen light, an old one I had brought home from work and lost months ago. It was lying in a shaft of milky light, resting in the corner of the door jamb and the wall. It had collected dust and hair, as if building a web for itself. I'd have to speak to the cleaning crew. Picking it up, I checked the batteries, startled by the thin beam of white light. I could have used the light in my search of the house, but then, fate seldom lets you have what you want when you need it. And then, standing half in and half out of the house, I heard something. A faint whine, tenuous and feeble. A scraping sound, like claws on earth. From beneath my feet.

A single siren sounded in the distance.

"Big Dog?" In my fear for Jasmine, I had forgotten about my other dogs. The whine came again, soft, pleading. I ran for the edge of the deck and leapt off. Wrenched my weak ankle when I landed. The breath shot from my lungs. I lost the gun, hearing it skitter across the rocks. *Some hero.* I groaned when a breath finally forced its way into my chest. I had strained my arm. My ribs, bruised before, made a soft creaking sound.

I had lived on this farm for nearly twenty years and had hurt myself dozens of times. But always before I had known Jack would be here soon to help me. Tonight, I was on my own. And I still hadn't found Jas. I lay in the gravel, shaken and bruised, the sound of my breath enveloped by the fog.

Headlights pulled up by the barn. Doors opened and closed. Jasmine's voice. Shrill and angry. Jas angry, meant Jas safe.

"Thank you, God. Thank you," I whispered, the prayer escaping with each tortured breath. I, who had closed my Bible the day Jack died and not opened it since. I, who was angry at God, alright, *angry* at God, first for taking Jack. Then for what Jack had done. *I* was praying.

The whine came again, low and pained from beneath the deck. Rolling back across the gravel, I flicked on the pen light. Two sets of eyes glowed redly back at me. So much for fate having a warped sense of timing. "Big Dog?" He whined, his tail thumping slowly. "Cherry?" Something wriggled and writhed near her, newborn, eyes closed. She panted hard, still in labor.

"Oh. Puppies!" I choked out. And then I saw the blood. Under and around Big Dig, dark clots and pools of it. And the wound on Big Dog's side, gaping red and raw. A hair-matted hole in the thin beam of light. "Big Dog" I breathed. And pushed under the deck.

The wooden deck was low, only eighteen inches or so above the ground. Last year's leaves, old straw, and cobwebs cluttered the space. I shoved with my elbows, pulled with my fingers in the dirt. My uniform top hung on a nail over my head and ripped as I moved. Footsteps thudded up the path from the barn. I heard my daughter curse as she stumbled over Hokey and Herman. Even more colorful language came from Topaz. I dropped my head and laughed, a relieved sound that echoed in the narrow space. "Jas!" I yelled. "Jaaaasmiiiine!"

A vehicle turned slowly up the drive, lights flashing.

"Mom! Mom!" Jas sounded hysterical.

But Jasmine was safe. *Oh, God, Jas is safe!* "I'm under here. Under the deck."

Bodies hit the ground, grinding into my trail. A punishing light stabbed at my eyes. The barn flashlight, its flare bright enough to perform surgery by, blinded me. I covered my eyes.

"No! Wait," I waved Paz and Jas back. "Go inside first, get the blankets out of my closet. Cherry's had puppies, and Big Dog's hurt bad. Call the vet. Tell him if he values Davenport business, he'll climb out of bed and get over here fast. Then set up the surgery in the barn. Now!" I added, when she hesitated after I spoke. Both girls moved.

The sheriff's car stopped in the drive. Feet shod in heavy boots crushed on the rocks. A low voice, authority and safety in its tones, asked questions. My girls, near panic, shouted frenzied explanations.

Jasmine is safe. Jas is safe. The words beat through me like my lifeblood.

I reached the animals, petted Cherry just as a bloody puppy popped out. Instinctively, I caught it. Cherry grunted, squirmed around and began cleaning her pup, warm and wet in my palm. I laughed again. And Big Dog licked my face, smiling through his pain.

"Lordy, Lordy, buckauger whoa."

I looked up, hearing Aunt Mosetta's voice roll in from the fog. Buckauger was one of the more colorful not-quite-swear words the old woman used.

"Hmm. Bet that just jarred her preserves," Nana added thoughtfully. Their voices came up the path from the barn, where Hokey and Herman still lay, mangled and broken.

"Dantucket, I say. Ain't seen nothin' like this since God made dirt." Mosetta's voice ebbed and flowed as if she shook her head while she spoke, sending her words first one direction and then the other. "Dan*tuck*et. Must a happen when we was watching The Price is Right for us not to be hearing these much shotguns," she said. Aunt Mosetta had once spoken like my Nana, gruff and crisp, but as she aged, she slipped back into the patois of her more impoverished youth, using words like dantucket, and the syntax of Dawkins County's African Americans.

"I'll call you in an hour or two, Mrs. Davenport," Doc. Ethridge said, slamming the hatch of his station wagon and cutting off the soft-voiced conversation in the darkness. I turned to him, half visible in the night. "I should know something by then, one way or the other."

His words were crisp and professional, but he ran his hands through his hair like a child faced with a test he hadn't really prepared for. Blood marked his cuffs, black in the darkness. He spoke to me but his eyes were on Jas, expression at once compassionate and firm. "We've done all we can here, Jas. Big Dog, if he makes it, needs more attention than you can give him. Not to mention a transfusion. You can come and see him in the morning . . ." The sentence trailed off unfinished, Big Dog's fate unknown. Her face pinched and pale, Jas nodded slowly. Her long hair was damp from the fog and plastered close to her skull, making her look sallow and colorless in the poor illumination. Topaz, standing just behind her, hands in her jeans pockets, shoulders hunched, looked no better.

And I wouldn't even contemplate what I must look like. Muddied, bloodied, and bruised, I was walking with a limp, had effective use of only one arm, and was breathing shallowly to guard against muscle spasms. Cramps clamped around my chest with each breath. I hadn't hurt this badly since losing my last baby, and that was something I didn't think about. Not ever.

It was the cold, more than anything, that made me ache. Cold and fear and the man in the Soiled Utility Room. *He had been here. He had done this. I knew it.*

"Call you soon, Mrs. Davenport, Jas."

"Thank you, Doc," I said softly.

"Anytime, ma'am." The Toyota station wagon rumbled to life and pulled slowly around the parked cars, easing past the deputy's vehicle and down the tree-lined drive. The headlights lit young saplings and a 'possum that scuttled across the lane, heavy with her young.

Shivering set in, starting in my shoulders and vibrating southward. Muscle spasms around my ribcage were so sharp that, for a long moment, I couldn't catch my breath.

Jasmine met my eyes in the night, a long, bittersweet stare. "You look like shit, Mama."

"You ain't mine, child." The words came out of the night, stern and hard as old stone. "But if you was, I'd box you ears, talking to you mama like that." Aunt Mosetta materialized out of the fog, an oak-brown woman with shawl and cane, shuffling about in red bedroom slippers and a pink chenille robe. Nana walked behind her. "They's ways a talking what's wrong, plague-on-it, an' they's ways what's right."

"Sorry, Aunt Mosetta, Mama." Jas shivered in the cool breeze, looking perfectly miserable. "I'm going to check on the horses and find a shovel." Her voice broke, a jagged, painful sound. "I don't want anything getting to Hokey and Herman."

"Put them dogs in a shed, chile. I'll sen' my Duke to bury 'em in the morning." Duke was one of Aunt Mosetta's grandchildren, or perhaps great-grandchildren.

I nodded, careful to move in tandem with my pain. "Do what Aunt Mosetta says Jas."

"But. . . ." Tears welled in her eyes, glistening in ambient light from the kitchen window.

"Please, Jas. Not tonight," I managed.

She sighed, a sound of real anguish, unlike the dramatic sighs of teenaged youth. "Yes ma'am." She wiped her face with the back of her hand. It was shaking and white and I could hear the tears in her voice.

"I got a tarp in my trunk, Jas," Topaz said. "We can . . ." she took a steadying breath, "roll them on it and pull the tarp to the carriage shed. Come on." She put her hand on Jasmine's shoulder and left it there, consoling.

"And, Jas, why don't you go to bed when you're finished, my girl. You look all done in," Nana said. "I'll take care of your mama for you."

Jas shrugged, dragged her eyes from mine, and followed Topaz through the fog. Mosetta and Nana took their places. "Don't tell Jas, my girl, but you do look like Big Dog dug you up and dropped you on the steps." I wanted to laugh, but the breath stopped in my throat.

"Humph. Trouble breathing?" I nodded, forcing movement through the pain. "Come on Moses, let's put this girl to bed."

"I'll make her some soakey. That put her to sleep," Aunt Mosetta nodded wisely.

"Give her indigestion, you mean. And nightmares. Make it whiskey. Neat. And don't you argue Moses, it's too late, too cold, and my girl's hurting. Come on Ashlee." Nana took my good arm and turned me toward the house. "I'll put you in a tub while Mosetta pours you some of Jack's whiskey."

"Don't like baths. Shower," I said through teeth clamped with pain.

"Not this time. You need to soak. And no arguing either." Nana half carried me up the steps and through the kitchen, the motion jarring me into silence. As we eased past Jack's golf bag, still standing in the hallway, the sheriff's deputy came out of the office, resettling his weapon in its holster.

"Mrs. Davenport, I've checked the house and it seems—"

"Sit down, son," Nana interrupted. Only my Nana could call a forty-year-old cop "son" and make him smile about it. "Mrs. Davenport's not well. I'll be back to talk to you in a minute. Why don't you make the officer a cup of soakey or something while he waits." The last sentence was said back over her shoulder as Nana led me up the hallway. I didn't figure the deputy would argue. Nana in this mode was like a rockslide. You couldn't stop it or change its direction, you just had to stand back and wait for the earth to settle.

"No soakey," I whispered, as Nana flipped on the bathroom lights.

Nana stopped the tub, turned on the hot water all the way and the cold water a quarter turn before she responded. Steam rose above the small pool in the tub bottom. I figured she meant to scald me.

"Why's that?"

"Got no coffee. No biscuits." Soakey was left over biscuits—the harder the better—a little cream and sugar and boiling hot, reheated coffee poured over the top. The mash was stirred and eaten with a spoon. Like Jasmine's breakfast combo, soakey was something I'd rather not watch being eaten.

"Humph. You do still have some whiskey?"

"Yes ma'am."

"Good." Nana unclasped my nurse's watch, removed my turquoise stud earrings, and dropped the pieces of jewelry into the bathroom sink. The watch was filthy, where I had dragged it through the mud and blood beneath the deck.

I looked down, taking in the rents in the knees and the ground-in mud and gore. The elbows of my scrub top were stained with dried blood. Nana stepped behind me, took the neckline of the scrub top in both hands and gave a quick jerk, separating the old fabric down the back seam. The top fell to the tile floor. My scant supply of skinny uniforms had just been diminished by one. "Your uniform's ruined," Nana said gruffly.

"So it is," I murmured as the pants followed suit. It seemed a waste, but at least it kept me from having to stretch or bend. I didn't think I could, not cramping. Moving efficiently, Nana stripped off the rest of my clothes and pushed me toward the whirlpool tub. I felt about ten years old. Since Nana was still in rockslide mode, I didn't disagree, just lifted a leg and stepped into the tub. Hot water swirled around my ankles. Nana *was* trying to scald me. With my good arm, I adjusted the temperature and supported myself as I stirred the water with a toe.

Nana squirted some perfumed bath gel into the stream. The scent of my favorite perfume bubbled up around me, a woodsy base overlaid with gardenia and a hint of spice. A delectable scent Jack had purchased for me on our honeymoon in Italy and replenished every year. I used the gel in the shower, and hadn't realized it made such mounds of bubbles in the tub.

As the water cooled, I sat and again adjusted the temperature, warmer this time. I had hated baths since I was a child, feeling trapped and slightly claustrophobic, entombed in the hot water and porcelain. But as the water reached the whirlpool jets, I sat back, accepted the whiskey neat from Aunt Mosetta and sipped, my eyes half closed. And the tension I had carried like a weight all evening dropped away, melted by the wet warmth that massaged my muscles and burned its way from my mouth to my stomach. Whiskey neat and a whirlpool, a new pleasure I had never tried.

Nana lit the candles on the vanity, scented, hand-dipped wax candles from England that had, until now, been a decorative touch, accenting the rose-colored countertop of the master bath. The electric lights went out, leaving me in the candlelight. The flames flickered and glimmered on the steam-damp brass and porcelain, tossing shadows and hissing in the steam. I drank the rest of the whiskey in a single gulp as Nana went to deal with the deputy. The glass clinked as I set it on the tile beside the tub and slid my hands beneath the swirling water.

I woke half an hour later as the whirlpool jets suddenly stopped and silence filled the dim room. Voices drifted in from the hallway. I recognized Macon and Nana and Mosetta. I wanted to join them, but whiskey and lethargy, heat and exhaustion, had drained me, holding me immobile in a hot wet tomb, just as in my childhood fears.

"It's all tied in with Davenport Hills, Mama Moses. And frankly, I wouldn't be discussing any of this had Ash not authorized me to."

"Why's that boy? You keepin' secrets from Mama Moses again? I thought you mama an' me done fixed that bad habit o' yours."

"No ma'am," Macon said quickly. "Attorney client privilege. It's the law."

Aunt Mosetta "Harrumphed," clearly not satisfied.

"The problem—or one of the problems—is something about the land itself and the equal value exchange that brought the land to Jack in the first place, although I admit I haven't found any irregularities in the paperwork so far."

"Tell you Mama Moses what a equal value exchange be, boy, 'cause so far, you talking nonsense."

"An equal value exchange is the way businessmen avoid paying sales taxes on certain business deals. For instance, if you bought my Jeep Cherokee, you'd have to pay sales tax, but if you gave me an acre of land in the middle of town for it, valued at the same amount as the Jeep, neither one of us would have to pay sales tax."

"Barter," Aunt Mosetta said. From my hot bath, I could almost see her nodding her gray head in understanding. Aunt Mosetta was in her nineties, but sharp as a scalpel.

"Right. Exactly. But some businessmen overvalue the price of a piece of real estate, or conveniently forget that there's something wrong with a property and exchange it for another property of greater value. Effectively, they end up cheating both their business partner and the state of the sales tax."

"I don't understand what this has to do with Jack," Nana said.

The whiskey and the pain held me prisoner beneath the water. I lifted my shoulders and cold air from the window over the tub brushed my heated skin. The window was ajar just a bit, and I wondered when Nana had opened it. Steam swirled up around me, a ghostly haze, half seen in the candlelight. Shadows played tag on the walls and ceiling, merging and parting like lovers.

"It's like this Nana. Let's say you have a piece of land with a cemetery on it, but it's overgrown with kudzu and honeysuckle, and even in winter, the stones can't be seen. And let's say you sell it to me for four hundred and fifty thousand dollars, knowing that I want to put twenty or thirty houses on it and tennis courts and a club house. But you don't tell me about the cemetery and halfway through the project I have to stop. Now I'm losing money. But it's too late to fix the problem because you sold the property I exchanged for the cemetery property. And maybe you've even gone out of business. You're long gone and the problem is mine. And so is the time-consuming financial burden of moving a cemetery."

"That's what Ashlee's man done? Sold some land that was different from what he represented it to be, and now it all coming to light, but he's gone?" Aunt Mosetta asked.

Water moved around me, covering my chin, hot and suffocating, but I no longer wanted out. I no longer struggled against the internal exhaustion and heat holding me prisoner. I just wanted to hear what Macon would say. Coward that I was, I couldn't have told them half as much. A breeze wafted past my face, moving the steam and the candle-light in bizarre patterns.

"I'm not saying Jack did anything wrong, Mama Moses. The piece of property in Charlotte that he exchanged for the old farms making up Davenport Hills was only in his possession for eight months. No surveys or other hard physical evidence suggests that Jack knew the piece of real estate he exchanged for the farms was an old chemical dump. It's likely that he didn't know that the Charlotte property was contaminated." Macon paused halfway through his little lie. Just a faint, half-beat of silence in the midst of his words. Perhaps he hadn't been a lawyer long enough to deceive with equanimity, to fabricate falsehoods on the run. Because Jack *had* known about the contamination. I was now *sure* that he had known.

"But the fact remains that the property is worthless. And the man who exchanged the Davenport Hills property is practically ruined. He's declaring bankruptcy and losing everything. His half of the exchange was a disaster." Macon's voice was different now as he broke the bad news, not the cool, even cadence of the courtroom lawyer, but gentle tones of family.

"And this is the man what killed Jasmine's dogs?"

"No. This is the man who has been calling and leaving the threat-ening messages I told you about. We don't know that he's the same one who killed the dogs."

Nana snorted. So did I. The sound came out as a soft breathy sigh that rippled the water beneath my nose. I knew who had killed Hokey and Herman. I had smelled him. Felt the prick of his knife.

"So. What are you doing to protect your cousins?" Nana asked.

"What." It was more demand than question, and my mind whispered,

Yes . . . what?

"I'm bringing a security expert to evaluate the alarm system for the house, and see about installing a system on the barn and the storage sheds. I'm going to recommend that Ashlee retain this expert's services and use him to look into any other problems, with the aim of clearing Jack's name. I think he intended to clear all this up before he died, and I wouldn't like to see Ash and Jas suffer from something that happens all the time in business." I snorted again, the water moving in faint circles. "And I'm looking into issuing a restraining order for William McKelvey. That's the man who feels he was cheated in the equal exchange." *Yes,* my mind whispered relieved. Macon continued. "Lastly I'm taking Jas and Ash to the practice range for target practice twice a week, starting tomorrow. Ah, today, actually."

"No," I whispered, sinking lower in the tub. I suddenly didn't like Macon Chadwick at all. Hot water moved across my lips as I frowned.

"That chile gonna have a fit. She neva did like guns. Don't reckon I much like 'em myself," Aunt Mosetta said thoughtfully. "But the Good Book say there be a time for everythin' under heaven. And I suppose that means guns too."

"Eat your ice cream, Moses."

"Humph. Would rather have soakey."

"Meanwhile," Macon said, "keep your eyes and ears open and tell me if anything odd or unusual happens around here. I can deal with it and save Ashlee a lot of time and trouble."

"This security expert. Who he be?"

"He's the best, Mama Moses."

"He a Chadwick?"

"I said he's the best, didn't I?"

I could hear the comforting, lopsided smile in Macon's voice. And yet . . . I lifted my shoulders again from the depths of the tub. Too faint a movement to reach cool air. My mind, as sluggish and lethargic as my body, struggled with Macon's words. Like a dream just recalled, like a jewel picked out by candlelight in the velvet darkness of a hand-painted box, something in Macon's story didn't add up. Something wasn't right. There was something else going on. Something besides the threatening phone calls and the obvious problem with the land deal. I knew it because the man with the knife had wanted a file. Permits. He was a new problem, self-proclaimed to be worse than McKelvey's problem. Macon knew nothing about him. And of the two, he was far, far worse.

The candles guttered, nearly going out as a sharp gust blew into the room.

CHAPTER SIX

I spent a restless night, starting at every creak and thump, watching the shadows play against the blinds. I didn't sleep, and fear left me exhausted. In the morning, with nothing solved and no rest, I crawled from the rumpled covers, dawn light striping the carpet through the blinds, throwing the room into a dull monotone, a sepia print. Like my mind when I tried to figure out what to do, washed out and limp and lifeless.

I couldn't go to the police. Not if I wanted to protect Jasmine from the effects of her father's . . . *what? What had Jack been up to that had caused this mess?*

But I had money. Jack had at least seen to that. I could hire the kind of protection most people could only dream of. I had never been bothered with decisions of this sort. Never troubled with thoughts of security or danger. That had been Jack's job. And Jack had let me down.

Muscles protested when I tried to force my body from the mattress, and it took long painful minutes to make it to the shower. Dual shower heads beat the stiffness from my limbs, pinkened my skin, drenched my hair, bringing life back into my body if not my soul. As the water pulsed against my skin, four phrases pounded against my mind, a litany, a solemn cadence, the remains of a half forgotten dream, mocking and curious, the questions in an unknown voice.

"What will you do with the years ahead? What will you do all alone?" And in syncopated beat, "How will you protect your little girl? How will you protect your child?" The words bludgeoned my mind as the water did my body. The dark and solitary mystery of the future. The fear of the present.

Avoiding all mirrors, I dressed in T-shirt, overshirt of warm flannel, and jeans and slipped through the house, leaving Jas and Topaz asleep, heading for the barn. It wasn't often I beat my daughter to the barn. I usually did small chores around the house, like making breakfast or actually hanging up my own clothes, but not today. Today I wanted the freedom of the outdoors. I had troubles, but I wanted to think of nothing, worry about nothing. Today, just for this moment, I wanted nonhuman companions and the feel of the sun, no matter how pallid a warmth, on my shoulders.

Leaving the house, I ignored the insistent blinking red light of the answering machine on the personal line as I had ignored it for days. *What will I do with the years ahead? What will I do all alone? How will I keep my daughter safe? How?*

The sky outside was pale gray, the sun weak, vague, and feeble, the world an uncertain old woman who can't remember what she planned for the day. A tentative ambiguous light, trickling down on the wet ground outside, a false sign of warmth. Jimmy Ray, relatively sober for a change, came running from the barn, his arms flapping as if he would take flight.

"She's down. She's gone down," he yelled.

Jas, I thought instantly. My heart like a fist, twisted within me.

"Mabel's down in her stall."

Relief thundered through me. With a silent gasp, I stepped off the deck and into the yard. The earth squished beneath my feet from the steady rain I had heard through my fitful dreams.

"Looks like her water broke already. I been here since 'bout four, and I done checked on her every half hour, so it can't be too far along," Jimmy Ray said, huffing and puffing and smelling of stale beer and day-old sweat.

A marionette with several strings cut, I ran for the barn, and a birth that stood a good chance of being difficult. This was Mabel's last foal, and at her age, it was possible she should not have been bred at all. His arms windmilling, Jimmy Ray followed.

Mabel was in the first stall past the tack room, her breathing deep and rhythmic. She was already in stage two of labor; the foal's forelegs, covered with a thick white membrane, were visible, sticking through the distended lips of Mabel's vulva. Her tail, which Jas and the vet had wrapped in preparation for the birth, was lifted high, out of the way. Her sides, rounded and ponderous, seemed to ripple beneath the patchy remains of her winter coat. With a heaving sigh the contraction passed; she pulled her hooves under her and came to her feet, an ungainly action, free of her usual horse grace. Mabel was taking a break from the task of birthing her tenth foal. She stood calmly at her feed trough and munched a mouthful of hay. Her black eyes were placid, her black tail held high like a salute, with the foal's feet sticking out behind like extra limbs.

Jimmy Ray and I stopped outside the stall. Resting my elbows on the wide shelf formed by the open upper door, I watched, evaluating Mabel as I had done so often for Jack. This wasn't the first time I had delivered a foal without my husband present. But it probably would be the last time. Unexpected tears stung my eyes.

Mabel, moving stiffly, turned around and stuck her soft nose into my hand, her warm breath whuffing against my fingers.

"You doin' okay, old girl?" I slid my fingers up along the ridges of nose, toward her eyes, gently scratching in the stiff mane. The mare lifted her head and placed it on my shoulder for a moment, as the heated horse smell filled my nostrils and my good arm came up around the muscular neck, slick now with sweat. She looked fine at the moment, as if the night before had been calm and peaceful, not filled with the sound of shotguns and the scent of death. Mabel breathed again, her nose in my hair. It was a melancholy sigh, as if she were saying, "Break's over. I better get back to work." A tremor ran along her body at the involuntary contraction.

Head tossing, hooves pawing, Mabel pivoted and moved slowly to the far side of the box stall and back, walking for a time until settling in the deep straw bed. She dropped slowly, curling one leg under at a time, easing down. Grunting already with the voluntary expulsive effort. In nurse-speak, Mabel was pushing. I didn't enter the stall. Mabel preferred to give birth alone, always had. I was just along in case there were problems. She huffed and pushed, and for a while, it seemed as if Mabel and I were the only two beings on God's green earth, locked together in the birth of her foal. The tip of the foal's nose appeared, wrapped tightly in the thick birth membrane. More of the legs.

The back door of the house slammed, the sound muted from here, and Jimmy Ray reappeared. I had forgotten him. Jas tore in to the barn, skidded to a stop beside me and gave me a perfunctory hug, one arm about my waist, her head above my shoulder. The same shoulder Mabel had rested on. And like the mare, Jas lowered her head and rested her chin there, her breath quick puffs from running. "She doin' okay?" she whispered. "How long's it been?"

"I think so. It's taking a little longer than with her last one, but it looks like she's just taking her time." I checked my watch. There was still blood in the groove where crystal met casing. Big Dog's blood. I hadn't noticed when I slipped it on. I guessed that Mabel had been in labor for perhaps fifteen minutes.

The long length of nose slid out, retracted a few inches, and slid out again. The bridge between the eyes showing clearly. Ripples of exertion flexed down Mabel's sides and flanks.

"Daddy said she was slowing down." A peculiar thrill, like the shock of nearby lightning, shot through me. Painful. Jas had been Jack's little girl. Daddy's girl. "I don't think he meant this though," she continued, her words a soft breathy sound in my ear. "How long has she been in stage two?" It was a professional question, clipped and concerned. My daughter, Jasmine Leah Davenport—the county's best amateur vet. I rocked my head against her face.

"I been checkin' her every half hour since four, so it ain't been too long." Jimmy Ray repeated, from above now, his voice filtering down from the hayloft over Mabel's feed trough. Jimmy Ray knew not to enter the stall. Except for Jack, Mabel didn't much like men.

Mabel's grunting deepened and the tremors quivering down her sweat-streaked body seemed to intensify. The foal started to move again, forced through the birth canal with steady, slick motions. "She's fine, honey," I said, my voice sounding distant to my own ears. "She's in no distress. She's just not in a hurry." My eyes never left the straining horse. My fingers curled into the wood of the door, as if by holding on I could assist the big mare in her labor. The foal's forelegs and the forefront of the shoulders were exposed. They were big and rounded for such a tiny horse, even in birth showing the strength of the breed that would come with maturity. The foal's feet were wet, with the fringe of soft horn hanging out beneath. Jagged, pliable skirts, designed by nature to protect the placenta and membrane from tearing in uetero.

The shoulders slid out and Mabel gave a single heavy grunt of pain, or satisfaction. Perhaps both. The big mare rested again, breathing heavily into the straw beneath her. Beside me, Jas opened the gate to the stall and slipped through, moving around the mare to the foal at her rear. Mabel, intent now on her travail, ignored her.

With delicate movements, Jack's daughter and mine tore the membrane covering the foal's nostrils and cleared the mucous from his breathing passages, a task Jack had always performed with such dexterity and gentleness—with fingers shaped and formed just like his, long and tapering and much stronger than they appeared. Her movements were so much like his that I wanted to cry just watching her. She had even remembered to slip on surgical gloves to protect the horse and herself. I hadn't had to remind her.

I checked my watch. Twenty-five minutes. Maybe more. The official rule of thumb for birthing horses is thirty minutes, no more. Any longer and a vet should be summoned. Mabel quickly passed that time limit, but she still seemed in no distress, just typically Mabel, slow and methodical about everything. And so I waited, putting off a call I didn't think we would need.

Mabel sighed again, resting her chin in the straw. It moved with each breath, silent, but still strong. Jas murmured soft words to mother and foal, pulling gently at the tough membrane, emptying bloody water into the straw bed, exposing more of the Friesian foal's black coat. All

Friesian's are as black as a moonless night, and the coats seem to throw back the light, as if glittering with stars. Mabel took a single, deep breath, lifted her head, and grunted. The foal slid free, his body and rounded massive hindquarters slipped out and bumped gently to the straw.

Jas ignored the cord hanging from Mabel, pulling instead at the membrane remaining on the colt. He jerked once and lay quiet. I watched Jas move slowly around Mabel, checking for signs of distress, signs of prolapse, signs of the myriad post-natal problems that threatened mares. Especially a mare as old as Mabel. Tears welled up and fell as I watched. Jas moved so much like Jack, so sure, so smooth and definite. No wasted motions. Finally she sat back on her haunches, forearms resting on her knees, her eyes on Mabel and the colt. I entered the stall and sat beside the mare's head, stroking her old bones and talking to her as we waited for stage three of labor, the expulsion of the afterbirth.

"Jack's Resurrection." The words were a ghostly echo from above. A second thrill, sharp and cutting, sliced through my chest. "That's what Mr. Davenport wanted to name it if it was a he," Jimmy Ray said.

Jas looked up and met my eyes. "That's what he said, Mom. Jack's Resurrection. Because he hoped this colt would revive the bloodline we lost to EIA."

Five years earlier, we lost our entire breeding herd of Friesians, except Mabel, to Equine Infectious Anemia. Ten horses had been put down and buried in a gully at the back of the farm. The loss of so many beautiful animals had nearly killed Jack. But . . . Jack's Resurrection . . .

Without a word, I rose from the bed of straw, and slipped through the stall door. Tears blurred my vision. My breath was a painful sob I couldn't quiet, racking through me, a harsh, heavy sound. I made it to the house. By feel to my bedroom, the bright cheerful room now a mockery. I closed the door with a soft thud, and sucked a shuddering breath into tortured lungs. "Jack's Resurrection," I whispered, tasting the salt of tears on my upper lip. "Jack's Resurrection. Yeah. Name a colt full of dreams and then leave me with proof of your lies and problems I can't handle." My cry was broken, the words fractured by tortured breaths, more groan than speech.

I sobbed, pain deep in my chest. My whole body ached, my throat a fiery agony. I fell against the wall by the door, blinded by tears and the vision of Jack as I remembered him, vibrant and gentle and loving. The Jack of my dreams, of my memory. But almost instantly the false vision was superimposed by the Jack I had discovered since. The Jack in the photos with Robyn. The Jack of the business world, the money maker.

The man who may have conspired to kill someone. I covered my head with my arms, blocking out the light and the truth of the sham he had been. The anger I had been denying myself, the anger that my pastor had once promised I would someday feel, when grief and shock began to wane, surfaced. In that single moment, I hated my husband. Hated him even more than I missed him. Even more than I had loved him. I cried, beating the wall of the bedroom with my balled fist. Cursing the man I had loved and who had left me. Until my strength finally gave out and I fell on the bed exhausted. I cried there, lying on the bed we had shared, until my throat was raw and my sinuses were clogged and Jack's pillow was wet clean through. I hadn't let Jas wash his pillowcase and it still smelled like him, earthy, with a hint of spicy-warm.

A single silver strand of hair, two inches long, rested on my left wrist. Jack's hair, caught in the pillowcase weave. I lifted the strand and cradled it in my hand. It was all I had left of him. The hair in his brush, the old sweat in the T-shirt he'd worn the afternoon he died. It was still hanging in the closet where I had put it, a memory I had buried my face in for weeks and cried as the scent brought him back to me. I knew that the smells would fade. Soon there would be only this single hair. The thought should have stimulated more tears, but my eyes stayed dry. I smoothed the hair with unsteady fingers. And wondered how I would survive without him. And how I could live with the knowledge of his betrayal.

The rest of the day loomed before me empty as a sandy, wind-swept desert basin, dry and harsh with far too much empty space to fill. The night beyond beckoned dark and hollow and cold, full of fear. My whole life was a barren wasteland. Climbing from our bed, I wiped my face on a handkerchief, once also Jack's. Blew my nose. And placed Jack's hair in an envelope and inserted it like a bookmark in my Bible. The Bible was closed, lying on my bedside table, a light sprinkling of dust on the cover. I hadn't opened it since the night before Jack died. I didn't plan on opening it again anytime soon.

Feeling empty, I went to the bathroom and washed my face, pulled on another T-shirt and retied the flannel one at my waist. Gathering up my keys and purse, I left the house, driving from the farm in the Volvo, not even recognizing where I was going until I was nearly there. The cemetery. The place where Jack was. This new Jack. The liar. The cheat. The man who had died.

I stared down the row toward Jack's grave, green grass in irregular patterns, gray marble headstones, silk flowers in plastic urns. The flowers were wired to the urns, which in turn were all wired into concrete anchors beneath the soil. It was a contraption designed to thwart the intentions of modern-day grave robbers, the kind who would drive up to a cemetery, park, and walk among the graves, plucking up the bouquets that honored the dead. The silk flowers ended up in flea markets or yard sales, the profit a bonus to thieves who had no more morals than to steal from the dead. I walked the rows of tombstones as the sun rose high, needing to see the marker with his name on it and the dates of his life cut into the stone. Needing to accept fully that he was really gone, the man I'd thought I had known. Really him, once and for all, buried here. Or needing desperately to find that it was someone else's life and death and lies. That the last miserable weeks of grief and fear, sleeplessness and utter agony were just a horrid dream and nothing else. Needing to prove that my anger was false and unnecessary.

But it was Jack beneath the soil. It was my husband. My fingers traced the letters of his name, the years of his short life. The stone was rough and cold in the chiseled shapes, and smooth and cold on the polished surface. And wet with dew that ran down the stone like tears.

Dew seeped from the grass through the denim of my jeans, chilling my skin where I sat before the stone. Is this the way he felt down there? This damp and cold? But then, he wasn't down there, was he? Only his body, moldering and withering. I was a nurse. I had seen bodies which had been dead for just as long as Jack. My mind veered quickly from the pictures, like a rat skittering down a frozen hillside.

"How do I accept your leaving?" I whispered through tears that slid down my face. "How am I supposed to accept the thorough and total finality of your death? The absolute fact that you will never, ever be there for me again. And the fact of your deception. Your infidelity. Your lies. Oh, God. So many lies." Tears fell on my hands and slipped across my skin, joining the cold dew. Making little iridescent puddles in the pale light of the rising sun. "How do I grieve? How do I hang on to my love in the face of all this?" I asked my dead husband. "Or does that have to die too? Does your death destroy both you and my love? My trust? All that was a part of our life together? And if so . . .what will I be then? *Who* will I be?"

I cried there, at the grave of my husband. Cried as the sun rose around me and burned off the last of the night-fog. Summer was coming, would be here soon. I could feel it in the rising wet heat that lay like a bath against my skin. I could see it in the mating dance of male cardinals, gathered in red clusters, screaming and fighting in mid-air, five or six of them battling for dominance. I could hear it in the hunting screech of a red tailed hawk. The far off stench of a skunk on the prowl.

Jack is dead. Jack is really dead. I sighed, the breath painful. Pushing away from his headstone, I went to my car. Stumbled over the gravestone of a child. Losing my way in the early glare, I panicked, hysteria gripping my heart as I looked around at the death. Death everywhere. Until I saw my car, just beyond a row of headstones. Runnelled with dew, windows almost opaque in the damp. Tears shimmering into rainbows at the edges of my vision. I fell into the safety of the Volvo, locking out the stone-hard evidence of mortality. I drove home. Home to my daughter and to whatever life I could make for myself in the reality of Jack's death.

Jas and I left the security expert checking the old system, various electrical tools scattered across the kitchen table, others hanging from his belt for immediate use. Macon had wasted no time in satisfying Nana and Aunt Mosetta as to our safety. And, as promised, the expert was a Chadwick, but a Chadwick several generations removed, with very dark chocolate skin and molasses brown eyes and an intensity unexpected in one so young.

Chadwick T. Owens—known in the family as Wicked Owens, a play on Chadwick that was more than appropriate—had been a troubled youth. In and out of gangs and involved in petty crime, he had been a resident of the juvenile justice system rather than the public school system until the age of fourteen. When he was accused of killing a man. Aunt Mosetta had hired a detective to clear his name. When the PI was successful, Wicked went to work for him to pay off his debt to the family matriarch. He'd been on the straight and narrow ever since, not that he'd had much choice against Aunt Mosetta's plans for his life. Though I had never met him, Wicked Owens was a near legend in Chadwick lore. One of the lost ones brought back to the fold.

He was in business on his own now, running Chadwick T. Owens Securities. He was one of the best in the business. Aunt Mosetta had surely known who the security expert would be. If I had thought it through, I would have known it myself. I took an instant liking to Wicked Owens, though he was too busy to do more than nod when Macon introduced us. He'd be around for a day or two, his little electrical devices probing and analyzing. I was obscurely comforted by the thought of his watching over us. Not that he would be any personal protection at all, Wicked being a small, wiry man, weighing not much more than Jasmine's new foal.

When Jas and I left at nine, he followed us to the cars, checked under the hood and beneath the vehicles before he would let us drive away. Cautious to an extreme, was Wicked Owens. As we drove off, he stood, arms akimbo, surveying the yard, the drive at the back of the house, and the house itself. He didn't seem very happy about it, but that was his problem. I had other worries.

Big Dog had survived the night. Doc Ethridge had him in the back of the vet clinic, in a little room off the surgery, his body bandaged and IVs running. Because Big Dog was too massive for even the biggest indoor cages, he was stretched out on a pallet in the corner. And although he was still woozy from pain killers, he thumped his tail enthusiastically when we entered. Jas dropped to the floor, running her hands across his body in her semi-professional way, murmuring endearments and scratching under his chin. I wished for a camera, so I could take pictures, just as I had when Jas was a toddler, first discovering a love of dogs.

She had been three, and Jack was training a spotted hunting dog, using an old shoe wrapped with feathers to teach the stray how to fetch. "Go get it boy," he said, throwing the old shoe as far as he could. And Jasmine, who had claimed the stray's affection, wailed at the top of her lungs because the dog loped off. Jack laughed that wonderful laugh and tossed Jasmine high in the air, catching her on the way down, turning her wail into laughter that matched his. Jas and Jack. Inseparable since her birth.

"Mrs. Davenport, the doc is free now."

I pulled out of my reverie and followed the veterinary tech to a cubbyhole where Doc Ethridge washed his hands at a large stainless steel sink. Water pounded as the vet scrubbed, using the same sterile technique as medical doctors, cleaning under his nails, pushing back his cuticles, rubbing at his wrists. And like medical doctors everywhere, he looked tired. Saving Big Dog had been an all-nighter.

Doc Ethridge was a medium kind of man. Medium height, medium weight, medium brown hair. But the circles beneath his eyes were dark brown with a faint lavender tint, and his skin was sallow, as if he hadn't seen the sun recently.

"Morning Mrs. Davenport. Have you seen Big Dog yet?"

"Yes. I did," I said. "And I want to thank you so much for saving him. I—"

"Well, he's not out of the woods yet," the vet interrupted, "but barring any complications, he should be nearly good as new in a week or so." I nodded again, feeling awkward. "He'll need some physical therapy on that hind leg, but it's something you can do at home. One of the shotgun pellets lodged up under his kneecap."

Doc Ethridge shut off the water and dried his hands in the sudden silence. "There may be some damage to the cartilage, and he may limp, but that's a fairly minor problem. A bigger one would be if his left kidney shut down. There were two pellets near the kidney's circulatory system." The vet dried his hands on brown paper towels and pointed to a dusty plastic dog kidney on a shelf. There were other various organs and body parts there, all neatly labeled according to species. His voice was an exhausted monotone, and I realized he was running on nervous energy and caffeine, explaining by rote.

"One of the pellets was lodged about here, just under the large vein that services the kidney. I removed that one. The other I left, lodged beside the renal artery, that's the major artery feeding the kidney. It was a judgment call I may live to regret, especially if infection sets in, but at the time, I was balancing between the damage I might do if I tried to remove the pellet and the damage if I left it." Doc rattled on, damp fingers touching his hair, adjusting the surgical mask still hanging around his neck, scratching his chest. "Quite frankly, infection seemed the lesser of the two evils." I wondered how many cups of coffee he'd consumed throughout the night, and how long since he'd had a full night's sleep. Propped against the doorway, I waited out his monologue. "But if his temperature stays normal, and if it looks like he's stable, he can go home in a day or two. If blood or pus shows up in his urine, he may need a positive contrast urethragram—that's an X-ray of his kidneys where we put in dye." Doc was really tired if he thought I needed the explanations. I resisted the urge to smile. "It's something we can do here; you can just drive Big Dog down, we'll sedate him, take the picture, then you can drive him home. I'll study the report and we'll decide what to do after that. I'd hate to go back in," a polite way of saying he might have to re-open the wound and perform a second surgery, "but that remains a possibility."

I nodded again while Doc Ethridge scratched under his arm. I wondered if he had a flea. That wasn't a problem medical doctors had to contend with very often, but a vet's patients were often creatures of the outdoors, like Big Dog. Then again, perhaps the itch was just a symptom of too much coffee and too little rest.

"Sheriff Gaskin's office called about your other animals earlier today. Seems like an animal rights reporter at the State paper picked up the story and ran it this morning. They've had enough calls to warrant a close look at the situation. He ordered autopsies and had the bodies brought in."

I dragged my eyes from Doc's scratching fingers to his face. I hadn't known of the sheriff's interest, hadn't seen him today. And then it hit me. Wicked Owens was in town. Did Wicked call up a reporter last night and get him to run the story? And did he then make dozens of calls to the sheriff's department pretending to be irate citizens concerned about dog killings? Or did he simply call up the vet's office, pretending to be someone from the sheriff's office, and ask for autopsies, saving time, a phone call or two and lots of red tape? Wicked had a reputation. Impersonating an officer of the law would be in character.

"He said you'd pay?"

I nodded after a moment. He was talking about paying for the autopsies. "Sure."

"On gross physical examination, it looks like both dogs died from shotgun wounds inflicted at close range, although there is some bleeding behind one of the dog's eyes, which could be indicative of a traumatic head wound. One of the dogs lost an ear. It was a clean cut, and because of the lack of bleeding at the site, I'd have to say it was most likely administered after death, to what purpose I couldn't say.

"The cat was probably dead before it was eviscerated. There are what look like tire marks up its back, maybe a crushed skull, broken spine. X-rays are being developed now on all three animals, and I'll know more this afternoon when I get a chance to open them up."

I asked, "Who at the sheriff's department called you about the dogs?"

Doc Ethridge made a let-me-think gesture with one hand and then shrugged, the motion exaggerated into a stretch by exhaustion. "I don't remember. Why?"

"Oh, I just wanted to call and thank them for their, uh, interest." Doc looked up at a sound in the doorway. Quickly, before he got away, I asked, "Did you see who brought the dogs in this morning?"

"Yes, ma'am, but I didn't get his name. Black guy, 'bout five-five. Must be new on the force, but with what little we pay them, the turnover's more than I can keep up with."

Wicked Owens was five-feet-five. And not well known in town. I groaned inwardly, hoping Wicked wasn't more trouble than he was worth.

"Doc," a tech said from behind me. "We have an accident victim at the back door. Black Lab, a big one."

"Get a gurney, I'm coming. Mrs. Davenport, I'll call tonight and update you on Big Dog and the others." And then he was gone, leaving behind the familiar hospital smells of medicinal soap and antiseptics, the less familiar smell of flea spray. And his itch.

Watching him scratch was contagious and I pulled at my scalp with sharp, uneven nails as I returned through the convoluted hallways to gather up Jas and drive home. The cat had been road kill, and that seemed significant. An afterthought? A lucky find that finished off a perfect evening? Or the incident that set the stage for the killing spree that followed? The cat could have been a separate incident entirely, carried out by kids who'd had more beer than their livers could metabolize. However, I had a natural aversion to the concept of coincidence. All the dead animals seemed to me the direct result of Jack's business dealings. Which meant that I needed to talk to Macon and Wicked about the man who'd threatened me. I didn't exactly look forward to admitting that I had been threatened at knife point and hadn't told anyone or called the police. It had seemed the only choice open to me at the time, back when I hoped to protect my daughter from the truth about her father. But before the confession session, target practice.

Target practice, for me, was a misnomer. I could point, aim, and fire, but I seldom hit anything I intended. Jack had always stayed well back of me on the rare occasion when he could persuade me to go shooting. But if it kept Macon happy I'd aim and fire.

Puckey's Guns 'n' Things was a ramshackle former sharecropper's cabin with rooms added over the years as Puckey's business and Puckey's family grew. From outside, the house was a confusion of building styles and materials, poorly constructed with ill fitting joints, warped boards and no particular color scheme.

Inside, it was much the same with floors slanted one way and then the other, odd changes in foundation levels, with single steps up or down between rooms, and the garish color scheme of demented, colorblind gypsies. Three front rooms were dedicated to the business, to handguns, knives displayed beneath locked glass, and to hunting equipment. The rest of the house was full of kids, cooking smells, dirty diapers, and Puckey's hunting dogs. It didn't sound like much, but Puckey had the finest selection of weapons and ammo in three counties.

Out back, Puckey had a custom-made target range. Puckey had allowed a builder to use his back property as a dump for over ten years until the county put a stop to it. There were four, large, irregular shaped hills behind Puckey's, composed of beams, carpet, old shingles, the occasional chipped tub, sink, toilets, tires, broken concrete, vinyl flooring, wet drywall, and anything else the builder had wanted to discard. Rumor insisted that bodies were buried in with the rubble, but the one time the sheriff had investigated the rumors, none had been found.

Over all the accumulated trash, Puckey had dumped dirt. Loads and loads of dirt, until the hills were smooth and compact. Grass, spindly pines, kudzu, and scrub cedar grew on the packed dirt, their roots holding the hills in place. Between the artificial hills and Puckey's peculiar domicile were rickety tables where practitioner's of the art of target shooting—or prospective clients—could place their gear as they honed or evaluated skill and equipment.

Man-shaped targets or round bull's-eye targets could be purchased from Puckey, along with advice and ammunition, after which it was a simple task to hang the targets on the small tree of your choice, position one of the rickety tables, and proceed to pepper one of the hillsides with bullets. In the damp of midmorning, Jas, Topaz, and I picked a hill, two tables, and placed targets while we waited for Wicked to arrive. I wasn't happy about our purpose. I still hated guns. But to protect myself and Jas, I might have to do many things I didn't want to do. Target practice might be only the first.

Though my ribs were an alarming shade of purple-black, and though I was so stiff I could hardly move, I loaded and emptied clip after clip of ammunition under the watchful eye of Wicked Owens. Taciturn by nature, Wicked quickly lost his reserve in his appreciation of Jasmine's skill and proficiency. He coached her on a variety of revolvers and semiautomatic weapons, even bringing several from the trunk of his car for her inspection and use.

When he watched me, he kept silent. His only reaction to my competency level was a tight mouth and obvious self restraint. I had never been a very good shot, and with my body so bruised and tender, I didn't hit a single target. At the end of our two hour session, Wicked coaxed me through the process of cleaning my 9mm, packed up his trunk and drove off.

His only and final comment to me about my shooting was delivered through the open window of his old Crown Victoria, the car idling with a powerful thrum. "Cousin Ashlee, it might be a good idea for you to consider using hollowpoints or starburst rounds. That way if you ever do hit anyone, you'll at least slow him down."

All in all, it wasn't a very promising recommendation, and yet, I felt more positive than I had before the practice. Perhaps it was the loud noise, the smell of boiled linseed oil and gunpowder, or the possibility of controlled violence held in the palms of my hands that contributed to my exhilaration. Not that I'd ever admit it, especially after all the years I'd professed my adamant hatred of guns. I was a nurse, dedicated to the preservation of life at all costs. I wasn't *supposed* to like guns. Or perhaps my "almost-elation" was the result of the intense, intimate, secret anger that was building within me. Anger boiling viciously under the surface. Anger against Jack. Anger, that he had bequeathed these problems to me. Anger that he had slept with Robyn and left the evidence where I would surely find it. Anger that had slowly encapsulated my grief, rendering it empty and meaningless. Anger that had no outlet. Or perhaps it was simply natural, because my home had been threatened, and God had built into the females of all species a drive to protect. A drive that brought out the primitive and the savage, and made all other emotions and needs impotent and unimportant. Whatever the reason, as we drove away from Puckey's I was more positive and in control than I had been since Jack died. This unanticipated feeling of almost-serenity left me ready to face Macon and Wicked about the man with the knife. The man who had peridontal disease. I was sure of my diagnosis. The stench was too strong to be anything else.

The girls and I stopped at Miccah's for salads on the way home, making great heaped mounds of assorted raw vegetables and meats and cheeses and carting them home to eat. We bought an extra one for Esther, and sandwich plates for Macon and Wicked. An offering on the altar of my guilt, or a cheap attempt to soften their anticipated irritation.

We paused at the mailbox for the day's assortment of bills and junk mail, and I was surprised. It was a new box. No sign of the cat's funeral bier remained. The metal was a shiny, glossy black. Jas didn't mention the box, so neither did I.

Nor did I mention the cream-colored, linen envelope that I discovered in among the advertisements. It had no return address. Just like the last threatening letter I had received. I folded the envelope and tucked it into my pocket so the girls couldn't get a look. Neither noticed.

Lunch was a noisy affair, with Wicked giving accurate, if unkind, descriptions of my inability to find a target, and me defending my poor marksmanship. I blamed all the missed shots on my bruised ribs, but discovered that excuses weren't acceptable to the crowd of gun lovers.

The girls giggled a lot, sounding like typical teenagers, which would have humiliated them had they been aware. Topaz spent the entire meal casting covert glances at Wicked, much to Jasmine's amusement. Topaz's fascination with the reformed black sheep of the Chadwick clan had gone unnoticed at Puckey's, but was clearly obvious over lunch, the girl staring moon-eyed at his every move.

Wallace and Pearl would have hysterics if they found out. Their daughter was destined for greater things than to be the kissing cousin of Wicked Owens. And they would likely blame me if the infatuation got out of hand. I'd have to mention it to Wicked if I could find the right time, place, words, and courage. Sometimes I hated being a Chadwick. At any rate, there was laughter and life around the circular kitchen table for the first time in weeks. It was good for Jasmine and it was good for me, even with the unopened letter in my pocket.

The rest of the day was pretty much awful.

To say that I was lectured by my Chadwick protectors for neglecting to mention the man in the Soiled Utility Room was an understatement. The diatribe didn't even fall into the same category. A holy rollin', hell and damnation sermon, delivered at the top of twin pairs of lungs would be more accurate. I was flayed, skinned, and beheaded like a catfish.

The punishment only grew worse when they opened the envelope I had hidden away. Just as I thought, it was a threatening letter, and like the first one, it had perfect grammar, no typos, and offered a glimpse into the new problems in DavInc.

Macon read the letter out loud three times, and each time his voice grew more frustrated.

Ashlee Davenport,
You have the permits and the file.
You hold your health and safety in your hands.
Guard them both well.

By the end of the third reading, I knew it by heart. Macon held the letter by the edges, and carefully set it aside for a later fingerprint analysis, a request Wicked made even before they opened the envelope. Like so many things in my life at the moment, this was a bigger issue than I could handle alone.

The confession session would have been amusing, but they called in Nana and Aunt Mosetta to render judgment, and the worry on my Nana's face was the real punishment. She wanted me to take Jas and move for a few days, until Wicked and Macon could solve this thing. "Head for the hills," was the way she phrased it. I had enough Chadwick genes to be stubborn. I might send Jasmine off for her safety, should she need it, but I was staying right here. Period. No one liked it, but they finally fell silent in the face of my determination.

We agreed that Jas and Topaz should go to the beach house with Mama Pearl—Wallace's wife, Topaz's mother—and stay for several weeks. As the girls had plans to go for seven days next month anyway, Nana thought it shouldn't be too difficult to convince them to leave early and stay longer. But she and Aunt Mosetta planned without thought for my daughter's wishes and her precious horses, and without considering Topaz's crush on Wicked. However, ensuring my daughter's safety took the spotlight off me, so I went along with their plans, knowing all along it wouldn't work. Even when they were younger, I had seldom been able to convince Jas and Paz of anything, not without Jack's authority to back me up. Now that they were grown, the prospect appeared even more daunting. The early vacation might never happen if the family matriarchs expected me to enforce their wishes.

Wicked wanted to teach me a few self defense moves, but my body couldn't take the strain. I was taking painkillers and started icing down my ribcage every few hours to cut the inflammation. I knew I would pay for the target shooting with hours of discomfort tonight. Any additional activity would have to wait at least a week.

The final result of my confession was much as I had thought it might be. I would stay home, take care, and contact Wicked if I felt threatened. The non-solution to my worries was pretty much what I had concluded on my own. Until Macon pinpointed the dangerous party sending the letters, isolated and disabled any danger presented by McKelvey, and found the foul smelling man in the ER, I would remain a target. I could prepare defensively, but there was little I could do to draw out my attacker and nothing I could do to outguess him. No one was happy with the situation, but I felt safer knowing Macon and Wicked were protecting me.

That night, my sense of safety slunk away, following the headlights of Wicked's car. He had repaired one of the security lights so the yard wasn't totally black, but the pool of darkness once lit by the other light was a black hole in my sense of refuge. The shotgun, which had only taken out the bulb on one creosoted pole, had damaged the socket in the other. Days might pass before it could be repaired. Days and dark nights. And, to make my sense of unease more acute, Wicked had expressed his displeasure with the layout at the back of the house. Although one could hear most vehicles approaching the house, they were visible only sporadically through the young trees lining the fence. If the car was quiet or the TV or radio was on in the house, there might be no warning of the arrival of visitors or enemies. I had known all that, but the fact of our isolation and lack of security had never mattered before. Now it did.

After the sun set, I wandered the lower part of the house, checking and rechecking the locks on the windows and doors, looking into the night, wandering past the steady red light of the security system. For years, the light had remained a steady green, unarmed in the safety and peace of the country, far from the crime of city life. The new red light was a constant rebuke against Jack. Whatever unethical or illegal activities he had been involved in, whatever lies he had told, now we were paying the price for his indiscretion. With every circuit I walked, my anger was building. How *dare* he. *How dare he die*, leaving Jas and me alone, in danger.

When I did lie down, the long hours passed with little sleep and bad dreams. The next night was no better. It would improve when Big Dog returned home. With Big Dog gone, I had no warning of strangers approaching the house, no real security. And that left us all in danger. Because of Big Dog's absence, McKelvey and friends had unimpeded access to my home.

The second morning, Jas found tacked to the barn door, a rancid, withering ear. Herman's ear. We had gone to the barn together before daybreak, and the dark-skinned ear stood out black and wrinkled against the white paint of the door, held in place with a red tack. There was no note tacked with the ear, but then, whoever left it didn't really need to leave words. He had accomplished much with very little. He had killed. He could get close to us. We were not safe.

Silently, Jas pulled it off and buried it over the site of Herman's and Hokey's graves to the left of the barn. After we brought the dogs home from the vet's, one of Aunt Mosetta's younguns had dug a deep, round hole, and we had curled Hokey and Herman around each other in the bottom, leaving them sleeping in death as they had slept in life. With the ear, they were complete and our job to honor them was done.

Hours later, after I finished going over the day's business with Macon and Esther, I returned to the barn. The sun had finally caught up with the season and I felt the return to early summer. It was warm enough to enjoy being outdoors but without breaking a sweat. And in front of the barn I discovered Jasmine, Topaz, and two little Chadwicks, the smallest pair being read the riot act by Topaz.

"And don't you act like little street niggers either."

I jerked at the word. *Nigger*. In my youth, it was a taboo expressions on Chadwick land. Like the term *boy*, it was demeaning and racially in-flammatory and *just. not. used.* Ever. Yet Jas hadn't flinched. And Topaz used the word with the liquid fluidity of long practice.

"You want a job, you'll work and work hard and do everything Jas and Mamash say. We Chadwicks don't shirk our duty, and we give good honest sweat for our pay." Topaz put both fists on her hips and bent over the two youths. "I find you layin' around or mistreatin' the horses, dogs, or cats, and I beat you both the first time." She paused a moment, ominously, and dropped her voice. "And I tell Mama Moses the second. You hear?"

Both kids nodded, faces subdued.

"What about snakes? Can we kill snakes?" the young man asked.

"Yeah, I hate snakes. They bite you," the girl said.

"Green, black, or any with stripes runnin' down this way," she demonstrated holding an invisible snake by its head and running a finger to its tail, "you leave alone. Any brown ones, you can kill, and any with

heads shaped like this." Topaz made a triangle with the index fingers
and thumbs of both hands. It roughly resembled the classic spearhead
shape of most poisonous snakes. I was impressed. Topaz was a city girl,
if you could call DorCity a city. But she knew her poisonous snakes.
With few words, she had divided safe from dangerous.

"What about rats?"

"Cats eat rats," one said to the other and shoved the offender's
shoulder. A pushing match ensued, brought to a quick halt by Topaz.
She grabbed one by his hair and one by an ear and shook hard. "I said
you act like niggers and I throw you to Mama Moses." The struggling
ceased instantly and I placed a hand over my mouth. I had seen Aunt
Mosetta stop a potential fight in a similar manner. Grabbing, shaking,
and issuing a threat. They say blood will tell, and Topaz Chadwick was
the living proof.

"They can kill rats, right?" Topaz asked Jas, not quite certain.

"Yes. And for a good days work you get paid good green money.
And all the real homemade lemonade you can drink. Nana said so."

"Yessss," the young man said. The other echoed his delight.

I put their ages at about twelve. The young man was bigger, the one
with the obvious fear of rats was the girl with her hair in corn rows.
Both had the distinctive greenish eyes of Aunt Mosetta's branch of the
family, and both froze when they looked past my girls and saw me.

It was an uncomfortable moment and I wasn't quite sure why, until
the little girl stepped past Jas and walked the short distance to me. She
held out her hand, very formal and proper, and took mine. "Miz
Mamash, I'm Demetria Chadwick, but you can call me Disa, and I'm
really sorry about Mr. Jack and him being dead and all."

I caught my breath, and for one awful moment I thought I might
cry, shaming myself and this beautiful, sweet child. And the bad thing
was, she knew it. *Oh God, why is nothing ever easy?* Disa gazed up at me,
watching the emotions pass, her face a solemn study, a child's face with
grownup eyes. I returned her gentle grip, and in the doing, felt a degree
of calm return.

"Thank you Disa. We all miss Mr. Jack." She nodded slowly, as if
she had been well coached for this moment.

"I'm Duke, Disa's brother. And I'm real sorry too, and I'm sorry
about the dogs. I dug their graves. I hope it was deep enough."

I shook his hand, measuring this young Chadwick who was
depended on by my Aunt Mosetta for such onerous chores as burying
dead dogs. He was sturdy, with a tight-coupled body and compact
muscles. He looked as if he would never grow tall, but rather had the
solid, meaty body of most horse handlers. There was something in his

eyes too that I liked. A directness, a composed and imperturbable strength. A look that said he had come to grips with the world and his place in it, and intended better for himself and his family. It was a look I saw often in Aunt Mosetta's family. I liked him on sight.

"I'm pleased to meet you Duke. The grave was prefect, and a kind gesture."

He nodded, a single quick bob of his head, and released my hand. "Thank you for the job, Miz Mamash."

"You're welcome, Duke," I said, finding comfort in the formalities. "But please, just call me Mamash. The Miz isn't necessary."

"No, ma'am. My mama, she say to call you Miz Mamash and don't nobody do different." He stood taller, his square little chin in the air, his eyes determined. "Miz Mamash, I need this job so's I can go to college, and I'll be 'spectful and work hard."

Another prepared speech. I had the feeling I would like the Chadwick who was raising these two children, and wondered when I might have met her. Or him. I'd have to ask, later, when they wouldn't have a chance to overhear and know that I couldn't place them on sight. Being a Chadwick held its own special conceit.

"Okay," Jas clapped her hands, attracting the attention of my small group. "Let's talk about rules. Number one: until Big Dog and Cherry get used to you, no petting. Big Dog is at the vet's but he'll be back in a few days. Cherry has new puppies and might snap for no reason. Number two: you never go into a stall unless I'm with you. Number three: never *ever* walk behind a horse. Number . . ." Her voice trailed away as she led the little band to the barn.

I wouldn't need to go to Nana's tonight after all. My grown and capable daughter had found her own Chadwick's to help out at the barn. I could put off for another day the resumption of another part of my life. The barn cats followed Jas, tails waving slowly, leaving me alone, always alone. A breeze flirted with the new yellow-green leaves on the trees overhead. A bird called. Laughter echoed up from the barn. The warm, musky scent of horse lifted to me. Fleas chased one another in the dust at my feet. It was nearly summer; flea time. The dogs were treated, but it was never enough. I'd have to spray the yard, the gravel drive, and beneath the deck where the dogs slept. Jack's job. So many things I needed to do now that Jack was gone, and only Jas, a drunken Jimmy Ray, and two children to help.

I sighed and went toward the barn. There was a day's work to do there, and only us few to get it all done. I didn't mind work. I didn't mind the fleas, the smell, the heat of summer to come or anything else about living on the farm. It was the place of my youth, the place mama and daddy had left me each spring when they took off for Europe or China or Africa for the year's three month long tour. It was home as no other place ever would be. But it was no longer safe for Jas and me. And I didn't know why. I looked up. Sunlight dazzled my eyes, a glistening brightness capped by the Carolina blue skies of a perfect, cloudless afternoon. It was an old cliché, this wondrous shade of blue. Poems had been penned about it, songs sung about it, and still the color could astonish and astound. A buzzard circled to the east, the jerky dip and curl of its flight pattern identifying it even in the distance. A mourning dove called once. Had things been as they once were, Big Dog would have trotted up from the barn, followed by Hokey and Herman, cats at their heels. But nothing was the same. Melancholy crept through me.

Yellow-green poplar leaves fluttered with the breeze. Smaller, greener oak leaves shivered in the warmth. Hickory and pecan, the last trees to leaf out, swelled with life, forming tight buds at branch tip. A horse in the yearling pasture called a challenge and stomped, another reared and bounced down in protest. A mock battle ensued, viewed piecemeal in the spaces between trees. It was a perfect day, except for the litany still sounding in my mind. *What will you do with the years ahead? What will you do all alone? How will you keep your daughter safe? How?* Awful words. As ugly and necessary as the buzzard in the distance.

Because there was nothing else I knew to do, I threw myself into mindless work, hoping something would come to me, some plan, some cerebral map to show the next step I was supposed to take. I worked up a physical sweat, but my mind stayed blank and paralyzed, as useless as a piece of farm machinery rusted in the rain.

At dusk, I took a break from hauling manure and rested my head against the white painted fence at the back of the barn to watch Jas work Mabel. Assuming the pose of cowboys in countless, I propped one foot on the lowest rung, arms draped along the highest, chin in hand. Dusty, dirty, exhausted, I was no closer to knowing how to protect my daughter than I had been.

Macon Chadwick could help against legal maneuvers and Wicked could make the house safer to hide away in, but knives in utility rooms were another matter entirely. I sighed—I had been doing a lot of that lately—and smelled horse, sweat, dog, and the potent aroma of dung. I could go to the police about the threats, I reminded myself, but then, Jasmine might find out too much about her father. Things I wanted to protect her from having to face, especially if Jack's crimes were felonious. And then again, perhaps these threats were something relatively minor.

A soft voice whispered in the back of my mind, *Knives against your throat aren't minor, my girl.* The voice, ironically enough, sounded just like my Nana.

Jasmine, lithe and graceful, fluid, and balletic, turned and turned in the ring before me. Her long, lean legs and sleek frame seemed to dance in the center of the practice ring, her arms held up and out with long line. Jas used no whip, but seemed to control a horse solely with her voice, the rhythms of her speech, the gentle pressure of her hands and the passion in her soul. She was so unlike me, this wonderful daughter of mine.

Jas was working the barn's newest mother on the long line, the foal at Mabel's heels. The young horse was dancing and prancing on unsteady legs, sniffing at everything, shying at most and generally getting in the way of Mabel's post delivery, slow, easy, workout. He wore a red halter that contrasted elegantly with the black sheen of his coat, and he rolled his big eyes as he took in the world, trying to decide if he would conquer it or fear it. Mabel was docile on the line, an old, feisty mare, ready for pasture or for young riders who wouldn't strain her aging joints. But Jas would never sell Mabel; Mabel was part of her earliest memories. The sole survivor when Equine Infectious Anemia swept the stable, Mabel had been in Texas, being covered by a Friesian stud when the other horses had been put down. Mabel *was* Davenport Downs.

The breeze shifted, cooling my sweaty neck. Tendrils of hair moved back from my face as night began to fall. Mabel snorted suddenly, arching her neck back, rolling her eyes, shifting to one side against the pull of the line. She wasn't looking at the foal still gamboling at her feet, but back at the woods on the other side of the ring. Upwind.

A low pitched growl rumbled beside me. I looked for Big Dog, but found only Cherry. Scant protection, her maternal instincts notwithstanding. I pushed away from the supporting fence. Mabel pawed the soft dirt of the practice ring floor, her nostrils flaring. Ignoring the long line. Ignoring Jasmine.

The remembered stench of rancid meat filled my head. I felt the cold steel of a sharp blade at my neck.

Cherry lunged like a big rat, teats dragging, her growl instantly frenzied barking. Mabel went up, raking the air with her front feet. Tangling Jas in the line she had been struggling to remove.

I whirled under the fence, stumbled into the barn through Mabel's stall door, the smell of death, sharp in my mind. The barn was dark and close, and the other horses were restive, picking up Mabel's alarm. By feel, I found the tack room and the light switch. The sudden illumination was disorienting, my eyes stinging with tears.

The cherry-wood finish of the 20-gauge gleamed, throwing back the light. I was surprised at the shotgun's weight. Remembered Jack's furious voice so long ago. "Brace it, damn it, Ash, or you'll knock your shoulder out of joint." Clicking off the safety, I ran for the practice ring, the screaming horse, and barking dog, smelling the foul scent I knew wasn't there. I hate guns.

No too-tall evil man stood at the ring, threatening my daughter. Nor at the far side of the ring where Cherry bounced up and down, the tenor of her bark proving she had cornered . . . whatever it was. *A man on the ground? Too low to see?*

Running, I circled the ring, halfway around recalling Jack's warning about the safety. I clicked it back on as the breath came hot and tight in my throat. My hands were sweat-slick on the stock. And still I couldn't see him. *Where was he?* I stumbled, nearly fell. The sunlight was almost gone. I shouldn't have switched on the light in the barn, it had stolen my night vision.

Mabel charged the fence beside me. Screaming. A black shadow with white-ringed eyes. Jasmine yelled, which I had never heard her do around a horse, her words unintelligible.

And then I saw it, bloody and frothing and clawing the air. Not a man. An animal. Black and white and fierce in the darkness. Cherry, teeth bared, ran at it and back, ferocious, frenzied.

"Cherry," I screamed. "Back. Get back." She hadn't been with us long enough to understand, and she ignored me, intent on the thing in the grass. My mind blanked out as it charged Cherry. She yelped, whether from pain or fear I didn't know.

I braced the stock as Jack had ordered and pulled the first trigger. The weapon was silent. *The safety. The safety. Oh God, the safety.* Fumbling, I found it, shoved the polished wood against my shoulder and fired.

I hit the earth, my head jarring hard against the fencepost behind me. A red haze misted at the corners of my vision, broken by sharp spots of white light. The thing on the ground turned and charged me.

Spreading my legs in the dirt, I sat up, aimed, and fired. The weapon kicked up and back, slamming into my shoulder. The animal flipped up and away. Spinning and twisting in the air. Landed beyond the verge of grass in the edge of woods where it first appeared.

"Mom! Mama! Mama! Jasmine's voice, so far away. A thin, muted sound in my damaged ears. And then she was there, beside me, knees in the dust, her voice still seeming to come from far off. A flashlight was on the ground beside her, beam shining off into the dusk.

"Mama! Mama!" She shook me and the pain was almost more than I could bear. I stopped her with a hand, cold fingers on her hot flesh. Rolling to the side, I retched. Nothing came up. Nothing but a bit of burning fluid, vaguely coffee flavored. I hadn't eaten all day. Forgot. "Is it dead?" I croaked.

The light beside me disappeared. A long moment later it returned, plopped to the ground beside me again and rocked before it steadied. A nauseating motion of light and dark. Hokey or Herman, or perhaps both, licked my face. I shoved at them, then at the ground and sat up. And gagged again. *Not Hokey or Herman. They're dead.* It was Cherry licking my face, grateful and proud, yipping like an untrained dog, ardent in her affections. Jack would never have tolerated such abandon. *Jack isn't here. Jack too, is dead.*

Jas was beside me, her hands again moving on me. "Where does it hurt," she demanded.

I laughed suddenly, an agonized cackle. It was the question I had always asked her when she was tossed by a horse or kicked or crushed against a stall wall. *Where does it hurt?* "All over," I said. "And you know what? I saw stars. Honest to God, I saw stars." And I laughed that crazy cackle again, breathing in with the pain. Broken shoulder? Maybe cracked ribs this time? No ribs could withstand so many assaults without breaking.

"I gotta get it away before Cherry takes it. Can you sit here by yourself for a few minutes?"

"Oh, sure," I said, breathy. "I'll . . . stay right here. After all, it wasn't rotten meat, was it?"

Jas touched my face like a mother checking her child for a fever, and then she was gone, taking Cherry with her. I did smell the scent of death then. The fresh scent of the animal I had shot. Typical scent under the circumstances. Not a danger scent. I lay back, my head on the ground.

I wasn't sure how Jas got me into the Jeep. I didn't remember the ride. I just woke up at Wallace's, my cousin and his wife Pearl helping me out of the Jeep and into a kitchen chair. My ears were still ringing, my hands white and shaky in the too-bright kitchen light . . . and I was hungry. So unbelievably hungry.

Dinner was on the table at my elbow, two small roasted birds and some roasted vegetables, and long strands of grass. Probably roasted fresh herbs. Pearl had been to cooking school, two of them, one in Paris and one in Hong Kong. She liked to cook with stuff she found in the woods. The smell was heavenly.

Wallace shone a bright light into my eyes and looked into my ears and pressed me all over as Jas had, and listened to my heart and my abdomen. Pearl bustled around getting an ice pack for my shoulder which was turning an alarming shade of lavender and black.

I would rather they just left me alone, or let me eat, or both. I was ravenous. And then I was sick again, retching up nothing, and the food didn't smell so good anymore. I ended up at the hospital, making a nuisance of myself, being X-rayed head to foot, having blood drawn, which I thought was a stupid precaution, and my urine checked, which was almost as bad.

Hours later, as Jas was tucking me into bed—my bed, thank God, not some sterile, too-hard hospital bed—she murmured, "All this for a damn raccoon."

A raccoon? A raccoon. I could have laughed, but my chest ached, and I really wanted to cry, not laugh. It had been a raccoon, masked, furred, inches high. Not a man who mistrusted dentists. Not a man. *Not. A. Man.* "Rabid?" I murmured, too tired to comment on her language.

"Probably," she said.

"Rabies boosters for Cherry tomorrow."

"Taken care of," my little girl said equably, "and the shotgun's reloaded, back in its place in the tack room."

Of course it was. All taken care of. Just like all my problems. Jack had once promised that he would take care of all my problems. Problems like the man with the breath of maggots who'd threatened me in the Soiled Utility Room with a knife at my throat. Jack had promised. Jack had lied. He had left me with an attacker who had a miasmatic case of halitosis. The slapstick aspects of it all weren't lost on me. And I hated my husband in that moment.

I fell asleep with Jasmine's hand in mine, knowing she was safe, aching like I'd been hit by a truck, though nothing was broken, at least according to the X-rays. My body claimed otherwise, but pain wasn't a reliable indicator.

I had to replace that shotgun with something more manageable. It was too big for me. Entirely too big.

In the hour before dawn, with a faint light graying out the windows, I sat up in bed, the motion slowed by pain. Three thoughts, occurring simultaneously, had wakened me, drawing me from the drugged darkness of morning dreams.

The man smelling of rotten meat was real. Flesh and blood real. His grammar proved that he wasn't the same angry man who'd threatened Jack on the phone. And he wasn't the man who had written the letters, those polite, well worded, calm letters. *How many threats were there? How many problems?*

CHAPTER SEVEN

Less than twenty-four hours later I was curled up on my bed, braced on pillows supporting my arm and shoulder. I was in too much discomfort to consider the satins and tapestries of my bed linens a luxury. At the moment, they were essential props, holding my body steady, and keeping me from falling over from the medication and muscle relaxers, helping me to breathe without pain.

I had been injured this badly before. On a farm that bred two-thousand-pound workhorses, there were always injuries. I'd been crushed against a stall wall, a full grown Friesian using me as a rump pillow. I'd been kicked more than once. I'd even fallen out of the loft one particularly silly day years ago when Jack and toddler Jas and I had played hide and seek in the barn. And, of course, I had lost my last baby here, slipping on the back deck and dropping the eighteen inches or so to the ground. It hadn't been a bad fall, but I was three months pregnant, and considered a high risk after two miscarriages.

When the pains started and the bleeding couldn't be stopped, my OB/GYN had taken the baby and my uterus. It was an accident I couldn't have prevented, but for which I'd never forgiven myself. I had wanted a large family. Jack had wanted a son.

This pain wasn't debilitating, but I'd learned to take time to recuperate. My body couldn't bounce back as it once had. Thus the day in bed—but it wasn't turning out as I'd intended.

Jasmine and Topaz were plundering my closet, emerging every few minutes with dresses held up against their bodies for my inspection: sequins, silk, gauze, floor length, tea length, and cocktail short. Dresses I hadn't worn since Jack died, and had no intention of wearing tonight, if ever again, though I hadn't convinced them of that fact, yet.

"Ohhh, Mamash, you would be positively delectable in this one."

I lifted a brow at the off-the-shoulder lavender silk Topaz held against herself. The floor-length gown stopped six inches from her ankles, demonstrating once again my limited height and proving that petite was just a polite way of saying short.

"Not bad, Mama. That shade harmonizes with the bruise on your shoulder. Like a tattoo or something."

I rolled my eyes, determined not to contribute to this ridiculous conversation, afraid that anything I said might aide them in their charade. I didn't want to spoil the moment. The two girls, friends again, were chattering away, giggling as only teenage girls can, and Jas had not a trace of grief on her face.

My room was littered with dresses and pantsuits draped over every chair-back, hung over all the open door tops. It looked like Mardi Gras and Halloween rolled into one, all because Jas had finally listened to the personal line's answering machine which I had ignored now for days.

Monica Beck—she had been Monica Schoenfuss when we attended Providence Day School, a private academy in Charlotte—had left a total of twelve messages reminding me about the special performance of the Charlotte Symphony tonight. And though I was so sore that I could scarcely move my right shoulder, and so loaded with medication that the room swam every time I moved my head, my girls were insisting that I attend.

They had called Monica, accepted in my name, made me stand in a pounding shower for almost an hour, dried and styled my hair in a tasteful chignon, and given me a make-over. I had to admit I looked fabulous. The weight I'd lost had trimmed my belly and upper arms, and the makeup the girls applied gave me a wan, delicate sort of beauty, unlike my usual tanned and wholesome looks. In spite of their makeover, I had no intention of attending the concert.

Jack had been a benefactor of the arts in Charlotte, donating more money to the symphony than some local families made in a year. He had been well known and well liked. And some of those casual acquaintances would not know that Jack had died, the obituaries not being mandatory reading among the moneyed crowd. I simply didn't want to go through an evening of torturous explanations.

"This one." Topaz held up a pantsuit I hadn't worn in years. Its wide legs camouflaged my rounded thighs and long flowing sleeves hid my upper arms, two "problem areas" I had worked to conceal all my life. The outfit was lovely, the rich fabric the dark sheen of peacock feathers at twilight. And I still had the mother-of-pearl necklace I had once worn with it.

"I don't know. It's awful small, Paz," Jas said, mirroring my own thoughts.

"Mamash is awful small, girl. You saw her when she got out of the shower. All tendons and bones under that white and purple skin a hers. She so skinny, only thing she got going for her is her legs. You got great lookin' legs, Mamash."

"I have fat thighs," I contradicted before I could stop myself.

"Men *like* fat thighs, Mamash."

"Daddy always loved her legs. Called her Thunder Thighs when he was horny."

"*Jasmine!*" Both girls laughed while I turned rosy beneath the pale makeup. Thunder Thighs was a private name. A name I had both loathed and loved. Loathed because I hated my big thighs, and loved because Jack always said it with such tenderness and seduction. I had forgotten that. Forgotten all about it. "Your father tolerated my legs, Jasmine."

"My daddy loved your legs, Mama. He told me so."

"He did?" There was a short silence in the room as I absorbed this tidbit of honesty. The girls exchanged a look I couldn't interpret.

"Yes, ma'am, he did," Jas said, turning her back to me and poking around in my jewelry case. Metal and gems rattled, trinkets from Jack, not the valuables which were kept in the safe.

"When . . . when did he tell you that," I asked, sounding far more casual than I felt.

Jas's shoulders moved up and down, a pearl ring on her finger, held up to the light. I don't know what she thought she might see. Pearls didn't sparkle.

There were so many things I wanted that I could never have, now. Little memories that were dimming. Memories of Jack and how much he loved me. Jack had claimed he loved my legs, but I'd never really believed him. Not when I longed for slim legs with svelte muscles and inches more of height. Memories of Robyn's beautiful legs in the hated photographs intruded. I blinked the thought away, wanting to remember only the good right now, for just this moment. Jack had told Jasmine he loved my legs . . . All these years he liked my legs. I slid a hand along the curved length, what there was of it. The motion hurt my shoulder. *He liked my legs.*

Through the medicated haze, I remembered the plastic garbage bag of pictures on the closet floor, hidden beneath winter boots. A thrill of fear shot through me and I sat up. But Jas hadn't burrowed there in her search for warm weather finery.

I lay back, fighting tears. All the years of loving had waited till now to become real to me. Now, when it was too late. Now, when he was gone and I couldn't ruffle his dark hair, shot through with silver, and see that wonderful erotic glint in his dark eyes each time he touched me. Now, when I knew about Robyn.

I closed my eyes, blocking out a world that was too big and dark and empty without him. A world where the Jack I thought I had known had never really existed. When I opened them again, the girls were arguing over underwear.

Jas had three bras over one arm, panties in the other hand; Topaz was trying to eliminate the white set. "Ugly. Just too ugly. And so . . . so plebeian. Now, the taupe set, that's classy. And new too. I think Mamash should take off the tags and slip into these, and that gold necklace with the yellow stones and she would be downright sexy."

I had to put an end to this now, before the girls had me in bed with some romantic stranger. This cooperation in decorating me was obviously a part of their mutual penance for arguing, but I was not their dress up Barbie doll. And I was not going to the symphony.

"Girls." They turned to me. Jas set her lips the instant she saw my face, and Topaz put her fists on her hips, dual belligerent poses. I wondered if Topaz would grab my ear and shake me before I finished what I had to say. At least they were friends again. "Girls, I'm not going to the symphony. I don't want to go. I hurt. It even hurts to breathe. And I can't drive with the pain medication. Understand?"

"We're driving you," Jas said stubbornly.

"Yeah. In the Volvo. We took it to the Majic Hands car wash. Got it washed, waxed, and vacuumed. Even got it deodorized so it smells like a Christmas tree."

"Topaz and I are going to drive you up, drop you off and go to a movie. Then pick you up at Monica's after the party. And if you get too tired, I'll have my cell and can pick you up early. But you have to go, Mama. You have to."

"No. I don't." And certainly to Monica's, who was a domineering, bossy, she-cat, chasing after anything in pants and catching most of them. She had even made a play for Jack years ago, when he was courting her husband Emory Beck and his investment group. And Monica had legs that would make Robin green with envy. *Monica and Emory had invested at Davenport Hills*, a small voice murmured at the back of my mind. *I might learn something if I went.* . . . Fat chance, I answered back. Monica had never told me anything I wanted to know; even as a teenager she had withheld information just for spite. "I'm not going."

The girls exchanged another glance. Something about that look finally penetrated. Something was up. My mind veered back to a romantic liaison with a sexy stranger. My stomach twisted in distress. Surely their new teamwork hadn't led them to do something horribly wrong. "What," I said, my voice severe. "What was that look about? You girls have something up your sleeves, and I want to know what it is. *Now.*" An uncomfortable silence stretched as they looked from me to one another and to the phone beside the bed. "What!" And this time there was that "I'm-in-charge, don't-mess-with-me tone," in my voice.

The one I always hated to hear Nana use. The one that always worked so well on me. It worked now.

Jas sighed. "It's supposed to be a surprise, Mama. About Daddy."

My apprehension faded, to be replaced by a different sort of worry. Jas climbed up on the mattress beside me. Topaz sat on the edge, her face solemn. "Monica and the patrons are giving Daddy a plaque at the Patrons' Party after the concert. For all his contributions over the years."

"Oh. Oh my." I was glad I was lying down, the pillows around me an urgent support as the room twirled once before growing still again. I felt limp and threadbare suddenly, like an old, linen throw in need of starch, a plain, faded thing surrounded by all this luxury.

"That's why Monica's been calling all week. She was almost frantic by the time I called her back this morning. Monica said you have to accept it posthumously."

"And Mamash, that woman could talk the ears off a mule on a good day," Topaz added, using one of Aunt Mosetta's favorite sayings. Jas agreed with a saucy grin, but there was an undertone of concern beneath it. She checked my brow again as she had done last night and half a dozen times since. It was the touch of the distressed, the frightened, and I understood it well. Perhaps better than she did herself, after reading and rereading the little booklet on grief given to me by my pastor, the newly Reverend Winslow, the day of Jack's funeral.

Most children, once they reach adulthood, begin to think of their parents as weak, helpless, and feeble. Jas had come to that point in life suddenly, brutally, and she wasn't certain I would stand up under the pressure. She was afraid I would die and leave her alone.

"It's supposed to be a secret," she repeated, whispering. She gathered up my hands in her own, her gaze on my fingers; her eyes rested on my left ring finger, naked now, without my wedding ring. She made no comment, concentrating instead on the conversation.

I wanted to hug her, reassure her that I would be all right. I chose a more effective, more difficult way of accomplishing that. I forced a smile on to my face and into my eyes, burying my own misery, my own aversion to what I was about to do. I took a deep breath. "Well, if you expect me to wear silk, you need to do something about my nails." Jas turned my hands over, nodding her agreement. "And the necklace I wear with the teal silk is a white mother-of-pearl choker." Topaz jumped off the bed and bent over the jewel box. Jas squeezed my rough hands. "The one that looks like small white bones. And the pearl earrings with the gold bands."

Suddenly the girls were bustling again, arguing good-naturedly about the tint of nail polish I should wear, and the shoes, and the movie they should see. I smiled and nodded and conceded to everything they wanted, sheltering them from my pain and the awful, tormenting sadness that clutched at me each time I thought about being alone tonight at the symphony.

I walked into the Blumenthal Performing Arts Center, feeling dwarfed beneath the lofty ceiling of the glass-capped Rotunda. The teal silk, fitting perfectly for the first time in ten years, was an unfortunate echo of the teal shade in the handmade Tatsumura wallpaper. I had heard the wallpaper described as being an acquired taste—a polite euphemism for the teal, orange, and white décor. But as no one else seemed to notice my color match, I tried to put it out of my mind.

The voices of the gathered concert goers rang and echoed, bouncing off the cream-colored marble, women's laughter high and piping, the basso of the men's a low rumble. Snatches of conversation surrounded me: golf, music, the investment potential of a new artist, politics as they impacted on the current financial situation, a new Thai restaurant, the price of land north of town, the expected profits of a new stock, a design house opening in the Dilworth community. Mostly though, money, the new southern etiquette. A generation ago, such subjects would have been taboo in the presence of the fairer sex, appropriate only after dinner over port and cigars, while the women-folk powdered their little noses and gossiped and did womanly things. Now, in this crowd of the elite, the women were equals in the conversations, offering advice, soliciting tips, gauging the margins of various investments.

I stood there, alone, conscious of my tender shoulder, ribs aching each time I drew breath, knowing I should be in bed instead of here in this vast, drafty place. The medication muting the worst of the pain added an isolation that left me feeling adrift and detached.

Wicked had tried to talk me out of coming. He had explained all the reasons why I shouldn't leave the farm, all the danger, which I saw perfectly well, thank you. But Jas needed me to do this. Jas needed me to take up my life and live again, at least on some limited level. And after all, no one except Monica and my family knew I would be here tonight, no one. I was as safe as I could be under the circumstances, and if I was going out into the world, this was the safest place anywhere, surrounded by the privileged few, the moneyed, the elite of society.

Wicked hadn't liked my plans, and Macon had sat on the edge of the kitchen cabinet, his lips pursed, following our conversation with narrowed eyes, his own opinion never voiced. Macon wasn't the type to talk until he was ready. And so here I was, alone in this crowd of high society snobs, so many like my mother, surrounded by noise and laughter and couples. Couples everywhere. And I was mate-less. I shuddered with my secret isolation while my heart cried out and I thought my face might crack open with the effort of maintaining a smile. Clutched in my hand were the two season tickets that would have seated Jack and me in the orchestra section, seventh row center. Jack's favorite listening location.

The girls had insisted that I bring both tickets so Monica could sit with me should her husband not be able to attend at the last second. But there, only feet away, was Emory Beck, resplendent in evening clothes, his arm around Monica, who wore the Beck sapphires against her milky flesh.

My arm ached and I told myself it was the bruising that caused the pain, not the absence of a husband by my side, an empty black hole that had once held life, sucking into it all light, all joy, all mirth and gaiety. Fleetingly, the anger I had nursed resurfaced and my false smile faltered. Jack had left me to face this too.

But Monica and Emory hadn't spotted me, and without greeting my old friend and rival, I slipped away. This was far worse than I had expected. I was quivering inside, trembling like a leaf in a frigid breeze. Yet my hand holding the tickets was steady and calm, the nails pared back, smoothed, and painted pale pink.

"I see you wore a rose." I whirled, nearly dropping the tickets. "It looks better in your hair than in the vase." The man was blond, with warm gray eyes and beautifully chiseled lips, the lower lip full and pink, in contrast to the thinner upper lip. His mouth curled into a smile, a sensual motion that startled me and brought a warm flush to my face. I took a quick, deep breath as I looked back into his eyes. There was a small pink scar in his eyebrow. "Alan . . ." The last name was a moment in coming. "Mathison?"

He canted his head in an abbreviated bow, the smile still in place. Lifting his right hand, he touched the rose Topaz had woven into my hair. It was one of the roses he had given me days ago in the Emergency Room, the blossom open to its widest now, full and ripe and crimson in my hair. I could smell its heady aroma, the rose an affectation I had allowed, as I had allowed everything else the girls wanted for me.

Alan had long, slender fingers, furred on the back with thin blond hair, and when he spoke, the smile was there too, in his voice. "I hope you removed the thorns."

"Yes, I did." I swallowed, my mouth suddenly dry. "And they are still beautiful," I added, remembering my manners.

"The thorns?"

I smiled then, my first real smile since I'd agreed to come out on this horrible night. "Those are sharp and painful."

Alan chuckled and my eyes were drawn again to his lower lip. "I got your thank you note. But you didn't have to. Really." His voice was grave and low, remembered from beneath the body of a car saying, "My wife. . . ." The memory restored my reasoning, putting things in their rightful place. Like me, Alan Mathison was truly alone.

"It was little enough for so many roses."

"Which were little enough for saving my life," he quipped back quickly, with a wicked little grin.

I looked away from his mouth and smiled again, taking refuge in propriety. "Do you attend the symphony often?"

"No." Leaning toward me, he rested his weight on a shiny black cane that I only now noticed, and lowered his voice. "Don't tell anyone, but this stuff puts me to sleep."

"Never," I said, putting my hand to my chest.

He chuckled again at my mock outrage, his voice still low. "I'm only here because my boss couldn't come, and someone had to represent the company at the Patrons' Party."

My smile faded, but thanks to my mother's rigorous training, the proper words were there, ready for use. "Onerous duty indeed," I managed. "Who is your employer?"

"I'm a vice president at Taylor, Inc. If you attend a lot of these things, you may know my boss, Jerel Taylor."

The name rang a curious bell. Jerel Taylor was a developer, like Jack, but had several generations of good green money to sustain his company. Taylor Developments, Inc. had expanded into half a dozen nearby states, buying up unused farmland and putting up regional malls and upscale housing. Jerel was also one of the investors financing Davenport Hills, along with perhaps a dozen of the other concert goers I would see in the theater or at the party afterwards. Jerel Taylor had been a difficult man to work with, demanding a say in the layout of the golf courses, making changes that the golf course architect had fought against and won. But it hadn't been a pretty battle. He was known to be an exacting taskmaster and a hard man to please.

Of course, Jack's opinion of Jerel had been phrased in terms a bit more extreme. I think his exact words were skinflint, barbarian, bloodsucker, cannibal, and criminal, interspersed with other, less favorable and more obscene descriptions. These judgments I kept to myself. "I've met Jerel, of course, and I'm familiar with the company. Have you worked there long?"

"Six years. Before that I was with several different investors and developers."

A low gong sounded, a melodious tone over the sound system. In the background, dissonant notes competed for attention, dueling in off key rivalry as the musicians tuned their instruments on stage. I hadn't even noticed the sound.

Alan looked at the two ticket stubs he held, and his full lower lip turned down a moment. It was wet, I noticed with a slight shock, and looked away. My preoccupation with his mouth was surprising and awkward. It wasn't a sexual response, I didn't detect that in myself at all. I wasn't ready for a man in my life yet, and fully recognized that I might never be. Yet, something drew my eyes to Alan's lips again. "I don't suppose you know anyone who might want an extra ticket? Jerel insisted that I take both season seats, but I'm just not ready to . . . ask anyone to join me."

Date. He meant he wasn't ready to ask a woman out on a date. I held out my own tickets, slightly crumpled now, from being held in my fist. "How about we try and scalp two."

It made Alan laugh again, and I quite liked his laugh. It was unaffected, not overly boisterous. Totally unlike Jack's gregarious, join-with-me laugh.

The crowd was moving slowly toward the open doorways, the vast darkened space beyond beckoning with wordless dissonance. Alan raised his voice and took my elbow, turning me toward the doorways with the hand that held his cane. "Better yet, why don't you join me. You can elbow me when I start to snore so I don't embarrass myself."

I took the tickets he proffered and checked the seats. His hand was warm through the silk of my blouse, the knob of his cane sharp against my elbow, and it occurred to me suddenly why my reaction to him was so intense. No one had smiled at me or talked to me about anything except grief or work or problems in weeks. And certainly no one had shown me the courtesy of guiding me toward an open doorway, his hand lightly on my arm. I was . . . *lonely.*

The memory of Robyn's love letters dangled in the back of my mind like bait on a string, adding another explanation, but I ignored the lure of bitterness.

Alan's seats were in the Mezzanine section, adequate, but not as good as mine. Surprising, because Taylor, Inc. could have afforded a seasonal box with no strain. But then, Jerel Taylor was known as a tightfisted man, and I doubted he had any appreciation of fine music. He probably preferred tunes that came out of a juke box, the kind with neon bubbles traveling around to the beat of some whiny song.

"Even better. Why don't you join me?" I heard myself say. Oh my. What had just come out of my mouth? Two voices, one sounding like my mother, the other sounding like my Nana, both gasped inside my head. Mother's was horrified. Nana's was amused. I decided to ignore them both, these two quarreling consciences.

"Better seats?"

"Much better."

"And you'll promise to elbow me when I snore?"

"Viciously."

Alan laughed, the sound rising above the noise around us. "Done. And I must admit I'm glad of the company, Ashlee."

"Me too, Alan." And I was.

He dropped his hand from my elbow, and balanced on his cane. With his other hand he stuffed the tickets into the front of his tux jacket with that motion that is peculiarly masculine, totally male. A little flutter of black cloth and then that shove, shove, shove movement. We were walking now, propelled by the swarm of Carolina's finest, crowded tightly together and pushed through the narrow doorways into the reverberant cavern that was the Blumenthal.

As we passed through the set of double doors into the softly lit theater, I felt a sudden chill on the back of my neck. A feeling like the touch of dead flesh, caressing, like the memory of some primeval fear left over from ancient times, a primitive instinct or rudimentary sixth sense.

Someone was watching me. The fine hairs along my spine rose stiffly.

Quickly, I turned, my eyes darting, to find only a crowd of nameless strangers, none paying particular attention to me. And then, at the edges of the slow moving mass, back where the lighting was less distinct, a dark form turned away and vanished into the mob.

A man. Medium height, dressed in a dark suit or tux. I hadn't seen his face. His movements weren't familiar, nor was his shape, but with his passing, my icy apprehension was gone. And then I saw Bret. While his face was indistinct in the semi-darkness, his eyes were on mine. I smiled. Bret nodded stiffly, his face unsmiling.

Alan and I moved into the auditorium, where the sounds of instruments being tuned filled the air with sharps and flats and asynchronous riffs of melody. I shook my head and looked back once more. It was the usual, eclectic crowd. No threat, no menace. Just dozens of people in formal wear and business wear, and Bret, elegant in evening clothes.

I was surely paranoid. It was foolish to think that anyone had been watching me in this crowded place, where no one expected me to be, tonight, so soon after Jack's death. Nerves. Silly, female nerves. A case of the heebie-jeebies left over from the raccoon and the remembered feel of a knife at my throat. *Unless Bret was involved somehow.* . . .

Determined, I put my fears from mind and found my seats. I could relax and enjoy this concert, or I could spend the entire evening jumping at every little thing. And since I was here, I decided on the music.

It wasn't as painful as I expected, sitting in our seasonal seats, seats Jack and I had shared for years. It was in fact, almost easy, with Alan sitting beside me, making soft little comments, his lips against my hair, the scent of his rose filling my nostrils. And if I enjoyed it a bit more than the average grieving widow, perhaps that mythical woman hadn't found pictures of her husband, naked in bed with her best friend only weeks after his death.

Alan was amusing, as only the well bred can be, his lips near my ear, offering up a soft and subtle commentary about the cellist's hair-piece, the violinist's torn petticoat and the guest conductor's tendency to sweat copiously, staining his tux in black-on-black rings. He was so amusing in fact that I scarcely heard the music in the first half and was surprised when intermission was called.

Fully half of the audience stood when the lights came up, making a long, tightly packed queue facing the entrance. It would be a madhouse in the ladies room, and since I didn't really care if my nose was shiny, and it would hurt to move, I kept my seat. Alan did likewise, stretching out his long legs beneath the matronly woman seated in front of him. His shoes were as shiny as the cane which he had hooked around his seat arm. "I must admit I'm glad that's over. Bach never did appeal to me. I'm sure I flunked the Bach portion of music appre' in college."

"Don't be so certain," I said.

Alan lifted his brows and cut his eyes at me. "No. Really. I do detest Bach."

"Noooo." I sighed out the word in real anguish. "I mean, don't be so glad it's over. My mother and father and Monica Beck are on their way over here. And I can tell they intend to give you the third degree. I'm sorry. I mean really, really sorry. Especially about my . . . friend." I didn't know what else to call Monica, but perhaps Alan understood. His brows went up higher, with alarm, amusement, or some less identifiable reaction. His lips, however, twitched. "I promise to be on my best behavior," he murmured. And then they were upon us as we both stood to face the onslaught. Pain caught my breath as I rose to my feet, and I held it until the electric agony passed and I could inhale again.

"Ash! Ashlee, darlin' I'm so glad to see you, and you look radiant. Simply radiant, darlin'. You've been workin' out, I can tell, and the results are marvelous. You look almost as tiny as you did back in high school. You must tell me what program you're on."

I almost said, "It's the grief diet, Monica, dear." Or, "It's the manure diet from the workout I got each day taking Jack's place in the barn, shoveling out poop and brushing down horses." But I didn't. I just smiled and pressed my cheek against hers and fought back tears.

"The girls promised me you would be here, and I must say, you look simply marvelous."

"So you said," I responded, thinking about the mottled black and purple bruise on my shoulder. A spurt of anger washed through me, hot and sharp. But Monica was chattering on.

"And who is this gorgeous man you have with you?" Her made-up eyes flashed down the length of Alan Mathison and back up again. "Oh, Ashlee, darlin', you do seem to get all the best ones. Except for you, Emory, you know you're the best, just the absolute best," Monica said, bestowing a kiss on his leathery cheek. Like me, Monica had married an older man, but in her case, her husband was a widower, alone and bereft and adrift on the world until Monica Schoenfuss entered his life. Emery Beck was wealthy and successful and firmly entrenched in Charlotte's moneyed circles. And many years her senior.

Rumor had it that Monica dallied with attractive men, having one affair after another on the side, but always careful to keep her marriage to the wealthy Emory Beck well protected. Her appraising glance raked Alan from mouth to shiny black shoes and up again, resting momentarily on the cane. I could have sworn the sight of it was an attraction in her eyes.

"Alan Mathison at your service ma'am. You can only be the famed Monica Beck. And may I say that Ashlee's description of you was both delightfully accurate and woefully inadequate? You are a vision, ma'am."

It was my turn to raise my brows. I hadn't said anything about the woman at all . . . had I?

Monica giggled. I hate it when women giggle.

"Oh, Mr. Mathison, I must say that, though it's awfully early for Ash to be dating, I can certainly see why she fell for your charm. Oh, indeed I do."

I jerked, my eyes moving from Monica Beck to my mother and back again. A flush started at my toes and rose on a tide of shock and horror. *Oh God. Oh God,* I prayed wordlessly.

My mother, the elegant and wealthy Josephine Hamilton Caldwell, stood less than a foot behind Monica, sucking in every single word, her plucked brows raised, her surgically altered eyes wide open in stunned surprise. I think I might have groaned.

"Mrs. Beck, although it would indeed be a delight to possess the interest of a woman of Mrs. Davenport's caliber, I must confess that our relationship is strictly professional."

"Oh?" Monica, my mother, and I spoke at the same time.

"Yes. I owe Mrs. Davenport a great debt. You see," Alan bent close to Monica's ear, though he didn't lower his voice. "Ashlee saved my life."

"No!"

"Oh, yes. Really. There was a horrible accident," Alan faltered, only for an instant, yet Monica leaned in closer and placed her hand on his black-clad arm. My mother leaned in closer as well. If she wasn't careful, mama would have to have her big ears reduced and pinned.

"My wife and my business partner . . . well, neither made it," Alan said, his voice husky and breaking.

"Oh, you poor man." Monica took Alan's hand with her own, just out of Emory's line of sight. Her breasts thrust forward as she inhaled and she actually batted her lashes at Alan. I hadn't seen anyone do that since Scarlett O'Hara flirted with Rhett Butler. My mother's eyes darted from Alan's hand in Monica's to me, her expression dubious, her lips slightly pursed. Mother had full, pouting lips, created by a surgeon, paid for by Daddy during plastic surgery number two. Or was it number three?

Alan patted the hand holding his own. "Yet because of, well, because of Ash's heroic measures, I survived. Quite literally, I owe her my life."

Didn't anyone but me see the slapstick aspect of this dialogue— Monica as Mae West, me as the mousy school marm? And then it hit me. Alan was protecting my reputation. I almost laughed, but it might have ruined his performance. Instead I said, "Oh, no. It wasn't really—"

"It was exactly really," he interrupted.

Alan, remarkably attentive to the reactions around him, smiled his easy smile and patted Monica's hand with his free one before he pointedly pulled away. "And I must admit another debt of gratitude, that Ashlee allowed me to join her here. Her seats are far superior to mine." He used his free hand to expose the corners of his own tickets buried in his inside pocket. "I've never heard the symphony from the orchestra section."

"Well." Monica placed her hand at her throat, calling attention both to her cleavage and to the Beck sapphires. The gesture was one my old chum had perfected in junior high school, when she had breasts before the rest of us. "I do hope you mean to attend the Patrons' Party at our house after the concert. Everyone will be there, Alan. May I call you Alan?"

"Of course. And, yes I'll be there, representing Jerel Taylor, who was unable to attend at the last moment."

"Wonderful. That's lovely." And my hackles started to rise. I had heard that tone in Monica's voice before, dozens of times, just before she got me in trouble. "And do you mind terribly bringing Ashlee in your car? I'm afraid Emory insisted on driving the two-seater. It's his new toy, you know. And Ash would be dreadfully crushed."

This was the first I had heard about a two seater, and Mama too. She turned her eyes on me. There was a spark of calculation in their green depths, and my heart did an odd lurch. Monica wasn't making a play for Alan. She was matchmaking. *For me.*

"You don't mind, do you?"

"Ash is perfectly welcome to ride with her family," my mother said. "As long as we are around, Ashlee will be well taken care of, I assure you."

Oh yeah? Since when? I thought, bitterly. And then shame washed through me. It wasn't as if my mother knew she was a poor parent. She simply never noticed that anyone else had needs. My father, ever the faithful follower, nodded. "Ashlee is our responsibility, Monica. I'm certain she shouldn't impose on strangers when ready transportation is available."

Their responsibility, my left foot! My parents had never worried about leaving me with others. I had been left with Nana every summer for years while they went gallivanting off to Paris or the African coast or Rio. This was a great time to be remembering their responsibility to me.

I lifted my brows and pressed my lips together, only faintly aware that I imitated my mother. Around me there was the inevitable round of introductions. I tried to decide if it was worse to be subjected to my mother for the ten minute ride to Monica's, or be thrust upon Alan.

The decision was taken out of my hands in one of those maneuvers that had resulted in Monica's high school nickname of Cat Woman. Monica made the decision for me, as she had made so many for us both, through twelve years of school. She paired me with Alan, deputized my mother and father to provide transportation for the sweaty, visiting maestro, and herded her little coterie away. I was mortified. Alan was chuckling as the intermission bell sounded.

We sat down again, with me feeling out-maneuvered, exasperated, and provoked. Alan, however, was still smiling a little half smile. "Quite the despot, your . . . friend."

It was said with the polite little pause I had used myself, and the comment brought an unwilling smile to my lips. "Is that a polite way of saying she's pushy? Overbearing?" I rubbed my shoulder through the teal silk. I needed the sling I hadn't worn because it was ugly and did nothing for my outfit but I had left it in the car, for use on the way home. What was that saying about vanity? My shoulder was almost broken and I was concerned about my looks.

"Exactly."

I had to force my thoughts back to the conversation at hand. What were we talking about?

Alan's lips stretched in a wider smile. "She's also very generous."

"Oh?" I had never in my wildest dreams considered Monica generous, so I must have missed a part of the conversation. However, I was willing to contemplate the preposterous. Aliens. UFOs. A government program to save taxes. Monica, generous.

"Um. She gave me to you when she wanted me for herself."

A small choking sound came from my throat and Alan laughed outright, a rapid ripple of amusement, his eyes on the mostly empty stage. "It's okay, Ashlee. I'm not insulted nor do I feel put upon. In fact, I'm honored."

"I'm so sorry, Alan," I said when I could find words. If I was a stronger woman, I'd never have let this happen. I'd have told Monica "No." *Hmm . . . There's a thought. No . . .*

Alan looked at me, and, reaching up, lifted a fallen rose petal out of my hair and placed it on my hand. "Don't be. I truly am honored."

Our eyes met and held a moment, until the house lights blinked and the curtain went up. Smiling his half smile, Alan settled back in his seat and lifted my injured arm up, resting it upon his own. It was as if he had read my pain and reacted to it, almost like a long-time friend . . . or a husband. The position was perfect, and for the first time tonight, the pain in my shoulder faded to bearable. And the pain in my heart disappeared entirely.

CHAPTER EIGHT

The Patrons' Party was a disaster. For a short while, Alan acted as a buffer between the curious, the cruel, the innocently unkind and me, until he was forced to plead exhaustion and find a place to sit. Either he was really in pain, as his pale face and tight mouth proclaimed, or he hated the synthetic camaraderie as much as I. Pleading discomfort, he slipped away, leaving me to the artificial affection of Monica Beck, and the treacherous hostility of my mother. I had once watched a documentary in which playful killer whales tossed a baby sea lion in a roaring surf prior to feeding. I felt like that baby sea lion, bleeding and menaced and dying. So I didn't really blame Alan for finding a tranquil corner and leaving me to the carnivores.

I avoided both women for an hour, as I waited for the presentation of the posthumous plaque. Mingling, I found refuge several times in the upstairs powder room, twice at the piano, where the sweaty, visiting maestro—whose name I never did pronounce correctly—flaunted his prowess, and once out in the Florida Room where shadows offered anonymity.

I wasn't handling the counterfeit consolations of my acquaintances any better than I had expected. And worse, every time someone innocently asked where Jack was, I had to fight back both a quick, rude response and tears. The Charlotte paper had carried only a small obituary for Jack, not the half page headline of the *Dawkins Herald*. Still, I would have thought gossip in this privileged crowd would have spread word of his death. These were the Patrons, for pity sakes. They were giving Jack a posthumous plaque. Didn't they understand that meant he was *dead?*

Several times after Alan left, I felt the cold touch of eyes on me, hostile eyes filled with malice. Yet when I looked around, there was only the usual crowd, or even a friend, smiling. Once, it was Bret McDermott, holding out a plastic stem of wine, his face unreadable, his greeting just a nod. Another time it was Monica herself, calling me to the front door to meet some important personage whose name I immediately forgot. And finally it was Senator Vance Waldrop. He had no reason to be in North Carolina, one state away from his own constituents, rubbing shoulders with money makers who, for the most part, couldn't vote in South Carolina. But Vance was a powerful man, welcome in circles that ranged far beyond the voting public. At least that's how I consoled myself when faint alarms sounded in my mind at the sight of him. *He shouldn't be here*, my mind whispered back, unconvinced. Too many of my husband's business partners were gathered here, and Vance in particular did not belong. He should be in D.C, wheeling and dealing, or at home with his wife. Not at this party, searching me out. And I remembered that Vance himself had told me to contact Bret and the Becks and my mama. What was it he'd said? Something about *old friends and family being the best in times like these*. What had he meant by that? I hadn't even known the senator and the Becks were acquainted.

Paranoid. That was me. Paranoid and alone and in pain.

Like my mother, whom I avoided with a practiced desperation perfected as a child, I eluded the senator successfully for the better part of an hour while Alan caught his breath and I satisfied the dictates of propriety by appearing to mingle—a thoroughly exhausting endeavor.

Yet, even with all that, the night might have been bearable had my mother not cornered me at last, demanding explanations and apologies, and issuing accusations, all concerning Alan. A mother was supposed to be supportive and compassionate; mine had never understood the concepts, viewing the world and its people as things to be used as needed and otherwise ignored. I had learned to live with her warped outlook, but it still hurt. She hadn't been to see me since the funeral. She hadn't called. She hadn't even sent an email. But then, that was my mother, selfish to the core. I was quite certain the thought of offering me support had never crossed her mind.

I survived the tongue lashing, and endured the Patrons' Party, for Jasmine and the plaque she wanted me to bring home. Nothing else could have pulled me through the polite torment. Toward eleven, I managed to elude my mother yet again, an accomplishment growing more difficult by the hour. I realized she was no longer wearing her glasses or contacts, that her once blurry vision and designer lenses had been replaced by 20/20 perfection, the result of a laser, her latest foray into the world of surgery. Mother was determined to be faultless, at least physically. With Daddy's money, she might be someday.

I had also lost the senator, Monica, and my father, who felt I had slighted my mama by riding to the party with Alan. Daddy had never let anyone get away with hurting his wife's feelings, though he allowed her to ride roughshod over the rest of the world with abandon.

Alone for the moment, I wandered out through the Florida Room, full of the hot house orchids Emory cultivated in his semi-retirement from the world of big business. The party had moved out here, and I slipped unnoticed past several couples talking about the weather, and out to the screened porch. It was empty, the breeze damp and warm as another of the contradictory fronts moved through the state. This one came out of the Atlantic, an early tropical storm that never quite grew into a hurricane before it slammed into the coast and moved north.

In the distance, highlighting the Charlotte cityscape of skyscrapers and twinkling lights, the storm still battered at the earth. Lightning brightened the frothing clouds again and again. Thunder rumbled, the sound muted by the miles. Separated from the city proper by acres of upscale housing and the ancient oaks for which the city was famous, it was still. Almost quiet. An occasional voice reached me from inside. The gutters lining the house gurgled softly. Raindrops trickled, collected in the curve of oak leaves, grew heavy, and fell in odd little splatters. Far off, a dog barked. Traffic sounds intruded sporadically.

As a full moon danced through fitful clouds, a gazebo appeared. It was painted white, a gingerbread toy, covered with an immense climbing rose bush, heavy with blooms. Inside, hidden from the world, was a swing, suspended from the overhead beams.

Pushing open the screened door, I went out into the porch and the garden beyond, up the steps to the gazebo. Amazingly, the swing was still dry. The scent of roses surrounded me, sweet and warm as the rose perfume Nana wore to church on Sunday, as the rose in my hair. I sat and pushed the swing into motion, rested my head against the wooden back and closed my eyes. The swing made a soft little squeak with each forward movement, the tiny little sound adding to the restfulness of the moment.

I don't know how long I sat there, swinging. I don't know when the peace began to fade. Nor when the apprehension first touched me. It was the unexpected chill of the party, and earlier at the symphony. The same urgent fear that made me turn and search the crowd for an enemy. I sat up quickly, eyes straining into the night.

The scent of roses was overpowering. A suffocating fragrance that seemed to close me off from the rest of the world. The darkness was heavy, a wet warmth, muffling all sound, closing out the world. I was alone.

Quickly, I stood. Moved for the house.

"Not just yet, lady." Whispered words.

A hand gripped me from behind. Jerked me back. Turned my wrist up behind me. It was a familiar move. I recognized it instantly from the Soiled Utility Room.

My breath shot out. My shoulder shrieked in agony, a burning pain. I gasped, my knees buckling. He dragged me back up, the torment of my arm a lever to his will. The hot scent of his foul breath blanked out the roses, surrounded me with the smell of decayed meat. Choking me.

He chuckled. "Lucky me. Finding you out here, all alone. Jazzy was worried you'd do this. Go off by yourself and grieve." He smeared out the last word, making it sound dirty and foolish. And then it hit me. *Jazzy.*

"What have you done with my daughter?" I ground out.

"Nothing yet, lady. Just sat behind her and that nigger cousin of hers at the movies. Listened in while they talked. I always did like 'em young. Course, older and experienced ain't bad either." He reached around me and squeezed my breast.

He wasn't holding a knife. His hands were free. I sucked in a breath. Opened my mouth.

"You scream, and I'll get little Jazzy tonight. I can do it, you know. I can find you and her anytime. Any place." He whispered the last word, a sibilant softness against my ear. I released the breath. Exhaled the scream silently. "Better. Much better." His hand moved across my body, the intimate touch of a stranger. I shivered in the wet heat. My right arm had gone numb.

"They need something you got, Ashlee. And it ain't this," he said, touching me again. "It's all them papers on Davenport Hills. Them files and permits." I gagged as his hand slipped into my clothes, touching my flesh. The rank scent of the man, rancid and sour, touched me everywhere, overpowering and foul. He laughed again.

"This is just fun. It only gets rough if you keep the stuff they want. And they's determined to have it all. Especially since you gone and hired that evil man. The little black guy. So, see can you remember. They want the papers, the file, the permits, and oh, yeah . . ." He pinched my nipple, pulling hard on the tender flesh. I bit my lips together to keep from crying out. "The original report. You remember all that, okay? Next time we talk, you'll give it all to me. Right?"

I nodded my head, a shaky motion, out of control.

"Good. You do all that, and I'll leave little Jazzy out of it. It'll stay just between us. You screw around with me, you try and keep something back, and I'll visit your little girl. I'll give her a night to remember. And while I'm doing her, I'll be sure to tell her how it's all because you wouldn't cooperate. How you hired some evil man to look into things you shouldn't. And how you could have protected her and didn't. And how her Daddy knew all about me killing a man for his business, and didn't do nothing about it. By the time I'm finished with your little girl, she'll know everything. And she'll hate your guts," he said, running his hand over my torso and down between my legs.

Hate your guts. A child's threat, made personal and violent.

He gripped my tunic; curled his fist into the fabric. Jerked. The silk tore. One long ripping sound, sharp on the night. I shuddered, my knees giving way. My hand, pulled up behind me, popped as my body slipped. There was no pain in my numb hand. Just the almost inaudible *pop* as bone separated from bone within a joint. "Next time—"

"Ashlee? Ash, are you out here?" Alan's voice. I shuddered again.

"Shit!" he said beside my ear, his breath strong and vile. And he dropped me.

I landed with a soft thud, a crumpled heap of nerveless, boneless flesh. Rose petals fluttered down from my hair. Soft footsteps beat against the gazebo floor, splashed once in the garden. *He was gone.* I sobbed.

"Ash?" Alan's voice came from the blackness outside. I took a breath. A breeze brushed my face. Rose-scented and fresh. No scent of putrid flesh. No sick scent rotten gums. *He was gone.* I lifted myself from the painted wood of the gazebo floor with my left arm. My right was useless, the nerves zinging with heat and electricity as feeling tried to restore itself.

"Alan? Help."

And suddenly he was there, a rush of dark cloth against my face. Smooth satin and rich summer-weight wool. Fine weaves. The fainter scent of aftershave as he settled beside me and lifted me close. "Ash? My God. Did you fall?"

I reached for him, clutching his lapel with my good hand. "A man . . . attacked me," I said, my voice quavering, tinged with near madness. *He was gone. I was safe.*

"Ash. Did . . . Did he . . ."

"No. He heard you call and he dropped me."

Alan closed his arms around me and pulled me against him, his jaw close to my temple. "Thank God. No one knew where you were and I thought you might have . . ." He stopped. I heard him swallow and take a ragged breath. Felt him look around in the darkness. "Ash, let's get you inside. I—" His hand touched bare flesh at my waist. He jerked back. "Ash?"

"He tore my clothes but he didn't . . . didn't rape me." Tears started as I said the word. The hateful, evil thing my attacker had intended.

Jas, my mind whispered. *I have to call Jas. Warn her . . .*

Alan moved in the darkness, his face patterned by moonlight peering in through the roses overhead. Silk slipped around me, warm from his body heat. "Take my jacket. We'll go in by the back way. Come on." Alan lifted me, leaning into his cane as my weight fell against him. I caught the turned post of the gazebo entrance and righted myself; heard Alan grunt softly with relief as I stood unsupported. His cane skittered across the floor with the hollow sound of a bass drum as he dropped it and picked it up.

A floodlight perched on the side of the house came on, a blinding illumination that exposed the damage to my right hand. My thumb was bent back across my knuckles, dislocated by my own weight. I stared at my hand as tingles like electrical shocks became sharper and more insistent, running through my flesh from shoulder to fingertips. Beside me, Alan sucked in a breath. "Shit, Ash. What did he do to you? It's broken."

"No. Only dislocated." But a bad dislocation, which I left out of my explanation. With my good left hand, I gripped the damaged thumb, pulled it away from the joint and back into place, pressing down onto the injured joint with the ball of my left thumb until it popped into place.

Ordinarily I wouldn't have had the strength to reset a dislocated thumb. But I had to warn Jas. I had things to do. I didn't have time for the dislocation, or the pain that enveloped me with the repair of the joint. Pain, more intense and powerful than the scent of the man. I sagged against the turned post, cradling my injured arm. So much for super-mom strength. Vomit rose in the back of my throat.

"You fixed it?"

"I think so," I said, swallowing down the pain, sucking in a deep breath, and taking a strange kind of comfort in the purely professional. "I have to have X-rays, though. I might have a nerve or a blood vessel trapped in the joint. But first, get me inside, please. I have to call my daughter. He said he was going after her."

"Your daughter? Damn, Ash. What kind of sick person did this?" Alan asked as he slipped an arm around me, supporting me down the two steps to the path.

With each step, the pain in my arm grew, collecting and amplifying like a powerful engine accelerating under strain. "Someone who's been stalking me," I answered, finding it hard to breathe. "He followed Jas and Topaz to the movies tonight and then . . . found me here."

Alan opened the screened door and moved me through the porch and the Florida Room into the kitchen and up the back stairs to the family quarters. Monica met us in the hallway, her hand pressed against her bosom. Typical Monica, pointing to cleavage.

Emory appeared in the hallway behind her. "My God, Ashlee," he said. "What—"

"A man attacked her out in your gazebo. Call the police, Emory."

"No. Let me have the phone first," I said.

"Right. Your daughter," Alan said.

"What—"

"Not now, Monica," Alan said, reaching behind my friend for the phone and putting me in a chair all in one motion. "What's the number?"

I gave it to him, and as he dialed, Alan continued to give orders. "Emory, go to another line and call 911. Make sure all the other guests are safe and don't let anyone out of the house until the police get here. Move it, Monica." He placed the phone in my hand as Emory and Monica left their bedroom like well trained servants.

I was crying now, from pain and delayed shock and from relief. It felt so good to be taken care of, to be pampered and protected like Jack used to do. *Jack who had caused all this.*

The phone rang twice. Then Jasmine's voice, full of laughter. "What now, Mom?" she asked, trying to be cute in that know-it-all way of teenagers. I was about to frighten her. But it was necessary, to keep her safe.

"Jas, listen carefully. When you were in the movies, did a man sit behind you and Topaz? A man with . . . A man who had terrible breath, like the smell of rotten meat?"

"How did you know that? Jeez that man stank."

"Listen to me, Jasmine Leah. He followed you. And he attacked me just now, out in the garden at Monica's. Whoever killed our dogs is a sick person," I said, tying in the two attacks, knowing for certain now that they were connected. "Do you understand what I just said?"

"Yes, ma'am." The laughter was gone from my daughter's voice. Jas was still and intent, focused on my words with all the fervor and passion of her youth. The man had killed her dogs. Instinctively, I had wielded the right weapon. Perhaps I had more of my mother's genes in me than I realized. "Did he hurt you?" she demanded.

"I'm okay. He dislocated my right thumb, but other than that, I'm fine. Another guest interrupted him before he could do worse. Jasmine, do you have your gun?"

"In my hand," she said, not commenting on my changed attitude toward guns.

"Don't try to drive with it," I warned, "but don't pull over or slow down, either. Not even for stoplights unless you get pulled by a marked car with a blue light. Go straight home. Do you hear me?"

"Yes ma'am."

"I'll call Nana and have her waiting at the I-77 turnoff. She'll call on your cell."

"How will you get home?"

That thought hadn't occurred to me, but before I could think of a reply, Alan said, "I'll drive you to the hospital and then home, Ash. It's the least I can do." He sat on the edge of Monica's bed and stretched out his bad leg, the crease of his pants razor sharp in the lamplight.

I knew that "the least I can do" referred to my rescue of him following his accident. I should have refused, as the rescue had been my job, but I was too battered in body and spirit to do the right thing and beg a ride from my mama and daddy. I nodded my thanks. "I have a ride, Jas," I said as pain shot up my arm—damaged flesh, shrieking in agony.

"A safe one?"

I smiled, pulling my arm in close. My flesh was warm to the touch, which was a good sign, though I couldn't find a pulse in my thumb and it was starting to swell. "I think so. You remember the man from the accident at Magnet Hole Creek and Trash Pile Curve? Well, I ran into him at the symphony and he's willing to bring me home."

"The guy with the roses?"

"Yes."

"He got a crush on you?"

"Jasmine!" I said. I didn't have time for all this again. She was in danger and here she was worried about my virtue.

"Cause if he does, he'll take better care of you."

Her words stopped me. "I wouldn't know. And I certainly wouldn't ask," I added before she could suggest it.

Jasmine laughed. I realized I was on speaker phone when Topaz joined in, the sound full of static and white noise. "Go get him, Mamash," she said.

I decided to ignore the comment. "How long before you reach the turnoff, so I can tell Nana."

"Better say forty minutes. The fog's getting thick and traffic's slowing down in town. If it's like this on the interstate, I'll stay slow."

"Good girl. Be safe, Jas."

"You too. And Mama?"

"Yes?"

"I love you."

"I love you too, Jasmine." Alan took the phone from my hand as I wiped away tears. I would have to tell Jasmine something about the danger we faced. Soon. Tonight, if possible. If I could find the words. I could procrastinate no longer, even if it meant admitting that Jack had been unethical. Jasmine's safety was more important than her vision of her father.

"Next number," Alan prompted. I gave him the numbers and he dialed.

Monica came in and placed a pill in my hand and a glass on the table beside me. "Tylenol. Take it, Ashlee. Your hand is bruising and it looks really painful."

"It's ringing, Ash," Alan said.

Monica acting as concerned friend set off all kinds of alarms in my mind, but the pain in my body overrode them. The pain medication I was taking for my shoulder was hours old. With no internal debate at all, I tossed back the pill and downed the water. Which wasn't water. It was liquid fire, burning all the way down and back up again as I gasped. Tears fell from my eyes.

"Vodka. The good stuff," Monica said. Her voice wasn't even smug. She was just informing me. I gasped again and gripped the phone. A delicious warmth shot through me. The phone reached my ear, propelled there by Alan's hand on mine. Nana had already answered.

"Nana?"

"Speaking."

"It's Ash."

"What's the matter, my girl."

A breathy laugh escaped me in a little puff of air and sound. That was Nana. Right to the point and all business. "Pretty much everything." As succinctly as possible, I told her what had happened and that Jas was on the way. Without comment, she listened until I finished with, "I need someone to meet Jas at the I-77 turnoff. A Chadwick. Someone we can trust."

"I'll handle it, my girl. I'll call Jas on her cell and set it up. And I'll stay with her until you get home. But she'll ask questions, you know that. What do you want me to tell her?"

"About Jack? As little as possible." The incredible warmth had reached my tongue, making it thick and suddenly unmanageable. It kept wanting to stick to the roof of my mouth. "I told her we had a crazy man following us. That should do for tonight."

Nana sighed, disagreeing, but not ready to debate my claim. Maybe she could tell that I wasn't exactly myself at the moment.

"How do you plan to get home? I know my dithering daughter isn't with you, because there aren't any hysterics in the background."

"Not quite. Alan's bringing me home."

"Alan?"

"Alan Mathison," I said, smiling up at him. His hand still held mine, keeping the phone against my ear. He smiled back, curling up those lips. My eyes fastened on them. His smile widened.

"Are you sure you trust him?"

"Oh yes. We've spent a great deal of time lately rescuing one another."

"Beg pardon? You want to explain that one?"

"Not really, Nana. My face feels slightly . . . um . . . numb." I blinked, and when I opened my eyes again, Alan was standing over me, no longer smiling.

"Ash?"

"I fell asleep, didn't I?"

"I guess that's one way of putting it. I told your Nana that I'd take care of you."

"Ash, this is dreadful. Just dreadful. That such a thing should happen here in the Bible belt of the nation," a familiar voice said at my side.

I didn't turn or glance his way. The warmth within me protected me from the fear hovering at my side caressing me with insistent fingers. The voice belonged to Vance Waldrop. Who was Monica's friend. And who surely had known I would be here tonight. Across the room was Bret, his lips pressed together in a thin hard line, his eyes grim. I looked away. My heart hammered within me, an uneven cadence that pounded in my injured hand.

Alan's eyes were on mine, reading, if not my exact thoughts, at least my disquiet. His grip on my hand tightened as Vance droned on. "This is exactly the kind of thing I've been telling my more liberal colleagues back in Washington. You have to make the punishment fit the crime. Keep the violent offenders behind bars for the full term of their sentences We have to—"

"Vance?"

"Yes, Monica," Waldrop said. "This is a terrible thing, and I know you must be terrified to have it happen in your own backyard."

"No Vance, I'm not. But I do want Ashlee to have a moment to change into something more suitable to wear to the hospital And I don't think she should strip in front of a US Senator. The tabloids would love it and the elections are coming up."

Monica was being foolish, worried about tabloid gossip when Jas was in danger. But then, Vance Waldrop, a powerful man with resources I couldn't even imagine, was bending over me. Bret moved closer. I pulled Alan's jacket tighter, scant protection, but it was all I had. My hand throbbed, and when I looked at it, the swelling made my head swim. I was far more than just *merely* bruised or *merely* tipsy. I put my good hand back into Alan's, thinking about the way the room seemed to spin. It didn't usually do that.

"Emory darlin', how about you and Bret taking the senator back downstairs and talk to the policeman. There's no reason Ashlee should be forced to give a statement here, when she could do it in the comfort of an emergency room."

Comfort? What was comfortable about an emergency room? And then I realized that I had spoiled Monica's party in a most improper and unbecoming manner. I'd had the bad taste to allow myself to become a victim of assault within sight of her home. Monica had a social fiasco to repair; having me here only prolonged the embarrassment. And Mama would be devastated. It was a miracle she wasn't here now, weeping and carrying on.

"I'll bring my car around," Alan whispered in my ear. I think I managed a nod in reply as Vance, Bret, and Emory left the room together, their heads close, the senator's full voice lowered to a whisper. Alan slipped out behind them.

"Monica," I said, speaking with a tongue that must now be shaped like a summer squash, "What was that pill you gave me?"

"Tylenol with codeine. Why?"

Well, that explained why the room was spinning. I blew out a breath between numb lips. There was no point in trying to explain to Monica that I needed the pain. Pain as a diagnostic tool would be a totally foreign concept to my thoughtless pal. "Don't tell mama," I said instead.

"Of course not, Ashlee, darlin'," she said, pausing in the doorway. "I've known your mama too long to do something like that. I'd have her crying hysterics and never get her out of my bedroom. I told her you'd puked in the garden. I don't think she'll be around."

"No," I whispered. "I don't suppose so." Mama had never been able to stand the smell of sickness. And Monica never could manage to act refined. Even when wearing the Beck wealth draped around her collarbone, the wild and rowdy party girl still chose the word puke instead of any of the more ladylike and tasteful terms she would have used had there been a man within hearing. And if Monica used the same word with mama, she must have blanched like a sheet. I wished I had been there to see it. The stress had probably sent Mama home with a migraine.

"Alan's a nice looking man, Ashlee. He's a widower, you're a widow. You're lonely, he's lonely." Monica was standing with her back to me, perusing her closet. It was bigger than my bedroom back home, which was probably necessary, as there were now two Monica's. *Crap . . . Two of them*. "I knew his wife, and she was a bitch, Ashlee, darlin'. Margie was in my book club. She wore the pants in that marriage, and made sure we knew it."

Monica looked at me over her shoulder, her expression cool. She was long and lean in her designer gown and emeralds. Beautiful and bitter and harsh, cutting as a bullwhip. *Two of them*. "You take good care of Alan. Keep him close by, you know what I mean?" Without another word, she swept out leaving a purple sweat-suit on the bed. I turned and closed my eyes. I knew what she meant. Alan had been right. Monica wanted him for herself, but she was being generous. She was *giving him to me*. The codeine and vodka made the whole concept amusing and fuzzy, insignificant and sad. What would I do with Alan? I didn't need a man.

"The room's cleared out," Alan whispered, waking me from a light sleep. "Do you want to go to Carolina's Medical Center? I think we could sneak out back with no one the wiser."

"The last part sounds wonderful," I mumbled, struggling to sit upright in the squishy chair. "But could we go to Mercy South instead?" I asked, speaking of the smaller, more exclusive, and therefore possibly less busy hospital in the south of Charlotte. I would wait for hours at the larger Carolina's Medical.

The pain in my hand had become as fuzzy as my mind, a soft, pliant, yielding, thrum of agony. All I really wanted was my own bed. And Jas by my side. And all this mess with Jack over, once and for all. "If wishes were horses. . . ." I mumbled.

"Then beggars would ride. I know. But you don't have to beg to go to Mercy South. It's on the way. Come on. Up you go," Alan said, pulling on my good left hand.

"My clothes," I whispered, not resisting and rising slowly.

"Well, you could put on the purple sweat-suit, but that which would mean a phone call or visit to return them. Somehow I get the impression you don't run in Monica's circles."

"Perish the thought," I said, reopening my eyes. When had I closed them? Alan and I were alone in Monica and Emory's bedroom. Alan was standing close, his face above mine. I focused on his mouth again, and was glad there were only two lips.

"Or you could simply keep my jacket. You look quite fetching in it actually."

I looked down at myself. "I look like a toddler playing dress-up in Daddy's coat."

"Yes. You do. Come on. We have a narrow window of time in which to make our getaway."

"Vance won't be pleased," I said, as Alan slipped his arm around me. "He's probably already called the press for an exclusive interview from the scene of the crime. He prolly—pro-ba-bly—wants me here to look abused and pathetic." The last word came out as "patetic", but Alan seemed to understand. I was growing more inebriated by the moment on the vodka and Codeine. If my thumb needed surgery, it would be hours before any self-respecting orthopedic surgeon would put me under. *Lovely. Just lovely.*

And suddenly I was outside, and closed up in Alan's car, a black BMW with leather upholstery and a sound system vastly improved by the medication and alcohol in my system. I hoped I didn't throw up all over the car's luscious interior. I slept all the way to Mercy South, waking only when an aide in a dark scrub suit rolled a wheelchair to the car. The ER visit was all a blur, the doctors and nurses uniformed paper-doll cutouts, all frowning at having to deal with yet another well-heeled drunk.

Within sixty minutes I was checked in, X-rayed, and released, an ugly splint on my thumb. Nothing was broken, nothing caught in between the bones of the joint. I had set it perfectly. The doctor in charge was amazed that a lush in an advanced state of intoxication had reset her own thumb. Alan explained that my good friend had slipped me the liquor, but the doctor didn't believe him. Or didn't care. He was a moonlighting resident, still working on his first hundred thousand, and he couldn't be bothered with lowlifes like me. And frankly, I was too stoned to care. I was also too drunk to care what the police officer thought.

He was even younger than the doctor, still trying to grow enough peach fuzz on his face to make it worthwhile to shave every few days. Tall, slender, and brown eyed, he took my report with all the passionate interest in his frame until he realized I never saw my assailant. After that he lost interest. It seemed I couldn't please anyone tonight.

Alan found my home, despite my disjointed directions and the fact that right and left ceased to have real meaning. I had never handled medication well, and the combination of Tylenol with codeine and vodka were worse than anything I remembered. It was only when we were rolling up the gravel drive that I remembered the plaque I was supposed to receive at the Patrons' Party. I never got it. Great. All this for nothing. Tears pooled in my eyes and spilled over drunkenly, though I managed to wipe them away before Alan saw.

Nana and Macon met Alan and me at the back door, Macon to assist me into a chair and Nana to look over Alan. She must have decided he was acceptable, as she let him in the house and gave him a glass of Jack's good Bourbon to sip on while she put me to bed. After that, I remembered nothing till the sun peeked through the open blinds and rapped against my skull. The sound was remarkably steady and firm, exactly like the feeling of my own pulse in my head and in my hand. A constant pain that pounded sharp and cruel against my brain and my thumb injury. I was wounded, and I had a hangover. What a way to start the day.

Nana had elevated my hand and iced it during the night, which decreased the swelling, but there was little I could do about the pain. Not with a hangover. I didn't trust ibuprofen or Tylenol, not with the vodka beating up my liver last night. So I just lay there, surrounded by the luxury given to me by cheating, despicable Jack, and felt sorry for myself, until Jas decided I had rested long enough and came into my room. At her insistence, I got out of bed and into the shower, the cold water helping with both the pain and my muddled brain.

I was in the shower when it occurred to me what I had to do to protect Jas. The mere thought of it brought tears to my eyes.

CHAPTER NINE

Only weeks after a husband's death, the ordinary widow would have been dealing with dozens of post funeral consequences and complications with insurance companies, credit companies, the Social Security administration, the IRS, and, for business owners, the employees out in the field. The ordinary widow would have been grieving for her husband, her altered life, and her lost dreams. But then, I wasn't an ordinary widow, was I?

I had Esther and Macon to deal with the legal matters, and a CPA firm and law firm to deal with probate and the legal system. And I had a husband who had lived a lie for years. Perhaps many lies. *That* I was dealing with.

Now, when I should have been grieving and putting my life in order, I was, instead, battling for my safety, for my daughter's safety, perhaps for our very lives. I realized I couldn't do battle sitting at home, wringing my hands, waiting for someone to discover the menace we faced and then protect me from it. The danger had escalated from threats to violence. It had become real. I had to go out and meet it. It seemed simple, really. I would just make a target of myself and respond when attacked.

I dressed in work clothes, knowing what I wanted to do, yet not knowing how to go about it. It was great to have a plan, or at least the germ of a plan, but I needed a beginning, a way to get started. Nothing came to mind. Before I could work it through, Macon, Wicked, and Esther summoned me to a meeting.

I was quiet as I sat at the head of the conference table in Jack's office where they placed me. Silent still, when Nana came in, Aunt Mosetta shuffling along behind her. Aunt Mosetta, in her nineties, was older than Nana, and her joints were always in pain. This was the third time—or was it the fourth—that she had left the comfort of her favorite rocker and made the trek to my house. By that alone, I knew this meeting was important. Perhaps the gathering could be the impetus I needed for my plan. It was time to lay all my cards on the table, as the old saying went, and I was quite sure that when I finished for the day and folded, no one would consider me a winner. I studied my family, knowing they would not make this easy.

Macon opened the meeting by explaining that he had called us together to give both a rundown and an update on the problems facing DavInc. He counted them off on his fingers like a grade school teacher offering a math problem to his class.

"We have two distinct problems. First, William McKelvey, who was put into bankruptcy when his part of an equal exchange proved to be a chemical dump. Because he would have difficulty proving intent to defraud, a suit would have been little more than a delaying tactic on his part, a bullying tactic meant to inconvenience us and slow progress on Davenport Hills—force us to settle. However, because Jack is no longer here to defend himself, and because the paperwork for Davenport Hills appears to be incomplete, we could conceivably lose in court, which would severely damage Davenport Hills, Ash, and Jasmine."

"Incomplete, how?" Wicked asked. He was stretched out on two chairs, his slim frame blocking the doorway, as if to prevent anyone from escaping. His position allowed him to see out the front windows of the conference room, keep an eye on the front entrance to the office, and watch the hallway all at once. Though he looked relaxed, his posture was deceptive. The small man was wary and watchful; a gun bulged at his shoulder, the holster fitting close to his body over his T-shirt, partly hidden by the work shirt over it. He wasn't blocking us in; he was guarding the door.

"I'm getting to that. Prosperity Creek runs through the property, creating several problems. One, a hundred-year floodplain that severely restricts the type of development allowed on the land extending out from the banks of the creek. Two, the land doesn't perk well," he said, meaning percolate, or drain, resulting in a standing water problem following heavy rains. These were common problems in Dawkins County and Jack had dealt with them a half dozen times over the years. Nana made an impatient twirling motion with her fingers to speed him up.

"Which brings us to our third distinct problem. Davenport Hills itself. When Esther and I started here together, the office had been ransacked. Permits allowing certain parts of the development are missing. Though Esther says Jack definitely applied for them, we don't know what he may have been doing with them in the days prior to his death, or where the permits are now. We're missing Corps of Engineers' permits, FEMA permits, and several State and County permits, all of which deal with the poor-draining, blackjack soil."

I nodded. Blackjack was heavy clay soil, the kind that absorbed rain water only slowly and when dried out, developed the consistency of concrete.

"Esther assures me that the permits were granted, and that Jack kept numerous appointments with inspectors from various agencies. But the record of which inspectors he met with, when the meetings took place, which permits were approved as applied for and which needed to be re-worded or altered, or were denied completely, has been lost. Esther can find no record of them. Either the file was stolen when the office was broken into, or Jack took them someplace. All this means problems. Big problems."

"So what do we do?" Wicked asked.

I smiled. *We*. The *we* of family—the Chadwicks. The pain in my body seemed to ease.

"We approach McKelvey. We tell him Jack has passed on. We ask first for more time, and then we use that time to find a way to clean up the Charlotte property and bail out McKelvey's finances."

"Wait," Nana said. "I'll run get my magic wand. And Moses, you go dig up that pot of gold you found under the rainbow last week. And Ash can wish upon a star." Aunt Mosetta cackled. Macon sighed. "Son," she said, "we have money, but it's all in land. And Ash is in danger *now*. Not five or ten years from now when we might be able to sell enough property to pay for a cleanup. You told me it would cost millions, Macon. Not the few hundred thousand I would be able to put together in three or four months."

"It's not a matter for miracles, Nana. Jack had a plan all mapped out, including a list of potential investors and a government cleanup program. It's both feasible and sensible, even in this economy, and it shouldn't cost DavInc a dime. Jack had been working on this problem for a long time. McKelvey's problems can still be handled if we go at it right."

"But McKelvey is the lesser problem," I said, rising from the chair where they had seated me. My thumb ached and throbbed, and my shoulder and ribs were stiff, but my pain was better than last night. With any other injury, I would have given myself time to heal in bed at least a day and icing down my tortured joints. But, I had no time to relax and get over last night's attack. Today, I had to protect Jasmine. "Last night, I was attacked. And although I couldn't see him, it was the same man who attacked me in the emergency room on my last night of work.

"Both times he did several things. He demanded the permits—which I am guessing is part of the missing paperwork—the evidence, and the files. He told me there was a bigger problem than McKelvey, as if he knew all about the man's threats and problems. This time, he threatened to rape my daughter."

Aunt Mosetta's eyes narrowed. Nana sucked in air with a soft hiss. A threat to family was not to be accepted. A threat to one Chadwick was a threat to all. And a threat to a Chadwick child was a call to war. With that one statement, I took total control of the meeting. I didn't know what Macon and Esther had planned for this conference, but it no longer mattered.

I continued. "I assume the evidence he wants is the evidence for the murder Jack mentioned in his letter. Have you found anything that might pertain to the death of an inspector?"

Macon shook his head and took a seat beside Aunt Mosetta, physically relinquishing control of the meeting to me. "No, nothing."

"Well, someone knows *exactly* what they want. And that someone is close to this family and to this business. Last night, the man who attacked me said I had made a mistake by hiring a evil man to work for me. I think he meant you, Wicked. Wicked, not evil." The room grew still around me as I let the words and their meaning sink in. To the rest of the world, Wicked was Chad or Owens. Even his old school friends called him Owens. Wicked was Wicked only to family. "Only family knew we had hired you."

"I told Sherman," Esther said softly. "He always wanted to be a private investigator." I knew what Esther meant, but I waited for her to explain. She bit into the eraser of her pencil, her eyes downcast. She was in yellow today, a bright, cheery color that matched the pencil in her mouth and contrasted well with the coral lipstick and nail color. After a moment she continued. "Sherman is retired, you know. And he sits down to the bus station most mornings with his cronies, shootin' the breeze till lunch time, when he has a sandwich and soup at the café."

She looked up at me. "I know Sherman is the world's worst gossip and I never tell him nothin' important, Ashlee, you know I don't. But I told him about young Chadwick. Even gave him one of Chad's cards. I'm sure he blabbed it all over the city by now. I'm sorry, honey."

I shook my head and rested my injured hand in the crook of my left arm, walking toward Esther. I smiled down at her, taking in the squiggles of the minutes she had taken. I wondered if she would include her own confession. "Everyone at this table has probably said something to someone," I said. "But he called Wicked by a family name. Did you tell Sherman he was called Wicked?"

"I purely don't remember, honey. I just don't."

The quiet of the room grew. No one looked at me now, lost in their own thoughts. I was grateful for the quiet, for the time it gave me. I knew that no one would like what I was going to do about the danger facing Jasmine and me. I didn't care for it very much either, but I didn't have a choice. The tranquil moments allowed me to generate some inner peace. To tell God what I had in mind. It wasn't prayer exactly. More of an information transfer and a request for protection. I walked to the head of the table, my back to the door. Wicked repositioned himself. Guarded. Careful. I could learn from his near instinctive movements. I had to learn. *Cover all the bases. Be prepared. Know what the other guy doesn't.* Jack's axioms. He had lived by them. Now I had to.

"I have always been a private person. I have never reached for the limelight, for the responsibility or glory of business or public life. That was Jack's joy, never mine. I stood by him, entertained for him, acted as his dutiful helpmate. I made the occasional suggestion, ran the infrequent errand and wrote the rare check, but the business was his. I never led the way in the day-to-day activities of DavInc. Now I will."

Wicked sat up. Macon grinned, his eyes narrowing. Nana nodded her head, as if she had known what I would say. Her reaction was surprising.

"Because the person who arranged these attacks on me is probably an investor, and because that list is fairly small, I have made a decision. As of today, I am taking over the management of DavInc and Davenport Hills. It is my intent to be public enough and loud enough to attract the attention of whichever investor is involved in the attacks."

Nana laughed outright. Aunt Mosetta clapped her hands in delight. They both looked pleased at my statement. Nana had always called me strong; now I would have to prove her right. I wondered how well nearly twenty years of sharing Jack's days, curling up together in bed at night, had prepared me for the challenge I had just given myself—the challenge of running DavInc and drawing out my attacker. I wondered if that part of it had occurred to my family.

"Ash," Esther said. I looked up. "About hiring the evil man? The only people who knew I was working again were Chadwicks—your family—and Sherman's cronies. And frankly, not one of them is in real estate."

I looked down at my cradled arms, resting against my body. It was the only part of my plan I didn't like. What if the dangerous threat I uncovered turned out to be family?

"So either a Chadwick talked, or a Chadwick hired a man with bad teeth," Wicked said, his head tilted thoughtfully, "or else your phones are tapped outside the confines of this house." He looked around the room, frowning. "I swept the place for sophisticated listening devices, but what if. . . . What if someone used something outdated? Like a tap on the lines?" He looked at the outdated answering machine. My mouth open in a little *ooohhhh*. Wicked smiled, glancing at me as he stood. The gun was clearly visible at his shoulder. "Could be. I like that scenario a lot better than one that includes a Chadwick. I'll check it out."

I inclined my head.

"There's one other problem. This security nightmare you call a house." Wicked looked at Nana, explaining. "Anyone can drive up, park, and get out without the occupants of the house being aware that they have company." He put a strong emphasis on the last word, as if he meant enemies, not guests.

"And?" she asked.

Wicked shook his head. "Dangerous, Nana." He turned to me. "You need an entire construction crew with a couple bulldozers to completely restructure the approach from the street—make a new drive, install a security gate at the entrance, and rig up a few cameras. Basic, standard stuff. You own a construction company; how soon can you get somebody on it?"

I sighed as I sat down, envisioning the secluded parking Jack had designed with privacy in mind, not security. Not attackers. "Jack used grading contractors for that kind of work and I don't want to use any of them. The subcontractors are behind as it is, what with me not giving Peter Howell the means to pay them for so long. If I pull someone off the Davenport Hills project to do me a personal favor, it would be . . . I paused. "It would be unprofessional. And I need these people to think of me as professional." Unspoken was the worry that one of the subcontractors might be part of the danger I faced.

"I have a friend but he's backed up for three weeks," Wicked said. "As a favor to me he's willing to take a look and draw up a preliminary plan. Maybe he can recommend someone who'll give it top priority, but I have to warn you, it's not likely we can start the construction tomorrow. Or even next week. And I don't like this, Ash. Not a bit."

There was a short silence as we all absorbed Wicked's warning and Macon retook control of the meeting. The rest of the little conference involved the mundane, not the dangerous, and it broke up quickly. Esther went to transcribe her notes, Nana and Aunt Mosetta left looking smug, about what I didn't know and didn't really want to know. Wicked pulled his cell to call his earth-mover friend, and Macon focused on his open briefcase.

I walked outside, looking for Jas. My plan to draw out my attacker included convincing my hardheaded daughter to go away for a while. It would make Nana and Aunt Mosetta happy to see me comply with their original plan of leaving town. Of course, they didn't know everything I was considering. And I hadn't figured out a way, yet, to tell them.

I found Jas working a young mare in harness. Friesians are workhorses, sturdy, long-winded, and muscular, best suited to trail-riding, long-distance riding, and pulling a load. They were good for light draft-work, to use horse lingo.

Friesians weren't big money makers, but Jack had sold several Davenport animals to restored, historical farms for plowing and pulling wagons for hayrides, and a rare, exceptional few for show and breeding. He had also sold some to amusement parks for open-air buggy rides, and one to a man who worked weddings, escorting the bride and groom in an old-fashioned coach from the site of the wedding to the site of the reception. Very romantic, and the flashy matched blacks who pulled his elegant equipage made his business flourish. Davenport stock had taken home blue ribbons in county fairs. Each Davenport animal had a specialty by the time they left the farm, but each knew at least the basics for working under both harness and bridle.

The mare Jas was working was small-boned for Friesian bloodlines, but she moved well and looked very showy pulling a lightweight training gig. Jack had contracts for selling seven horses for city buggy rides in Charleston come next spring; Jas had a summer's work to do in preparation for the final sale. It would be hard to convince her to go away. I was afraid I'd have to pull rank on her and order her to the beach. Did other mothers have a difficult time getting their daughters to stop work and go have fun?

I propped my elbows on the highest rung of the big training ring and watched my daughter work. The mare was a three-year-old with a glossy summer coat and a thin layer of glistening sweat. Jas looked like a nymph perched on the tiny seat, the delicate wheels whirring to either side. Her face was serene and intense as she watched the hooves, gait, and hindquarters of the mare only inches in front of her. Checking for God only knew what. It looked perfect to me, but when it came to horses, my specialty was birthing and general health, not training.

When she finally stopped the mare, pulling gently on the traces, the training buggy rolled to a stop, and Jas looked pleased. The mare stood patiently as Jas left the lightweight rig, tilting her head to move the thick, unruly mane out of her wide-spaced eyes. Jas sauntered up to the mare's head and offered her a quarter of an apple, which the mare took with dainty lips.

"Not bad," I said. It seemed a safe enough evaluation.

"Not bad! She's coming along great!" Jas said, wiping her face with the inside of her T-shirt. Like the mare, she was bathed in a fine, glistening layer of perspiration. "We start with a heavier rig next week. The farrier's coming Tuesday to fit her with her first pair of work shoes. Daddy had high expectations for this little lady. He'd be so proud." A faint whisper of dread murmured through my veins. Yes. Jack would have been proud. Of the mare and of this tall, lovely young woman who was his daughter. Jas met me at the fence, gripping the top rung in strong hands. "So. What?"

She knew me too well, could tell there was something on my mind, and would know in a New-York-second if I lied to her. Instantly and entirely, she would know. I held in a sigh.

Behind her, Duke entered the ring, unhooked the simple harness and led the mare to the barn. He was at ease with horses, as if he had lived here all his life, instead of working here only a few days. The mare nuzzled his shoulder, nudging with her head for a treat. When Duke offered her nothing, she snorted into his hair as he led her away, the snort half-affection, half-pique.

"If you think you're going to talk me into leaving, you can forget it," Jas said. It was amazing how she could sound both complacent and dictatorial at once. A no-nonsense tone more suited to the pulpit than to the horse training ring. "Nana already tried to talk me into leaving, and I told her 'No!' too."

I looked at my child and managed not to laugh. She looked so stubborn and determined and defiant. And Nana had been running her mouth again. I brushed a lock of hair behind Jasmine's left ear and waited her out.

Jas tugged her lower lip between her teeth several times, pulling and releasing, pulling and releasing. "I know about the threats. I saw the dogs. I found the ear, for God's sake. I'm not leaving my horses for some maniac to shoot them down with a shotgun." She paused as if she expected me to debate the issue. When I didn't, she propped her fists on her hips. "No way, Mama. I'm not going. Not even for the week I had planned."

I still said nothing, having learned years ago that silence was the best way to deal with Jasmine's stubborn streaks. Argument was futile. It was difficult enough to change her mind when she was a child and I was bigger than she. It was nigh unto impossible now that she was grown. But there had to be some way to force Jas to do what I wanted this time. I had to get my daughter to safety. I couldn't worry about her getting in the way when my enemy decided to attack. I had to have my mind free of worry about her, so I could concentrate on the danger. Why had I not taken a firmer hand with this child of mine years ago? Why had I left the more difficult aspects of discipline to Jack? And how could I get her to do what I wanted without telling her everything . . . Like the fact that her father was less deserving of respect than he had seemed.

"Besides. I've written to a trainer," Jas said, her tone a bit less belligerent. "Elwyn VanHuselin, from Holland. Well, Holland originally, but he's been in Kentucky for six years. And I have to be here to help break him in, introduce him to the horses and our computer system and everything." Jasmine's eyes were dark, like Jack's, a wide brown ring of iris and black pupil.

Suddenly I missed my husband terribly. Suddenly I could have forgiven him anything if only he would return and stand here with me, watching our daughter become a grown woman.

"You sound awfully sure he's coming," I said softly.

"He's between jobs. When Lacey's Forever On was injured just before the nationals, the owner discharged Elwyn, even though it wasn't his fault. So I think it's a good bet he'll come."

"Lacey's Forever On was a Hackney, Jas, and worth ten times the value of our Friesian's. Which means your Elwyn would be taking a considerable step down to come here." Jas stared at me, her face flushing, a hint of guilt in her dark eyes. Instantly, I was on my guard. "Jasmine Leah Davenport," I said slowly. "What have you got up your sleeve?"

"Daddy left me the horses, right? In his will?"

"Riiiight," I said, drawing out the word, trying to second-guess my volatile child.

"So if . . . if I, like, wanted to sell off most of the Friesians and start a line of something else. . . ." Her voice trailed off, the final notes filled with guilt and some other emotion as well. Frustration? Anger? And then I remembered a series of dinnertime conversations, the ones where I mostly just listened while Jack and Jas talked horses and the future and bigger and better horse dreams. Jas had wanted competitive harness animals. Jas had wanted to make Davenport Downs into a name to be reckoned with. And Jack had said, "Maybe, Jazzy Baby. Maybe some-day."

"Your father," I said, ordering my thoughts. I had come prepared to fight a mental battle with Jas for her safety, not explain her father to her. It took a moment to shift gears. "Your father used horses as an outlet. A part-time hobby that was never expected to make a profit. He was happy if it paid for itself. But it was just for fun, Jasmine. He didn't mean to deprive you of your own dreams, he simply didn't want to make horses his own dream."

"That's just it," she said, her voice becoming passionate, pulsing with some new emotion I had never heard from her before. Intensity. Need. The Big Dreams of Youth. The frustration was still there, buried beneath the desire in her voice. "*DavInc* was daddy's challenge. He had DavInc to pour his money into and try to build into something special.

And I have Davenport Downs. That's *my* dream," she said, palms pumping into the fence rung. "I want . . . more."

I pushed the strand of loose hair back behind her ear again and smiled. "Sweetheart, you can do anything you want with the horses. They're yours. And frankly, I have no desire to take on the horses when you go away to school in the fall—" I stopped. "You are still going away to school in the fall, aren't you?"

Jas grinned and caught my hand, which had come to a stop in the air beside her face. "Yes, *Mo-ther*. I'm definitely going to school in the fall. Soooo. It wouldn't upset you if I sold all the horses? Except for Mabel and her colt, of course, and maybe one or two others. And used the money to buy some Hackney mares or some other breed for breeding stock?"

I almost told her she knew next to nothing about Hackneys, the delicate smart-moving breed that was a pricey favorite in world-class competition rings. But why bother? That was why she wanted Elwyn. Instead, I took my plunge. "Jas, you can do anything you want with the horses if you'll go away for a few days."

"Done. But it'll have to wait. I have to get the Friesian's ready to sell. I mean, I'm too busy to go away right now. Okay?" Jas had that half pleading, half demanding tone so common to teenage girls. It signaled her willingness to negotiate, at least on the small points.

I sighed. It had never been fun forcing Jas to do anything, but this was life or death, and I had no choice. There had to be something I could say to convince her to leave without frightening her to death. Something. "Jas—"

"Look, Mom. If we're separated, then somebody, this man who is threatening you, and who followed Topaz and me to the movies, could use me to get at you, right? I mean, he could follow Topaz and me to the beach and then just, you know, take us. Course, we'd just shoot him, but how would he know that? Right, Mom?"

The picture Jas painted was sharp, strong, so real, that I took a step away, my eyes on hers. She was right. The man who had attacked me would do that. He would. I remembered ache of my shoulder wrenched up behind me. His hands on my body. The sound of my clothes tearing. I remembered his threat against my daughter. What he would do to her . . . I could picture things happening as she described. I could envision the man approaching my girls, a casual stranger, armed to kill. I could see him hurting my baby in some far off place where I couldn't protect her, while I was safe at home, waiting for an attack that never came. Asking Jas to go away could be foolish for both of us. We might be stronger here, on Chadwick land, together. But how to protect her? And then I knew. "Alright, Jasmine. You don't have to go away."

"Yesss," she said, throwing a fist into the air like a prizefighter winning a match.

"But you can't leave the farm, either," I said, steeling myself to tell her a truth I would rather have hidden from her.

"What? What do you mean, I can't—"

"The man who followed you and attacked me . . . He threatened to—" I stopped, not able to say the words, "—to beat you, Jasmine," I temporized. "And I believe him."

Jas blanched, the expression on her face moving from shock to a very adult anger and mature comprehension in an instant. "What else did he do to you? I thought you said he only dislocated your thumb. Did he . . . Did he *hurt* you!""

"He didn't have *time* to hurt me more," I said, surprised at her reaction. Jack had always talked straight to Jas, spelling things out with almost brutal honesty. I had never been able to talk to her in the same way; it wasn't in my nature or my upbringing to spell things out to anyone. It was in my nature to protect those I loved. Something stirred down inside me, like truth waking from a deep slumber. It had something to do with honesty and protecting those I loved . . .

Jas bent and stepped between the rungs of the fence. "What did he do to you? What?"

I stepped back, but Jas stopped me, taking hold of my injured arm and hand, probing both with practiced fingers. Her eyes were on my face, intent and as searching as her fingers. Her eyes asking the question for her. Imploring. *Did he rape you?*

I opened my mouth to answer and the truth fell out, truth I would have spoken to another adult, to a friend, not my baby. "He tore my clothes. He. . . ." I swallowed. "He touched me . . ."

"The sonofabitch," Jas hissed, her eyes flashing, teeth bared.

"And then he threatened to . . ." I took a deep breath. ". . . to rape *you*, Jasmine."

Jas snorted, sounding much like her horses. She was angry, not afraid, and I laughed, a short bark of sound, startled. What had I expected? Hysterics? This was my *daughter*, not my mother. I paused, surprised. *Not my mother.* Not Josephine, who had been protected from reality for years, protected by my father, protected by me, insulated from the problems and ugliness of life. This was my strong, independent, self-confident *daughter.* I reached up and brushed the errant hair back into place, watching her as she watched me, reading my thoughts. I had always treated her with kid gloves, protecting her, when she needed it even less than I. My daughter. *Not* my mother. I nodded, coming to a lot of conclusions at once. "You move about in the county, so you make a better target than I do. So, you don't leave the farm *at all*. Understand? And you don't talk about it on the phone. Wicked thinks our phones might be tapped." Jaz cursed again, startling me, and I laughed. "Do we have a deal?" I asked. Truth. Honesty. Not mollycoddling. Just the real, blatant, unabashed *truth*. This was the baggage I had carried from my youth, learned at my parent's knee. Fear of truth, fear of sharing the realities of life. Giving them subterfuge and lies cloaked as tactful evasions and—

"Deal? Hell no," she spat.

"It's that or I have Wicked pack you a bag and drag you to the beach and handcuff you to the TV set," I said, fighting a smile. *How's that for honesty and blatant truth?*

"Jeeez, Mom, it's like I'm being punished or something."

"Take it or leave it, Jas," I said firmly.

"So, I'll take it," she said, instantly, her voice only mildly sulky.

I narrowed my eyes at my daughter. She smiled ingenuously and lifted her brows. "I said I'll take it." From the start of the conversation Jas had been willing to negotiate on the small points—like living on restriction—so long as she got to stay home. And I realized then that even with all the truth and honesty and the great revelation I had experienced in the midst of this conversation, Jasmine Leah had gotten her way. *Again.*

Sometimes great revelations aren't what they're cracked up to be. I still hadn't won. But then, I was new to this idea of brazen honesty and adult conversation with my child. Maybe with practice . . .

My visit with Nana and Aunt Mosetta was no more productive than the one with Jas had been. The two older women were bickering when I entered the old Chadwick farmhouse, their garrulous voices carried on the warm air.

There was something special about old farmhouses—even refurbished, renovated ones. Sunlight streamed in through ancient blown glass panes forming irregular patterns on wide pine plank floors, picking out the grain in the aged wood, reviving the worn patina. Diffuse beams fell gently on vintage, hand crocheted pillows, cozies, doilies, and lace tablecloths, brightened faded upholstery on plump armchairs, softened sturdy side-chairs. Even the smells were old house smells. Camphor, cedar, coffee, fresh bread, and lemon wax. Everything radiated warmth and comfort, even the cracked, grizzled voices coming from the kitchen.

"You knowed better than to talk to Jasmine Leah. That girl her mama's problem, not yours."

"Her mama would let Jas get away with murder. And Ash will never tell her about the problems. I had to say something."

"I'm not seen' where you done too good wit' her yourself. She done tol' you no, she ain't leavin'."

"She'll come around. You wait and see."

"You puttin' in too much flour. You biscuits be hard as rocks."

"My biscuits are always just fine, Mosetta Chadwick. If you want to criticize, get up out of your rocker and make 'em yourself."

"My arther'itis actin' up in my hands. You know I can't be making no biscuits."

"Drink some whiskey."

"That your cure for everythin'. Drink whiskey for a cold. Drink whiskey for a fever. Drink whiskey to make you sleep. Give whiskey to poor ol' Ashlee in the bath and plague-on-it 'bout drown dat chile."

I laughed at that one and stepped into the kitchen. Flour was scattered across wax paper on the hundred-year-old work table, a kettle steamed gently on the stove and fresh coffee gurgled in the drip pot beside it. Aunt Mosetta sat in a rocker in a shaft of sunlight, her gnarled hands in her lap. Nana stood in front of the biscuits, white to the elbows, a frown on her face.

"You could'a rung the bell. I nearly jumped outta my skin, my girl," Nana said.

"Huh. You neve' jump for nothin. Jesus come back not make you jump. You jist scairt 'cause you got caught talkin' is all," Aunt Mosetta said.

I laughed again and Nana's frown grew sharper. "Yes, ma'am. I heard. But if it makes you feel any better, Jas let it slip first." I crossed the room and hugged my nana, though she stood stiff as a dime store Indian in my embrace. "It's okay, Nana. I've never minded you talking to Jas. You fixed so many things that my own mother did wrong, I figure you'll help fix my mistakes with my own daughter."

"Huh. You give that ol' woman a big head ever' time you come down here. Dantucket, she hard enough to live with as it is," Aunt Mosetta mumbled. But she had a smile on her face, and she looked pleased at my words. A compliment to one Chadwicks was a compliment to both.

Nana unbent enough to kiss my cheek, a rare gesture for the hard-bitten woman. Words had always been easier for Nana than physical contact. "Your mother was always making mistakes, my girl. I had no choice but to butt-in unless I wanted you growing up just like her, cold and malicious and catty as a she goat."

"She goats not catty. She goats jist mean," Aunt Mosetta said.

"Like I said," Nana agreed, rolling the dough over once. It landed stiffly and flour flew.

"Well, Jas isn't going to the beach," I said.

"Why that is? You her mama. You say she go, and she gots to go."

"Jas pointed out that if we separate, we may be better targets. Someone could get to her first. Probably easier at Surfside Beach than if she's here."

"Huh. That chile jist conjured you, Ashlee Chadwick."

I always loved it when one of these fine women called me a Chadwick. They could say anything, tell me anything, and still make me smile.

Nana nodded. "I don't suppose she mentioned what Wicked said about hiring them a bodyguard to look after them at the beach."

I sat on the bench that ran along one side of the worktable. It was an old textile mill bench, a long log split in half, flat side turned up, rounded side toward the floor with peg legs inserted in holes. The wood was worn slick and smooth from countless bottoms, as familiar to my fingers as the contours of my own face.

"No," I sighed. I remembered the look Jas had given me at the end of our conversation, when she knew she had won. Had she mentioned the bodyguard or had I thought of hiring one myself, there would have been no argument about her safety at the beach. I could have shipped her off and known she would be fine. Bodyguards. What a strange concept for one who lived in the security of farm country.

There was, however, a bright side to Jas winning the argument. "She didn't mention bodyguards. But I admit, part of me is satisfied to have her close by where I can keep an eye on her. If we decide on a bodyguard, he can protect her here easier than at the beach where there's ten thousand other kids to get lost among."

"Huh. Pitiful argument, my girl. Jas just got around you is all."

"Gots her way around both of you, seems like to me," Aunt Mosetta chuckled.

Nana dusted off her hands and reached for the glass with which she would cut perfectly shaped biscuits. "Mind your own business, Moses."

"Jas wasn't the reason I came out to see you." Even to my own ears I sounded guilty.

Nana set down the glass. "What nonsense are you getting into now?"

I took a deep breath. This was woman's talk. The part of my plan I didn't get around to describing in the meeting. "I don't mean to worry you, but besides running DavInc, I've decided to . . . ah . . . reenter society. I know it isn't proper so soon after Jack's death, but—"

"But you figure to make a complete spectacle of yourself, draw out this person and then stop him," Nana interrupted. "As if going into business isn't a big enough attraction for all concerned. You'll hang yourself out like bait on a hook every which way but Sunday."

"Well . . . Yes, ma'am." My face flushed. It had sounded more workable in my mind than it did coming from Nana. Yet, Nana's tone wasn't totally censorious.

"Well, you do what you want, Ash. You pretty much always do. And you know I never cared a hoot about what the society types thought. But you work out an ending to your plan before you go attracting attention. You figure out how you're going to recognize this person before he gets to you, and how you're going to stop him. You hear me? Don't get sloppy."

"Yes, ma'am," I said. But I knew I wouldn't. I had looked at this thing from every angle. There was no way for me to be prepared. I'd just have to hope I could handle whatever happened when it happened.

Nana shook her head and went back to her biscuits. "You never could lie worth a toot."

From her rocker Aunt Mosetta chuckled, "But she got spunk, your girl. She got spunk."

The phone rang, thankfully putting an end to the gossipy little chat. Nana dusted off her hands and picked it up. "I'll never get these biscuits baked."

"They gonna be hard as rocks anyway," Aunt Mosetta said.

"Hush Moses. Hello." After a moment of silence, Nana said, "Yes, Macon. She's here. You heard the rest of this half-baked scheme of hers? She's going to re-enter society to flush out the persons responsible for this mess." After a moment Nana grunted and looked over at me, a half-grin on her face. "Yep. She is that. And more. Ashlee, Macon wants a word with you."

Those cryptic statements might be taken several ways. I took the phone. "Macon?"

"Ash, you wanted to take over the business, here's your chance. It looks like there's some trouble out at Davenport Hills."

A short flare of fear shot through me. "What kind of trouble?"

"Bret McDermott from the bank, a representative for some of the investors, and Rolland Randall the Third are out there sticking their noses into everything, asking questions, getting in the way of the workers and the heavy equipment, and generally being pains in the butt, to quote Peter Howell. He wants some official backup and he wants someone to answer their questions."

Bret was at the development? Why? After a moment, I asked, "Are your ready to provide any answers? You haven't had long to look at the books."

"I'm game if you are. The main thrust of our response will be that you are in charge. We may not know all the answers, but we are working through all the problems."

I looked down at myself. My work boots had been left at the front door. Otherwise, I was in old, worn jeans, an old flannel work shirt over one of Jack's old T-shirts, and no makeup at all. Come to think of it, I looked like I belonged on a construction site. *How would Bret react to seeing me there? I'd have to watch his face. . . .* "I'm on my way." I looked at Nana as I replaced the receiver. Whatever I was feeling must have shown in my face as wide-eyed terror, because she chuckled. She was white to the elbows again and the cookie sheet was neatly lined with thick rounds of dough.

"You'll do just fine, my girl. Just fine." She looked at me slyly, a grin showing a silver strand of dental work on one side. "As long as you don't pretend to be your mother and shove a cookie in everyone's mouth."

I smiled back. "Point taken, Nana. I'll call you when I get back. Let you know how I did."

"Better than that. Come to supper. Bring Jas and Macon and that Wicked boy. We'll have us a little party to celebrate your reentry into society." She put a little bite into the last three words, as if she was giving me a warning or trying to prepare me for something. And she was right. The next few hours wouldn't be easy, nor would the next few days.

In the south, it was still proper to mourn a loved one for months, a lost husband for a year. I had broken all kinds of social taboos just returning to work and being out in public again. The tongues would wag off at the roots when the Dawkins County gossips discovered I had been out at Jack's job site, thumbing my nose at the world and throwing my weight around like a man. But the Dawkins County gossips would be no competition at all for my mother. It took little effort to imagine her dismay, her consternation, her very horror at the thought of my going into public again. My Mother was the last of the die-hard Southern ladies, the kind who grew up wearing white gloves to church and social functions, wide brimmed hats in summer, girdles all year round. The kind who stood by her man through thick and thin, who affected a demure and helpless stance, and yet ruled the roost with a manipulative and pitiless hand. It would be a safe bet to say that I was scared witless of Mama's reaction to my decision. But then perhaps I could discover and disarm the threat to my family before she discovered I had put aside my mourning.

When I got back to the house, I washed off my work boots at the spigot by the screened porch. The mud had been nearly ankle deep and the wet made leather look nearly new. Inside, I listened to the personal line's answering machine as I applied a bit of lipstick and powder, combed my hair and raided Jack's half of the closet for a jacket. Monica had called, inviting me to a luncheon with friends. I could think of nothing so boring as a luncheon with Monica and her society pals. I found a navy blazer I liked and slipped it on, putting Monica out of my mind. The weather had turned cool again, and as the sun set, I would need some extra warmth.

Jack had been a tall man, but slender, and with the cuffs rolled back three turns and the collar turned up against the chill, I looked the part I wanted to play. A bit vulnerable, a bit delicate, but ready to work and prepared for the world of business. If I also managed to look like a twelve year old playing dress-up in Daddy's closet, well, I'd just have to live with it.

Macon met me in the office doorway, scanned me from head to foot and gave a shout of laughter. I lifted a brow and said, "We'll take the Jeep. It'll speak to the workers and subs, something about who's in charge and pays the bills. And Macon," I tapped my chest, "I'll drive."

"Yes, Ma'am. Whatever you say ma'am. And I suppose it could be worse. You could have worn a pony-tail and popped bubble gum."

I grinned unrepentantly, wondering if I showed molars on one side like so many Chadwicks. I grabbed Jack's briefcase.

"They'll never know what hit 'em, Mrs. D. Your Nana herself couldn't have dressed for the part any better." It was the first time anyone ever called me Mrs. D. I quite liked the name. It fit the new persona I had put on with the jacket and the work boots. A new name for a new life.

CHAPTER TEN

It was a short drive to Davenport Hills. Just a few miles north on I-77, I saw the first dignified billboard, if one could call a real estate advertisement the length of an 18-wheeler dignified. It showed a view of a golf course, a lake, a palatial home and two happy, tanned, and fit forty-somethings acting like love birds, heads touching, watching a sunset. Typical advertising, no gimmicks, no slogan, just a description of the amenities and the price range, the happy couple doing the rest to lure the interested. Jack had hated paying for advertising, even though the industry relied heavily on it to attract the better paying moneymakers of society.

Seeing the sign brought my first pang of fear, making me remember my own emptiness. My widowed isolation. The coarse, bitter taste of being utterly and completely alone. The feel of Jack's jacket against my body only made it more difficult to keep my eyes free from tears and my mind sharp. I was afraid. And I wondered if the men I would be meeting would be able to tell.

It was acceptable to look a bit vulnerable at first glance, another thing altogether to make my first appearance at the development shaking and in tears. Gripping the wheel, I drove in silence, breathing deeply, flooding my system with oxygen, searching out a calm place inside myself. I thought sleeping in a house with no husband and no Big Dog to protect me was difficult. This bearding the lion—and the subcontractors—in their dens was much worse.

Macon turned pages beside me, his eyes intent on the figures of cost sheets and the wording of contracts, constantly speaking to inform me of some fact he thought I might need to know in this showdown with the investors. Taxes, amenities, utilities, and road surfacing were only a few of the topics he touched on. I was grateful for his steady conversation and the opportunity to calm myself. As Macon talked, the sun slid behind a cloudbank, darkening the world. A front was moving in, promising more rain. At least it was coming from the south and would leave warm temperatures. This unexpected cool spell might be good for killing off insects at night, but I was ready for the heat of summer.

I-77 rolls through miles of timberland, farmland, and pastureland, broken by mobile homes with tires on their roofs, the rare evangelical church in desperate need of a paint job and an access road, and rarer intersections offering fast-food, gas, and textile outlets. It was far from the crime of inner-city housing projects in either Charlotte or Columbia, and yet close enough to both to make the commute bearable. Davenport Hills was an attractive locale to transplanted Yankees looking for a safe place to live, one with the comforts of city life in a protected, country setting. It was a secure community for the wealthy, carved out of the rural South.

We turned off the interstate just inside the county line, Macon still talking about his files, and solutions to problems. I listened as I drove the country road past a cattle farm, soybean fields, and acres of newly planted cotton to Davenport Hills. Macon was deeply buried in the files and folders in his lap and on the floor around his feet, and didn't look up to view the bucolic setting.

I had acquired a measure of calm by the time the landscaped brick entryway came into view. I didn't really know how I wanted to approach this first trip to Davenport Hills. I didn't know who I wanted to be. I hadn't had much time to think about it. I knew I couldn't be my mother, and I didn't know how to be my Nana. I would just have to feel my way through it all and discover myself as I went.

The guard in his little booth did a double take at the sight of the Jeep, and because we had never met, he came to the doorway instead of waving me on through. He had the former-cop look, and though he was past law enforcement retirement age, he was vigorous. About fifty-five, he showed a little gray at his temples, and the extra padding at his waist that cops acquire sitting behind the wheel eight hours a day. He ducked his head as I lowered the window. "Ma'am."

"I'm Mrs. Jack Davenport, Officer Reynolds," I said, reading his engraved brass nametag. Putting my right hand through the window, I shook his. "And this is my lawyer, Macon Chadwick." The cop's eyes traveled to Macon, took him in at a glance and raised his evaluation from black street kid to black ACLU. It was a common failing among law enforcement to view the world and all its inhabitants from the aspect of street crime. To them, people fit into categories rather than existing as individuals. The narrow-minded thinking that kept them alive on the streets was difficult to shed after twenty-five years as a survival mechanism.

I continued, "You'll be seeing us both a good bit in the next few months. You may want to issue Mr. Chadwick a sticker for his truck window, but you can handle that later. For now, if you'll just put us both in your logbook, I'd be grateful."

"Yes, ma'am, Mrs. Davenport. I have you on listing already. But your lawyer will have to register when I can record his vehicle description and tag number. You can set it up anytime, Mr. Chadwick."

"Thanks, Officer," Macon said.

"Can you tell us where Peter Howell is, please?" I asked, feeling very in control and very insecure all at once, my head swirling with facts, figures, possibilities, and my growing fear.

"He's down at the new golf course, ma'am, with the architects."

"And is RailRoad the Third and his little group with him?" I asked, calling Rolland Randall by my daughter's mildly disparaging title.

The name amused Officer Reynolds. A glitter of something not-quite-nice sparkled in the depths of his eyes. "Yes, ma'am. Mr. Howell was giving them a tour of The Swamp in his four-by-four when the thing got stuck and they all had to walk out. Ruined that fancy lawyer's expensive shoes, I'm afraid."

My lips twitched. "Has Mr. Howell's vehicle ever gotten stuck before?"

"No ma'am. It was the damnedest thing. I had to call a wrecker to pull it out." Officer Reynolds' grin was positively evil. But then, RailRoad the Third had that effect on people. After only a short acquaintance, they often wanted to see him suffer.

"Thank you, Officer Reynolds."

"Call me Joe, ma'am.

"Thank you, Joe. And I go by Ashlee, or Mrs. D., if you prefer," I said, using the new name for my new persona, whoever she might become.

"Have a nice visit, Miz. D., Mr. Chadwick."

I raised the window as we pulled past the guard booth. That hadn't gone badly. Joe had seemed nice enough, and his eyes hadn't bugged out of his head to see me in Jack's Jeep at Jack's work place. He seemed to accept me out here in no-woman's-land. Of course, the real test would come with the workforce and the subcontractors. They would be the real judges and arbiters of my presence on the job site. And of course, I would have to deal with the investors.

I drove straight down the four-lane boulevard of Davenport Hills, and still Macon droned on about prices and specs and linear foot costs of road surfaces. The center island and both sides of the road were heavily landscaped with azaleas, dogwoods, Bradford Pear trees, monkey grass and flowers. Groupings of beech, poplar, oak, and maple marked the entrance to the side streets or cul-de-sacs, bearing names like Cavendale Drive, Mosstree Court, and Crow's Nest Circle. Interspersed were green areas, tennis courts, and the open acres of golf course that peeked out at the road. Natural and artificial hillocks added balance and privacy to the houses closest to the boulevard. Huge rocks dug from foundation space or blasted from roadways made rock gardens. Acres of grass were watered by underground sprinkler systems fed by the runoff below Willow Lake, a state watershed project that just happened to be in Davenport Hills. Even in the drought months of July and August, Davenport Hills would look green and fresh.

Mercedes, Jaguars, BMWs, Volvos, and high-ticket American-made cars of the development's early customers passed us on the wide sweep of road. Some were driven by Realtors, others by well-coiffed house-wives on their way to the day-spa or the book club. Most looked bored and out of sorts as their faces flashed by. It could be such a drag being rich.

Part of Jack's dream for Davenport Hills was the business sector, which we passed early on. In one area, just off the entrance, was a series of quaint-looking shops for the hairdressers, maid services, laundries, and pizza parlors that were necessary to maintain a modern, upscale residential area. A progressive child care center and elementary school was part of the county's plans for next year. The biggest draws of the entire project, however, were the golf courses.

Designed by Cavenaugh and Wright—an up and coming arch-itectural firm specializing in golf courses—they were championship quality, Jack's pride and joy. The first course had opened two years ago, attracting nationwide attention in *Golf Magazine*. The second eighteen-hole course was due to open next spring, but underground springs, standing-water, and constant rain threatened delay. The problem with standing-water was so severe that subs and employees had named the course The Swamp. Jack had been working through the problems the night he died.

I followed the boulevard beyond Phase Three of the development, leaving behind the landscaping, upscale housing, parks, and the paving. Bumping over gravel packed red mud, I trailed tracks of heavy equipment and trucks through dense trees, along ponds edged with water grasses and cattails, and over manmade dams. A red-tailed hawk holding a field mouse watched my progress from the dead branches of a lightning-struck oak. A small doe and spotted fawn bounded across the rutted car path behind us. Wildlife, driven out by man's pursuit of a nature he could control and exploit. The ground became increasingly muddy, the tires slipping until I shifted into four-wheel drive. Macon was no longer studying his papers. Instead, he was staring out over the liquid ground around us.

"Your husband thought he could make a golf course out of this?"

I shrugged, concentrating on the road—what there was of it. "Jack always kept a pair of work boots behind the seat. They may be a little large for you, he wore a size eleven, but you're welcome to try them."

"Yeah. Thanks." Macon's voice was tinged with distaste. I wondered if it was the thought of wearing someone else's old shoes, or if he was just fastidious about mud. Vehicles appeared through the trees as Macon struggled to put on the boots. Three cars, two trucks and a wrecker were parked in a small clearing. Several men stood to the side.

"I don't suppose he kept a pair of waders? These are new jeans," Macon muttered.

"That's the beauty of denim. It washes well."

"That's the kind of thing your Nana would say," he grumbled.

"Thank you. We're here. And it looks like we interrupted a meeting of minds great and small." I pulled the Jeep beside Peter's gray company truck, parked, and got out. Macon was still tying the laces on waterproof boots that dwarfed his feet. Spotting Peter, I moved away from the trucks. There was a makeshift table constructed from saw horses overlaid with a battered exterior door, the surface covered with plans, some rolled, some held flat with calculators and briefcases. Peter stood with his back to the table, surrounded. Except for the one or two in the trees to the side, the men circled him, looking for all the world like a pack of dogs holding wounded quarry at bay. I didn't like the look of the group. They were hostile and combative, body language straining for a fight. My eyes narrowed in the glare as the sun came from behind the clouds.

I recognized Bret McDermott, his arms crossed, legs planted in the mire. Though dressed in a suit, Bret had sensible boots on. Another man, his suit muddy to the knees, was shouting, my husband's lawyer, the ringleader. There were at least six men in work clothes and boots, and two more in suits, none of whom I recognized. Peter saw me coming, but I waved him to silence as I walked up, unnoticed by RailRoad the Third and his little coterie.

"I have a problem with the entire layout. I don't care how much planning went into it, I want it changed," he shouted. "Moved off this wet quicksand to someplace safe for normal human beings. This so called golf course is a disaster!" The skin on the back of his neck was red, his hair was mussed, and there was mud up one arm as if he had fallen and caught himself with his elbow and his knees. Poor RailRoad. His dignity and authority were sorely shaken, and it was clear he was trying to recapture them both by shouting at Peter. It was also apparent the men had discovered the problem Jack had been working on before he died. The golf course could not be built as designed. To avoid the wet ground, it would have to be turned at an angle between the eighth and twelfth holes and completely redesigned.

Golf courses are usually built along the natural contours of the land. Jack had explained to me that when this one was originally drawn, the state had experienced a severe water shortage for eighteen months, and the water table was so low that there was none of the muck visible today. Turning the golf course would mean starting from scratch, a costly proposal that would result in changes to the established lots bordering the course. It was a design flaw that should have been avoided by Cavenaugh and Wright—and proper earth core samples. For the design professionals to have made such a costly mistake, Jack must have been overworked in another part of the development, and Cavenaugh and Wright must have been just plain stupid.

The architects would have to redraw everything, losing housing sites in the process. I couldn't remember exactly how many, though Jack had explained it to me. A new road would have to be built to make up for the change in layout, and the proposed modifications would be expensive, but in Jack's briefcase I had his preliminary drawings. I had seen him put the velum overlay sheet away in the fold of the lid less than an hour before he died. And I had seen it again the day I discovered the photographs of him and Robyn. I knew the changes could be made, if I could just remember all the details he had explained. Every other part of the night he died was graven into me like the dates on his tombstone. Surely I could remember this small bit.

RailRoad had gone on with his rampage while I thought. The circle of men had closed in on Peter. ". . . and as head of the legal department and one of the investors, I want you replaced."

Investors? I hadn't known RailRoad was an investor in Davenport Hills, but then there were several companies I hadn't recognized on the investor list. RailRoad was bullying my husband's favorite and most capable employee. *My* favorite and most capable employee. Peter didn't have to stand for it and neither did I.

"Your handling of this matter has been inept from the beginning. I don't know what Jack Davenport was thinking when he hired an incompetent like you—"

"He was thinking that Peter Howell was highly recommended, ethical and capable," I said, a bit too loudly.

The men turned toward me. I hadn't meant to shout but my words rang out. Peter Howell exhaled with relief. Macon reached my side, but I didn't look at him. I kept my eyes on RailRoad. He had good dental work. I knew because his mouth was open, offering me a clear view of his back teeth. RailRoad had been Jack's lawyer for over ten years and, as Jasmine said, he was a slimy character. He could easily be behind the attacks I had suffered and the letters I'd received. I took a quick look at Bret. His face gave nothing away. No shock at seeing me here, no anger, no remorse, no fear. I returned my attention to RailRoad who snapped his mouth shut.

"I don't appreciate you berating DavInc employees, *mister*, investor or not. If you have a beef with this company, then you have a beef with *me*, not with Mr. Howell. That's number one. Number two, is the conflict of interest you just mentioned. I have just decided that it's not ethical or proper for DavInc's legal council to also be an investor."

I didn't know where all the terminology was coming from, perhaps from years of listening to Jack talk about the problems and personalities on the job, perhaps from some place deep inside that had been preparing for this moment for days. But the words were there, as clear and concise as if I had memorized them instead of just thinking them.

"Therefore, as of this moment, I'm canceling your retainer. Neither you nor your firm will have anything further to do with this company." I felt myself redden, a pink heat that started at my toes and flushed its way north. Suddenly I was angry. It was the slow and fear-filled anger spawned by the attacks on me, the protective anger generated by threats to my life and my family. A heated anger like red-hot coals ready to burst into flame. It was a fiery anger, unlike my usual, tepid self. I liked the feeling. It was one of power rather than helplessness.

RailRoad was stuttering. A vein stood out on his temple. "Don't have a stroke standing here. It would be a real pain getting an ambulance back in these trees," I said. "When you leave, Mr. Macon Chadwick here will follow you back to your offices and prepare to go over all the company's legal papers to date. He'll be taking over for your firm."

"You can't fire my firm, lady. We have a contract." His face twisted as he spoke and a thin white line drew itself around his mouth as the blood was forced from his skin. Clinically, I wondered what blood pressure medication RailRoad was on, and if he'd taken it today. "And there's nothing illegal in my financial involvement in this project."

"I didn't say illegal. I said it's questionable and I don't like it. And because DavInc is now *my* company, and because *I* make the decisions, I've decided to terminate our business arrangement. Macon?"

"Yes, Miz. D. His firm's contract with DavInc was up over two months ago, and Mr. Davenport was in negotiations with Mr. Randall before he died. There's no problem with changing firms, contrary to advice your former legal council just offered."

RailRoad leaned closer, his face a ghastly red. "Senator Waldrop's not going to like this. Do you understand what I'm saying? He's – going – to – be – pissed." The widely spaced words hung in the air, reverberating through the clearing.

I should have been terrified at the mention of Waldrop, one of the men who seemed to be pivotal in each of my problems, but I was too angry to care. To use one of Aunt Mosetta's terms, I was mad enough to spit fire, no matter *what* the senator felt. I smiled thinly, putting my fists on my hips. I was making an enemy, and I knew it. But I had wanted to draw out my assailant by kicking up a fuss, and this was killing two birds with one stone, getting rid of RailRoad, and being as public as I could get. The man who threatened my daughter would hear about this. The whole county would hear about this.

"Macon, will you kindly follow Mr. Randall back to his office," I said without taking my eyes off the lawyer. "I want you to take immediate possession of all legal papers in Mr. Randall's possession. I realize you may need further assistance from your firm for this project. Please feel free to call on Chadwick, Gaston, and Chadwick for whatever you need. And consider yourselves under retainer by Davenport, Inc."

"Yes, ma'am." I could hear the grin in Macon's voice, but I was careful not to look his way. If RailRoad was involved in my problems, Macon would now have means to prove it.

"Listen, little lady. As an investor I have certain rights—"

"Yes, you do. But shouting at an employee and interfering in the performance of his duties isn't one of them. And you may address me as ma'am or Mrs. D. Not little lady, honey, or dear as you have so often in the past. Is that understood?" Before he could respond, I went on, surprised that I still had control of the situation, except that I was using my official voice, the one for offensive drunks, the one I felt safe using when cops were in the ER to back me up. Macon and Peter were my backup here, but that didn't seem to matter to the men I faced or to me. This was *my* development, damn it, and RailRoad wasn't going to run me off it. I took a deep breath, feeling my chest muscles pull against the fabric of my T-shirt. My ribs and shoulder felt numb; I was too angry to distinguish the pain in my hand from my pounding pulse. "Now, how 'bout you taking off. And the next time an investor requires a meeting with DavInc, call Esther and *schedule* one. With *me*. Understood?" I turned my back on Railroad, facing the other men.

"I realize the quarterly reports are late, due to the death of my husband. However, even the government gives a company reorganization time, and as a courtesy, I'd appreciate the same from the investors. Esther will have a partial report out next week, outlining the changes in the golf course and the projected cost. I believe this is a fair request to make.

"Mr. Wright," I added, finally recognizing the younger of the architectural firm's partners. He was medium build, wearing a Gortex golf jacket and casual shoes that had probably cost a small fortune. Now they were muddy and ruined. He had a ridge of beard along his chin and a chilly look in his eyes that I didn't know how to dispel. If his firm pulled out it would cripple development for months. I just hoped we owed them money. If so, then I could count on them hanging around for at least a while. "If you would be so kind as to stop by the office tomorrow, I'll have Jack's drawings of the proposed changes to both the golf course and to Phase Four of the development. Peter and I will go over them with you. Say, two P.M.?"

Wright finally nodded, a curt jut of his head, but his lips stayed tight. I hoped he wasn't one of those old-fashioned, controlling types who believed a woman's place was in the home and who would be happy to see one fall flat on her face in the business world. He glanced at his watch, a clear signal that I was taking up too much of his valuable masculine time. Fixing on my sweetest smile, I said, "If you have another appointment and have to leave, I'm sure we all understand. Don't let us keep you, Mr. Wright."

Wright didn't like being dismissed but he took the hint, folding up his plans with a flourish. He was muttering beneath his breath as he walked to his car, but I didn't try to understand what he was saying. I had the feeling it wasn't flattering.

Macon followed RailRoad past me to his car. The muddy lawyer was stiff with outrage, but containing it, at least for now. A moment later, Macon brought me the business cell phone and Jack's old briefcase. I accepted both and he drove away. I kept my eyes on the men remaining. I met the eyes of each. They were oddly quiet, standing in a semi-circle watching me, as if they were waiting for a signal to eviscerate me. I hoped it would be only figuratively and not literally.

Bret McDermott, while characteristically solemn, tilted his head, acknowledging my assumed authority. A secret ally? One of Vance Waldrop's pals? A young man I didn't recognize stood stunned and silent. I didn't know who had sent him, but when I met his eyes, he scurried off, moving in the wake of RailRoad and Wright with unseemly speed. He climbed into a state government car, and I assumed he was one of Waldrop's aides. I wondered if the taxpayers had financed his trip from Washington. I figured I could expect to hear from the senator. *Joy, oh, joy.*

Mr. Wright looked up as he was climbing into his car. "The office, two P.M.," he said, apparently having made up his mind about me. I nodded. I really would have to learn the man's first name. Peter's beeper went off, an urgent voice calling him to another hotspot. He gave me a little half-salute and said, "I'll come by the office or call first thing in the morning," as he jumped into his mud-caked truck and spun off down the twisting path. Not once did he get stuck. Two other men trailed to the trucks, decreasing the numbers left in the attack circle.

My gaze met clear gray eyes, twinkling with amusement. Fine skin crinkled at the outer corners; his lips, delicately chiseled, turned up in a faint smile. *Alan Mathison.*

Without turning my head from Alan's gaze, I set the briefcase on the makeshift table, holding the phone in my injured hand, against the brace.

Bret walked to his car, patting my arm on the way past. Silent as usual, he drove away, trailed by the last of the assault team. and suddenly the little group of men was gone, and I had time to wonder what significance the appearance of Senator Waldrop's aide and Bret might hold in light of my suspicion that an investor had been involved in the killing of an inspector and the threats to my daughter and me. I watched the last of the vehicles drive out, slipping in the mud.

The last of my anger evaporated. I was alone with Alan Mathison. "Jerel Taylor sent you." It could have sounded rude, but the words came out almost as a question. His smile faded.

"Actually, I've been put in charge of all Taylor, Inc.'s South Carolina projects and interests. Including the apartment complex that will adjoin Davenport Hills," he said. "I asked for the position this morning." He spoke his words carefully, as if they were imbued with something more than just the surface meaning.

After meeting me at the symphony, spending the evening with me. A faint blush lit my cheeks. I looked down, focusing on the cane at his side, dark wood splattered with mud, different from the one he had used with the tux. Because I didn't know how to respond, I said, "I understand there has been some legal maneuvering between our two companies about that apartment complex. Something about a restraining order against Taylor, Inc?" I let my words trail off. Jack had talked to me often about his work, his plans, and problems. I had retained a lot of the one-sided conversations. "The dual role of Taylor, Inc. as both investor in Davenport Hills, and competitor, was part of the problem."

Alan nodded. The small pink scar hidden in his brow was all but grown over with fresh blond hair. "I was hoping the, ah, *new management* would come to terms with Taylor, Inc and avoid any legal unpleasantness."

I smiled at the polite little expression. He didn't smile back this time, just kept his eyes on mine. "Actually, the new management," I said, using his words, "would also like to avoid any unpleasantness. Frankly, Taylor, Inc.'s financial input is necessary to the timely completion of this project." I thought that was pretty good business lingo, and Alan must have thought so too, as he quirked a grin and banged the cane on his leg in a little tattoo. The action dislodged a glob of mud on the tip. I cocked my head. "If Taylor, Inc would supply specs and drawings of the proposed apartments, and agree to keep the designs extremely upscale and in keeping with the original format of Davenport Hills, the new management would remove the restraining order."

What I asked was only fair in light of the shoddy workmanship that went into most apartment complexes, and the consequent effect on Davenport Hills' resale values. A poorly constructed apartment complex and low rents could bring in crime and the undesirables that the snooty Davenport Hills residents paid to keep out. Unfortunately, what I asked for was exactly what Jack had asked for originally from Jerel Taylor and been refused. Things had gotten nasty and Jack had gone to court to stop the building.

"I don't suppose the new management would simply take my word for it that she would be pleased with the development?" Alan said, the twinkle back in place.

"No, I'm afraid not."

"In that case, may I suggest that we retire to Miccah's for a pitcher of beer and a careful study of the materials in my truck? Man to man, as it were." Amusement was bright in his voice and eyes. I was being challenged, *mano a' mano*. It was a new experience for me and I rather liked it. In fact, I rather liked this wheeling and dealing in the business world.

Perhaps I had a knack for it, a quick way of handling unpleasantness, or at least putting it on the backburner. Of course, my enjoyment might have diminished somewhat had I lost the recent encounter. But I had won, and winning was addictive. I crossed my arms, the movement sending a sharp pain through my shoulder. For a moment, I had forgotten about my injuries. "Are you going to call me little lady?"

"No ma'am," he said gravely. "I believe the correct form of address is ma'am or Mrs. D."

I nodded, fighting a grin. "Is Jerel Taylor to join us?"

"No ma'am. Why spoil a perfectly good business meeting? And besides, I now have complete autonomy in dealing with decisions pertaining to South Carolina. I'm in the midst of setting up a satellite office in Dorsey City to work from."

"Local competition?"

"Friendly competition."

"Good. Dawkins County needs good, *ethical* developers and investors."

"Yes, ma'am. I aim to please."

A drop of rain landed on my nose. The front was moving in fast now, the air warming. I didn't really need Jack's jacket in the rising heat of late afternoon.

"Well, as I seem to be stranded without transportation, and in the spirit of fair play, the new management of DavInc would be delighted to join Taylor, Inc.'s representative at Miccah's to go over plans. But I warn you." I held up a finger. "I'm not buying. And," I held up a second finger, "two beers and I lose all restraint."

Alan laughed out loud, the sound frightening a flock of starlings into noisy flight. I hadn't realized how quiet it had become when the other men drove away. Surrounded by the well-grown poplars and oaks towering over us, the location closed off from the rest of the development, we were quite alone. His laughter died away. "What you're saying is. . . ."

A strange tension filled the muddy clearing after his words. My breath came short, and I was certain my cheeks were still flushed. "That one's my limit," I said. "So you may want to make it a small pitcher."

Alan smiled a bit sadly, as if I had answered wrongly. His expression was peculiar, and I wondered what he had hoped I might say, and then I decided it might be better if I didn't know. "Agreed." Turning his back, Alan walked to his truck and opened the door for me. "Ma'am." He invited me in with a gesture, his face smiling once again.

"Thank you," I said, as I climbed into his truck.

CHAPTER ELEVEN

I created a minor sensation in Miccah's for the next two hours. Alan and I appropriated a large table on the glassed-in porch, one whose surface was well lit by the western sun, even behind clouds, yet was close enough to the bar and waitress station for quick service.

Miccah's was patronized by a varied group of townsfolk, some in business suits, some in work or sports clothes, farmers, shop owners, doctors, lawyers, mill workers, secretaries, and hair dressers all gathered in little groups, like high school kids in the lunch room, each little "clique" watching the other, all hungry for food, gossip, and camaraderie. Even in the rural South, people went home to families and dinner around the table less and less often, opting for other, livelier pursuits, with no dishes to wash. Alan and I gave them something new to talk about. But between introductions, greetings, belated condolences, and down-right nosiness on the part of DorCity's gentry and moneyed professionals—during which I deliberately sniffed our visitors' breath—we actually covered a great deal of information.

Alan had his pitcher of beer—a small one—and I sipped a glass of wine and nibbled on nachos with jalapenos and cheese as we went over the specs for the apartment complex planned by Taylor, Inc. Blueprints, topographical surveys, and aerial photographs were scattered across the table. Advertising layouts, Realtor contracts, Alan even showed me renter's contracts. It was amazing cooperation from Taylor, Inc, a company notorious for its high-handed operating style.

It gave me a good overview of the extensive condo, townhouse, and garden apartment complex planned by Taylor, Inc. There were tennis courts, two pools, a fully staffed clubhouse, a bicycle path and jogging track, two playgrounds, and a two-acre lake. It was all tastefully done and would coexist nicely beside Davenport Hills. Jerel Taylor was sparing no expense in his development of the former hay farm that would become his newest South Carolina project. I couldn't see why he had resisted showing Jack these plans. His stubbornness had resulted in delays for his own project and steep legal fees. But then, according to Jack, Taylor had never let good sense stand in the way of pride. There were still unanswered questions of course, things Alan had left out of his impromptu presentation, but I had offered no information in return; it had been a one-sided conversation. I wondered what I hadn't been told.

And then I had an idea. "When Davenport Hills applies for a city charter in five years time, will Jerel resist being incorporated?"

"Probably."

I smiled into my wine glass at Alan's honesty.

"With few permanent residents and a mostly transitory tenant population, I don't see the need from our point of view. It would mean higher taxes and regulation, and I know Jerel wouldn't like that."

"True. But there would be police and fire protection offered by the new city. Garbage pickup, access to the cheaper electricity and gas rates negotiated with Duke Power by Jack this spring, just for starters."

"Okay," he conceded, "but those higher taxes are still a problem."

"Lower liability rates," I finished smugly, proud I had remembered some of the facts Macon had tossed at me on the ride to Davenport Hills.

Alan laughed, attracting the attention of the waitresses and of Bret McDermott who had just stepped through the entry door of Miccah's for his usual evening meal. I paused when I saw him enter the door, his banker's black replaced by jeans and a Polo shirt. This was the first time I had been to Miccah's at dinnertime since Jack died. I had forgotten Bret ate here every evening. He found us in the smoky shadows, his eyes moving over Alan, the papers between us, and me. Curiously calculating eyes, cool and restrained. Beneath his gaze, I suddenly felt guilty sitting here, in a public place, only weeks after the death of my husband. Making a spectacle of myself, just as my Nana had said. Guilty and afraid.

But then, that's exactly what I had wanted, wasn't it? To draw attention to myself and to Davenport Hills. To seize the attentions of the man who attacked me and those who had sent him. To make him come for me.

And then what, my girl. The words and tone were Nana's, the phrase with which she had questioned countless harebrained schemes over the years. The words calculated to make me poke holes in my own thinking. Usually, Nana's stern voice urging me to think, worked. This time it didn't. It served only to make me stubborn. After all, how else could I protect my daughter?

I waved Bret over. "Bret, you remember Alan Mathison from the meeting this afternoon." If my husband's old friend heard the subtle scorn in my voice, he gave no indication. Alan stood, the two men shook hands, and Alan asked Bret to join us. He settled on the booth seat beside me. A few moments of manly chitchat later, I was finally allowed into the conversation. I really hated being the little lady in a group of men.

"So. Mrs. D.," Bret said, a faint smile playing on his mouth. It was the first time I had ever seen him display humor, or even any awareness of the concept. He was a distinctly serious man. "I hope you'll accept my heartfelt apologies. I had no idea Rolland was going to light into Peter Howell that way. I should have put a stop to it. I'm sorry," he said, his words slow and his high Dawkins accent very strong.

In Dawkins, there are four distinct accents. Mill-town, farmer, African American, and high. The high accent is a rougher version of the typical Charleston accent, the result of so many Charleston patriarchs vacationing here in the summers before malaria-carrying insects were controlled in the Charleston swamps. Many liked Dawkins and just stayed on. High Dawkins meant money and connections.

"I dialed Peter and made peace. I hope *you* will accept my apologies as well."

I didn't know what Bret wanted, and I was uneasy, but I tilted my head to show I held no hard feelings. "RailRoad is difficult to halt once he gets started." Bret smiled at that. "And I appreciate that you called Peter. He's a good man," which seemed a safe enough statement.

"Yes. He is," Bret agreed. Again, his face showed nothing but the cool expression he had worn at The Swamp and again when he entered Miccah's.

I could think of nothing else to say, and it seemed an appropriate moment to excuse myself: the sun was a dull orange ball hanging below the last of the clouds, Miccah's was filling up with diners who needed the seating space, and I had accomplished my goals. I had taken the reins of DavInc, and either done really well today, or made a complete fool of myself. There was no way for me to know. Either way, I had come out of hiding. Both actions would be bait for my attacker, and had exhausted me simply because of their unfamiliarity. It had been a long and emotionally draining day, so difficult that I couldn't decide if I was afraid any longer.

My exhaustion and the fact that Jasmine and Topaz had just entered Miccah's—quite obviously looking all over the place for me—convinced me my meeting was over. Jas looked like a thunder cloud, her face dark with anger, her eyes flashing as if they might shoot lightning. I assumed some of her friends had spotted me with a strange man and made a surreptitious cell call, alerting Jas that her mother was out with a man. "Well, I have a daughter to feed," I said, falling back on every Southern woman's finest excuse, family. "So if you gentlemen will excuse me." I stood in my corner of the booth as I spoke, my knee brushing against Bret's. Both men came to their feet, Bret moving into the aisle as if I had made a shameless and unwelcome pass at him. He was still as shy and gauche as a grade school boy.

I didn't look up at him, afraid I might smile if I did and insult the man. His years of business success had taught Bret nothing about women. Bret's feelings toward me had always been ambivalent: a bit old fashioned and judgmental in viewing me as a working wife. There were other emotions as well, better hidden. Jack once teased me that Bret had a crush on me. One of those full-blown, sleep with your picture under my pillow, do you love me, yes, no, or maybe, check one, crushes. I never believed it till now; Bret did have a strange expression in his eyes

As I stepped into the aisle and picked up Jack's old briefcase, I looked up at Alan. "DavInc will be happy to drop the restraining order against Taylor, Inc.'s development if you agree to send me a letter outlining the proposal we discussed. Do we have an agreement?"

Alan hesitated, uncertainty glimmering deep in his eyes. I understood his hesitation. It was one thing to go behind the boss' back in an informal meeting in a restaurant. It was something else entirely to commit the offense to paper. "Agreed," he said with a sigh. "I had hoped to put off testing Jerel's promise of a free hand in South Carolina, but it might as well be now as later. I've yet to hire a secretary, and my typing skills leave a lot to be desired. I hope a delay of several days won't slow down the process of having the restraining order lifted."

"I wouldn't think a few days would make a difference to the restraining order." I waved to the girls and saw them start over to me. Jas was glaring, looking over the two men. Bret she dismissed as too familiar to be a threat; it was Alan she focused on.

"I'll notify Macon and he can begin the paperwork. Of course," I said with a sweet smile, "I'll have to approve the specs before any legal changes can take place. Just to make certain that I understood everything we've discussed, and that there are no substantial differences on paper. I'm quite new at this, you understand."

"Of course, Mrs. D.," Alan said, matching my smile. "I'll messenger the specs over to you in a few days."

"Not likely," Bret said. "DorCity doesn't have a messenger service. This isn't Charlotte, you know." Poor Bret. He was always so serious. "In fact, we don't even have Taxi service. The last one closed down in the seventies when the price of gas went through the roof."

"Really?" The twinkle was back in Alan's eyes, as if he, too, found Bret plodding and humorless. He ran a hand over his flat stomach. "Big business makes me hungry. Sure you won't stay and join me—us," he added, including Bret, "for supper?"

"Thank you, no," I said. "Gentlemen, it's been a pleasure."

"Mrs. D," Bret said, with his attempt at levity.

"Ma'am," Alan said. "Your humble servant."

I rolled my eyes, tucked Jack's briefcase beneath one arm, took Jasmine's hand in my left and Topaz's in my right as they reached my side. I pulled them outside. The rain had slowed, leaving a fine mist in the air, scented with honeysuckle and exhaust fumes. Puddles glistened in the potholes of Miccah's parking lot, reflecting the security lights. Darkness had fallen.

"Macon filled us in about this afternoon. He said you really nailed old RailRoad to the wall," Jas said, with fierce pleasure.

"We'll discuss that later. Right now, I want to know what you're doing off the farm."

"I had to pick up some feed. Jimmy Ray showed up drunk after lunch, and we were running low. Since Daddy died, we haven't received a shipment and I called two days ago but they haven't gotten back to me with an explanation."

It was an innocent excuse, and there *were* four, fifty-pound bags of feed in the back of Jack's Jeep, next to and piled on the jump kit. But I'd thought Jas understood that she had to stay on the farm. "Right," I said, still looking into the back of the Jeep, suddenly feeling my weariness in every muscle and joint, every tendon, even every eyelash. I was tired down to my bones. Too tired to think straight. But, I had to deal with Jas. Now. If my plan was to work, my daughter had to be safe. "So. You needed feed. The fact that someone called you from Miccah's, and told you I was here with a man had nothing to do with your trip to town."

"I told you she would see through it, Jas," Topaz hooted. "She got you, girl."

Jas' hand rested on the Jeep door, keys dangling. Her expression was part guilt, part defiance, the reaction glaringly visible in the dark of the parking lot. "How did you know?"

"I took a wild guess." It was something Jack might have said, or Nana, but never me. Not until now. Jas unlocked the doors and we all climbed in, My daughter fighting a slow, unwilling grin. I figured, why stop now, and went on, sounding more and more like Jack as the words left my mouth. Maybe I had delegated all the discipline to Jack out of laziness and not inability.

"I thought you understood that I will not be dating unless we talk about it first. And I thought you agreed to stay on the farm until I straightened out this mess with DavInc."

"But—"

"No buts, Jas. You spent the last ten years of your life trying to convince me you were grown up enough to be trustworthy. You said your word was your bond, which means once you give it, you keep it even if keeping it's hard."

"But—"

"You broke your word. Not because I was in danger and you were coming to my rescue. Not because some great moral imperative overrode the necessity of keeping your word. You left the farm and broke your word because you didn't trust me." I let the last phrase hang in the air.

The warm front had moved in and I was perspiring in the layers of shirts and Jack's jacket. Jas said nothing, just sat in the driver's seat, staring out at the drizzle, her bottom lip held in her teeth. It was a mannerism that meant she was thinking over what I had said. Finally Jas looked at me, her mouth turned down in a frown that could have been either anger, frustration, or shame. "You were having a business meeting. Right?"

I nodded.

"I'm sorry," she said.

I turned in my seat. "I'm so hungry I could eat a horse."

Jas smiled that unwilling smile again. It was an old joke on the horse farm, and she answered with the ritualistic answer. "Which one?"

"The Italian one."

"Pizza or subs?"

"If my vote counts in this little mother-daughter dialogue, I want pizza," Topaz said.

"Little Caesar's or Pizza Hut? I'm buying," I added. "And it has to be enough to feed Nana and Aunt Mosetta and Macon and Wicked and anyone else who shows up. Nana's having a party tonight." A party I could have done without, tired as I was, but no one said no to Nana.

The girls conferred as the Jeep motor purred and Miccah's parking lot filled up around us, spilling over into the bank's lot to one side. I watched each new arrival, as I hadn't been able to do inside the restaurant or while Jas and I were having our mother-daughter dialogue, as Topaz had called it. Few of the men who went into the restaurant glanced at the Jeep. I knew most of them, which gave me a measure of confidence; I could concentrate on the strangers. My stalker was just hired help, his vocabulary setting him apart from the letter writer. I wondered how many newcomers had severe periodontal disease. Did cops allow a "sniff test" of possible suspects?

The thought made me laugh. It was all so ludicrous. "Pizza Hut," I said to cover the laugh and settle the dispute. "Drive. I'll call it in."

We picked up six large pizzas, called Nana to tell her we were on the way, called two of Jas and Paz's friends to join us, and headed home. I relaxed in back, nibbling a slice of Supreme pan pizza with extra jalapenos.

I had done alright today. Averted one crisis, concluded another, fired RailRoad, and acted in a professional manner. If I made any mistakes, no one had been rude enough to tell me. The result of the success was dry eyes and exhaustion that thrummed through my veins like pain. I was a nurse, not a female version of Jack. I took care of drunks, gunshot wounds, kidney infections, earaches, heart attacks, and other assorted medical problems. I knew next to nothing about finance, land, water rights, rights of way, advertising or running a business. Mentally, I cataloged what I had learned today, and it all boiled down to one fact. DavInc investors were all so busy protecting their little patches of turf, they couldn't compromise without a lawyer to hold their hands. They were legalistic and dogmatic. Unless you got one of them off alone, they rapidly developed a pack mentality. The scene at the golf course hadn't been pretty, a group of rabid wolves snapping their jaws at Peter. And worse, I didn't know how much of my success handling today's crises had been beginner's luck. I'd had the element of surprise when I showed up at the development; tomorrow things might be considerably different. By tomorrow, all the investors would know that I was taking over. Even worse, I still didn't know what my stalker looked like. I could have been within feet of him today, and if he had been downwind, I wouldn't have noticed him at all. Which made me grin. Sillier and sillier. . . . I smiled and closed my eyes.

Somewhere between the Pizza Hut and home, I fell asleep, a slice of pizza in my hand. By the time the girls turned on to the gravel road, the cheese had dripped into the weave of the denim on my right leg, and then cooled enough to pry free with little residue. I woke feeling positive, hopeful, and inordinately refreshed from my catnap. For the first time, I was not weighted down with the fear and loneliness that were my legacy from Jack. I could do this. I could run DavInc, solve Jack's problems, and protect my daughter. I could.

At seven A.M., I was up and dressed in jeans, boots, and T-shirt, eating a muffin at the kitchen sink. There had already been a call from Bret, asking to speak with me about a private matter. And a message left over from last night, from Monica, wanting to know why I hadn't returned her call. Jas had been up for two hours and was at the barn with Duke and Disa, feeding the horses. Macon and Esther weren't due for another hour. It was peaceful and calm in the house. A refuge from the world.

I had the kitchen window open to let in the last, cool, night breeze, and a bite of cream cheese and muffin in my mouth when the irregular rhythm of a diesel engine reached me. A strange car pulled down the drive. I swallowed the bite whole, choking as I attempted to see the car through the trees. It was red. *Did killers drive red cars?* I swallowed again, trying to force the bite of muffin past the lump of fear in my throat.

Without conscious intent, I ran for the office, to Jack's gun cabinet, and pulled out the 9mm I had slept with for several nights. I checked the safety. The clip. And I swallowed and swallowed, trying to down the bite of muffin. I tried to take a breath, fighting for air past the lump of dough lodged in my throat; I couldn't get enough air to cough. Tears burned, caustic and sere for not being shed. *People choke to death this way.* Food stuck partway down, the esophagus swelling shut around the mass, obstructing the airway. My heart was a beating pain in my chest. I closed my hand on the 9mm. Holding the weapon down beside me, I ran for the kitchen. Struggling against the panic spreading out from my throat. I grabbed my hot tea. Tepid now. It went down fast, lubricating my throat, wetting down the muffin. Tears which I no longer cried for Jack, trickled down my face, blurring my vision of the uninvited guest. Finally the bite of muffin moved. I swallowed harder.

The diesel motor stopped, silence and morning air pouring through the open window. A car door opened. I swallowed the last of the tea. The liquid blocked more air. A hot sweat broke out on my body. My heart was thundering, which meant part of me was in a full-blown panic. *People panic when they suffocate. They panic when someone is trying to kill them too.* Another part of me looked on clinically, evaluating. *So. Either way, this is what it feels like to die . . .*

Panic numbed my hands and I dropped my mug. It shattered beneath my feet, scattering porcelain in razor sharp shards. I couldn't see the guest. He had parked behind the Volvo, and I wasn't watching as he exited his car. I swallowed again and again. And the muffin went down. Sucking in a breath of precious air, I thumbed off the safety and jerked open the door. Blinked through my tears into the morning light. And focused. On Robyn.

"Oh. . . . Ash." Her eyes were on the gun.

I looked down into her face, down because she was on the step below me. She was still as lovely as the day she left town for Atlanta. As beautiful as the photos of her in Jack's arms. I swallowed convulsively. My tears still ran. I lowered the gun toward the floor and turned away.

"I just got in from the trip." Her voice quavered. "I drove straight in from Atlanta."

Suddenly she was in my house, closing the door, enfolding me in her arms, Offering me the solace one woman offers another after a spouse has passed. I stiffened in her arms. Pulled back. Still breathing in loud, desperate draughts of air. Shaking. My heart still thundering as panic bled into some other emotion. Part shock. Part relief. Part fury.

Backing away, I collided with the kitchen table and nearly fell. Carefully, I thumbed on the 9mm's safety. Placed it on the table beside me. Looked into her lovely, lovely face. Some women are beautiful in an overt, sensual fashion, women like Sophia Loren and Vivien Leigh. They have a kind of beauty that is enhanced in strong light and picked up by the camera. A kind of beauty that glows every time a man is near. Others are simply pretty, like Jodie Foster or . . . or me—a kind of beauty that needs skillfully applied makeup and might not be seen at all without it.

Only a few women in the world are truly lovely, gentle of spirit, tender and warm, like the character of Melanie in *Gone With The Wind*. Delicately featured and so well put together that no individual feature stands out. Like my daughter. Jas has that quality of loveliness. And so did Robyn. It was one thing that drew me to her when we first met, that gentleness of spirit.

It was a gentleness totally lacking in the photos of her with my husband.

My shaking worsened. Cracked porcelain crushed beneath my boots. My throat ached as if it wanted to close up again each time I pulled in a breath.

"Ashlee?" Concern in her voice. And just a little fear.

I turned away, wiping my face, my hands trembling as if with palsy. Shock faded. My anger grew. *How much had Robyn known about the murder?* I should have considered that before, and hadn't, not even after the discovery of the photographs. It had never occurred to me that Robyn might have been in on the problems with DavInc. *Had she typed the murder letter?*

"A gun? Ashlee, what—"

"Get out of here." My words ground out, rough, coarse, full of pain. "Get out, Robyn."

"Ashlee?"

"I found the pictures. You remember the pictures, Robyn?" I asked, my voice low, a harsh, grating sound. "Well, I found them. Just a few days ago, I found them in his desk drawer. Photographs of you and my husband." I didn't look at her, didn't think I could. I inhaled and air burned my throat where the bread had scraped it raw. I wanted to ask about the murder, but I couldn't force my throat to make the necessary sounds. Silence stretched between us.

"Ashlee?" She was crying now. With my back turned, I could hear it in her voice. I couldn't look at her, my once best friend. "Please, Ash. . . ."

"Go away, Robyn. Just go away." Whispered words.

Long seconds passed as I fought with the need to weep, holding it in so tightly it burned in my heart with white-hot heat. Behind me, her breath caught and shuddered. Her feet shuffled sounding uncertain and oddly forlorn. The door opened. Closed. I could hear her crying all the way to her car, great broken sobs. The diesel roared to life, backed slowly away. She was gone. I stood in the silence of my kitchen, hearing the house creak and settle, picking out the mewling sound of Cherry's puppies on the screened porch. Listening to each sound and to nothing. The last tear fell, splattering on the back of my hand. My eyes dried.

In Jack's office, the phone rang. Jack answered, as he had every day since his death. "You have reached Davenport, Inc. Our regular office hours are eight-thirty to five-thirty, Monday through Friday. Please leave a message and someone will contact you as soon as possible. Thank you for calling Davenport, Inc." The tone sounded, A-flat and plaintive.

"Well, well. Ashlee Davenport. Sticking your toes into the water, are you? Testing the temperature? Dangerous business that, getting involved in your husband's problems." *Who was this? The man from the Soiled Utility Room?* I remembered his words, whispered in the close confines there and again in the gazebo. "Remember what you were told? To take good care of the file? Losing it isn't a very good start, Ashlee. When you find it again, I hope you will remember that it belongs to my friends and me. And I hope you don't ask the wrong questions, or get too curious. Because then you'll be in trouble, Ashlee, baby. Very big trouble."

The phone clicked off, the final tone sounded. I could hear my breathing, coarse as a bellows in the silent room. *How had he known I didn't have the file? What did I do today that gave it away?* A cold chill settled in the pit of my stomach.

"I'll find your damn file. And I'll find you." I heaved a breath that burned against the abraded tissue of my throat and left me coughing. "And when I do, you'll wish to God you had never been born. I promise you that," I finished. In the silence of my house, I laughed, a stubborn sound, as hoarse and guttural as my words. Pure Chadwick. Picking up Jack's gun, I walked back to his office and raided the gun cabinet for a holster. Made for another of Jack's weapons, it wasn't a perfect fit for the 9mm, and it certainly didn't fit me. But it worked well enough.

Locking the gun cabinet with its expensive collection, I went back to my bedroom to change. I needed a thicker knit shirt to protect my skin from the leather holster's chafing. I needed to wash the tears from my face. While I was splashing cold water against my reddened skin, the man's words came back to me. The threats, the diction; the grammar. The man who'd attacked me twice had used poor diction and grammar. *Not this caller.* Proof perfect that the man who was after my daughter and me wasn't working alone. This time it was one of the bosses.

I pulled one of Jack's jackets over my gun. I had a busy day ahead.

I left a list of instructions for Macon. Number one was to apply to the sheriff for a temporary gun permit that gave me legal permission to wear the 9mm in the ill-fitting shoulder holster. I needed the permit fast and didn't have time to take the eight-hour course. Second was an order to hire a bodyguard for my daughter, someone innocuous who could double as a stable hand. The third order was to dig faster into DavInc records. My appearance at the development yesterday had rattled someone's chain. Between taking over as the company's legal consultant and handling all my personal needs, poor Macon would have a busy week . . . okay, month. My legal fees would go through the roof. And I didn't care. When I had done all I could to protect my daughter, I went to the barn. With Jimmy Ray on a binge, the chore load seemed especially heavy, even with school finally out for the summer and Duke available to work. He had proven an invaluable addition to the farm, though I would have to keep an eye on the littlest Chadwicks to ensure their safety.

I spent the long hours of the morning working in the barn, shoveling manure one-handed, stretching tight muscles, working out my anger from seeing Robyn. I was also giving Jas the time she needed to contact prospective buyers for the Friesians she wanted to sell, and time to locate Elwyn VanHuselin, the trainer she wanted to hire. Selling the Friesians would mean the presence of strangers on the farm, which I didn't like at all. However, within another hour, I'd been assured that the bodyguard would start first thing in the morning, and Jas would then be as safe as I could make her, short of locking her in the old root cellar at Nana's.

Just before two, during a late lunch, Wicked stopped in to talk. I was alone in the kitchen, drinking a bowl of Campbell's chicken noodle soup and a mug of hot tea laced with a shot of Jack's whiskey. My throat still ached from choking on my morning muffin, and liquids eased the pain. Especially the whiskey. The whiskey-tea was Nana's recipe, of course, but I had to hand it to her, it worked. It even helped to alleviate the discomfort of my bruised shoulder, dislocated thumb and the sprained ankle I was still walking on.

Wicked came into the kitchen from the office, made himself a sandwich from my supplies in the fridge, poured himself a cup of hot water and dropped in a tea bag, all without a word of greeting. I wouldn't have taken him for a tea man. Coffee or beer, yes, but not tea. He added a shot of Jack's whiskey to his own mug, making himself at home in my kitchen. Well, he was family, after all. He took a seat at the table, propped his feet in the chair across from himself, and took a bite of bread and chicken salad.

"Not bad," he said, around the mouthful.

"I'm glad you think so. *Me casa, su casa.*" Even with the bruised vocal chords, he could hear the irony in my tone.

Wicked grinned unrepentantly and took another bite. "That's what I figured."

"Haven't seen you around today." With Jas in the house busy on the phone, and Duke and Disa now familiar with the routine of the barn, I hadn't talked much all morning. My throat was still tight with pain. I sipped tea to lubricate it.

"Been busy tracking down the bugs on your phone lines."

"The bugs . . ." I drank more tea as elation washed through me and was gone. "You find something?" Bugs on the phone meant a Chadwick wasn't involved with my problems.

"Yeah, but it was hard as hell to locate. 'Scuse the vernacular."

I gestured for him to think nothing of it. He took another bite as I waited for him to continue. He swallowed and rinsed the sandwich down with whiskey-laced tea. "What you got is a cobbled together system, one not approved by Ma Bell. In fact some parts of it are illegal as hell. Someone went into the box on the street and wired in to both the business line and your personal line. Ran a wire down to a tape player loaded with a twelve-hour tape, and a digital box that records every number dialed in or out. Basic set up," he said, "but put together with a mishmash of parts, as if whoever put it together did it in a hurry with stuff he had laying around."

I listened, sipping my tea. I should have been angry. I should have felt violated, horrified and shocked . . . and fierce and triumphant that the enemy's attack had been discovered. But all my deeper emotions had boiled away at the sight of Robyn, and what was left was a dry dullness.

"It's is a federal crime, carrying a hundred thousand dollar fine and ten years in jail, well, unless a president does it," he gestured wryly with his teacup, "in which case only the penalty is harsh words from the opposing party." I chuckled dutifully and he went on. "Somebody's mighty interested in your life and what you have to say, cuz, and that somebody's been making regular trips out to exchange discs. It's not something you can do by remote, not on this setup." Wicked ate the last bite of his sandwich. I got up and made us both another cup of tea. Wicked added a healthy dose of whiskey to his cup, less to my own. "Shame to waste good whiskey in tea," was his only comment. I wondered why he didn't drink it straight, but talking hurt too much to lavish precious words on unnecessary conversation.

" 'Course, the phone tap was the easiest part of my little survey. The hard part was locating the transmitter in the office."

I put my mug down hard. Hot tea splashed out over the tabletop. "Tell me," I croaked.

"Something wrong with your voice?"

For a detective, he wasn't terribly observant. "Laryngitis," I lied.

"Yeah, well, sorry you're sick. You don't look sick. Anyway. These little babies are higher tech and easy to set up once you have access to a site. You just unscrew an electric outlet and screw in a new one. One that not only lights up your lamp, it also transmits every word you say to some undisclosed location and a digital, voice-activated recorder."

I knew that someone had been in my house, roaming around, touching my things, I had known that by the way the office had been ransacked. And they had been listening in on every word spoken in the office. I should be ticked. But all I could see, suddenly, was Robyn's face as it had looked, shocked and hurt and grieving. *For me? For Jack? For herself.* I sighed, the breath long and mournful, as I waited for Wicked to continue. He seemed vaguely disappointed that I hadn't responded to the violation of my home and my privacy in some more concrete fashion—fireworks or fear, not a sadness that couldn't be explained by his news.

"There were two of the little buggers. One at Esther's desk—and let me tell you," he interrupted himself, "she's pretty pis— ah, she's real unhappy to find out about it. It seems your colorful little Esther sometimes talks love talk to Sherman when she's alone in the office." Wicked looked like his name, mischievous and naughty, like a kid caught teasing his little sister.

"Love talk?" I managed.

"Yeah, you know, like those numbers people call. Dirty talk."

"Esther? *My* Esther? Talks dirty on the office phone?" Here at last was something that had the power to break through my unnatural calm, something innocuous and unimportant, an amusing little slice of life leaving no one in any danger, where embarrassment was the only negative outcome. I could, in some strictly subjective manner, recognize Esther's violation of privacy, and empathize with her. But I couldn't stop the way my lips tried to turn up at the corners. And I couldn't banish the twinkle in my eyes. Esther and dirty talk? *To Sherman?*

"Exactly," Macon said, grinning his naughty-boy smile. "I left the system in place in case we decide to use it on this end. Set up something to draw out your stalker."

I nodded. My throat was getting better as I sipped warm tea, or else, thanks to the whiskey, I just didn't care as much about the pain. I had no tolerance for alcohol, and warmth burned through my stomach, heating its way out to my limbs, my skin. It was the warmth of anger, replacing the dull emptiness of the morning. It was the warmth of resolve. And of course the warmth of whiskey. It was the first real emotion I had felt since Robyn drove away. I gestured to the fridge. "No listening devices in the house?"

"Not a one. Clean as a whistle. And yours and Jasmine's cell lines are clean too. You have to make any calls where you don't want to be overheard, use the cells."

I nodded.

"You planning to use that gun?"

"Yes," I said, surprising myself.

"To shoot or to toss at someone?"

"Very funny," I croaked, my voice giving out when I tried to speak too loud.

"Then you better get in some practice," Wicked said, loading a slice of bread with Miracle Whip and chicken salad.

"This afternoon, after my meeting with Peter and the architects. Around five?"

"Count on it. I'll meet you at Puckey's and supervise. And help patch up anyone you accidentally shoot when you miss your target by a mile."

I mimed firing a gun at his head.

"Not me. I'll stay well away from your target. If I can figure out what you're aiming at."

Rolling my eyes, I got up from the table. I had a meeting to prepare for. I wasn't happy with the thought that someone would be listening in on the conversation, but since I didn't know what my assailant was listening for, and since I wanted to be provocative enough to draw him out, I had no choice but to hold the meeting in the non-privacy of the office. At the kitchen door, I stopped. "How far from the transmitter can the recorder be? How far from here?"

"Distance wise? About a half mile, but that depends on its frequency and any interfering FM activity, like cellular towers or radio stations, or even a busy highway with a lot of cell phone and trucker's CB radio activity."

I pointed to the front of the house. "I-77 is that way." I pointed to the living room. "WTZY is that way. That leaves only two directions to consider."

"True, which means only about a hundred locations if you didn't count the trailer park across the train tracks. We'd never find it, Ashlee."

"Yeah. You're right," I whispered, one hand against my painful throat.

"If you intended to paint a bull's-eye on yourself and attract the attention of the man who pulled a knife on you, now's your chance. Just be careful."

"Good advice. So tell me how to be both a target and careful at the same time. In fact, tell me what the man is looking for and I'll just blurt it out right away and get this over with."

Wicked shrugged. "That's Macon's department. You loaded him down so much with work yesterday, he might not find the problem for years."

"Thank you so very much for that happy tidbit. If that's the last two slices of bread, get a fresh loaf out of the freezer, and be sure to clean up after yourself. I'm not your mother."

"Yes, ma'am. Will do," Wicked saluted me with the sandwich and took a big bite. Family could be such a pain.

CHAPTER TWELVE

It was an emotional experience for me, opening Jack's briefcase again, touching papers he last touched only moments before he died. Emotional and painful and confusing, making my hands tremble, and my throat close up tighter. It was a pain I hadn't expected. It was a pain I'd thought burned away in the heat of my anger against Jack and his lies and his mistress.

Though I had touched the briefcase the day before, today the leather seemed different, worn and soft, distressed by years of banging around in the back of one work truck or another. It was like the touch of an old friend; its smell was wood shavings and Jack's own, unique scent. The feel of the papers inside was like the remembrance of death. This was the last thing Jack had touched the night he died. The last thing I touched the morning I discovered his infidelity.

I held the papers, smoothed them in my hands. Remembered Jack's voice as he discussed his plan for the Swamp and the golf course it would become. And when I was ready, I joined the men in Jack's office for another test of my authority as the de-facto leader of DavInc.

The meeting went well: Evan Wright and his senior partner Angus Cavenaugh, and Peter Howell and his immediate assistant Bill Berkowitz being agreeable to one another and receptive to Jack's drawings and notes on the golf course changes. The topographical map coincided well with the proposed changes, matching closely with the new positions of the greens suggested by Jack the night he died. I hadn't realized the breadth of Jack's plan, nor his grasp of the problem, until I sat back and watched the men—golfers all—react to the new concept.

"This fifteenth hole will be absolutely awesome—"

"Unless you play a hook instead of a slice, in which case you are screwed."

"Yeah, and water hazard on the thirteenth. . . ."

"The three new ponds circumvent the wet ground problem, spring heads, runoff. . . ."

"It's gonna cost, though."

"Jack knew it would. Look at these figures. . . ."

I concluded the meeting at four-forty-five, convinced I had averted another disaster. For a moment I found myself less angry with Jack. He had been trying to clear up some of his problems when he died. He hadn't meant for me to be forced to deal with them. He hadn't meant for me to suffer. Of course, if that were true, he wouldn't have left the photos of Robyn in his drawer. And with that thought, the residual pleasure of the meeting fled. Robyn with her long sleek thighs and her enraptured face. *Damn. . . . Just . . . damn.*

I met Wicked at Puckey's just after five and fired off ten clips of ammunition, five with the 9mm I wore beneath my left shoulder, five with the 9mm kept in the Jeep's glove box. I thought the session went well. I hit the target twelve times, once in the concentric circles. My best record ever. Wicked, however, left Puckey's with a glower. Twelve out of one hundred forty rounds was, evidently, not a promising score to the Chadwick's best shot. I thought it was great and rewarded myself with a can of albacore tuna and a glass of wine for supper. I told myself the wine was for medicinal purposes, like the spoonful of whiskey at lunch. But it was really just for the pleasure, the meal sliding past the roughness of my throat with ease. Tuna and wine. Pure heaven.

I went to bed early, feeling more peaceful and positive than I had in days, but strange dreams plucked at my mind, disturbing my sleep and drawing me up out of slumber from my much needed rest. Odd, muddy dream fragments, part memory, part fantasy . . .

Jack and Robyn standing on a red mud beach, alone, gulls keening overhead, the surf booming. Embracing, oblivious to the sea. An immense wave rose and threw them to the earth, swept them into the sea, screaming for help. Waves scoured away the red mud, erasing even their footsteps.

Alan Mathison in a muddy tux, standing beside his ruined car. Bending over me, asking me to go to the symphony with him. Marjorie Mathison, screaming as the wreck lifted from her dying body. Muddy water swirling around her body.

Senator Vance Waldrop with his mouth full of sugar cookies, confused as the cookies turned to mud.

The shards of visions became a longer dreamscape: Jack, Angus Cavenaugh, and me, on a golf course. Jack putted the ball and it rolled two feet before stopping, well short of the hole. "Slow, Ashlee. A wet course is so slow."

Angus said, "But the new plan completely circumvents the wet ground problem."

Nana, who was suddenly standing with us, handed me a cup of coffee and stared down at the green. "Wet ground is useless for farming. Good for nothing."

The dream segued into Aunt Mosetta, trying to climb on old Mabel, one foot in the stirrup, her house shoe firmly planted in the steel support, as the black mare nipped at her, sidling away. Aunt Mosetta hopped along in the mud on one foot, trying to keep pace with the prancing horse. Her other slipper sank deep into the wet earth with each step. "Con-sarn-it all," she muttered as she hopped around.

I was standing on the golf course at Davenport Hills, my feet sinking into the mud, slowing my progress. Just ahead, RailRoad the Third was taking a bite out of Peter Howell, huge jaws clamping on Peter's shoulder. I couldn't save him. I couldn't reach Peter in time. Blood spurted, great, scarlet gouts of it, spattering my shoes mired in the thick, red mud . . .

I woke up, sweating and gasping. Sucking in air that still burned my injured throat. Air lightly scented with death, rotten and crawling with maggots, like something out of a nightmare. Shaking, I pulled the 9mm from beneath my pillow, checked the clip and the safety, the faint metallic sounds loud in the quiet house. Bands of light fell across my comforter. The security lights were both repaired now, the outside illumination casting shadows.

The clock in the hall ticked loudly. When we first hung the antique clock on the wall, I had trouble sleeping at night. For a week the sound kept me wakeful. Now I scarcely noticed the ticking except when uneasy dreams plagued my rest.

Out on the porch, puppies whined and Cherry went out the doggie door to relieve herself, the little flap of wood swinging noisily. Big Dog would be home soon, perhaps by morning. The doggie door would have to be enlarged so he could seek shelter while recuperating, yet have privacy from Cherry's litter. I made a halfhearted mental note to have someone enlarge the flap.

Overhead, the beams creaked in Jasmine's rooms. Soft strains of music drifted down from my daughter's domain. She often played the radio late into the night, PBS and soft jazz.

Jack's dream words came to me again in the darkness, twisted in the covers, his gun in my hand, a round in the chamber. *"A wet course is so slow."*

I knew it was significant, but I didn't know why. Mud and water in every dream. Mud and water and a million and a half dollar golf course designed by Cavenaugh and Wright and redesigned by Jack Davenport on a little scrap of paper just before he died. Sleep was elusive.

The next day, I persisted in my plan to make a target of myself, to make enough noise about Davenport Hills to draw out whoever was stalking me. I still had no idea what I would do when he came after me—I'd have to wing it. But there was danger in my half-baked plan—a real chance I would have to face my stalker and his cold blade. A chance I could be hurt, badly.

After feeding the horses and conferring with Macon and Esther, I drove out to Davenport Hills. The warm front had brought more rain, a tedious, constant shower to erode the saturated ground. Driving slowly, I cruised along the main boulevard, giving my mind free reign as I observed the development. I was hoping some thought would come, a solution to my problems formulated out of restless dreams, a subconscious revelation about mud and water.

The development was bisected by Prosperity Creek, a wide, meandering stream that eventually emptied into the Catawba River. The hundred-year floodplain spreading along both sides of the creek had doomed large portions of the land to be labeled unfit for development, and this wide strip of land was the location of most of the parks, playgrounds, and tennis courts. Broad sections had been left natural, with cattails and marsh grasses growing in wild profusion.

Today, the ground along the creek was soggy, a sticky muck runnelled with fresh ruts where rain had gnawed into the banks and eaten away at the overpasses. It wasn't a pretty sight and, in several places, it looked as if the deterioration could quickly become a problem. The muddy ground bothered me and I slowed the Jeep, taking several side trips down the length of the creek, stopping often to get a clear look. I made a note to discuss the creek with Peter, and drove on, eventually reaching the marshy ground of the second golf course.

Prosperity Creek and Magnet Hole Creek came together near the boundary lines of the Davenport Hills property. The two creeks joined on the edge of a two thousand acre parcel of land planted with pines for the paper industry. Jack, Peter, and the surveyors had ridden over every acre of the Davenport Hills property prior to signing the original purchase deal. Because the creek was such an outstanding feature of the tract, Jack and Peter had followed it for miles beyond the Davenport Hills property, upstream and down to be prepared for future problems.

Friesians from Davenport Downs had carried the men along the banks and through the woods with no loss of stamina and with great endurance, giving Jack the idea that they might do well in long distance, overland races. The blue ribbons and silver loving cups brought home by his best animals were testament to the inspiration of that ride years ago.

The only part of the ride too difficult for the horses was the land at the confluence of the creeks, the only part of the property not touched by bulldozers and construction crews. The only part of Davenport Hills left totally natural and wildly beautiful. To this day I remember the look on Jack's face when he described what Peter and he found when they forced their way in on foot.

A great wash of sand twelve feet high and forty feet wide marked one side of the confluence. A small forest of downed trees and brush marked the other. Smashed and broken branches were crushed into the crevices of a massive rock that had been pushed to the surface eons ago, or dropped by a great flood in some prehistoric disaster. A dead raccoon was twisted into the debris. A wild turkey hung suspended, long dead, bones exposed by scavengers. Tangled undergrowth climbed the eroded banks; huge deposits of yellowish and gray clay lay exposed in the bare spots. Blacksnakes and water turtles sunned themselves. It was wild and beautiful and dangerous, and I could tell by Jack's face that he coveted the patch of land for its violent character and unrestrained spirit. I had known that Jack would never touch the few wild acres.

Robyn had been with us that day, sharing a meal, sharing Jack's enthusiasm and his eagerness for the new project. I wondered if they were sleeping together even then. The memory of Robyn soured my mood, darkening my thoughts like the lowering clouds darkened the day.

Turning into the final phase of Davenport Hills, I followed the truck path into the future golf course. Thick mud sucked at the tires, forcing me into four-wheel drive and, even with the increased traction, the mud-bath-of-a-road was difficult to navigate. Peter Howell, the surveyor, the architects, and the grading subcontractor were all standing in the drizzle, their hands in their pockets and mud up to their ankles. Several plot maps and sets of plans were protected beneath a temporary roof, a tilted sheet of plywood, supported on crossed 2x4s, over the makeshift work table. Rain dripped off one side.

I braked gently, letting the Jeep suck down into the mud as it halted. Pulling out an umbrella, a silly little thing given to me by my mother a few years ago as a Christmas gift, I stepped onto the boggy ground, opened the umbrella, and shook out its ruffles. It might be macho to stand around getting wet, but as I had nothing to prove, I intended to stay dry.

"Gentlemen," I said as I reached the little group.

"Mrs. D.," they chorused.

"Ma'am," someone added a beat later.

It seemed my preference for titles had been made known. "How does my husband's plan stand up under the light of day and the wet of rain?"

"So far," Peter said, "the preliminary drawings look like they'll eliminate most of the drainage problems. We may lose the three lots we talked about yesterday, a loss of over three-hundred grand, not even factoring in the added costs of re-surveying the course and putting in the new road. But it looks reasonably feasible."

Reasonably feasible, huh? Yesterday it had been great. Perfect. Wonderful. Today, it was reasonably feasible? What was Peter trying to tell me? I nodded sagely, as if he had said something profound. "The state's still reimbursing us for the roads, so that much of the added expense is covered," I said thoughtfully, giving myself time to think, watching the subs. They were men's men, brawny, dressed in denim and logger's heavy boots. And scowls.

And it hit me. A fine group of men's men, standing in the rain, having a talk about the manly subjects of moving earth and re-sculpting the topography of the land, and little old me with a ruffled umbrella intruding on the masculine powwow. I started a slow burn, and looked at the surveyor and the grading sub, narrowing my eyes at them, widening my smile, ladylike in the way that Scarlett O'Hara was ladylike when she closed a business deal. Predatory. "I would certainly appreciate the lowest cost possible for this portion of the project, gentlemen. *So far*," I said, with careful emphasis, "you both have done well by DavInc, and I think a little compromise on profit margins would be a fine return," I finished, twirling my pale pink umbrella. The "so far" was an almost-dare, and they knew it.

Okay, so I was baiting them with my female-ness, a plump little hen crashing an all rooster party, watching for a reaction. I really didn't want to play this game, the game of manipulation that women played with men, a game of reward and punishment, the game played because men didn't respect straight talk from women as they did from other men. The umbrella threw water droplets in an arc around me. Spattered the men. Peter grinned and looked down at the mud. Cavenaugh and Wright, the golf course architects looked on with interest.

"I don't expect you to eat your shirts, but some consideration on this matter *is* expected," I said into the silence of the morning. "And any cooperation at this juncture would make a difference down the road. DavInc would very likely remember your assistance in some future tangible way." Umbrella-twirling aside, I was surprised and pleased at the words flowing from my mouth. This was *me* talking, being reasonable and sincere, with just a hint of steel in my voice, the tone I used when I negotiated with a noncompliant patient. I turned to Waddell Youngblood, the grading sub. He was staring down, frowning, scuffing his toe in the mud, moving earth, even in his off time. "Wade."

He kept his eyes on the rut he was building, ignoring me. Waddell—Wade to the boys—had a world-class beer belly. "Wade," I said more firmly. "It's been hard since Jack died. I want to keep this project going for all the subs and contractors if I can. I don't think it would be fair to anyone to dump this project, declare bankruptcy or sell out, although frankly that would be a lot easier than trying to finish all this." Out of the corner of my eye, I saw the surveyor flinch at the thought of bankruptcy. Peter Howell turned away, hiding a smile.

"I'm doing the best I can to step into my husband's shoes and save this project. He was always fair to you subs, standing behind you when you needed help, loaning money when you had a temporary short-fall. He wouldn't want me to leave you hanging with bills unpaid, or sell out to another developer who might bring in his own subs." Waddell Youngblood's eyes crept up and met mine briefly. I sighed. Wade was not a happy camper. Wood Blankenship, the surveyor, lived up to his own name, his face carrying all the emotion of a superior poker player. He was giving nothing away. Neither were the others.

"Okay," I said, suddenly not caring if I appealed to their manly pride or not. "It's like this. Money's tight. I don't want to slow down business taking new bids from subs all over the state to open Phase Four and redesign this golf course. I could, but I'd rather not. I'd rather count on all you boys being fair and helping out in this tight spot, redesigning this golf course."

Angus Cavenaugh pursed his lips and studied the muddy mess on Waddell's shoes. He was waiting his turn as I dealt with a first class redneck.

"I'd rather be able to say to the new man at Taylor, Inc., that I have the best, most reasonable subs in the state. I'd rather put in a good word for you all, instead of having to be brutally honest and maybe cost you a bid for the apartment project going up next door to Davenport Hills."

That got all their attention. Finally. "Thought Mr. Davenport had put a restraining order on Taylor's project," Wade mumbled.

"He did. The new man and I came to a satisfactory agreement yesterday. Provided he doesn't back out, the court order will be rescinded effective the day I receive a written proposal, as early as next week. It would be sooner, but the man needs a secretary." With those words, I had a thought. If you can't beat 'em, buy 'em out. "Wood, your wife was part of the administrative cuts made at Bowater last year, wasn't she?"

Wood Blankenship was a long, lanky fellow with dull red hair and a wad of chewing tobacco in his cheek. We attended the same church, and even on Sunday, he carried the chaw, the soft packet of flavored tobacco leaves tucked into the back pocket of his suit pants during the sermon. "Yes'am. She was." Wood had inherited financial problems from his father, and it was an open secret that he had taken a beating when Flo lost her job. He had four kids, three in college, and a house to pay for. Losing the second income had been a blow to the family.

"Tell her to call Mr. Alan Mathison. I'm sure Taylor, Inc. has phone lines by now. Tell her to say I referred her. Some of you met Mr. Mathison out here the other day. Blond guy in a hunting jacket?"

Waddell grunted and raised his brow in a partial sneer. Wood's eyes lit up. "Thank you Mrs. D.," he said, not looking at his surly friend. I had the feeling Wood was about to sell Waddell out. "I'll tell her to call. Well 'scuse me folks. I got work to do, trimming down a bid. Uh, later, Wade."

Bingo. Wood Blankenship stepped from the group to his truck. He wasted no time getting to his calculator and the topographical maps drawn for the original phase four project. I had made a friend. Wade went back to playing in the mud, his brow furrowed down over his eyes. Wade was a little slow today. I turned away. "Peter. Anything I can help you with?"

"Got it covered, Mrs. D."

"I imagine you expect some consideration from Cavenaugh and Wright, as well." Cavenaugh's voice was laced with the faintest trace of ridicule.

"Mr. Cavenaugh, what kind of trees do you see around you?" It wasn't the non sequitur it seemed, and the instant spark of light in Cavenaugh's eyes proved it to me.

I hadn't studied the trees around us, but Cavenaugh had. Trees that were able to thrive in wet ground were specific according to species. I knew that because Jack and I had discussed it one evening when we were planning the location of our home. I had been big with child and drowsy and contented, all curled up in our big bed, plat maps spread out all over my tummy.

He told me our house would have to be further away from Nana's than originally planned, because certain trees were growing where we wanted to locate the barn. Those trees meant the drainage was poor. Jack had seemed like the most intelligent man I'd ever known; the best man I had ever known. Seemed like . . .

Cavenaugh lifted a brow and glanced at the trees. He wasn't surprised at what he saw. He knew what I was driving at.

"If Cavenaugh and Wright had done their jobs, and not missed an obvious sign that the ground would have drainage problems when the drought passed, we wouldn't be having this last minute fox-trot, and I wouldn't be facing a costly problem. There should have been drainage adjustments made when the topographical survey was evaluated for this project. That was your job, not Jack's. So, yes, I expect some consideration. A *lot* of consideration."

Angus Cavenaugh opened his mouth, closed it and pursed his lips again as he thought through the implications. Finally he lifted an arched, aristocratic brow. Waddell sneered. Though the men were impossibly different, their mannerisms were similar, and so was their meaning. The little lady should be home, birthin' babies and cookin' an' such. I bristled, but managed to keep a tight lid on my rising temper, knowing I had to get out of here fast, or risk blowing my top and losing whatever I might have gained in the last few minutes. Peter, however, was having a ball, a wide grin on his face. "Peter, call my cell if you need anything. And, at some point, we need to take a look at Prosperity Creek. I spotted some extensive erosion problems from this heavy rain."

"Yes, ma'am. I'll take a look at it today and come up with some recommendations. Get back to you soon."

"Fine. I'll be at the office, gentlemen, awaiting your bids for the restructuring of this project." If I'd had a hat, I might have tipped it. Lacking that, I twirled my pretty little umbrella once more and slogged my way through the mud back to my Jeep.

I was sweating and damp and shaking all over at my own audacity. The last time I had talked down to a man like that it was to a half trained ER doctor who had callously told a family that their mother, a seventy year old woman, was dead, and that they had done all they could, but her heart just stopped. The woman was, in fact, sitting in another room, waiting for her family to take her home, her wrist bandaged up to cover the stitches suffered from a fall. The doctor had not bothered to verify his patient's name before he called a family conference. The family had been hysterical, the woman's husband on the verge of a heart attack himself. Not a pretty picture.

But when the young doctor tried to blame an even younger nurse for his own error, I had faced him down, and set the record straight in front of witnesses. The doctor had never forgiven me, and I had never forgotten the incident. Now, I had faced down a group of hostile men and walked away in one piece, the nominal victor.

Climbing into the Jeep, I sat, my feet hanging above the ground, out of the mire, and paused to consider what I had just done. I tried to convince myself that my success wasn't so impossibly strange. The attitude I had adopted both with the doctor and the men in the clearing was the same one I'd used in dealing with recalcitrant patients over the years, the moderately drunk, the needle-shy, the overanxious, the belligerent, the oxygen-starved, all reacted well to the strong mother image who explained the reward and punishment aspect of life. My method could be summed up in the image of Nana, a trimmed switch in her hand, a resolute look in her eye. "You reap what you sow, my girl. Now, bend over and take your punishment or go home to your mama.

No other choices." Not the stick or the carrot, but the choice between punishments.

To see it work in other areas of my life was astounding. I should try it on Jas. Closing my umbrella, I started the motor and pulled the Jeep around, turning the vehicle out of The Swamp. I had accomplished something else as well. I had discussed the water problems in public. If the men who were after me heard about it, and if my dreams had been trying to tell me something I knew, but didn't yet recognize, *and* if the mud and water of Prosperity Creek were really the heart and soul of Jack's problem, then my stalker might pay me a visit. If . . . if . . . if.

I fingered the 9mm belted across my torso. Hidden beneath Jack's jacket gave me an ace. I would have to use it at close range, if I needed it. I probably wouldn't hit anything more than twelve feet away. Any closer, the attacker would have a good chance of killing me before I got the gun drawn and ready to fire. I needed some hand-to-hand combat training, sneaky little things a short, slightly rounded female could pull on a bigger opponent. I stretched my shoulder and ribs, pulled against the thumb joint inside my brace. The pains were still there, the muscles so tender any roughhousing would be agony. I wondered what nasty little tricks Wicked could teach me. And I wondered if I would be able to move tomorrow at all.

Back at the farm, I met the new security guard. He was six-foot-four, with a chest like a beer keg, a trim waist and hips, a firm butt, and gorgeous blue eyes. Any objections Jas might have put up about being trailed around by Bishop Jennings—Bish to his friends and clients—evaporated when she laid eyes on him. The attraction was clearly mutual, the heat practically sizzling between them. *Lovely.* Just *lovely.* All I needed was a doe-eyed Jas, too interested in a firm body to pay attention to any strangers on the place. I managed to catch Bish in a stall shortly after the two met, and threaten to cut short the possibility of any descendants if he laid hands on my little girl. After my success in The Swamp, I was feeling cocky.

Bish politely informed me that he didn't screw clients, a frank statement that made me blush. So much for feeling cocky. Of course, his declaration didn't touch upon what might happen after the job was over. The temperature between the two promised that whatever happened would be like a fireworks warehouse set to the torch. It had been that way when I met Jack. And I had been the same age as Jas.

However, his employee status did relieve my mind in the short run. And if there *were* problems, I'd just turn him over to Nana and let her jerk a knot in his chain. She didn't allow cocky employees or unsuitable suitors either. Nana would straighten out the boy just as she had Jack when she first met him. I'd like to be a fly on the wall for *that* straight-talking conversation.

The rest of the day was marked with mini-crises. A back-loader was driven off the job site by juvenile delinquents during lunch break and ended up in Prosperity Creek. It wasn't my fault. It wasn't my liability, either. It was the fault of the driver who'd left the key in the ignition.

Waddell Youngblood needed two thousand dollars to pull the piece of heavy machinery out of the creek and get it repaired. Muddy water had been sucked into the engine, and the shop wanted up-front money. No credit for Wade, not in this part of the county. Sheepishly, he came to me. I loaned the money to him. Chadwicks have always been generous people. Especially when proven right. I could have given him an I-told-you-so stare but I didn't want to pay for the pleasure. You reap what you sow, and the Almighty seemed to be in a tooth-for-a-tooth mood.

The second little crisis was the sub who put in the foundations for Davenport Hills. The boss hadn't been aware that a woman had taken over the company. When he discovered the fact, he and his crew walked off the job, refusing to "work for no female, no way". I immediately called another sub, a man whose file had been sitting in Esther's desk drawer for months because she "had a good feelin' about this boy". He accepted the job, sight unseen, for his original bid, and was on the site before close of business, scoping out the previous sub's work and planning his takeover. He looked like a hardworking, earnest sort, and I liked him as much as Esther had.

The sub who walked off the job wasn't so well pleased; he'd assumed I would be unable to find a crew replacement. According to Peter, he'd expected to be begged back by a desperate female with tears in her eyes, urgent entreaty in her heart, and bucks to spend. I popped his bubble, not taking his call when he asked Esther for me. Macon, working in the office, grinned at my refusal, his expression proud. *You reap what you sow, my girl.* Nana had been right.

The third crisis was a lunchtime message on the office answering machine. It was the whispered voice of my second stalker, cultured, grammatically correct, not the country boy language of the Soiled Utility Room and the gazebo, but just as frightening. Just as dangerous. "Ashlee," he whispered. Listening, I stared at Macon, his eyes holding mine. "You were a bad girl, Ashlee. You used the file. You talked too much. Your time is up. Someone will come for the file soon. I suggest you don't resist when he asks politely, Ashlee, or it'll be Jasmine's turn." The line clicked dead. Without a word, I left the room as Macon replaced the digital drive with another, saving the whispered tones for the cops should we go to them. But how do you catch a phantom you can't see? How do you prepare for the unknown?

I considered calling the police, but there was nothing they could do. We had a dozen prospective suspects—investors all—for a crime that *may* have been committed against an *unknown* inspector *sometime*, and amorphous phone threats. The police would only be helpful in catching someone after we unraveled my business problems, or after an assailant killed me. A heavy weight of fear lay on me. I jumped at every sound, every quick movement for the rest of the day. My mouth dried in terror a dozen times. I reached for the 9mm twice, uselessly. The usual mini-crises of an ordinary day on a farm continued, one after another, all day long.

The next involved good ol' Bish of the tight buns and trim waist. Jas came upon him holding an unexpected prospective horse buyer in a headlock, while the man's hysterical wife pulled a pretty little pearl handled, snub nosed .38 and prepared to shoot out Bish's left kidney. The couple from North Carolina had arrived four hours early to look at Charisma—Jack's best, long distance, prizewinning mare—and her foal.

At my urging, Bish finally released the stranger. He even apologized to the man when Jas explained that buyers often arrive because unethical breeders would drug a half-wild or mean-as-sin or sickly horse before a customer arrived. It was an unethical practice to unload an unsalable animal off on an unwitting buyer, yet, the old saying said it all. Let the buyer beware. Thankfully, the couple was not the type to hold grudges. Once I explained that my daughter's life had been threatened, and groveled a bit, and we'd consumed some of Jack's best Glenfiddich scotch, they bought the mare, her young foal, and two geldings. And left happy.

The next crisis was based on a previous one. Jas took a flat-bladed manure shovel to Bish, hitting him first in the face with the business end, then poking him several times with the rounded-off handle in the center of his rippled, muscular belly. My daughter told her bodyguard in no uncertain terms that this was her barn, her customers, and her—expletive deleted—horses. And if he laid a hand on anything or anyone without her prior express approval, or without her life being in danger, she'd shoot his—expletive deleted—testicles off. Trust Jas to use proper medical terms even in the midst of a heated temper. The expletives were the only surprise, and I wondered how much their use was due to the other heat flaring between her and Bish.

Assorted minor crises popped their devilish little heads up during the rest of the day. Petty little difficulties like Esther's old-fashioned adding machine blowing the small rubber belt that turned the roll of paper. The machine was outdated, and the office supply company had to order the part. A five day wait to replace a twenty-five-cent part. And of course, Esther didn't want a new one. She liked the old one.

Then her computer had a glitch and she was unable to open the employee payroll file. Two hours later it changed its mind, but by then Esther—dressed today in vibrant blue—had calculated all the employee's weekly paychecks using Jack's old handheld calculator. Esther wore bifocals and wasn't particularly happy about having to read the tiny numbers on the minuscule LED screen. Stressed from the close work, she was in a snit, slamming things down on her desk, answering the phone in frigid tones to suppliers and customers alike, and even wearing shoes, a bad sign to those of us who had seen her in a fury.

I left her to Macon, wondering how much of her bad mood was due to the recorded "love talk" Wicked had reported. I might know nothing about business, but I knew when to give Esther her space.

And then Monica showed up. She had never been to visit me, except for the annual Christmas party given by DavInc. She brought the plaque that I should have picked up at the Patrons' Party, a long trip she could have avoided by simply mailing it to me. I didn't know what to make of her presence, but I was too busy to deal with her today. I had Esther tell her I was out at the job site. Just a little white lie.

Late in the day, Nana decided it was time to bush-hog the front forty. The old John Deere had other ideas. It kept belching great clouds of gray-black smoke that had nothing better to do than infiltrate the office and choke us all. The smoke was less offensive once she got the stubborn tractor going, but then we had to contend with the noise—a mighty roar up close to the house, a more tolerable growl when she turned the tractor the other way. A slow, rhythmic intrusion on our busy afternoon.

On top of all that, and in the midst of the sale of Charisma and the other horses, Doc Ethridge brought Big Dog home. Limping, shaved, stitched, tongue lolling happily, he bedded down on the porch with Cherry and her pups. He had his own water and food bowl, perched on top of the box used as a birthing den by the feisty mother, positioned so none of the smaller dogs had access to his medicated food and antibiotics. It was a perfect setup for the recuperating dog, except for the fact that I had neglected to have the doggie door enlarged. There was no way Big Dog could squeeze through the small flap in the screening. Every time he whined, someone—me—had to go to the porch, open the door, escort Big Dog out into the yard, and reopen the door when he was finished. Doc had been able to save Big Dog's kidney, and considering the number of times the shaggy mutt needed to go out, the kidney was working perfectly.

It was a relief to have Big Dog home. I hadn't been aware how much I depended on his fierce bark to warn me of approaching strangers. I had missed his gentle attention and protective presence, his warm snout thrust into my fist, his liquid eyes and lolling tongue. But Big Dog had changed. He was still the easygoing, gentle giant of old for Jas and me, but now he hated men. All men. Macon, Wicked, Bish, and Duke included. He lowered his ears and tail, growled in the back of his throat in warning and barked his fool head off when they came near. His main concern was Cherry and her new family. So long as all males stayed away from the screened porch, Big Dog was okay. If they got too close, he got noisy. And I got a throbbing headache.

I shooed the DavInc crew out early, telling them to take the rest of the day off, canceled target practice, didn't mention self-defense moves to Wicked, and gave myself a break. The gesture seemed to mollify Esther somewhat, but did little for Macon. He left complaining that the EPA permits weren't satisfactory, the survey maps provided by the Federal Emergency Management Agency didn't match the maps drawn by Wood Blankenship, and the Storm Water and Sediment Erosion Plan hadn't been approved by the Corps of Engineers. And we still hadn't found the permits allowing Davenport Hills to exist. "Don't worry about it, y'all," Esther said as she sailed out the door. "If there was one thing Jack Davenport always kept up to date, it was the permits. They're all here somewhere. You just have to keep looking. RailRoad the Third probably hid them somewhere just to spite you. Or maybe he filed them under 'mud'. Hah!" Esther's idea of a grand joke was somebody burdened with a problem she didn't have to handle.

Finally the house was vacant, with Wicked and Bish out in the barn looking after Jas, Big Dog's bladder empty, and Cherry happily nursing her puppies. If only Nana would find some other acre of pasture to mow, it would be perfect. The smoke and noise were awful.

Pouring myself a glass of wine, and cutting off a hunk of jalapeno pepper cheese, I sat down to take my first break of the day, and to nurse my headache. The cheese was tangy and soft and hot on my tongue, just the way I liked it, and the wine was crisp and dry with a sharp, sweet aroma. I unstrapped the gun from my chest and dropped it on the table, leaned back and stretched. My groan echoed through the empty house. And Big Dog whined.

"You just went," I yelled through the wall. Big Dog's bladder wasn't impressed. I took a sip of wine. It was a Riesling Jack had kept for clients and investors, but Jack wasn't here. I decided if investors couldn't drink colas and coffee, they didn't need to do business with me.

"No," I shouted at Big Dog again. I knew he could hear me. And I knew the Vet hadn't taken him out every few minutes. Big Dog was acting spoiled. "No, Big Dog! No!" Big Dog answered by putting his huge paws up on the sliding glass door and scratching like mad. He really did need to go out, it seemed.

Out front, Nana had decided to be a pest as well, interrupting her usual pattern of up and down mowing. She hadn't moved from the house-side of the pasture in minutes, ignoring the rest of the half-mile-long field. The noise and smoke roiling past the windows were thick and stinky.

Big Dog whined. The John Deere roared. My head pounded.

I sighed, closed my eyes, and placed my glass on the table, creating my own little crisis. I hit the edge of the plate of cheese, broke the fragile stem and spilled the over-priced wine. Glass and pale wine ran together across the wooden top. "Damn." Tears gathered at the corners of my eyes. Hot, salty tears like the ones I had cried when the muffin got stuck in my throat and cut off my air. And Robyn held out her arms.

I threw myself from the kitchen chair and wrenched open the sliding glass door. Big Dog was scratching at the yard door, whining. A tear fell and I wiped it, hot on my shaking hand. "Okay, okay. We'll go out." My throat spasmed, the words low and dull. I wiped my face again. "But we have to come to some kind of understanding, here, Big Dog. I am not going to be at your beck-and-call for the rest of the week. You—" Big Dog licked my face, cutting off my tirade. He was standing before me, up on his hind legs—his injured hind legs—his face on a level with mine. He grinned at me, liking the taste of my tears as he lathed my cheeks. My tears fled. I put a hand on Big Dog's head and scratched behind his ears. He whined with pleasure once, then the tone changed and he looked toward the yard, his whine a soft, desperate sound. I laughed.

"Okay. Okay, okay, okay." I squatted, helping the huge canine drop to all fours. He licked my face one last time, waggled his shaved tail and walked back to the yard door, the one Cherry could have gone through with no effort, but was inches too small for Big Dog. My fault. I could have, should have, had it cut to fit, and maybe Big Dog knew it. I walked to the door, opened it and followed Big Dog out into the yard. He looked at me once, lifted his injured hind leg close to his body in a protective position, and took off at a hobbling run.

"Big Dog, you get back here! Now! Come!" I demanded. Big Dog hobbled toward the front of the house, looking over his shoulder at me like we were playing some kind of stupid game. Even injured and moving on just three legs, Big Dog could cover some ground. I ran after him, into the tractor exhaust, shouting. My voice was too low to reach the disobedient dog over the roar of the John Deere. Rounding the corner of the house, I spotted Big Dog, waiting, impatient. He was either feeling frisky enough to play tag, or he was trying out a Lassie imitation. The one where Timmy has fallen down a well, and Lassie goes for help . . .

My irritation mutated into fear. *Nana*. Nana was in the front field. Mowing the front forty with an ornery tractor. One that hadn't circled the pasture in minutes. Long minutes.

I sprinted past Big Dog, rounded the front corner of the house, and ran into a blue fog of exhaust. Dropping my head lower, I ran for the noise, Big Dog at my side.

CHAPTER THIRTEEN

Just inside the fence, half visible through the small saplings lining the pasture and the haze of tractor smoke, was the John Deere. It was traveling in a circle covering perhaps half an acre, the bush-hog's fierce steel blade churning up dirt and debris from the well-mowed ground. No one was driving. Nana was nowhere in sight.

"Nana," I whispered, and stopped. There had been cases like this before in the county. Just last year, an old farmer, driving an even older tractor, had been clearing an overgrown field when the rusted metal tractor seat broke off. He had fallen behind the tractor, landing in front of the attached bush hog. Like being run over by a giant lawn mower, he had been pulled under and devoured by the heavy-duty blade. Marking the spot where he landed was a damp, bloody strip of land. A twisted belt buckle, part of a shoe, a few pieces of bone and a scrap of hair was all the Rescue Squad collected on their foot-by-foot search of the accident site.

Big Dog limped into the cloud of engine smoke. I could see only a vague outline until the John Deere moved downwind, completing its counter-clockwise arc. The injured dog was standing over a body. "Nana." I must have shouted. My throat closed up again, this time in panic. The body moved. The tractor headed back again.

I ran for the two forms in the path of the tractor. My heart pounded, an uneven rattle in my chest. I don't remember climbing the fence. But I was suddenly there, standing over them. No blood. No body parts missing. Nana was shouting, her words lost in the rumble of the big diesel. One arm stuck out at an obtuse angle from her body. She was trying to crawl from the path of the tractor, trying to point with her chin. Grabbing the hand holding her weight, and having no idea what internal injuries I might be affecting, I half dragged her from the pasture, back to the fence and the scant safety it afforded. A bush-hog blade can chew through small trees in seconds, reducing them to chips. If the tractor decided to head this way, the fence didn't stand a chance.

Carefully, I eased her to the ground. Nana was gasping, blue around the lips with what I hoped was emotional shock and pain, not blood loss or severe oxygen deprivation from an MI or a punctured lung or. . . . The tractor roared by.

I reached for my gun, intending to fire it to attract attention, but I had left it on the kitchen table. Great. Some hero. "Big Dog. Go get Jas. Go get Jas!" Big Dog turned yellow eyes from me to the tractor and back again before glancing in the direction of the barn. He didn't move.

Jack and I had expected to spend weeks teaching Big Dog the all our names, but it was an easy process; the smart mongrel had learned each name in only minutes. Jack would say, "Go to mama. Go to mama." And then I would call the dog over. We would repeat the process by saying "Go to Ash. Go to Ash," so he would know who was being searched for no matter which name was used. What a bizarre memory to be having in the midst of an emergency. I never had problems focusing on a patient in the ER. Of course, I'd never had my Nana to take care of there, either. "Go get Jas. Go!" Big Dog didn't want to leave Nana, but he was a working dog, not just a pet. He dropped his skinned tail low and headed for the barn in a rough three-legged run.

The tractor reached its farthest boundary and began its curving trek back. It was really moving. I watched it a moment, trying to determine if its circular motion was fixed or changing. The wind shifted, taking the fumes and dust away. I could hear Big Dog bark, back at the barn. *Good dog. Steak for supper tonight.* The tractor's path was a widening circle, the steering wheel apparently stuck at an angle, though I couldn't understand how that was possible.

Nana was still talking, her words rough and broken, as if she had screamed and screamed alone and in pain and no one had come. Her voice was nearly gone. Stooping down, I concentrated on my patient. She was lying on the ground, eyes wild, breaths far too rapid and shallow, her color ashen. A trickle of blood seeped from her upper lip. Her right arm stuck out from her body at an abnormal angle; a conspicuous hump was situated between her collarbone and shoulder tip, deforming the shoulder. An anterior dislocation. Painful, but easy to repair.

Standing, I put my foot in her armpit and pulled the arm steadily out and forward. Beneath my instep, the bone bumped back into place. Nana made a strangled sound as I folded her arm across her stomach and tucked her fingers into her waistband to stabilize it. She was suddenly breathing easier, and she made little mewling noises of pleasure.

I checked Nana's pupils, which were a little slow to react but were equal in size. I counted her pulse, which was irregular and fast, but slowing, even as I counted the beats against the second-hand of my watch. Her respirations were slowing too, growing deeper. Moving my fingers gingerly through her dirty, disheveled hair, I found a bump above her left temple. Not the best place for a blow to the head.

The tractor went by again, throwing dust and grass shavings into the air. Even with all the rain of the last few days, the bush-hog could make dust. Moments later, it headed back, its course wider than before. I wondered how I would get Nana to safety if it headed straight for us. I couldn't pick her up, and doubted I could drag her. I couldn't leave her to call for help. Maybe I would get lucky and the tractor would run out of gas.

Big Dog stuffed his wet nose into Nana's face and whuffed. "Mama!" Jas shouted. I stood and waved though the trees. Jas, Wicked and Bish were approaching at a run, Wicked in the lead, Jas in the middle, and Bish bringing up the rear, his gun drawn. Great. Maybe he could shoot the tractor, like a rampaging buffalo. I had a mental image of a tractor on its side, bleeding gasoline and various fluids into the pasture. Idiotic laughter gurgled from my throat, my Nana in pain at my feet and an out-of-control tractor bearing down on us.

Wicked vaulted over the fence and bent over Nana, started to lift her.

"No." I put a hand on his arm. "Don't move her. She may have internal injuries."

"But—"

"You think you can catch that tractor?" I asked. Wicked focused on the runaway piece of heavy machinery. "Remember how to shut it off?" Wicked was a city boy, but he was also a Chadwick, and every Chadwick had done two things: ridden a horse and been taken on a tractor ride. It was a childhood tradition. Wicked's eyes grew wide as he understood what I was asking.

Jas and Bish reached me, Jas dropping down beside Nana and repeating my nurse's routine. Bish looked for targets.

"I think so, but—"

"Be careful when you jump on, Wicked Owens, "I interrupted, and nudged him away with my hip. "The fall might hurt you but the shave afterwards will kill you." I laughed again.

"Yeah. Right," he muttered, watching the huge machine rumble past. Reluctantly, he jogged for the John Deere. Seconds later, a blessed silence descended over the farm.

"Jas, go get some blankets. She looks shocky. Call for an ambulance."

"I'm not going to no hospital," Nana said, her voice raspy and stubborn.

"'Fraid so, Nana. You got a bump the size of a small squash on your noggin," I countered, matching her Southern lingo. I slipped a hand beneath her work shirt and prodded her ribs.

"All I need is a little rest. Stop that. It tickles." She pushed at my fingers exploring her sternum. No bumps, lumps, or obvious malformations. I moved to her abdomen.

"Mom. Her ankle's swollen."

I felt down Nana's right leg, pressing and prodding, following the natural contours of bone and muscle and tendon, all the while watching Nana for signs of discomfort. There was no change in her expression, which was good, but the left leg was a different matter. Nana's knee was swollen and painful to the touch, so was her ankle.

She groaned and laid her head back as I unlaced her work boot. "Jasmine," she whispered. "You do what your mama said and call an ambulance. Then you go tell Moses I'm all right. You tell her not to worry. And while you're there, get me some clothes. Your mama's probably gonna cut these offa me and I have no intention of being driven 'round in my undies." Nana's voice grew stronger as she spoke, but her color was still ashen. I didn't like the way she looked, and wondered how long she had lain here, alone in the pasture, being chased by a tractor before Big Dog had come to her rescue. And how much longer she would have lain there had I not bothered to let my dog out.

"Pack her a bag," I mouthed at Jas. "She may be staying."

"The hell I will," Nana said. At least there was nothing wrong with her eyesight or hearing. I looked hard at Jas, pointedly insisting she do as I said, using one of those "mother looks" that communicated so much more than mere words. Pulling her cell phone Jas nodded and headed for nana's house at a run. Bish grunted and walked to the tractor. He was still looking for the enemy, but at least his gun was holstered.

"You make me stay in that hospital, I'll cut your inheritance in half, my girl."

"You already gave me my inheritance, Nana. Besides, a doctor will make that decision."

"Then you call Wallace and tell him to get himself down to that hospital. I want a Chadwick to take care of me, not some fool stranger. Pay me back for some of that education money I spent on him." Since I knew good and well that Wallace had long ago repaid Nana, with interest, for every penny she had spent sending him to medical school, it was an easy mental leap to intuit Nana's real intention. She thought she could boss Wallace around. What she didn't know was that unlike the young man she had helped raise, the grown up Dr. Wallace Chadwick was no pushover. She would have little recourse against any decision he might make regarding her care. Nana suddenly rolled to one side and vomited on the ground. Vomiting wasn't a good sign in a patient with a head wound.

Brown fingers slipped in beside mine and stabilized Nana's head as she retched. Wicked nudged me out of the way, much as I had him, pushing with his hip. I checked Nana's pupils again. Still equal, thank God. But slow.

"Ash. Someone tampered with the screws on the tractor seat," Wicked said, his voice soft and low. "Is this the first time anyone has used the tractor since the night the dogs died?"

"Yes." Nana spat into the grass, wiping her mouth with a sleeve. "First time."

"What did they do?" I asked.

"They removed the screws, all but two, and they were loose. The vibration of the engine shimmed them free. I can tell by the shiny metal around the bolt holes."

"Wasn't runnin' right either. Better get a mechanic to check it out," Nana said, as she rolled back and closed her eyes. "How long's this arm gonna hurt?"

"Several weeks," I answered. "Two weeks really bad." My thumb had been a peculiar exception to the rule about pain following a dislocation. I'd been fortunate. I didn't think Nana would be. "You shouldn't plan on doing any heavy work for six weeks. And even if that ankle isn't broken, you won't be walking around much."

Nana snorted. "I'm a tough old broad, my girl. I don't need an ankle to run a tractor. Or an arm either." Wicked pressed his lips together and shook his head. I shrugged. She was a Chadwick, the name practically synonymous with the word stubborn. I wasn't about to argue while she was lying in an over-mown field, covered with dirt, smeared with blood and in pain. In fact, maybe I'd let Jas argue with her. My daughter had better success manipulating Nana than I.

"I'll call the cops as soon as Jas gets back with her cell," I said. I looked toward the house. Jas should have been back with the blankets by now. My daughter had handled enough crises on this farm to know to grab the blankets and make her calls on the run. Jas knew shock could be— Slowly, I stood, a strange sensation running along my nerves. Jas should have been back. *Jas was in the house. Jas was alone.*

"Big Dog," I whispered. "Stay. Guard." I pointed at Nana, breaking into a run in the same instant. Through the fence, I was halfway to the house when I heard the words behind me.

"Ash?"

"Jasmine. . . ." And the sound of running footsteps as Wicked and

Bish echoed my flight. I slammed through the back door at a dead run and through the kitchen, my eyes adjusting to the dimmer light of the house. And I smelled it. The stale, rancid smell of my attacker.

Scuffing sounded over the pulse beating in my ears. An angry groan. A man's grunt came from my bedroom. The place where the blankets were stored in summer. *He had Jas.* I caught myself on the hallway door casing, seeing a dozen things at once. The broken window beside the office door. Golf clubs scattered across the hall floor. Jack's golf bag on its side. The vase Alan had given me, shattered into a thousand pieces. The gun I had left on the table.

I couldn't use the gun. I might hit Jas. Quickly, I bent and lifted a club, grabbing the grip two-handed. And dashed for my bedroom.

He was on top of her. Tearing at her clothes.

She was gasping, blood on her face.

I pulled the club back and swung, the whoosh of air the only warning. He started to turn, lifting his head. The club made a *thwacking* sound, whipping down. Wrapped around his neck.

My speed carried me past him. Giving me only a glimpse of his face. Brown eyes. Oily hair. I landed hard against the bedside table. The lamp fell and cracked, the shade flying.

He made a strangled sound, rolling from Jas. Clutching at his neck and the club wrapped around it. *He had a gun.*

"Ash! Down!"

I dropped, falling across Jas. Protecting her with my body. Gunshots exploded over me. Someone cursed. Something fell, a hollow, booming sound. Footsteps pounded. Wicked screamed. Breaking furniture and shouts sounded.

"Mama! Mama! Mama! Mama!" Jas panted.

"Jasmine. Jazzy Baby." I pulled her into my arms and scuttled backward like a crab into the closet. Into the dark. We huddled, our arms around one another. The fight receded. We were closed in a shell of refuge, protected by the dark. "Are you okay? Did he. . . ."

"No," she said through her sobs. "You . . . you g . . . got here in . . . in time."

I pulled back. Even in the dark of the closet, I could see blood on her face, a bruise on her cheek. The wild look in her eyes. "He hit you," I stated.

"Yeah," she said. "I think he broke my nose. I haven't had a broken nose since I was six."

"Son of a bitch," I whispered, the words fierce. Jas tightened her grip on my arm.

"Ash?" Bish's voice. "Mrs. D.? He's gone. He got away. And

Wicked's been shot."

Icy shock rushed through me. I didn't want to leave Jas. . . . I pulled her to me in one final hug. "Are you sure you're alright?"

"Go help Wicked." Her voice was shaking, but calmer, as if she had absorbed some strength from me, like the mother's milk I once fed her. "Go."

I crawled from the closet. Bish was leaning over Wicked in the hallway just outside my door. I shoved him away. "Call 911. Bring me my cell and my gun off the kitchen table. And then go stay with Nana. Take the blankets."

"But—"

"No buts, damn it. *Move.*"

"Yes, Ma'am."

I ripped the brace from my hand, turned on the overhead light and assessed Wicked. He was conscious, his eyes looking up at me, pupils equal and reactive. He was breathing fine. Blood stained his shirt. Gripping it, I ripped the buttons off, exposing his chest. Pain raced up the length of my damaged thumb. The man with the gun would have raped Jas and shot us both. I knew that. Bish and Wicked had saved our lives. Tears welled, blinked viscously away. I probed his chest, searching for entrance and exit wounds.

Jas crawled from the closet, wiping blood and snot from her face. She was shaking, needing something to do, some way to channel her fear. Bish placed the phone and the 9mm on the floor beside me. "Jas. Take the gun," I said. White-faced in the unforgiving light, Jas took the gun and removed it from the ill-fitting holster. Checked the safety and the clip. Her hands steadied as she worked. Bish took the blankets and ran for the pasture.

I found an entrance wound on Wicked's chest, just inside and below his left nipple. Directly over his heart. He met my eyes, his own steady and wide. "Mama Moses kick my sorry ass if I die and leave you to deal with this shit," he said, sounding like the kid from the hood he had been so long ago.

"Well, don't die then," I said, giving a shaky laugh.

"Good idea."

I knew in that moment that I had used up my quota of luck escaping danger. My attacker had come for the file I didn't have, evidence I couldn't identify. He had nearly raped my daughter. Now it was kill or be killed.

Ninety minutes from the time I first discovered Nana lying in a field with a tractor headed her way, Nana and Wicked were on their way to Wallace's emergency room, me crouching over Wicked all the way,

Jas following in Bish's car. As soon as we wheeled them through the doors to the ER, they became Wallace's problem. *I* had to deal with the police. Again. And this time, Sheriff C.C. Gaskin came, wanting to interview all of us and then see the crime scene.

Jas was more help than I. She had seen the man at close range, while I could only tell the officers that the attacker had brown eyes and needed to wash his hair and brush his teeth. When the sheriff had finished with us, Macon took him away and filled him in on the problems at DavInc. Or at least the problems he thought he should share. Sheriff Gaskin wasn't a happy man when the interview was over; none of us were. There were too many things we hadn't told the police about Jack's business, too many things that didn't add up in the sheriff's eyes, holes in our stories. I couldn't worry about that at the moment, however. Later. Maybe later.

The waiting room filled up with Chadwicks over the next hour—most of the Dawkins County crowd coming to show support. Even a few from Ford County showed up to keep watch until the medical verdicts were delivered. Between Aunt Mosetta's branch and Nana's branch, there were over a hundred Chadwicks within easy driving distance.

Toward dark, I informed them that Jas had a broken nose with no deformity, and Wicked had a rib cracked in two places, but no internal damage. The bullet had entered at a sharp angle, bounced off his ribcage, circled the outside of his chest, under his skin, and stopped near his spine. Wallace had popped the .32 round out with a blade and tweezers, ordered antibiotics and dressings and pronounced him well enough to go home. Nana had a concussion, a broken ankle, and a badly wrenched knee. No one would be dying tonight. Still, the Chadwick kin waited around, gossiping and catching up on family business and the latest family news. They had shown up for a wake and acted almost disappointed when there wasn't one.

Unfortunately, someone had also called my mother. Josephine Hamilton Caldwell blew in just before dark, weeping dry tears. After all, why muss a perfectly good makeup job? Her emotions were seemingly shattered, and yet not a single perfectly coiffed hair was out of place. Careful to wrinkle neither her linen suit nor the corners of her surgically altered eyes, she fell prostrate into the bosom of her family. On that note, Jas, Wicked, Bish and I left. We had horses to feed, a bed to make up for Wicked, and supper to prepare. My daughter needed the solace of her horses and the safety of family. Wallace, who was getting off at dark, volunteered to take care of getting Nana home as soon as her soft cast was ready. She'd be treated by an orthopedic doc for the break later; the soft cast was temporary support.

I just hoped the sheriff's deputies would be through gathering evidence and taking fingerprints at my home. We all needed some peace. They were. Back home, Bish nailed a board over the broken window, checked and armed the security system, and took care of the cops and the horses. He didn't really want to leave Jasmine, preferring to hover over her and assuage his guilt for allowing her to be attacked. But he didn't argue either, when Jas and I gave him orders. For a city boy, he was really rather useful, even following Duke's orders at the barn.

By ten P.M., I had my injured crew bedded down, Jas in my bed so she wouldn't be alone tonight, Wicked and Bish in two adjoining guest rooms. Making sure I was armed, I made the quarter mile drive to Nana's to check on her. There, I discovered a surprise. Several actually. The long driveway was choked with cars and trucks and Chadwicks, and no one looked ready to leave. Some of the prospective mourners had dropped by the farmhouse after leaving the hospital. If they couldn't have a wake, then they'd have a party. One visitor had even moved in.

I hadn't seen Joanetta Chadwick, Wallace's mother, in years, but she was firmly ensconced in her old bedroom under the eaves, determined to nurse Nana back to health. Whether Nana wanted her to or not. Wallace had chosen the better part of valor and high-tailed it back to his home and the gentle embrace of Pearl, leaving his mother to handle things at the family farmhouse. It was one argument I was not mediating. Instead, I turned for home, but stopped in the side yard when I spotted Duke, Disa, and perhaps a dozen preteen kin, playing children's games. With Alan Mathison.

"You put your right foot in. You take your right foot out," they all sang, some in tune, most not, but with Alan's pleasing baritone leading the way. "You put your right foot in and you shake it all about . . ."

It looked like he'd shaken most body parts several times in the last hour, as he was sweaty, breathless, and exhausted. "You put your right hand in. You take your right hand out. You put your right hand in and you shake it all about. You do the Hokey Pokey and you turn yourself around. That's what it's all about."

Suddenly, I joined in. "You put your whole self in. You take your whole self out . . ." The children all turned toward the back of the line and giggled. I joined the row of children and shook my hiney on the proper line, braving the dark of the outdoors and the touch of some really filthy little hands. And feeling a moment of happiness as I sang. I needed the release. I needed the laughter. *Jas . . . alive. With only a broken nose.*

"You put your whole self in and you shake it all about . . ." Alan Mathison's eyes met mine in the dark, his lips turned up in laughter. Even in the night, I could see the devilment in his eyes. And I forgot the simple lyrics. "Okay. Enough," I shouted, clapping my hands. "Everybody. Hide and seek. Tomeka Chadwick, you're "*It*". Hide your eyes and count to ten. Everybody else, hide. *Go!*" Alan's charges scattered, squealing with laughter. Their squeals were more melodic than their singing had been.

He took my hand, pulling me into the darkness of Nana's overgrown sasanqua bush. Untrimmed for thirty years, it towered over the eaves of the house and bloomed all winter long, a profusion of huge pink blooms. It was also a great place to hide for the game. Two little Chadwicks crouched beneath us, giggles muffled behind dirty hands.

"Alan," I said when I caught my breath, "what—

"I brought by that spec letter for the Taylor development two hours ago," he interrupted, his voice breathless. "You weren't home, so I followed all the cars here. I've eaten two huge pieces of cake, six chicken wings, a half dozen cookies, a delicious piece of chess pie, and been introduced to more Chadwicks and Chadwick kin than I ever hoped to meet. I've also been looked over from head to toe by your Nana for the second time, and been told that I would do, whatever that means. I was afraid to ask. Is it always this way around here?" His lips were close to my temple, laughing into my hair, his voice soft,so Tomeka wouldn't find us in the waxy green leaves. A child shifted beneath me, hitting the back of my knee, throwing me forward. Alan caught me around the waist, steadying me. So quick, that simple touch. So unexpected.

I gasped softly. "Shhhhh. We don't want to be *It*," Alan whispered.

I nodded, concentrating on his words rather than the warmth of his hand still on my waist. "The spec letter?"

"Yeah. Jerel wasn't too pleased that I prepared one, but I reminded him I was supposed to have total discretion in South Carolina, and that if I fell flat on my face, it was my problem and my job, and he could fire me if I screwed up and lost him money."

"And?"

"And he told me it would be his blankety-blankety-blankety pleasure to can me if I did."

I chuckled.

"Shhhhh."

"Sorry."

"And I wanted to thank you for sending Flo Blankenship to me. She's far too qualified for the job I offered her today, but if this division takes off, she'll be the best executive assistant I could hope for. She starts in the morning."

"You're welcome," I said.

"She's not a spy, is she?"

"No," I chuckled again. This time a junior Chadwick shushed me from below.

"Family? A distant Chadwick, maybe?"

"You've been here a while. You see her around?"

"No."

"Then she's not a Chadwick. I think every Chadwick for fifty miles made the trip to see if Nana was about to die."

"Ahhhh," Alan said.

Someone spit a long dark stream of fluid off the farmhouse porch into the sasanqua. We all moved back a few paces, into the foliage, out of range of the tobacco chewers on the porch. A long chaw after dinner was a quaint custom that was yet to be bred out of some branches of the Chadwick clan, and I didn't suppose that anyone wanted to reform tonight.

"In the interests of fair play, I'll be sending the county's best earth movers, graders, and surveyors your way," I said softly, trying not to think about the hand still on my waist, or the warmth at my back that was Alan Mathison.

"No need. I'll be taking bids for subs."

"Lowest bid for graders will land you with Turnipseed and Son."

"You're joking," Alan said.

"Nope. Turnipseed is a common and respected name in these parts, mister," I whispered with mock censure. "Unfortunately, these particular Turnipseeds spend so much time in a bottle, they never finish a job. You'll find it cheaper, smarter, and more time conservative to go with somebody else."

"I'll keep that in mind." Alan's hands tightened on my waist in warning. Tomeka was doing a duck-walk past the sasanqua, squatted down, resting on her ankles as she waddled past. Her head was turned away, looking beneath the porch.

"Gotcha! Gotcha!" she shouted. Four or five screaming little Chadwicks of every skin color burst into the light falling from the porch, all running every which way like chickens.

"Got all of you. Help me find the others. My mama's yellin' for me," she shouted.

From inside the house, I could hear several mothers calling for children. Small bodies ran for the house, the porch, and their respective families, including the two from beneath my feet. As they emerged, the filth of an evening's play clearly visible, I could hear the outraged exclamations of a mother or two. It was dirty on a farm. Kids were supposed to get grubby and stinky. I was sure it was a rule, written down somewhere.

The game over, Alan and I emerged from the shadows. He dropped his hand from my waist to rest both of his on his cane. I hoped he couldn't see my blush in the diffuse porch light. "I must admit, Mrs. D, that was the most unusual business meeting I've ever attended." He handed an envelope to me. "I hope to hear from you in a day or two."

"Macon needs a day to look this over, and then we'll call the judge and find out what we have to do to drop the restraining order. Jack signed the original, but since he's . . ." *What? How do I say it?* I swallowed with difficulty. ". . . not with us now, I assume the judge will let me sign the release, or whatever." I looked away, my flush fading at the thought of Jack. It wasn't right, my talking to this man. But then, it wasn't right what Jack did with Robyn, either, was it? I looked at Alan. There was a hint of understanding in his face that caught at my heart. A flash of tears drenched my eyes, and when I spoke, my tone was harsher than I intended. "I'll give your new secretary a call as soon as I know something. Now, if you'll excuse me, I have to get my Nana to bed."

Alan inclined his head, smiled that exquisite, sensitive smile of his and stepped away. I had the feeling I had been gauche, perhaps even rude, yet I didn't know how else I might have responded to his . . . *what?* Alan Mathison was a former patient, a new businessman in town, a competitor. He had been friendly, kind. And, like me, he was alone in the world, trying to build a new life. Alan was not an investor in Davenport Hills. He had, in fact, worked at Taylor, Inc. for only six years. The list of investors for the project had been drawn up years prior to Alan's employment. Of all the people in my new life, he was the safest, while not exactly an ally. Great. I had insulted a new friend by my tone, if not my words. I'd have to encourage Macon to speed up the process of withdrawing the restraining order. A little cooperation from DavInc would go a long way toward rebuilding any bridges I just singed. I watched him walk away, moving to his car in the dark, his limp pronounced.

Climbing the front steps, I went to work cleaning out Nana's and Aunt Mosetta's visitors. By eleven, I had Nana's foot and knee iced down, a Darvocet in her system, the dishes washed and put away, and the house straight. Exhausted, I left Jonetta, Aunt Mosetta and Nana arguing about sleeping arrangements and went home. Nana didn't want to be babied or spoiled, and she certainly didn't want them sleeping in her room. Both Jonetta and Aunt Mosetta wanted to be close in case she needed anything. I figured they could bicker about it alone as well as they could with me in attendance. I needed a break. It had been a long, wearing day.

Back home, Big Dog needed attention, both medical, and the loving kind that included a steak and lots of scratching. He had gotten dirt and dust in the puckered, healing incision running the length of his side; it looked inflamed. I gave him his overdue antibiotic, cleaned his wound with warm water and antibacterial soap, then fed him a cold sirloin steak I had picked up at BiLo. While he ate, I scratched his ears and belly and back, all the while telling him he was a sweet-smoochums-of-a-hero-dog. He ate up the attention like the protein, licking me almost as thoroughly as he did his bowl. Bish had tried to feed him, but Big Dog's new hatred of men had not abated in the least following the afternoon's excitement. He didn't like the bodyguard.

Finally, close to midnight, I found time to open my email and snail mail. Sitting curled up in the center of my bed, I was surrounded by soft rose satins and beige silks and locally woven brocades, all in muted patterns and stripes and flame stitched designs. Jasmine snored gently beside me. The broken lamp had been replaced. The bloodstains removed with the rugs or washed up. *Had Macon cleaned up? Or one of the celebrating Chadwicks?* All evidence of the attack on Jas had vanished. All but the swelling of her nose, and the uneasy dreams which played beneath her eyelids. I watched her for long minutes.

In my email, there was a note from Monica, telling me she was thinking about me, which I found hard to believe. Most of the rest was spam. In the snail mail, there was a card from one of my cousins in California. It was a delayed condolence, a floral Hallmark note with a scripture verse on the inside. I put the card on top of the bills, tossed the ads into the trash and opened the large manila envelope sealed with two-inch-wide shipping tape. There was no postmark, and I wondered how it got through the mail. From inside I pulled an 8x10 full color photo. It took a moment for me to process the pictures, to make sense of the lines and forms and colors.

It was Hokey and Herman.

Blood ran in rivulets reflecting back the flash, glistening. A dark red stain. The dogs were freshly dead. Or perhaps still suffering. I dropped the photograph as if it burned me. Inside, I felt no heat at all. I was cold. So very cold. My fingers, poised above the photo were white and pasty. I blinked. Took a breath, shaky and stiff, feeling the pain in my ribs for the first time in hours.

There was a paper clip at the top, the metal curl touching Hokey's ear. Forcing myself to touch the vile thing, I flipped it over. On the back was a typed note.

Did I get your attention?
We want the EVIDENCE, Ashlee, dear.
IT'S TIME. You've been
A VERY BAD GIRL.

Shivering, I pulled the blankets up to my neck, dislodging the pile of bills and advertisements and the up-ended photo. They all slid to the floor in an untidy pile, the picture on top in all its gory glory. Ugly. Ugly thing. Fury whipped through me and vanished.

The lamplight was a soft pool on the ceiling. The clock ticked softly in the hall. The delicate tint on the walls wavered and swirled as tears filled my eyes. I was alone with all this. I was really, really alone.

CHAPTER FOURTEEN

The phone rang before six, when only a faint light tinted the sky gray. My face was turned into the pillow, my breath warm on the satin case, my dreams sharp shards drifting across my memory, slicing, cutting. On the first ring, I opened my eyes, and I could have sworn my breath stopped. It had to be the curser. It had to be Bill McKelvey. It was too early for anyone else.

Beside me, Jasmine snored softly, tangled in the sheets. On the second ring I threw off the comforter, springing up like a much younger woman. The shock of my landing traveled up from my heels to my neck, a quick, stabbing pain in my strained ankle. I bared my teeth in a grimace. I must have looked like an aging lion, mane tangled and sleep-tossed, running down the hallway.

I didn't want Jas to hear the voice. I didn't want her to hear the threats. I wanted to protect my daughter from this man and the filth he spewed. Fury sparked in me like fire, a blaze of rage. Damn him! *Damn* this man who thrust himself at me through the dark of sleep! A low sound like a snarl puffed from my throat with each breath, with each step. Part rage. Part pain.

I picked up the receiver before the fourth ring. A fierce calm descended upon me then. Frigid. Cold as the arctic steeps. As cold and impenetrable as a glacier. "This is Ashlee Davenport," I said, my voice thick with hostility and sleep.

"I want to talk to Jack."

It was him. The man who cursed, the foul-mouthed man who threatened and swore. It wasn't the man who spoke softly and pricked with a knife and murdered my dogs. It wasn't the cool, calculating threat of the Soiled Utility Room, or the violence of the attack upon Jasmine. It wasn't the pure evil of the photograph of Hokey and Herman delivered in a plain envelope. But it was a threat I could put my hands on. Reply to. Deal with. And *damn* him for this harassment. "Jack. Is. Dead," I said distinctly, icy restraint containing my fury. "He has been dead for weeks."

The pause on the other end was sharp, disbelieving. A short hiss of shock. After a long silence, he said, "Dead?" And there was the resonance of despair in the simple word, the sound of an intimate and personal ruin.

"Yes. Dead," I said, hearing the fury in my voice. "And I know who you are, William McKelvey. I know about the deal between you and my husband, and the equal value exchange that went wrong. I know about the toxic waste landfill you got stuck with, and the financial problems you are having. I know all this," I ground out, my hand clenched on the receiver. Jack. It was all because of Jack. "My lawyers are looking for a solution for you. But until then, you will *not* call this number again. Do you understand?"

"Dead?" he whispered. And then McKelvey's voice changed. "No! *No!* He's not dead! He's . . . Damn it! You put him on the phone! Put him on!" McKelvey screamed. "Put the son of a bitch on!" I held the phone from my ear. It was a howl, a wounded wolf, berserk with pain and anger and something . . . not quite sane. The hairs lifted along the length of my neck.

"He's gonna pay, do you hear me? He's gonna pay. He can't do this to me. I want—"

Softly, gently, I hung up the phone. The click stopped the awful screech mid-word. I stood, still and cold, shivering in the early morning cold and the sudden silence of the office.

McKelvey would not be an easy man to deal with. The phone rang, the shrill tone making me jump. Reaching over, I turned down the volume on the machine. I wouldn't hear Jack's voice answer. I wouldn't hear McKelvey's deranged threats. Padding softly, I returned to my room.

With McKelvey's threats recorded on the answering machine, and with all that had happened to me in the last few days, Macon was able to get Judge Yarborough to issue a fifteen-day restraining order against the man. The order could be renewed at the end of fifteen days, and again every fifteen days after that, until the situation was cleared up or until McKelvey went over the edge. Not that a restraining order was much protection. I knew exactly how safe a woman was from the determined pursuit of a dangerous man. I had tended the damaged and injured for years, those battered women who had looked to the law for defense. Restraining orders were simply a paper hurdle, easily overcome.

I made certain Bish stayed with Jas at all times. When she went to shower, he waited outside the bathroom. When she slept, he took the room across the hall. The enforced intimacy and the relationship blooming between them was a problem I would have to deal with later. For now, I depended on Bish's earlier claim. "I never screw clients." It wasn't much.

But my Jazzy Baby was strong and resilient; she bounced back quickly, laughing easily, her old self. The nightmares were mine. And the fear. What if I hadn't gotten there in time? I wore my 9mm to the barn, to the office, to Davenport Hills, to the bathroom, to everywhere, awaiting an attack for which I couldn't prepare. Two days passed. Then another. Late in the day, after dealing with the ordinary crises of Jack's work-a-day world, I was taking a quiet break over a glass of wine and a slice of orange. I had missed my glass of wine the day of McKelvey's attack, and there hadn't been time since. I wanted to savor it.

Jas and Bish were down at the barn, entertaining a prospective client at the training ring, putting Annie Oakley's Hope—a flashy four year old—through her paces. Annie Oakley had taken first place in two shows as a three year old, drawing both a hackney cart and a traditional Friesian gig. And though she had taken time off from competition to heal from an injury to a front hoof, she was now in good health and fine form. Without her corrective shoes, the mare was beautifully balanced, versatile, and quite the show off.

Everyone from the office was gone. I was alone in the yard with Big Dog, my glass of wine in one hand, the orange in the other, and a trickle of juice beading on my chin. Big Dog was marking the entire yard, lifting his bad leg, pausing for moment, and then moving on to another spot he had neglected for the duration of his convalescence. Doggie version of reestablishing his territory. He had been out only twice all day, and he had saved up for the extended evening rest time, marking the tires on the Jeep and the Volvo and Jas' little truck and Wicked's Crown Vic and Bish's snazzy Corvette. He also marked the monkey grass, azaleas, and the patch of freshly planted mums from Jack's funeral. It was a sign of my ambivalent grief that I didn't chase Big Dog to a more appropriate spot. I just sipped my wine and watched him mark the yard.

Standing in the driveway, I heard the car engine. It was moving steadily down the drive as I turned to watch, a big, seventies model, pearl colored Cadillac with bright chrome wheels sparkling in the evening sun. I knew the car. I knew the driver. It was Reverend Perry, coming to offer his condolences and pay his respects. He had been the pastor of First Baptist Church for over twenty-five years until he retired three years ago. He had baptized me, married me to Jack, baptized my daughter, and watched over my spiritual health ever since I could remember. He had been the spiritual heart and soul of DorCity for a quarter of a century, and he would have buried my husband, had he been in town when Jack died. Though retired, Reverend Perry had been my first choice for the eulogy and the funeral sermon, the one person outside of family I had tried to reach the night Jack died. But the good reverend had been in Mexico, building a church and hospital, leading a three month mission trip. Reverend Perry hadn't been available. And now, here he was, driving down my drive, prepared to console the grieving widow and pray with her and share in her sorrow. It wasn't a role I could play anymore. I wasn't grieving. I wasn't in sorrow. I no longer knew what I was.

"Big Dog," I called. He looked from the approaching car to me and back again, wagging his tail in recognition. He knew Reverend Perry and liked the older man; his recent hatred of men would not be extended to the missionary pastor. But then, everyone liked Reverend Perry.

"Big Dog! Come!" I commanded. He sighed, the pink, scarred flesh on his side moving despondently. "Come!"

He came, loping erratically on three legs, pausing to nuzzle my hand before he climbed the steps to the screened porch and through the doggie door Bish had enlarged in the last two days. Greeting Cherry's puppies, Big Dog sniffed each, exhaled happily and settled in beside the terrier mom. They made an unlikely looking family. Cherry, all of ten pounds with milk-filled teats, lay on her side. Big Dog, neutered, shaved, weighing in at over one hundred twenty-five pounds, curled up beside her. Four fast-growing puppies climbed over mother and adoptive father with abandon.

Reverend Perry's tires crunched on the gravel. I put my wine glass and well gnawed rind of orange on the step and walked to the preacher's car. He looked good, especially for a man in his seventies, skin tanned by a Mexican sun, muscles hardened by physical labor. His blue eyes flashed behind the window as he opened the car door. Gentle eyes. And even that contributed to my feeling of ambivalence, that Reverend Perry should be here, so full of love and gentleness.

He was dressed in jeans, a work shirt, and running shoes, the soles silent on the gravel drive. Odd dress for a pastor out on his ministerial rounds, yet the required dress code for a retired missionary carpenter. "Ashlee." Gentle voice to go with the gentle eyes and gentle smile.

Tears pricked at my eyes. Seeing them, he folded me against his chest, a fatherly gesture, full of compassion. "I got in the day before yesterday," he said. "I'm so sorry I wasn't here, Ashlee. I would have seen you through this. I would have been here for you."

I don't know why, but I broke down. Or, I do know why, but I was surprised at the rush of misery I unleashed on his chest. Violent, intense tears, a terrible anguish. Twisting my fists into the fabric of his shirt, I cried in real grief for the first time in days. Big, despairing tears mourning my lost dreams, my empty life, and the innocent joy I had once known. Tears that mourned Jack. The Jack I had known and loved and lost so totally. Reverend Perry murmured soothing words, stroking my hair, patting my back, rocking me like a father with a wailing child. "It's all right, Ashlee. It's going to be fine. You just cry it all out and we'll pray together. The Lord will take all your heartache and sorrow upon Him." Words I half heard as he soothed me and I sobbed.

Long, long minutes later, he handed me a tissue and helped me wipe my eyes, patting my cheeks and chin with slow, easy pats. Reverend Perry was like that, slow and easy and steady and thorough. Finally I smiled up at him and managed a shaky laugh. "Even my own father didn't let me cry like that." I blew my nose and wadded up the tissue.

"Yes. I've met your father, remember. At your baptism, and again at your wedding." Reverend Perry's eyes twinkled blue as an afternoon sky, though behind me, the sun was setting, tinting the heavens plum, pink, and gray. "A bit . . . cowed as I recall."

I nodded. "My mother . . . Well, you know."

"Yes. I know your mother well." He handed me a second tissue. I blew my nose again. "She never recovered from the betrayal of Pap Hamilton."

I looked up, surprised, and then blew my nose one last time, hard. "What do you mean?"

"I taught religion to your mother in high school, watched her mature. A beautiful girl, she was. Her father's passing was a hard time for her. There was scarcely an outward change in her at all. But the day Wallace moved in and the talk about Pap Hamilton started, she began to change. She grew hard and flighty and cold. Before that, your mother was a warm, gentle young woman."

It wasn't a side of my mother I had ever seen. And I didn't know where this talk of my mother was coming from when I had assumed the reverend was here to comfort me about Jack. I nodded, confused.

"Your mother never forgave her father, Ashlee. She never forgave him for the pain of his deceit and deception. And it's that unforgiving spirit that made her so hard and unyielding." Reverend Perry gently squeezed my fingers. "Ashlee. Robyn came to see me."

I don't know what my face showed other than clear and complete shock. The reverend nodded, his eyes on mine. It was impossible to look away from Reverend Perry's blue eyes. Always had been. He patted my upper arm in a way I usually hate, and smiled again. I couldn't even respond. I just stared at him. "She told me what you said. What you had discovered."

How dare she! The thought washed through me like a tidal wave, obliterating everything before it. I took a deep breath, as painful as the words he had spoken. How *dare* she!

Reverend Perry went on, reading my emotions, seeing my soul as clearly as if I had no skin stretched over it. As if I were a cancer he diagnosed and excised, digging around inside. I pulled my hand away. "She came to me some years ago, when she and Jack were ending their affair. She came because she couldn't deal with the guilt and the pain and the lies that stood between you two. She knew she had done you a great wrong." His words rocked me.

Anger roared through me. I stepped back, a single pace from the good pastor, my eyes on his face. "You knew," I whispered, my words faint and breathless. "You knew and didn't— You and who else?" The words ripped from me, rough, fierce, coarse as a rusted rasp. "Who else knew and didn't tell me?"

Reverend Perry's blue eyes bored into me, steady and firm. He patted my arm, and I jerked away, waiting for the answer to my question. Waiting for my world to totter and lurch once again. "Only me, Ashlee. So far as I know, I was the only one they ever told. And so far as I know, no one else ever guessed."

I swallowed down the taste of bile, burning acid. "And you decided not to tell me. You decided to keep it a secret all hidden away and buried like the *filthy* thing it really was." The words heaved in my chest. I could hear the sound of my breath, rough and harsh, like something external to me, foreign and malignant.

Reverend Perry kept his eyes on me. Too blue. Too piercing. "And if I had told you about the affair, when it was over and done, what then? Would you have left Jack? Destroyed your family? Agonized over the dishonor they did you as you tried to rebuild your life alone? Would you have tried to work it out? Or suffered with it for all the years you had left together?"

I tore my eyes away from the reverend. Away from the truth in his blue gaze. He had always been good at making me see truth even when I didn't want to. Now, of all times in my life, I didn't want to hear his version of *truth*. I stared out over the farm where I had lived my life with Jack.

In the distance, an early owl hunted, gliding through the trees, silent, wings outspread. It was a big owl, gray in the falling light. By day it might have been strawberry blond or striped gray. Landing, it weighted a branch, folded its wide wings, and perched, watching the pasture and woodlands below. Patient. Waiting. Just like Reverend Perry waited for my answer.

Swallowing again, I gripped my upper arms as if I was cold, holding myself together by force of will. Seconds ticked by as I struggled with my fury. Finally, my anger began to ease, and it was my hurt, my wounded spirit, that surfaced. I remembered the disbelief, the intense pain I felt when I saw the photographs of Jack and Robyn. Searing anguish; numbness that followed. I remembered the peculiar thought that the photographs had burned out my grief like a surgical cautery. Finally, my eyes still on the owl, I said, "I've thought about that. Thought about what I would have done had I been told back then. And I might have left Jack for a while. And I know I would have suffered." Tears began to form again, and my owl wavered though he didn't move.

"But I also know I would have worked through it. I would have been able to forgive him, and I would have gone on with my marriage. And yes it would have been hard. But at least it would have been a living, breathing person I had to forgive, and not just a memory. At least Jack would have been here to work through it with me. Here for me to yell at and even hit if I wanted to. Here to shout back. To explain. To say he still loved me. Instead, I'm alone. And I was alone when I found the pictures of Jack and Robyn in his desk drawer, right there, easy at hand, where he could pull them out and stare at them and fantasize over them." Tears pooled in my eyes, a glimmering wetness that obscured the world. I took a deep breath. "Dozens of well-fingered, well-worn photographs of my husband and my best friend having sex."

I looked at Reverend Perry. It was clear he hadn't known about the photographs.

"I'm alone with that," I said, my throat tight. "Alone with my anger and hurt, my absolute knowledge that my husband never put Robyn away. That she was always there in his mind and his heart and that I was never enough for him. So don't come here ready to help me forgive an old sin, Reverend Perry, because the sin isn't old and dead. Not to Jack. And not to me.

"It's a fresh sin I'm dealing with. A fresh betrayal that Jack kept close to his heart, hidden and precious, right there in his desk drawer so that if anything ever happened to him, I would have no choice but to find out all about it." I wiped my eyes, finally, with the back of my hand. Cocking my head, my breath strident, I looked away from the compassion and the tenderness in my old mentor's eyes. He had come to offer a shoulder to cry on, words of wisdom. Yet, the sin and the situation weren't exactly what he had prepared for. I wasn't exactly what he had prepared for. Had I changed so much? My tears dried, leaving my eyes hot and burning, fiery as the setting sun that silhouetted my owl.

"Jack never left *anything* to chance. Not ever. He *left* those pictures, *kept* those pictures, exactly where he wanted them. Exactly so that I would find them. A punishment to me because I had kept him from his true love. Or perhaps it was a punishment to us both. Either way, he left them there on *purpose*. I've had to accept that, and use the knowledge to make me *strong*."

"Strong or hard?" Reverend Perry countered gently, reminding me of my mother in his story. I blinked into the trees and found my owl again. He was eating, now, a mouse held in his claws, his beak dipping and tearing. Remarkably like what the good reverend was doing to my soul. I shrugged, my eyes dry, my heart as hard as Reverend Perry had suggested. "Will you let me pray with you, Ashlee?"

"You can always pray for me Preacher." Not catching the distinction, or choosing not to, Reverend Perry took my hands. I kept my eyes on the eating owl. I had never watched an owl dine. The predator bird was delicate and fastidious as it shredded the still wriggling animal.

"Father, we come to You, flawed and wounded . . ."

I wondered what it was eating. I originally thought mouse, but it was too large.

". . . grieving and angry. We stand together, two in Your Name as the scriptures say . . ."

Perhaps it was a young rabbit. Or an opossum that fell from its mother's back.

". . . asking intercession for Ashlee, who has withdrawn from You."

Not really, Preacher. Not withdrawn from God. Just withdrawn from Jack. I wanted to say it. I wanted to interrupt. But I didn't.

"She is empty inside and alone. Bleeding, the prey of angry thoughts . . ."

Perhaps it was a young squirrel. They sometimes fell from their nests and died from the elements or became dinner for some predator. It was bleeding, dead now, which was what Reverend Perry was saying about me, inside. Interesting comparison. Me and the owl's supper.

"Give her peace, Father, the peace that passes human understanding. Your peace . . ."

The owl lifted off its perch, the tree shaking with the loss of its weight. The big bird dropped several feet, spread its wings and beat the air. A scrap of dinner dangled from its beak.

". . . help her find the way to grieve, and give her insight into the nature of her love for Jack. A love that was itself pure, though the recipient of that love may not have been . . ."

The owl angled its flight through the trees, its path so smooth it appeared to pass through the branches rather than around them.

". . . in the Name of the Father and the Son and the Holy Ghost, Amen."

"Amen," I said. And wondered what he had prayed.

He patted my hand and walked to his car. He opened his door and put a foot inside. Then he looked up at me. "You can come to me any-time Ashlee. Whenever you are ready to talk. Even if it's the middle of the night, you can call. I'll be here. And I'll come." I nodded stiffly. The car started, the door closed, and the car pulled down the drive. I went back to my wine, turning my back on the drive, picking up the water-beaded glass. Putting it to my lips. Sipping, I sat down on the step, my back to the receding car, my shoulder against the corner board of the porch wall.

The sun was setting fast now, a great orange ball settling into a wide, plum-colored sea of low lying clouds. Dropping down over the rim of the world, and plunging toward night. It was stunning. Reverend Perry was gone. So was the owl. The air was still and cool, the heat melting from the world. I was too warm to shiver.

Voices echoed from the barn: Bish and Wicked's deep notes, Jas' lilting laughter. A car roared up the drive, moving fast. Back tires fish-tailed on the loose gravel. The preacher's car? It sounded similar, though less patient, engine racing. Something he forgot to tell me? Some nugget of wisdom he thought might pull me back into the fold? Make me forgive the unforgivable? I looked through the trees as a pickup roared up the drive, one of Jasmine's friends, I thought, speeding like a dirt-track racer, grinding ruts in the gravel. Jack had complained about them, lecturing the boys who came to call. Now I would have to do the honors. But tonight . . . I was just too tired. I drained my glass, the wine tart on my almost empty stomach. The truck stopped. The door opened, its engine still running. I stood and put down my glass. I didn't really want to be difficult. I didn't want to make a scene. There had been too many of those.

Big Dog growled at a running figure. A man, not a boy. I could hear the slamming pace of his hard soled shoes crunching gravel.

Before I could react, he was on me. Picked me up by my arm. My body left the ground. Space and time went thick and viscous, like clotting blood. My feet flew. I watched them, as if they were something apart from me. Out of my control. They kicked the porch screen, im-pacting with twanging snaps that loosed it from the supports. I was irrationally distressed at the damaged screen, more concerned about it than afraid for myself. And then my complacency shattered. I slammed against the porch screening. In almost slow motion, I bounced off, seeing the sky and then the grass.

Big Dog went wild, a howling bark. Ramming himself at me. His
claws scratching the metal mesh at my face. Forgetful of the new doggie
door.

"You bitch! Where is he?" The voice was low, as guttural and harsh
as my dog's. And just as mindless with fury. My eyes widened. Sucking
in air like a drowning victim, I could think of nothing to say. *This wasn't
the man I was trying to draw out. This wasn't the man who smelled like death.* The
world grew darker and slowed, moving in half time, like the arrested
motion of an old film out of sync. "Where is he?" Teeth bared at my
throat. Human teeth, snarling. His hands twisted, bruising. I should have
fainted or screamed. Instead, the shock gathering at the back of my
throat broke free. And I giggled. I didn't mean to. I tried to hold it in.
But it burst through my lips in a helpless little titter. A rush of
vulnerable, tiny notes, nervous and frivolous. I swallowed the sound,
biting my lip.

His eyes opened wider, wild, maniacal eyes. He crushed me against
a post holding up the screen porch. Secured me there with the press of
his body. His breath gusted against my face. *Not rancid. Mints.* Big Dog's
claws ripped through the screen at my side, piercing it. I thought only a
steel blade could pierce the metal netting. I giggled again, uncontrolled
and shaking.

"Where is he! Where is he, you bitch!"

The weight of his body was suddenly gone. Lifted away from me. I
fell to the gravel beside the porch steps. Catching myself. My palms
bruised and cut by the sharp stone.

I heard a grunt and a thump. The attacker slammed to the ground
only feet away. Bish dropped atop him, pulling the man's arms up and
back. The man cried out, his wail like a wounded animal. Big Dog
bolted through the torn screen. Launched himself at the man on the
ground and sank his long teeth into the handcuffed arm. The man
screamed.

I sank to the ground, a hand over my mouth, covering a fatuous,
witless smile. Thinking how I should be afraid, even now that it was all
over. But somehow, I wasn't frightened. There hadn't been time for me
to respond. Maybe it was the wine that caused my detachment. If so I'd
have another glass, I thought, as I sat on the ground. Maybe two . . .

I put my arm around Jasmine who was making as much noise as
Big Dog and his victim, screaming and crying and prodding me all over.
This semi-medical examination was becoming a habit. I'd have to give
her some pointers. Jas poked too hard.

I drank a second glass of wine as we waited for the cops. And a third glass as my attacker was searched, identified, read his rights, and placed in the deputy's car. It was Bill McKelvey, the curser who threatened me on the phone. The man who blamed Jack for his financial problems. The man who had seemed not quite sane. He was still raving even now. And Big Dog was still barking a constant, frenzied, verbal attack, though Jas had him on a heavy-duty leash tied to the porch. My canine protector hated William McKelvey. As he barked, I considered the possibility that McKelvey had killed Hokey and Herman and shot Big Dog, had tacked Herman's ear to the barn door and sent the awful photograph. Even through my wine haze it didn't add up. If I could only focus; I wanted to work it through, wanted to think. Instead, I drank more wine.

By the time the deputy drove away, McKelvey in his car, blue lights flashing against the trees on the drive, I was well along on my fourth glass, humming an old hymn off key. Happy. Content. *One bad guy down. One to go.* And then the phone rang. I never would have answered had Jas not insisted. Which meant I would have missed out on the rest of the day's fun. God—had to be God to organize things so cleverly—had even more planned to enliven my evening, and by then I was just drunk enough to enjoy it. A tad unwillingly, I picked up the personal line. "Ashlee Davenport, although I'm a Chadwick at heart," I said, winking at my daughter. Jas rolled her eyes and looked at Bish. Something about that look bothered me, but before I could figure out what, Macon spoke.

"Ash. It's Macon."

I knew that. After all, I had drunk only . . . was it four glasses?

"There's been a break-in."

"Of course there has," I agreed. My words slightly slurred. "And we got him."

"How did you know that?"

"I was here."

"But . . . the break in was at the office. At Chadwick, Gaston, and Chadwick."

"Nope. It was here at the house. Only he didn't really break in 'cause Bish and Big Dog jumped on him, and he's on his way to jail. Only," I confided, "I think he's lost his cookies—no. Not his cookies. That means he threw up. He's lost his marbles. And I think he'll go to the state mental facility unless his family gets him sent to wherever they send crazy people in North Carolina, cause he's lost his marbles. Am I repeating myself?"

Macon chuckled. I could picture his lopsided mouth with all the molars exposed on the left side. Or was it the right? "Ashlee. Are you inebriated?"

"You always were so very polite," I said. "Even as a child. An', yes. I think I am drunk. You wanna talk to Wicked?"

"Please." I could hear amusement in Macon's voice, and thought that maybe I should be insulted, but we Chadwicks were too well bred to be insulted over trifles. I lifted my chin, handed the phone to Wicked and went down the hall toward my shower. I nearly fell over Jack's golf clubs. Wonderful things, Jack's clubs. I might never move them. I might need them again one day. I giggled and it didn't sound like me at all. I was polluted. Sloshed.

Moving slowly, I turned on hot water and pulled off my soiled clothes. My arms where McKelvey grabbed me were painful. It seemed all I did these days was get bruised. I had to start taking better care of myself real soon.

Hot water pounded down over my head, diluting the worries of the long day, easing the cramp of muscles crushed and squeezed by my husband's business partner. *One down. One to go.*

I smiled into the steam and the pounding water. Yet, somehow I wasn't the least bit surprised when the shower door opened and Jas pulled me out into the cold room. I stood there, naked and dripping, as my daughter said, "Mom. They caught the guy who attacked us."

CHAPTER FIFTEEN

With all the dignity I could muster, I drank down a quart of coffee. I had chosen a bad night to overindulge, but how was I to know that a man with severe halitosis would break into Macon's office tonight? I had assumed that being prayed over and then apprehending one bad guy would be sufficient excitement for one night. I hadn't expected to participate in a line up.

It was a singular experience. Mostly sober, wide awake, with the beginnings of a throbbing headache, I walked along a line of men and sniffed each. One man smelled of unwashed body, rank and gamy. Another smelled of old beer. Two were relatively pleasant, though one of them wore too much cologne. It had a musk base, thick and cloying. I wandered what form of wildlife such a scent was supposed to attract.

The fourth man smelled of decomposing meat. Rank and potent.

In front of him, I paused and sniffed again. It was the same foul scent, the harsh, putrid reek of the man in the Soiled Utility Room and the gazebo. Lifting my eyes, I stared at him. Standing beneath the number 4 sign was a lanky, rope-thin man, tall, with evasive brown eyes and a stubble of brown beard. He had a bruise on his right cheek, which could have been made by a golf club. A second bruise marked his Adam's apple. Four scratches cut into the flesh beneath his left eye. *Jasmine's fingernails.* She'd scratched him. I smiled and it wasn't pretty.

His hair was short in front and on the sides, longer on top and greasy; he wore jeans and a plaid shirt, the sleeves rolled up, exposing tattoos. There was nothing remarkable about him other than the foul smell. And that meant what? That my worries were over? Or maybe it meant nothing. I felt curiously unaffected by the sight of the tattooed man, as if his capture had nothing to do with me. Perhaps I was beginning to react to the long days of unremitting stress, shutting down all but the most essential emotions, experiencing wide swings from feeling nothing at all to the near hysterical giddiness of McKelvey's capture. How long could I live under stress before I broke down totally?

The man beside me twitched and I looked up into his eyes. He bared his teeth at me in a grin, exposing red gums, bleeding and raw. He was laughing at me. The stench was staggering.

I turned to an officer, glad of the residual wine floating in my system. Glad of the distance the alcohol and the stress offered me, the insulation from the proceedings. Each moment seemed separate and disconnected, the world around me moving in disjointed blocks of time, like the individual frames of a video on pause.

"This one. Number four."

The deputy nodded and moved toward the prisoners. Behind me, a door opened and Macon entered the room. My lawyer was smiling and gesturing. "Ashlee. In here."

"Here" was a small, cramped consulting room crowded with a conference table, half a dozen gray plastic chairs, Macon, Wicked, Bish, Jas, and Sheriff Gaskin. They all looked pleased, as if in choosing number four I had accomplished a neat trick and they wanted to congratulate me. Much like a dog that had finally caught a Frisbee.

The room was close and overheated. My headache bloomed into a monster, pounding against my skull. Pulling out a chair, I sat down and waited. The sheriff, his deputies and I were getting quite chummy. "Jasmine picked out the same guy," Macon said.

And then it finally hit me. *Two down.* Jasmine was safe. I discovered it was possible to be both exuberant and nauseated at once. *Jasmine was safe.*

"Our man isn't talking," the sheriff said. "He's asked for a lawyer though, and says he has something to trade. Name's Clevon Dixon, but he goes by the name Tattoo or Stinky. Familiar?"

"No." My head pulsed with pain and my arms felt hot and tender where McKelvey had twisted them. I could trace the shape of his hands on my arm by the pain. "I need some Tylenol. Anybody got any?" No one did, and the Sheriff continued.

"Clevon has a list of priors going back to his teens, but he ain't bright enough to be in charge of what's been going on here, Miz Davenport. Not all the things your lawyer and my men have been telling me. I figure Clevon's working for somebody else. He knows the ropes though, and I have a feeling he's willing to cooperate. Ashlee, you got any opposition to my working a plea bargain if what he's got seems worth a trade?"

It was Ashlee now, instead of Miz Davenport. We were definitely getting too chummy. "You do what seems right Sheriff. Though I'd appreciate it if you tell us before you let him loose." I looked up at Macon. He nodded, apparently agreeing with my statement, and the little meeting was abruptly concluded. Sheriff Gaskin opened a door, letting in a cool draft of air, and dashed off to do whatever it is that sheriffs do. He was a busy man. I just wanted Tylenol.

Following a brief, whispered conference with Macon, I stood and joined Bish, Wicked and Jas. Assuming we were no longer needed, we wandered through the Law Enforcement Center, out into the parking lot. My headache was worse, and I'd have gladly given up a back molar for a headache med. Alcohol had never agreed with me. The world staggered and swayed. My stomach was queasy. Only knowing that my daughter was safe helped.

The trip home was a seasick agony I attempted to sleep through. I rested my head against the seat and closed my eyes, trying to block out the young people's conversation. I was somewhat successful, until I realized Jas was talking about her father. "He knew about Mr. McKelvey's toxic dump, didn't he? He knew about it when he traded for it. And he cheated that man." Her voice was cool, sounding very adult. Only a mother would have noticed the resonance of desolation and disenchantment. I fluttered my fingers at Macon, giving the lawyer the right to speak. Jasmine had the right to hear some of the truth, even if it hurt.

"We don't know, Jas. But it seems likely that he knew," Macon said kindly. "In his defense, before he died, he was working on a solution. And to give your father credit, he also was finally in a position financially to make things right with McKelvey. The profits from the development of Davenport Hills had reached a point where he could have taken back the land in Charlotte, and provided McKelvey with recompense for his financial loss. The way the deal with McKelvey was structured, it appears your father had planned a bailout for him."

I sat up at Macon's words, tying to focus in the darkened interior of the Volvo.

"That doesn't make him any less of a thief," Jasmine said softly.

I opened my mouth to defend Jack, but closed it. There wasn't anything I could really say. All the phrases that came to mind sounded trite and banal in the hollow silence of my mind. In the darkness, I reached over and took Jas' hand. She squeezed back, as if she understood my concern and wanted to reassure me in return. In an uncertain quiet, we traveled the miles home.

Bleary-eyed, half-awake in the morning light, I stumbled to the shower. Ten minutes later, Jas' words penetrated, but even awake they made no sense. Something about being late and red-necked turkeys shooting each other. I'd never heard of a red-necked turkey, but I had no intention of watching them kill one another. Surely I'd missed something when Jas rolled me out of bed this morning, talking non-stop. When I stepped from the shower, she was there to feed me coffee and English muffins, dress me as if I were a doll, explaining all the while. "Mother," she said in that patronizing my-mother-is-a-moron tone that teenage girls use when their mothers display unwitting ignorance. It was a tone I hoped she would outgrow before I had to say something to her about it. "I told you about the turkey-shoot the day of the concert. It was one of those messages you didn't bother to listen to. The Rescue Squad is hosting a turkey-shoot to launch a fundraiser. Remember?"

I didn't. But I nodded anyway, and dutifully put my arm through the sleeve of the shirt she intended me to wear.

"They're naming the new building the Jack Davenport Rescue Squad Building Number Two. It's in Daddy's honor, not that he deserves it, and *you* are the guest of honor today. I told you all about this. And now you're going to be late. How much wine did you drink last night?"

It was more accusation than question, and I meekly answered while stepping into jeans. "Four glasses. Which was three too many," I admitted.

"Yeah, well, McKelvey bruised the heck out of your arms." She handed me charcoal gray cowboy boots, ones Jack bought me for Valentine's. They had red hearts and roses twining up the sides. Very campy. "I hope he and that bastard Dixon rot in jail for what they did to you."

I didn't know where Jas learned such language; I should have put a stop to it. After last night, however, I wasn't the best example. Meekly I took a boot and braced myself for her response to my words. "Macon bailed Mr. McKelvey out this morning."

"What!" Jas' dark eyes were wide and shocked.

Reaching down, I stroked her hair. She was kneeling, boot in hand, at my feet. "I asked Macon to handle it last night. It's part of the plan he and Esther devised to reimburse McKelvey for his loss in the original exchange, for two of the farms that became Davenport Hills. Macon came up with a bailout plan based on your father's notes," I added gently.

Jas looked away, picked up my left foot and pointed it into the boot. "Yeah. Well. Maybe my daddy wasn't all he was cracked up to be."

I obliged my daughter by stepping into the boot, my toes sliding down the shaft to the arched bottom. Then I squatted beside her and took her face in my hands. "Jasmine Leah, your daddy wasn't perfect. Nobody is. And I suppose it's possible he knew about the toxic dump before the property exchange." Jas looked away. Gently, I pulled her face back. "But long before he died, your father was working on a way to rescue McKelvey. Your father had written to the state of North Carolina to inquire about federal bail-out programs to clean up toxic waste sites."

Jas finally looked up from my booted foot and into my face. Her eyes were wounded and aching, and no matter what I might really know or suspect about Jack, I couldn't let my daughter be totally disillusioned. I just couldn't. Perhaps it was a weakness, something in my Caldwell or Hamilton genes, but I had to protect Jas, even if it meant defending Jack. "Your father put his company and his reputation on the line to get help for McKelvey. And frankly, he didn't have to help the man at all. Legally, he could have let McKelvey flounder and drown all by himself."

Jas blinked and absorbed the words I had just uttered. And with the words something twisted deep within me, the truth of my own statement forcing its way into my mind, settling in. Jack could have let McKelvey hit bottom. From a financial and legal standpoint it might even have been a wise move to step back and watch the man fall. But he hadn't. Jack had stepped in and come up with a rescue plan. I didn't have time to think it through right now. I didn't have time to accept the truth of my own words. Staring into my daughter's soul, I went on. "Macon and Esther discovered your father's notes and copies of the correspondence dealing with the bail-out, some moneys of which will eventually come from Davenport Hill's profits. It will be expensive, especially in light of the water problem at the golf course."

"The Swamp." Jas said, mocking the title and her father both at once.

"Precisely. But the plan was your father's. And I okayed it yesterday."

"It doesn't make Daddy any less of a crook," she said stubbornly.

It looked as if I would be here a while, so I re-positioned my weight, sitting back on my rump, and got comfortable. "Jasmine, remember when you nearly killed Mabel?"

Jas looked up quickly, her face stunned. I had never before mentioned the foolish mistake that almost cost Mabel her life. "It was an accident," She whispered.

"Yes, it was. But you knew better than to give Mabel whole carrots. You knew she ate like a pig. You knew to slice the carrots both lengthwise and in half. But you wanted to go to the movies with Topaz and Mama Pearl, and you were running late. You knew better. And yet you didn't slice the carrots."

She whispered, "The new James Bond. I wanted to see it . . ."

"More than anything," I finished for her. "And when you got home, what had happened?"

"Mabel had colic. She was down in her stall" Jas shook her head as if to shake away an ugly memory. "Daddy and Doc Ethridge saved her." Tears glistening in her eyes.

I smiled at my daughter, took the right boot and slid it over my foot. "Your father never said a word to you. He understood. He also understood when you put yourself on restriction and didn't leave the farm for three weeks. He understood when you decided on veterinary medicine for a career. Your father understood the concepts of penance and restitution, Jasmine. He was practicing both penance and restitution to McKelvey when he died."

After a long silence, Jas finally spoke. "I think I understand what you're trying to say."

"Good. I think I'm beginning to understand a little too. Unfortunately."

Jas looked at me quizzically and when I didn't explain, she said, "Put on some makeup and I'll meet you at the Jeep. Okay?"

"Okay. Are you signed up to shoot?"

"Of course." Jas rose from the floor in a single, lithe smooth motion, pulling me up after her. She took a deep breath and said, "I'm my father's daughter, aren't I?"

The words were progress in the right direction. "Yes Jasmine Leah Davenport. You are."

Thoughtfully, Jas checked me over from head to boot, nodded in approval and left my room. After a moment, I went to the bathroom and applied makeup, covering my pale skin and hollowed eyes, the bruised look left from weeks of grief, anger, and last night's wine. I kept my mind blank, not thinking over the words I had shared with Jas. I wasn't ready to consider anything good about Jack. I wasn't ready to give up my anger and bitterness. I wasn't ready to forget that my husband had been a liar, a cheat, and a thief. And perhaps a party to murder. What was the term? Accessory after the fact? I wasn't ready to forgive the photographs of Jack and Robyn that rested on the floor of my closet in a plastic grocery bag. I wasn't ready. Not today.

Because Jack and Jas were crack shots, and because turkey-shoots were a favorite county fundraiser, I had attended numerous similar events. Contrary to the name, no turkeys were ever shot. In fact, the only turkey involved in the contest was the twelve-pound smoked one given as a prize to the best shot in each age category; second place was a small, honey-cured ham. Today's category tournament prizes were donated by Bi-Lo, while the overall winner would receive a gift card for Puckey's

Guns and Things.

The fund raiser was held behind Hargett's Truck Stop at the junction of 901 and Gordonville Turnout. Centrally located in Dawkins County, Hargett's was a watering hole for local men on their way into and out of one town or another on farm business, a place where they could stop, have a strong cup of coffee or a beer, and catch up on local news and gossip. Find out who was selling what and for how much, or what they'd take in trade for it. Hargett's advertised the coldest beer and the worst boiled peanuts in the state, but their real draw was the vast array of tobacco products. Cigarettes, snuff, chewing tobacco, cigars, and pipe paraphernalia was stacked floor to ceiling on aisle two. Cartons of tobacco-based products were sold by the case to enterprising types who wanted to risk the law, cross state lines and sell at a tax-free profit.

There was a cooler along the back wall with beer and wine, milk, cheese, and sandwiches prepared daily by Mrs. Hargett. Motor oil, fishing tackle and lures lined one aisle, and live bait hopped crawled, or swam. Saddles and used tack took up one corner near cowboy hats and work boots. Minuscule bathrooms, cleaned and scented with Pine Sol, were in the back. Snacks were behind the counter with hotrod, hunting, and porn magazines. Ice cream and school supplies, sunglasses, muscle rubs, aspirin, Pampers, Mentholatum, and Tums were bestsellers, scattered in no particular order on the shelves.

A dusty twenty-point buck with a red bandanna around its neck presided over the scene, and Hargett himself ruled the roost from his swivel chair behind the cash register, an illegal sawed off shotgun beneath the counter for the foolish stranger with larceny on his mind. It was hunt and search for what you wanted in Hargett's, or ask Hargett. He'd scratch his chin, ponder, and finally point you in the wrong direction. Most times it was faster to find what you wanted on your own in this modern-day remnant of a general store.

For the Rescue Squad's fundraiser, Old Man Hargett was donating eighty cents on the purchase of each beer sold, twenty cents on each cola, ten cents on every cup of coffee. He'd make a profit and the Rescue Squad wouldn't have to handle the cash. It was a generous arrangement for both sides. Food was provided by a variety of vendors, the most popular being the whole roast pig offered by June Bug Gordon. Because June Bug was a Rescue Squad member, and because his son had been saved by the Rescue Squad from drowning when an earthen dam broke several years back, he donated the whole pig roasting on his traveling barbeque, all proceeds to go toward the new building. The carcass, slow cooking since yesterday, was turning on the spit at the back of June Bug's pickup truck. The aroma of roast pig was mouth-watering delicious, the scent attracting heady for a mile around. The financial and culinary arrangements were typical for turkey shoot fundraisers.

It felt strange to be a guest rather than one of the hosts; Jack and I had often organized Rescue Squad fundraisers. Someone else had handled the advertising, had arranged with Puckey for the ammunition. Someone else had talked to liability insurers. And someone else had handled all the last minute delays and headaches and errands. Not Jack. Not me. Phillip Faulkenberry was the new captain of the Rescue Squad, and quite obviously in control of the arrangements. He was carrying an air of importance around like a badge of honor, shouting answers to questions, giving instructions, and pointing out the location for the P.A. speakers.

Phillip strode up, his long legs covering the packed earth at what, for me, would have been a fast jog. "Ashlee! You made it!" A big smile wreathed his face, deepening weatherworn wrinkles into deep crevices, bracketing his mouth. Phillip pulled me into a hug, my cheek to his rib cage. "I'm so glad to see you. I know this is a hard time, but everyone's been asking after you, hoping you'd be here. You are staying long enough to give out the first place prize, aren't you?"

"She'll be here," Jas said, at my side. "Nice to see you Mr. Faulkenberry."

"Good to see you too, Jasmine. Where's your shadow?" Phillip asked, and then roared at his own joke. "You know. Topaz? Shadow?"

"Oh, I got it, Mr. Faulkenberry," Jas said, her eyes slitting. " 'Cause she's blacker than I am." Jas was protective of her cousin, and any slight to Topaz was an insult to Jas. Of course, being a Chadwick made her super-sensitive to racism in any form.

Phillip, however, was immune to Jasmine's ire. Still chuckling at his whimsy, he slapped me on the back and strode off. "Ya'll have a good time. I'll see you at the finish, Ash."

"You know," Jas mimicked, "Topaz? Shadow? Ugh. Idiot redneck."

As racial slurs went, I had heard worse, but I kept my peace. "I'm starving." Okay, I also know when to change the subject entirely. "How soon will the pig be ready?"

Jas checked her watch. "Soon. But if you beg real sweetly, I'll bet June Bug'll slice you off a taste right now. He always does. And don't worry, Mama, I'll be polite. I wasn't about to stomp down on old Faulkenberry's instep."

"Good," I murmured. "Let's go get a barbecue sandwich." The food at turkey-shoots was always luscious, savory, delicious—most any synonym. It was also high in fat, cholesterol, and calories. Now that I had most of my appetite back, I would have to be careful not to overeat and regain the weight I had lost grieving over Jack. I enjoyed the comfortable fit of my old jeans.

There were over two hundred participants signed up for the turkey shoot, which made this an all day, jam-packed affair. There were eight rounds with twenty-five participants in each round, all shooting 12-gauge shotguns loaded with birdshot. The targets were turkey-shaped, attached to wooden frames, and each participant would get three shots, instead of the usual single shot. Two rounds would shoot at once, while a harried announcer tried to keep pace on the ancient P.A. system. Two sets of judges controlled the show from the safety of a judge's stand and observers watched from the sides behind a heavy duty rope, hung with yellow caution flags.

Bales of hay were set around the gravel lot for atmosphere and vehicle parking was haphazard, with pickups and rusty camouflage hunting trucks predominating. There was a traveling carnival set up to one side for the kiddies with a small Ferris wheel, a toddler-sized roller coaster, tilt-a-whirl, and other rides, most of which should have been outlawed as unsafe a decade ago. The smells of popcorn and cotton candy were drawing a young crowd, children pulling at their parents' hands in anticipation. The carnies were barking out their attractions.

I would be awarding the prizes to the best shot in each early category round of the turkey-shoot, as well as the best and second best shots in the final round. In between handing out awards, I was free to share the day's festivities with the shooters and friends. My duties had been explained to me on the trip out, my daughter's voice reflecting that you-should-know-better tone again, the bane of mother's everywhere. Perhaps because I hadn't planned for the orgy of food and gunpowder, the mass of people or the noise, I was able to relax and enjoy it all. I hadn't brooded about it or been given time to dread it, and because I hadn't had to plan the event itself, I could revel in the simple pleasures of the day. Sunshine beat down, warming me. Hugs and well wishes from old friends met me at every turn. Roast pig and big fluffy buns, ice cold Diet Coke and homemade ice cream dipped from the churn filled my stomach, pressing against the waist band of my jeans. And my stinky-smelling-stalker was in jail. My stress began to seep away.

Whichever investor had been behind the actions of Stinky Dixon had two choices: to attack me personally or hire another front man. I didn't think Stinky's boss would risk personal involvement, especially before hundreds of witnesses, most of them my friends and family. And there would be no repeat error on the night of the Patrons' Party—I wouldn't be alone. With Chadwick's all around, and because Stinky was in jail, I felt safe. I even left my 9mm locked in the glove compartment of the Jeep. Not even the presence of Bret McDermott and my suspicions about the man made me regret the decision to abandon the gun. I needed the leisure and the crowd. I needed the freedom from worry and fear.

The danger to Jas would soon be at an end, McKelvey's threats were being dealt with by Macon's capable hands, and, so long as I didn't think about Robyn or Reverend Perry's visit, I was just fine. The beer Bish brought me in a paper cup helped, too. He might have an eye for my daughter and an unfortunate tendency to forthright speech, but he did know how to quench a thirst. The beer also did wonders for my nagging little headache. All in all, it was a lovely day.

By four P.M. I had given out three prizes for the best shot in preliminary rounds, handing over a turkey or ham and offering a short congratulatory speech to the winner. Not being accustomed to public speaking, I didn't know where the words came from, but judging from the smiles on the winner's faces I must have done fairly well. Each little speech was a variation of:

"It is my pleasure to award you, Jimbo Kendall, this prize the preliminary round of the Rescue Squad's turkey shoot. I have to admit I couldn't hit a tractor-trailer if I was locked inside one, so I especially admire a close, clean win. Again, congratulations and we all hope you'll hang around for the Champions Round to take place near sundown. Meanwhile, enjoy the festivities and the good food." My words, amplified by the county's sound system were scratchy, squally, and full of feedback, but no one seemed to care much so long as I smiled real wide and clapped the winner on the back as I handed him his turkey and his family snapped photos for the family picture album. At which point I'd shook the winner's hand and wandered off for more roast pig.

I caught sight of Jas and Bish several times during the afternoon, the bodyguard torn between watching my daughter's lovely, playful face, and scanning the crowd for possible assailants. The boy was smitten, and Jas was more than a little aware of him, but Bish was focused on Jasmine's safekeeping, and the crowd itself was a sort of protection—any assailant would have a well-armed mob to contend with. Jas was as safe as she would have been back home in her barn. At least until nightfall when the dark took back a measure of protection.

There were a few unpleasant moments in the long, noisy hours of the afternoon. Patty Gaskin, the sheriff's wife, snubbed me at the cooler while serving up colas and canned beer. And later on, Matilda McConnell, the mayor's wife, pretended that she hadn't heard me greet her. These were reactions from so-called "ladies" of the old school who felt I should have stayed home in widow's weeds, grieving with the blinds drawn. It was what I'd expected. Oddly, it didn't hurt. In fact, it was curiously liberating, the silent condemnation freeing me from shackles I hadn't known I wore. Independent and unrestrained, I wandered the grounds watching everything and everyone, engrossed in my unexpected freedom, pausing only to give out prizes.

At five P.M., the prize I gave went to Jas for her bull's-eye shot on the turkey-shaped target; she beat out twenty-three men and one woman in her category. Because it was Jas competing, I watched through the entire round, and as turkey-shoots go, it was exciting.

Afterwards, Phillip Faulkenberry and Nana took the obligatory photos for us, Nana from a seat of honor with the Chadwicks. Jas smiled for the cameras as Bish stood in the crowd behind Nana, his face beaming. I liked that in the bodyguard—that he could watch Jas beat a bunch of men in a traditionally masculine sport and feel proud of her success. I also liked the fact that he stood behind Nana. There was something respectful in his choice of position. Then, blinded by the flash, I hugged my daughter and wandered back into the crowd.

There were few of my darker-skinned cousins present, not that I had expected many. Topaz had once explained it: "You got a couple hundred white country boys loaded up with liquor and guns and all that's missing is the white sheets. Not interested." 'Nuff said. Even Wicked was back at the farm, putting locks on the doors to the outbuildings except the barn.

Alan Mathison won the last of the preliminary rounds, beating out Bret. I hadn't bothered to check the list for any names except Jasmine's, and I couldn't hide my surprise as I handed Alan his prize. He, however, was as gracious as ever, accepting his turkey with a smile and an elegant little bow of his head. He stood out in the crowd of Dawkins County regulars like a Thoroughbred in a corral full of mules, though I was, of course, too polite to say so from the podium in front of a live mic. As the final round of the turkey-shoot began immediately after, I had no time to carry on a conversation. Instead I pressed his hand and said, "Good luck."

"Wait for me after the shoot? I need to speak with you, if you have time."

"I have time," I said, and fought down the silly little blush that threatened.

"Good. Actually, you'll have to wait anyway, to award my prize."

"Think you're going to win, do you?" I said, laughing at his audacity.

"Of course. I always win." He covered his heart as if swearing fealty. "Always." His expression was one of wounded surprise and pretended hurt, as if I was supposed to know he was a winner. "And I'll dedicate my win to you," he said, the phrase sounding courtly.

"Oh. Great. Beat my daughter and then credit me. Thanks but no thanks."

With a roguish grin, Alan ran for the shooter's box. The Champions Round consisted of eight participants, the winners of the preliminary rounds. Each shooter fired three shots in three rounds. The first round went to Alan, the clear winner. The second round winner was King Kirby. He'd missed in the first round, but settled down and shot steadily in the second. The third round was a dead heat with Kirby and Alan placing their shots so close they couldn't be judged.

The crowd cheered wildly, pressing close to the sidelines, half of them drinking beer, the other half sipping from bottles hidden in small brown paper bags. Fifty percent of the adult crowd was drunk as skunks, another five percent was only about half drunk, leaving only the churchgoers sober. I was glad I wasn't working the ER tonight; there would surely be accidents when this crowd drove home. The highway patrol already had vehicles stationed at the intersections, waiting eagerly for DUIs or wrecks. They would give a lot of breathalyzers tonight.

For the final round, bets were placed, most for Kirby, a known sharpshooter, though a few went for the new man who was cool and relaxed under pressure. After the shots were fired, Alan stood flatfooted, his hands steady, waiting for the judges to declare a winner, and I studied him. He was dressed in skintight faded jeans, worn cowboy boots, the heels rounded, and a faded denim shirt. No hunting boots or cowboy hat like the rest of the country crowd. Just Alan Mathison, smiling that subtle smile, his lips perpetually up turned at the corners.

Not once did he glance my way. Alan kept his eyes on King Kirby, who was sipping a beer, an empty one by his side. After several minutes, the judges agreed to disagree, and admitted that they couldn't choose a winner, a non-decision that riled the bet placers. To settle the crowd and satisfy the contestants, the final ruling was a one-on-one competition, another three-shot round to determine the contest winner.

While the judges set up fresh targets and re-inspected the weapons and ammunition to make sure all was fair, the two contestants wandered off, Alan toward the extra Porta-Pot toilets set up in the darkness, Kirby to his truck. I chose not to follow either man, walking over to Nana to make sure her toes weren't swelling beneath her cast, taking the opportunity to chat with Uncle Horace and Aunt Mosetta and hug all the cousins I hadn't seen in days. I also took the time to reorganize my thoughts. A vision of chiseled lips turned up at the corners kept intruding. Even when I tried to replace their image with another, the smiling lips would reappear.

I spoke with Mick Ethridge who told me a joke that both began and ended with the words "No shit, Ashlee. I tell you true." I accepted a hug from Irene and Buddy Rodgers whom I hadn't seen since the night Alan's wife died in the accident at Magnet Hole Creek. I stood for a while in silence with Bret McDermott, letting the evening breeze cool my face. I wondered if he had heard about the capture of Stinky, and if it worried him. And I wondered if the sheriff had been able to find out whom Dixon had been working for. I didn't want it to be Bret.

"Your little girl is a fine shot, Ashlee," he said.

"Yes. She is." I picked out Jas in the crowd. Bish was leaning toward her, his head close to hers, listening, his eyes on the crowd. Jas laughed up into his face, her eyes sparkling. No trace of the attack she had suffered remained on her face. Even her swollen nose had gone down.

"So is Mathison." Bret's voice was conversational, with no emotional overtones.

I flushed as I looked out over the shooting ground, remembering those lips. It wasn't a comment I had expected. "Yes he is." My voice sounded wooden, but Bret seemed not to notice.

"Ashlee, I know it's too soon, but eventually you'll want to . . . date again."

I jerked my head to look at Bret, but now he was staring out over the crowd. I looked away, following Bret's eyes, if not his line of thought. The sun was a burnt red ball in the west, lighting thin strips of clouds with feverish color. Long, diffuse shadows formed across the bare ground. Security lights began to glow overhead. "And, well," he said, "uh, Alan Math—"

"Ladies and gentlemen," the words squealed through the PA system, interrupting Bret's words. "The final round of the turkey-shoot is about to begin. Let me start this round by saying how much we appreciate the presence of each and every one of you here today. And although we're still working on the final tally, we think we raised somewhere in the neighborhood of six thousand dollars today, enough to break ground on the Jack Davenport Rescue Squad Building."

The crowd began clapping about halfway through Phillip's little speech, drowning out any further attempts at conversation. I smiled up at Bret and shrugged, not real surprised when he didn't smile back. Bret had obviously worked up the courage for a special little chat and didn't appreciate being thwarted. With Dixon in jail, perhaps he had decided to approach things more directly. If he was Dixon's boss. I tried to place Bret's high Dawkins accent in with the stiff tones of the man who had called me once or twice. It didn't quite fit, but then, Bret didn't have to be alone in this, if he was involved at all.

Phillip continued as the swell of foot stomping, rebel yells, and applause died down. "Now, if the judges are ready—and I can see they are—we'll begin the dead-heat shoot-off between Alan Mathison, a newcomer, and King Kirby, last year's winner. Ashlee Davenport, how 'bout coming up here to view the final round from the podium? Let's give a big hand to a fine little lady. Ashlee, we're all here because of Jack's vision, Jack's dream of the state's best educated, best prepared, all volunteer Rescue Squad." There was more foot stomping and hollering, as I elbowed my way to the dais. Podium was a fancy term for four sawhorses overlaid with 2x10s and plywood. Although the platform wasn't sturdy, I climbed up and stood with Phillip, waved to the crowd and refused the opportunity to make a speech.

"Are the contestants ready?" Phillip bellowed through the mic. Along with the rest of the crowd, he had visited the beer keg, and though he handled himself well, he was two sheets to the wind and flushed with success. No one, including Jack, had ever raised six thousand dollars at a turkey-shoot. Not even close and Phillip had imbibed a self-congratulatory drink or two. "Are the contestants ready?" he boomed again. Children in the crowd raced and ran, the adults pressed closer to the ropes at the sides.

At the shooters' table, Alan flexed his fingers, bending them back from the palm. Rolled his head back and forth. Checked his weapon. I caught sight of Bret in the crowd, his eyes stormy. Beside Alan at the long table, was King Kirby's prize 12-gauge and an open box of ammo. But no Kirby. A strange disquiet rippled through the crowd. Alan stretched his shoulders, his eyes on the targets fluttering in the breeze. I caught sight of Bret again, looking around.

"Will the final contestant please take his place at the shooters table? The words echoed through the crowd, vanishing over the treetops. But still no King Kirby. Alan looked around, met my eyes and lifted his brows, as if to say, "What now?" I shrugged back.

From the row of pickups, a child yelled, thin voice triumphant. "Here he is! Here he is! I fount him!" It was the same tone of voice a child might have used had he discovered the prize egg at an Easter Egg hunt. Kirby was stumbling, confused, bleary eyed, and he didn't smell too sweet either as he made his way to the shooters' table. Former appearances to the contrary, King Kirby was drunk as a skunk. He had been discovered beside his truck, most of a beer spilled down his shirt, passed out cold. He couldn't stand up straight and kept reaching up with both hands, holding his head. I sympathized with the headache. I knew what a glass too many could do to an alcohol-induced headache, and Kirby's was clearly caused by more than one too many.

Half the crowd was highly amused at Kirby's attempts to find his weapon. Others, ones who had bet he would win the overall championship round had other reactions. None pleasant. When it became clear that King Kirby, the county favorite, could not safely compete, the judges halted the competition, awarded Alan the first place gift card to Puckey's and gave Kirby's wife, Arnette, the second place prize. It was an ignominious ending to an otherwise successful day.

The crowd thinned out rapidly after Kirby's downfall and I headed for the Jeep where I sat in the dark sipping a cup of lukewarm coffee, one brewed early and parboiled the rest of the day. It sat heavily on my pork-filled stomach.

Jas and Bish met me in the gravel lot, her upper arm gripped firmly in his hand as he scanned the crowd for attackers. I kicked open the Jeep door and slid my feet to the ground in one smooth motion. The cab light and the metallic sound brought Bish to a halt. Instantly his hand moved to his left shoulder and the gun that rested there. It returned to his side the moment he recognized me. My daughter's protector was nervous. *Good.* Scowling, Bish loaded us all in the Jeep and started the ignition. It was impertinent to assume he would drive, but I didn't really care as long as he kept my daughter safe.

Alan appeared in the headlights, waving an arm. In the other was a shrink-wrapped turkey. Bish braked and rolled down the window. "Fancy shooting, Mr. Mathison," he said. "Congratulations."

"Thanks. Too bad it wasn't against sober competition, but that's the result when you mix liquor and country boys. My daddy was a country boy, so I know. Sorry, do I know you?"

Bish stuck a hand out the window and shook Alan's. "Bish. Friend of the family."

"Nice to meet you Bish. Ashlee, I hope you'll allow me to donate a smoked turkey to the next Chadwick family reunion. I hate smoked meat." He opened the door, passing the bird across Bish to me. It was too big for my lap. It needed its own seat. Seatbelt, too. In the event of an accident, Alan's gift would go sailing through the windshield like a cannon ball. "Ashlee, when it's convenient, I need to discuss the Taylor development with you. We've run into the same kind of groundwater problems that Davenport Hills is having and I'd like to hear your input and how Jack handled the permit problems."

I almost said, "We don't know if there *were* permit problems at Davenport Hills because the permits are missing." Instead I said, "Sure. When?" The heavy turkey was putting my legs to sleep. I'd be paralyzed before I got home.

"No time like the present. Now?"

"I could drive Jas home, Mrs. D. Take her to see Nana. Feed the horses."

"Perfect." Alan crossed to the passenger door and opened it, lifted out the turkey, and I slid to the ground. Then he placed the turkey in the seat and strapped it in. Almost as if he had read my mind. "I'll bring Mrs. D. home in about an hour. Okay?"

"Fine Sir."

CHAPTER SIXTEEN

"Ash?" Alan gestured with his palm up toward the mid-sized Nissan truck. It wasn't American made—a serious flaw in this part of the county—but it did have the requisite gun rack in the back window and a white metal tool box stretched across the bed.

Suddenly, I was obscurely uneasy, the feeling murky, uncertain and clouded. As I climbed into the cab, I realized that part of my difficulty was because I had left the 9mm in the Jeep all day, knowing I was safe in the crowds of locals. It was still there. Dixon's boss would know by now that he was in jail, perhaps ready to talk. If he reacted tonight, on the miles of dark country roads would be an optimum time to attack. And here I was. Unarmed.

Up ahead, Jas and Bish pulled into the line of traffic, leaving me alone. Alan closed the door, insulating me in silence and giving me a moment to think. It seemed only fair to tell him about the attack on Jasmine, the danger to me, and possibly to anyone in my company. Fair, but difficult, and I wasn't certain I would find the words. "Miccah's is the only place in the county for decent food, and after a day of nothing but roast pig and beer, I could use a good salad. You?" Alan asked as he climbed into the truck.

"Yes. Fine." I figured the ten I still had in my jeans pocket would cover that well enough—if Alan still wanted to be seen in public with me after I enlightened him as to my troubles that is. He started the little truck and whipped it diagonally through a muddy ditch and out onto the road. The motion of the truck threw me up toward the roof and slammed me back down, jarring my shoulder. For once I was glad I was short. An inch more in height, and I would have had a concussion.

Alan hadn't struck me as the type to cut across a field to reach a road, but then I didn't know the man well except as a patient. Bracing myself on the dash, just in case Alan tried any more shortcuts, I began describing my little problem. "Alan, about Bish."

"Your daughter's bodyguard."

"How . . ." I stopped, having no idea what to say next.

"Everyone in the county knows you have problems Ash. Someone killed two of your dogs, there have been threatening letters, phone calls.

Rumor even has it you beat a man with a tire iron for attacking Jas. So when Bish appeared on the scene, everyone assumed he was a bodyguard. He's too good-looking to be a replacement for your handyman."

"Golf club," I said, still surprised. Gossip was a full-time occupation in some circles of small-town life, so I should have known there would be talk. I should have expected that conclusions would be drawn, right or wrong, about my troubles.

"Beg pardon?"

"I beat him with a golf club. Not a tire iron."

"Ah." Alan glanced at me and then to the road.

"My point is that I might not be the safest person in the world to be around. And I left my gun in the Jeep."

Alan laughed, glancing my way again. Several of the vehicles ahead of us turned off onto the road past the airport—such as it was—toward Cliff Notch, a small township in the south of the county. The road ahead in front of us was dark and empty. "You've been carrying a gun?" His tone was curious and vaguely amused, not insulting as I might have expected, none of the "macho man to the helpless foolish little female" in the tone. "Can you shoot?"

"Not worth a toot," I admitted. Alan laughed again. "But I feel safer with it, somehow."

"Makes sense. I'd feel safer with a gun too, in your circumstances. Not that it's any of my business, but I am curious."

It was my turn to use the overworked phrase. "Beg pardon?"

"Why is someone threatening you? What exactly is the problem? Not that I'm prying or anything, although I am."

I settled back in my seat. "To be honest, I don't know."

"You're right," he said quickly. "Too personal. We could talk about the weather then. After today, listening to farmers talk, I know more about the weather and its effect on crops than I ever wanted to. Did you know that cotton balls really do get rotten and that when they get rotten, you really can't pick the cotton?"

"No," I said with a half laugh. "I mean yes. But I meant what I said; I wasn't trying to be evasive. I really don't know why I'm in danger."

Alan was quiet then, the tires a soft hum on the newly paved road. "You want to talk about it? You don't have to worry about it going any further. I don't live here. I don't gossip, at least not under normal conditions. The only reason I listened about you, was . . ." He paused. I waited, wondering where this confession-and-answer time was going. DorCity's lights loomed in the distance, a yellow glow against the clouds. The sky looked like rain again. Perfect recipe for rotten corn, rotten hay, or rotten soy. It was actually too early in the year for rotten cotton. "We have some things in common, Ashlee." I turned my attention back to Alan.

"We've both lost spouses recently, although I admit my marriage was down the tubes anyway. Margie and I had been talking to a counselor before she died, not that it was doing any good. We were ready to separate before the accident. She was . . . She was seeing someone else." Alan shook his head and braked, stopping at the first red light, the one outside the old Sky City, its empty windows boarded over with warped and rotten plywood. I didn't know what to say.

"We're both alone, you and I. Both in the construction business. And of course there's the fact that you saved my life. We have that in common." He gave a half grin and put the truck in gear. Traffic had increased and surrounded us. Ahead, the warning lights at the railroad crossing began to blink and in the distance, a train's whistle sounded.

Alan floored the Nissan and beat the lowering crossing arms by seconds. "In Charlotte, the trains are all overhead, out of the way." He said. "Here you have to wait if you get caught. So, anyway, back to the subject at hand. All the above named reasons aside, I listened to the gossip about you because I was interested in you."

A flush started at my feet and wavered up my body, settling in the palms of my hands and the pit of my stomach. Miccah's big, billboard appeared, showing a huge steak, shrimp, crab legs, and a wine bottle. We turned into the parking lot and found a slot near the door. Alan killed the motor, leaving us in silence. His hands still gripped the wheel. The motor pinged as it cooled.

"I know it's too soon for you Ash. But I'm interested in you not as a nurse or a rescuer, and certainly not as a contractor or developer. I'm interested in you as a woman. I won't push. I promise. But I'll be around. And when you *are* ready, well, I'll be here." He looked at me then and I met his eyes. My flush faded. I gripped my hands in my lap; they suddenly felt cold. "I promised you a salad and a business conversation. Still game?"

I nodded, recognizing the confusion that had claimed me with his words. What was I supposed to say to his confession? What was I supposed to feel? Alan came around and opened my door, stepping back so I could slide to the gravel parking lot. In silence, we entered Miccah's, the long whistle of the train piercing the night.

Over a bottle of wine and a couple of Miccah's shrimp scampi salads, heavy on the garlic, Alan asked pointed questions about the accepted ways of doing business in Dawkins County. Questions about the capabilities of subcontractors and job site supervisors and the poli-

tics of small town business. I offered what answers I could. Though
Alan probed delicately, I couldn't discuss my worries about DavInc and
about the threats against Jas and myself. We did discuss the standing
water problem at the golf course and the methods I was employing to
deal with it, but we never mentioned potential permit problems at the
project, and we reached no conclusions. The conversation became no
more personal.

It was only on the way home that I realized several things. The one
hour I had expected to spend had stretched to nearly two. And I had
enjoyed myself far more than I should have. The words Alan had
spoken came back to me as the miles of darkness swept by. *"We have a
lot in common."* It was true. We did. And I'd had a good time with Alan
Mathison. As we passed the old Holiness to God Freewill Evangelical
Baptist Church, I finally broke the silence. "Alan?"

"Um?"

"We never did solve your standing water problem in the Taylor
development, did we?"

He laughed low, his chuckle soft, a contented sound. In fact, it
sounded just like I felt. Warm and— "Nope. But then, Jack was putting
in a golf course when he had drainage problems. I have to worry solely
about housing and the situation is different. I would appreciate any
thoughts you might have, but another day."

"Okay." The only thing I knew about Jack's business had *something
to do with murder.* But that was something I couldn't say to Alan. "I'll
mention it to Macon, see if he has any ideas."

Alan reached over and squeezed my fingers. "Thanks Ash. I'll
admit I want this development to succeed for the most selfish of
reasons. And it will be a lot easier to accomplish if I have your help." He
squeezed my hand a second time before turning into Chadwick Acres,
not releasing it to complete the turn. He slowed the car as we passed the
upscale brick homes and manicured lawns, as if he wanted to prolong
the moments left to us. And he slowed even more as gravel ground
beneath the tires in my drive, his hand warm and my feelings tumbling.

The security lights blinded us as he parked the Nissan, turned the
key, and sat back in his seat. I could feel his eyes on me. "Ash, if you
ever want to talk about what's bothering you, you can. To me. Not as a
competitor, but as a friend." I nodded, feeling the burn in my face, the
frantic pace of my heart. He pulled me to him across the bench seat and
pressed his lips against mine. My blush faded away. His lips moved
against mine, his tongue stroking the place where they met, still closed.
And I felt a curious . . . nothing. After a moment, I gently pressed my
open palm against his chest and pulled away. "Good night, Alan."

Breathless, I slipped from the truck and ran to the deck. I stood in the shadows as his truck pulled down the drive.

The warmth of his touch was still on my skin when I walked into my house and discovered the break-in. My home had been burgled. I instantly realized that I hadn't set the brand new fancy alarm system. They don't work if you don't turn them on. *I'm an idiot.* Tears in my eyes, I walked through the house.

The thieves had been thorough. They had broken a window and climbed in. It hadn't been difficult. I had forgotten to leave Esther a note reminding her to set the alarm when she left for the turkey-shoot, and as it wasn't Esther's job to remember, she hadn't. Foolish, foolish, foolish of me. My eyes burned as I looked around at the destruction. They had made off with Jack's big screen TV, the smaller TVs from the bedrooms, the office computer, the broken adding machine, and the answering machines. They even took Jack's golf bag and his clubs. I stared at the empty place where they had stood, in the way, and felt tears gather. It was as if with the golf bag gone, Jack was really gone as well.

The silver from the dining room was gone, all of my jewelry from the bedroom, both the costume and the flashier pieces, and Jack's gun collection had been taken too, the locked cabinet broken open, splintered. Of my jewelry, only the pieces stored in the safe had escaped theft.

The thieves had made an attempt on the safe. There were bore holes around the combination wheel drilled by a fairly competent safe-cracker. The safe had withstood the assault, as Jack had known it would. The surface of the safe was scarred, however, as if the frustrated safecracker had beaten it with a crowbar.

I stood in the center of the office, surveying the mess they had made, expecting somehow that there would be more destruction than there was. But there was only the smashed front of the gun cabinet, papers scattered across the house, and a little mud scuffed at the back door.

Macon, Wicked, Bish and Jas were there, waiting for me. Our insurance agent had come and gone as had the police, both showing little concern, both leaving blank lists to be filled out with the missing items. The extra cars were parked in front of the office on the other side of the house, shielded from the drive when Alan had kissed me.

Sitting in a kitchen chair was Bret McDermott. He had heard the call over the police scanner and had driven out to lend his support. That was his claim. But Bret seemed to be near me whenever I had trouble. He looked at me strangely when I came in alone and late. The look made me feel guilty, as if I had committed a sin. As if he knew of the intimacy I had shared with Alan. Of that kiss. Yet, he said nothing. He walked closely behind me as I wandered through my violated home to survey the damage and loss. Warily, I accepted his presence, wondering why he was really here. With Dixon in jail, was the investor behind it all finally coming forward to handle things personally?

I said little, crunching broken glass beneath my boots, running a finger through black fingerprint dust remaining on the china cabinet, staring dry-eyed and empty into my bare jewelry box. I shivered as if with cold, because Bret was there. Surely Bret hadn't hired Dixon. Surely. I wished he would go away. I was afraid of him. I no longer knew who he was.

Instead he hung around, helped fill out the paperwork, poured me a glass of wine I didn't want, and generally made himself conspicuous. Close to two A.M., I made him leave. Him, Macon, and Wicked, who no longer needed my nursing skills, locking them all out of my unsafe home and setting the alarm before falling into bed, numb and exhausted. And finally after the long day of publicly displayed strength, I gave way to tears.

"Mom?" Jas woke me at six-thirty, the clock by my bed giving lie to the darkness of my room. A thin gray light brightened the windows only faintly; rain thundered down on the roof outside, sounding as if a waterfall emptied itself onto the roof. I pulled the covers over my head hoping Jas would just go away. It was a great day to sleep in. "Mom." She shook my shoulder. "Mama, I have to go to Charlotte. To the airport."

I lowered the covers, finding her in the half-light. Already she smelled of horses. "Why?" my mouth was dry and uncooperative, the result of wine with shrimp scampi salad. I was surprised Jas could stand to be so close to me. I slid my tongue over teeth that were wearing fuzzy slippers. Vile. Positively vile.

"Elwyn is coming. You remember me saying I had written him?"

I nodded trying to place the name. Elwyn was the world-class trainer, I remembered. Elwyn Van something. The one Jas was willing to leave her horses with when she went off to college. The one who would eventually take her and Davenport Downs to world-class competition. "Yeah. So?"

"His plane lands in an hour. His letter accepting my offer was lost in the mail and took forever getting here. Anyway, it came yesterday while we were at the turkey-shoot. He accepted and he's on the way now. So I'm going to pick him up. Okay?"

"Take Bish," I said as I pushed up from the pillows. Jas sat back away from me and I didn't blame her one bit.

"Okay. And when I get back, we need to talk. About Bish and the beach trip, and stuff."

I didn't particularly like the "and stuff" part, but I nodded, and Jas bounced off the bed.

"Great. And Mom, would you have the cleaning crew clean out the extra guest room? The salary I promised Elwyn included board for the first three months. I'll be back in a couple of hours. Bye!"

And Jas was gone, taking with her the cleaner scent of horses and the answer to a very important set of questions, one of which was "What salary?" Another, "Who's supposed to pay it?" But then I figured I knew the answer to that one anyway. Me. Throwing off the covers, I headed for a shower and toothbrush, both of which I desperately needed. Carefully, I kept my gaze from the empty jewelry box. It was still dusty, smeared with fine powder left by the police.

Jimmy Ray was at work this morning, moving slowly and favoring his head, but getting the horses fed and into their respective pastures in the pouring rain. He had worked all day the day before, following a list left by Jas, directing his diminutive helpers, Duke and Disa, through the schedule. Neither had been kicked in the head and killed, none of the horses had been over-fed and gone colicky, and the barn hadn't burned down, all of which made yesterday a success.

Today was similarly successful, albeit muddy, with the single exception of an encounter between Mabel's teeth and Duke's shoulder. The aging mare had previously reserved judgment on whether or not Duke was a man, and while she kept a wary eye on him, had not shown her usual man-hating tendencies. In the half-light of dreary morning she finally decided that Duke was a member of the hated species. When Duke got too close to her colt, Mabel snorted, lunged, and nipped at Duke with all the ferocity of a protective mother. I was too far away to intervene and managed only a gasp. Duke jumped back, Mabel's big teeth leaving a raspberry abrasion as they snapped together.

At which point, Duke dropped Mabel's lead. The canny old mare took the rare opportunity for a quick gambol down the driveway, her colt at her heels. I released my indrawn breath. Duke and I exchanged longsuffering sighs. "Stay here," I said. "I'll get her."

While Jas could have caught and retrieved Mabel quickly, it was a long drawn-out process for me to get her back to the barn. After an hour of cajoling, chasing through the rain offering treats and threats indiscriminately, I finally got her locked safely in her stall. Leaning my spine against the locked door, breathing like a bellows, and dripping rainwater steadily into the clean hay at my muddy feet, I allowed myself a rare daytime tear. The reason for my self-pity was ridiculous. After all that had happened, the threats, the misery, the fear, I was missing my dogs.

It was the first time I'd really missed the playful Hokey and Herman. The first time I even allowed myself to admit I loved the frisky mutts. It had been the two dogs' job to herd reluctant horses where humans wanted them to go. Except for eating me out of house and home, entertaining me with doggie antics, and contributing to the flea problem, herding had been their talent, taught to them by Jack and Big Dog, who was still recuperating.

I tilted my head back, staring overhead, the shape of the opening to the loft wavering in my tears. Perhaps one of Cherry's brood could be trained to herd. Dogs worked better on cattle than on horses, but they were still a great help on a horse farm. One of Cherry's pups showed every sign of having been sired by a large-sized dog, his feet already like saucers and his ears nearly dragging the ground. The thought of the puppies cheered me somewhat, and, wiping my eyes on a sleeve, I trudged back to work.

I spent the morning at the barn and lunch at Nana's tending to her itching foot, trying to convince her not to remove the cast with a ball-peen hammer. Early afternoon was dedicated to showing Elwyn around the barn, the grounds, and the books. With the computer gone, the books for Davenport Downs were relatively simple—the hard copies stored in an upstairs bedroom.

The rest of the day I spent with Macon. It was another day of problems, typical small calamities, but the ones brought to me by Macon were by far the worst. His first words to me were, "I've been looking for days, but I still can't find the necessary permits from the Corps of Engineers to move earth or build around Prosperity Creek. It's possible Jack never got them."

It was a bald, uncompromising accusation. Even *I* knew this would be a far worse problem than Mabel playing tag down the driveway. I sank down on a kitchen chair, putting my head in my hands and resting them on the tabletop. *Why had Jack done this to me?* "What are we going to do about it?" I finally asked, my words echoing in the hollow of my arms.

"I've already asked for all the part-time people who fill in at the office to come here, under the direction of Donaleen, the paralegal who does our title search work. With the extra help, I'll be going through every piece of paper turned over to me by RailRoad the Third. Donaleen is going directly to the source, and find out if the Corps has anything on file. It means alerting them to the possibility of a problem, but we have little choice, Ash."

I nodded and lifted my head. "What are the ramifications if Jack didn't file a development plan with the Corps?"

"Steep fines. And I mean really steep. Steep enough that you might have to have political clout to work around them. But that's not all. I think you should see this."

I followed Macon to the office, which was marginally neater and cleaner now, since Esther and the cleaning crew had been to work for hours. The burglars had left a mess, and Esther had obviously spent the morning reorganizing her office after the most recent ransacking.

Macon led me to the safe, which now hung open. "Esther and I went through the safe when you hired me, but only a cursory examination. This morning we went through it thoroughly. We found these." *These*, were the metal canisters that had stood in the safe for ages, and a small stack of official looking papers. I looked up at Macon. Esther, dressed in a vibrant pink outfit, stood in the doorway, pad in hand. Her expression was somber. She was wearing shoes. Somehow, that alarmed me more than her serious demeanor. "Ash. How long have these canisters been in here?" Macon asked.

"They were the first things Jack put inside. That and my good jewelry."

Macon sighed and knuckled his kinky hair with a fist. "I think they point to the murdered inspector. And by the way, Wicked's been here to disable the listening devices. I don't know what anyone would make out about our discovery by what we've said this morning, but I didn't want anyone knowing the full extent of this. Any use you might have put the bugs to is forfeit, but you need security more. Wicked was putting together an operation to draw out the bigwigs behind Dixon, but even he agreed. This takes precedence."

"Sit down, Ashlee," Esther said, guiding me to a chair. I sat. "Now, you let Macon explain it all, honey. And then we'll find a way to deal with it. It'll be alright." Esther's mothering me in the same way she once mothered Jack was reassuring *and* frightening. It reminded me that Jack was gone, and that whatever they told me rested squarely on me. Alone.

"The soil sample containers are the kind used by DHEC to inspect core drillings on land that changes hands for development. For example, at Davenport Hills, Jack called in DHEC to do a large-scale inspection of the soil before he could do *anything* else. And the soil had to pass the inspection. *The soil itself*, Ash."

"Okay," I said. But I didn't understand and they both knew it.

"I'm talking wetlands, Ash. When land anywhere is developed for the first time, it has to be proven *not* to be wetlands."

"You mean the drainage problems?"

"No," he said. "A high percentage of Dawkins' land is blackjack, with drainage problems, especially near creeks. I'm talking about official *wetlands*, the kind protected by the Federal Government." Suddenly I remembered my dreams. Jack telling me about the ground.

"Every developer has to submit a plan to DHEC and request an inspection. *First.* Before anything else. If the soil is proven to be wetlands, the development can't go through. Period. Under the current Washington administration it's almost impossible to develop wetlands. But the point is this. Jack got the land inspected as per regulations. The inspector's name was Charles Whitmore. And he died shortly after the inspection."

"How shortly?" I asked, feeling a familiar dread settle around me. I had lived with the soil canisters for so long that I never really saw them anymore when I went into the safe. And these tall metal canisters were the evidence we had needed?

"He inspected the land on a Tuesday. He died the following Friday night. His soil samples and a typed report were found on the secretary's desk the next Monday morning when she got back from a long weekend. He died in a one car accident and his blood alcohol level was three times the legal limit."

I must have looked confused, because Macon elaborated.

"Charles was an alcoholic but he'd been on the wagon for years. And he never—never, Ash—typed his own reports. His secretary did. The secretary was so suspicious, she made another inspector compare the soil samples with the final report. They matched. The soil was suitable for development."

I shook my head. It sounded as if everything was fine. Charles started doing his own typing. So what was this problem that had Esther wearing shoes as if this were a funeral?

"This is a copy of the report his secretary found on her desk." Macon handed it to me and I flipped through the pages. All neatly typed. "And this is what Esther and I found in the safe, with the soil sample containers. It wasn't an actual report, just handwritten notes, so we both overlooked it the first time we went through the contents." Macon handed me a yellow legal pad, edges curled with age, the pages covered with diagrams and chicken scratch any doctor would have been proud of. There were four small maps as well, covered with notations. I didn't bother to read it. I rested both reports on my lap, waiting.

"This *handwritten* report is very negative, Ash. It states that Charles found large portions of the old plantation and the farms that now make up Davenport Hills were unsuitable for development. I have a contact in DHEC who owes my father a favor. She's going to fax him a sample of Whitmore's handwriting if she can find one."

"But if the soil samples matched the report . . ." I started.

"They did. But these are the samples Charles Whitmore actually collected, Ash. They are numbered as to where he collected them, and they have his initials on the stickers. The small maps and handwritten report matches the canisters. The notes are in the same handwriting as the report. I think someone killed Charles. And switched the reports, the samples, the maps, everything. I think Davenport Hills is wetlands, Ash."

"Jack knew," I said softly.

"Yeah. He had to. Perhaps even Bill McKelvey, your telephone admirer, knew. Or at least guessed. And that was why he said he could ruin Jack in court."

"And the Davenport Hills development . . ."

"Is a done deal, which in some ways may help our case. Every part of the property has felt the blade of landscapers and earthmovers. The land is radically damaged. Eighty percent of the development is complete. That puts a whole new spin on the problem." Macon was poker faced, his tone giving no indication what he was feeling. "And lastly, Jack is dead."

I shook my head. Macon was feeding me so much information I couldn't process it all. Wetlands? I pressed my lips together tightly to hold in thoughts I wasn't ready to speak.

Macon smiled then, a hard, brutal smile. "Having a state senator as an investor could help here, as long as the press doesn't notice and start screaming about political cover-ups and favoritism. Senator Waldrop could intervene and smooth things out for DavInc and Davenport Hills. So long as you and he are bosom buddies. Or perhaps cookie buddies."

Realizing Macon had been talking to Nana, I shook my head and offered one of my mother's smiles, a sickly unconvincing attempt that never reached my eyes. The expression reminded me of Reverend Perry's visit, and the paltry smile faded. "I'll start baking cookies."

Macon laughed. It wasn't the same laugh he had brought to work on his first day here. It was older, strained, fierce, and worn, as if his time here had aged him. On his face was an expression I had often seen on the faces of my Chadwick kin, familiar, protective, stern, and strong. It said, "This is family, and family sticks together." It was also an expression I had seen once before on my cousin's face. Years ago, on the day I last remembered seeing him before all this began, standing thigh-deep in the big swimming pond, his fists on his hips. Suddenly, that day came flooding back, fragile and uncertain, softened at the edges.

The Chadwick's and our strange "color scheme" had been accepted by most of Dawkins County. The fact that we were multi-racial and shared certain genetic patterns back a few generations wasn't universally liked but was ordinarily tolerated, for the political and financial power of our family, if not for more personal reasons. Under normal conditions we had no trouble with the less broad-minded citizens, but that hot, dry day had been an exception.

Wallace, two of his half-brothers, and a sister, Willie Mae, Uncle Horace's granddaughter Mindy, and I were taking a break from the heat, swimming in a pond fed by a creek that was still running. Elsewhere it had been dry for weeks and the ponds on neighboring farms were drying up, the earth cracking open, the crops baking in the fields. Cattle and chickens were suffering from the heat. Several surrounding farmers faced ruin if rain didn't come soon.

The tension had reached a boiling point in local bars where fights had broken out over little or nothing. There had been a murder/suicide of one farmer and his wife, and the stress and frustration had been clear even to us children. Hence the whoops and hollers and splashing and general roughhousing as we younger Chadwicks let off steam. Unfortunately, the noise level had attracted three neighborhood boys, out hunting quail in the off-season.

They had cornered Mindy in the shallow water, the older boy pulling at her bathing top talking dirty and threatening my blonde-haired, blue-eyed cousin. The two younger boys stood knee deep in mud and pond water, two air-rifles held on us Chadwicks as we watched Mindy and her tormentor. Helpless, all of us. Until Macon hit one of the young guards with a well placed rock thrown overhand, hard.

The resulting fray had left the three interlopers with black eyes, broken noses and mud-clogged gun barrels. The outgunned Chadwicks won a decisive victory, celebrating with a watermelon stolen out of Aunt Mosetta's garden, and Macon had been the hero. Proud. Protective. Stern. Standing in the center of the pond, smiling that lopsided smile. His expression back then had been like now. A Chadwick, responding to a threat against family. Strange that I hadn't remembered that incident, that moment, until now.

"I'm not saying you have to kiss the old goat's backside or even feed him cookies, I'm saying you might have to pull a Nana on him."

I cocked my head.

Macon chose his words carefully. "Explain to him the unquestioned benefits of lending his support with DHEC and the Corps of Engineers before this problem becomes a press problem. He'll know the part about journalistic investigation should he not handle this thing well, of course, but as an investor, his butt's in the sling already. If he doesn't help us, and we have problems, he'll be nailed to the wall with us. Something like that. Get the point?"

"I think so," I said, seeing the young Macon so clearly in the grown man standing before me. "But, Macon, what if Waldrop was one of the investors involved with the murder?"

"So what? If he screwed up that big, he can take his lumps along with the rest of us." It was a callous remark, reminding me of the child Macon, rock in hand. I shook my head and put the reports to the side. The idea of dealing with Vance Waldrop like Nana would was terrifying. Perhaps I should bring along a plate of cookies, just in case.

"Of course, I may yet uncover the paperwork for the Corps, so don't make any plane reservations for DC just yet. But do keep it in mind."

I nodded. "I'll do that. You need anything right now?"

"More space. Can we use the living room?"

I seldom thought about the living room, the twenty-five by nineteen foot space where Jack and I entertained important guests and had the social functions necessary to running DavInc. It was the location of the company Christmas parties. I hadn't been in there since Jack died. "Help yourself. TVs gone, of course, thanks to our robbers, but you can bring in tables, chairs, whatever you need. Rent them if you like."

Macon nodded, his eyes searching mine. He was watching me closely, studying me, and I didn't like the expression on his face. "When's the last time you got a full night's sleep, Ash?"

"1982. Jasmine had the flu and I got it from her. Slept twelve hours straight," I said, the comeback snappy and quick. "You never get a full night on a farm, Macon. You know that. I'm lucky if I get six hours."

"Ash. You look like hell. Have you glanced in a mirror lately?" His voice was gentle. Concerned. And that should have made me feel reassured, more secure, but it didn't. It made me angry. Coldly, unreasonably angry.

"No. But I've looked in Jack's gun cabinet and my silver chest. Into my jewelry box and into Jasmine's eyes. I've looked down at Jack's headstone, and into my husband's illegal business dealings. I've held my daughter while she cried, and walked through an empty house and slept in a lonely bed. Something's gone from them all, Macon." I stood, pushing against the table with my hands. "My life isn't what it once was. I'm not who I once was. Everything is changed. You can't expect me to look like a beauty queen after all this."

"Ash, I'm not denying all that. But you could pass for Frankenstein's wife about now. You need rest."

"I agree. And when Jasmine and her future are safe, I'll get some. I promise." I walked away from Macon, back toward my room and the solitude I could find there. "Let me know about DHEC and the Corps of Engineers and what you discover."

"Yeah. Sure."

"Night, Macon."

"Night, Ash."

Elwyn VanHuselin and Bish were now both living in my house. The sound of running water indicated that Elwyn was showering off the effects of travel and a day spent traipsing through Carolina red mud. Bish was folding his laundry, his door open. And Jas was sitting on the edge of his bed, watching, her face winsome and fresh and soulful. And very much in love. She didn't see me slip back down the stairs and into my room. I didn't announce myself. When I stepped out of the shower, long, hot, steamy minutes later, Nana was sitting on the vanity seat I seldom used, her cast propped up on the tub. She held an untwisted metal coat hanger, stretched out, in her right hand; the far end of the long metal wire buried beneath her cast. Scratching.

I wrapped up in a towel, tossing a second one over my head. "You moving in too?" I asked. It sounded surly, even rude, but I didn't care, I was too tired to care anymore.

A strange grin spread across Nana's face. She continued to scratch. "My, aren't we touchy," she said laconically. "You do have a houseful."

I rubbed the towel over my wet hair, blocking her out. Found a terrycloth bathrobe and pulled it on. With my back turned, I shaved my legs. I hadn't shaved them since the symphony so it took a while. All that time, I ignored Nana. And all the time I ignored her, she was smiling that strange toothy smile. I know. I peeked at it in the various bathroom mirrors. It never wavered.

Nana sipped from a mug. It had the words "I'm not old. I'm just grouchy!" printed on the rim, over a likeness of the actress who starred in the movie *Throw Mama From The Train*. It fit Nana, especially tonight, the peculiar expression on her face. Beside her was a second mug, a refill or one for me. I would have ignored it too, except it smelled so good. "You want to tell me why you're so touchy tonight? I mean, besides the obvious reasons of grief and exhaustion and no sleep."

"Not really," I said, dropping one towel and pulling a comb through my hair. The mug held chicken soup. Homemade. Thin broth with noodles nesting in the bottom and herbs floating. Fragrant steam rose toward me. It smelled wonderful. I put down the comb and secured my hair back with long pins. Dabbed my face with night cream. Macon was right, I did look awful. Bruised crescents hollowed under my eyes. My cheeks were sunken in below bony protuberances and I had developed a sharp vertical line between my brows. I smoothed more night cream into my face, as if by pampering my skin tonight, I might make up for weeks of neglect.

The mug of soup had scented the entire bathroom. It smelled heavenly. My stomach rumbled. "That for me?" I finally asked, my voice gruff and curt. It was the same tone I'd used as a child the one time Nana had slapped my face. Sassy, she'd called me. And though she didn't slap my face this time, she didn't answer either. Just cocked a brow. I cleared my throat and tried again. "The soup smells really good. Is it for me?"

"Yep," Nana said, wasting no words. "But I'd stir it up first."

I noticed the spoon and a napkin on the sink edge, stirred, and sipped. The soup was delicious, even the hint of bitterness from the floating herbs. Sage, maybe, and tarragon, some parsley. Wonderful. I ate fast and slurped the last noodle out of the bottom. I was still hungry. I rinsed the mug at the sink and used it to drink a glass of water and then another.

"Thought so."

I lowered my mug, brows raised.

"You didn't stop to eat today did you, my girl?"

"It was a busy day, Nana—"

"And as if that wasn't bad enough, you didn't bother to drink any water either, did you?"

"Well . . ." I stopped, surprised. It was true. I'd taken time to water the horses, but hadn't bothered to drink any myself. All day.

"You're dehydrated. That's why you look like hell."

I turned to Nana. "Macon's been telling tales, hasn't he?"

"Yep. He come to the house right after y'all talked. You drink some more water. A couple of those should make a start on rehydrating you."

I drank six mugs-full just to show Nana I meant to take care of myself. All but the last two were vaguely chicken flavored. My stomach felt full beneath the robe, taut and rounded. And, strangely, I was suddenly sleepy. It had been a long time since I had been sleepy. I yawned.

"Go on. Get in bed, my girl," Nana said. "Moses said you'd sleep if I fed you some chicken soup. I'd have thought whiskey would work better, but maybe she's right this time."

I yawned again and nodded, finding my bed in the semi-dark room. Without even pulling down the covers, I crawled in and closed my eyes. I never noticed when Nana left. The next thing I knew, it was daylight again.

Feeling more like my old self, I rose, drank half a dozen glasses of water, dressed, ate a muffin and two fresh peaches, skin and all, and beat Jas to the barn. I didn't want to work in the office today, and I certainly didn't want to go to the development that was the source of all my problems. I wanted to bury myself here, in the uncomplicated joys of barn and horse.

By early afternoon, Jas, Bish, Elwyn, and I had worked up powerful appetites. Jas had always worked like a fiend when surrounded by her horses and Bish took his cue from her, straining his muscles and working up a sweat. Elwyn was a surprise. He rolled up his sleeves and pitched right in, not even seeming to mind that he was working with workhorses instead of his more elegant Hackneys. He helped Jas put the horses through their paces, made good suggestions on which horses should be sold to make room for more, curried, fed, hosed down and chased just like the rest of us. He seemed determined to make this his new home.

Elwyn was a diminutive man, blond-haired, small-boned, and quick. He moved like a bird, always searching out the next chore, discovering where tack and medicines and feed were located. Claiming the hard copies of the horse's records to study until we could replace the computers. I admitted to myself as I watched him work that I hadn't expected to like him, but I did, very much. And Jas thought the sun set on his shoulders, which was all that really mattered.

Nana, Aunt Mosetta, Wicked, Topaz, Esther, Macon, and the crew from Macon's office joined us for lunch, and Elwyn put away enough KFC to feed two men twice his size. The moment Macon and the legal types returned to work, and Wicked went back to whatever he was doing, Jas and Topaz sprang their latest plans on me.

"Mom, Paz and Bish and I are going to the beach today. Well, tonight actually. That is, if you'll trust us enough to let us go down and spend the night alone? Cause Mama Pearl can't come until tomorrow, and you know you've been trying to get us to go, even making Bish work to get us there, which I think was really low, but then I'm not a mother. So can we?" Jas asked, both accusing and begging at once. Typical teen. I'd be glad when she outgrew this stage.

I took a sip of Diet Coke and put down my chicken leg. I waited to answer, feeling a little proud of myself. The old Ashlee would have felt guilty at Jas' little speech and hastened to make everything right, kowtowing to teenage emotional blackmail. The new Ash resisted manipulation.

"Is this your way of asking me to do you a great big favor or your way of complaining?"

Jas looked up at me, surprised. "Well, I mean . . ." She stopped, stunned. The silence in the kitchen was absolute. After a long moment, Topaz spoke. "Mamash, would you consider letting us go to the beach without a chaperone?" Trust Paz to cut right to the heart of the matter.

"To be honest, you girls are old enough. But because Dixon hasn't given away who his boss is, and because the bail hearing is set for Tuesday, and because he'll be free soon, you need a chaperone. And although Bish carries a gun, he's young. No substitute for Mama Pearl or me. So. This time, no."

I thought I had done rather well with that explanation, sidestepping the over protective, apron strings accusation I could sense was coming next, and offering justification for my decision. I rewarded myself with a nice big bite of my drumstick. I wanted Jas away when Dixon was let out of jail, but I didn't want her alone in an empty house with Bish. Topaz was no chaperone for that kind of situation, though I was wise enough not to say so.

"So will you drive with us to the beach, help open the house, and stay with us for a couple of nights?" Jas asked sweetly.

Checkmate. "You little stinker," I said with a breath of laughter. "You've been talking to Nana. She wants both of us gone when Dixon gets out of jail."

"Told you so, Jasmine. Those two old women been stickin' their noses in all kind of things, tryin' to get things done their way," Topaz said, disgruntled.

I smiled back, my mother's cookie-eating smile. "However, since I want you gone too, I'd be delighted to chaperone you to the beach. When do we leave?" And so it was that I left my house to the care of Elwyn VanHuselin, a thin-bodied stranger with the familiar smell of horse about him, and a brogue that seemed to calm the horses and Jas better than anything I had ever seen. I had no doubt that Jas would never have gone to the beach if it hadn't been for Elwyn's presence at Davenport Downs. I owed the little man.

My life was taking sudden turns, quick, jerky changes left and right, leaving me feeling like a soldier dodging bullets on a battlefield. Perhaps the analogy was apt. Until Dixon's boss was in jail and Jack's business problems were solved, I was on the defensive and in danger.

I might have resisted Jasmine's ploy and forced the girls to remain at home another day had Stinky Dixon not been getting out of jail.

Sheriff Gaskin had informed Macon they could no longer deny bail to the malodorous man. And although Dixon had given the sheriff the name he wanted, the sheriff refused to share it with my lawyer or me. Even Nana couldn't pry the information out of him. Not until they had investigated more and possibly charged the men involved. That's what he said. The *men* involved.

Macon had asked the sheriff for protection for Jas and me. C.C. had laughed as if Macon was making a joke in poor taste. "This is a poor county Macon. I don't have enough deputies to patrol the out-lying areas as it is. Sorry."

It was almost a shame how pleased my family was to see me getting out of town. The trip to the beach was unexpected and hastily planned, but it was critical to Jasmine's safety. To keep Elwyn safe, we dropped Big Dog off at the vet and sent Cherry and the pups home with Duke and Disa for a few days. I hoped that time spent with the puppies would insure the mutts a good home. Sneaky, but so what?

I made a few calls, telling people I would be unavailable for a few days. Esther volunteered to check the personal line's answering machine while I was gone, as well as handle the daily running of the business. She was capable, and unnecessary guilt about the last break-in had made Esther agreeable to almost anything. I could leave everything in her hands. Wicked was pleased. He would have two days to work on security for the house and office and clean out the phone system, which was still bugged, without putting us in danger while he worked.

With the sun setting in the rearview mirror and the Volvo piled with linens and floats and collapsible beach chairs, I headed for Myrtle Beach—well, Surfside. Ahead of me Jas and Topaz rode in Topaz's Mazda, Bish drove his Corvette, and I was blissfully alone for the three hour trip to the beach. Not so, once there.

We had no more than driven up in the driveway when two other vehicles pulled up behind us. Three boys, two white, one black, piled out of the first car. Two black boys and three black girls climbed out of the second. A third and fourth car turned down the drive. Adolescent radar at work, the teenagers descended on us like ravening beasts, helping us carry the groceries to the house, then helping us discover what we'd brought. If I hadn't demanded the boys help finish the unloading, there wouldn't have been a chip or cola left. The rest of the night was pure teenage torture. It was after two A.M. before I ran the last visitor off and fell exhausted into my vacation bed. Mama Pearl loved the responsibility of taking the girls to the beach each year. Pearl could have it; I wanted my home. But at least Jas was safe. Dixon was getting out of jail soon; I could handle anything for the forty-eight hours until Pearl got there. At least that's what I told myself.

Lying in the dark of the vacation home, streetlights filtering through the shade casting half unfamiliar patterns on the ceiling, I thought of Jack. Perhaps it was the scent of briny air, or the soughing of the wind through stunted trees. Perhaps it was lying in the bed, the bed we had shared through so many beach vacations. Perhaps it was the absence of the golf bag that used to rest beside the sliding door each time we were here, but now were likely in some pawn shop, some other man gripping the custom made clubs. Like Jack, they were gone forever.

Perhaps it was all the changes in my life in the last few days. All the things I had found out about Jack's problems. All the changes in my household and living arrangements. Or perhaps it was Reverend Perry's prayer. Or this trip to the beach. Or Alan's kiss . . . Or, perhaps, it was simply time. Time to remember. Time to forgive. Time to grieve. So much had happened in the last weeks, so much discovered, so many awful revelations. So much of my life exposed as lies, stripped away, memories tainted by truth. Somewhere in all the lost dreams and hopes, was Jack. The Jack I thought I had known. The Jack I knew I had loved.

Tears pooled in the crevices of my face and trickled s lowly into my pillow. Warm, salty tears, not the hot, burning tears of anger, but real tears, real grief. It was a release, lying in the darkness on this half-familiar bed, my body tired, my mind confused, and I couldn't have said why. I only knew my anger was suddenly gone. I was free from it, liberated, as if shackles had been loosed around my heart; it took only resting in this bed, miles from home.

For weeks I had run from Jack, from his memory, from his loss, from his betrayal and the ugly truths of his hypocrisy and deception. I had become cold and hard and unfeeling, shutting away all the warmth I had felt when he was alive. Lying here, wide-awake in this bed, I knew I had been foolish. Discovering his infidelity with Robyn had only bruised my love for Jack, not destroyed it. I still had to deal with my loss. I still had to face the fact that he was gone, the fact that there could be no healing of my marriage. The fact that now, nothing would ever be resolved between Jack and me over Robyn. His death was irrevocable, unalterable fact. I missed him. His warmth curled against me in the night. His ready humor. His skill in dealing with the problems of our everyday lives. His certainty dealing with the bigger problems on the various developments.

He hadn't meant to die and leave me burdened with the situation at Davenport Hills. Perhaps he hadn't meant for me to discover the photos in his desk. But now both problems were mine to deal with and grieve over. Not Macon's or Esther's. Not Reverend Perry's. Not

Jasmine's. Mine. Mine alone. I wept quietly in the hours before dawn, curled into the crisp sheets, curled around Jack's pillow and my pain and loss. Wept for the love I had lost—the pure love Reverend Perry had prayed about. And because of the long lonely hours, a healing finally began. I discovered a peaceful place in my soul, a place I had forgotten, a place I hadn't visited in a long while. A place of prayer and serenity. Of stillness and calm. Near dawn, I slept.

With dawn, the rat-race of teenage visits began again.

After ten hours of teenagers and outdated rock and roll, soul, and hip-hop, Mama Pearl arrived. She was a day early, tooling up the drive in Jasmine's little truck, the bed loaded with more supplies. Her early arrival left me free to drive home if I wished. I gave her my little pearl handled 9mm, just in case my troubles had followed me here. Pearl accused me of being paranoid, which was true, but she took the gun. I packed my bag and left immediately.

Long, lonely hours of flat, sandy beach terrain, moss draped oaks, and tourist-y small towns, rolling sand-dune-hills, and then pine covered red mud hills flew by as I drove home. With each mile, I grew more certain of one thing. My lost life deserved my grief, as did my lost husband. My pain deserved the right to be experienced, felt, explored, and tasted. Jack may have been less than I thought him to be, but I had loved him and that love deserved mourning.

CHAPTER SEVENTEEN

I sat on the swing, swaying slowly in the dark, listening to the silence of the house, the calls of night birds, and crickets chirping. No radio or TV audio filtered through the house. No laughter of teenaged girls. Only the repetitive call of a whippoorwill, the far-off calls of owls, one to the east, one to the north. A distant dog's territorial barking. The occasional stamp of a horse in the barn, the sound transmitted on the still air. The soft groan of the swing supports. I hadn't turned on the security lights, and the full moon made unaccustomed shadows in the yard and against the house. I didn't listen to the answering machines. I simply sat in the silence of the porch, surrounded by the soft sounds of my world.

Elwyn had gone out, after explaining that the phones were out of order. Wicked had been running checks on the system and, because no one expected me back, hadn't finished.

I should have been concerned about security, sitting in the dark, but no one knew I was here. No one knew I was alone. This gave me protection as much as the alarm system I had activated when Elwyn left. Eventually, I would go out to the car for the cell phone and the second gun locked in the glove box, the extra 9mm in its ill-fitting holster. In my one trip from the car, I had carried luggage, not my small portables. I was safe, sitting in the dark, strangely and peacefully safe.

The moon hung low on the horizon, a silvered orb, glistening, dappled, and mysterious. So bright, it threw shadows, long and lean, the poplars striping the lawn like thin slits opening into the netherworld. Bats dipped and flitted, hunting. A luna moth, silver-green in the night, beat its wings disconsolately against the screen. Dying. It seemed that around me everything was dying or leaving me to face the night alone. My mouth twisted wryly. *Such morbid thoughts.* Not like me, not really, just the aftershock of leaving Jas at the beach, driving away from the seascape without her. Driving away and coming home to an empty, silent house. Morbid, but normal. Just like it was normal for night birds to call and crickets to sing and luna moths to die. The moths, so delicate and elusive, don't even have a digestive system. They live long enough to mate and die, about twenty-four hours. It was *normal* for it to die so young. But not normal for Jack. A man was supposed to live at *least* to his early seventies. Especially one who didn't smoke or drink to excess and who exercised regularly. Jack had been an anomaly. Dying young.

Leaving me to uncover his secrets one by one, the deceptions of his business life, the deceptions of our marriage. Paying the price, as he had taught me so long ago.

A truck turned into the long drive, the smooth purr of its engine pulling off the road announcing a visitor as clearly as a phone call would have. I sighed, knowing somehow exactly who it was. Alan. He had called before I left, wanting to talk, and I had put him off, as I had put off Bret McDermott and Monica who still wanted to take me to lunch. None of the three had been happy about waiting, proclaiming worry for me in my grief. I had promised to call each of them as soon as I returned from the beach. I hadn't. I didn't want to. This wasn't the night to deal with unpleasantness. This wasn't the night to cause disruption in my unexpected, tranquil peace. I needed this night alone, to come to terms with my sudden and startling emotional evolution. I had to deal with my feelings about Jack before I could deal with other's feelings about me.

Alan wanted something from me. Something I wasn't ready to give. Perhaps it was easier for men to set aside their grief, to put away feelings and get on with their lives. Or perhaps Alan's marriage had been as empty he claimed, dead long before the accident that plunged their car off the road into the creek bed. Maybe he was ready for a new relationship.

But I wasn't. Jack hadn't been all I'd thought he was. In many ways, the man I loved had been a lie. But my love had been real, and, for all its weakness, so had his love for me. Love doesn't die easily. And so I wasn't ready for Alan. Not yet. Perhaps not ever. The Nissan truck pulled up behind the house, its lights off before it rounded the curve in the drive. The engine died into silence, parked between my Volvo and Jack's Jeep.

I thought about slipping into the house and pretending to be gone or asleep early, but both options were just lies and cowardice. I might as well get it over with now. No sense in putting off the inevitable, although I did suddenly understand the attraction of a Dear John letter.

"Ash? Is that you?" Alan shaded his eyes and squinted into the darkened screened porch, finding the motion of the swing in the moonlight. "I called Nana. She said she talked to Jas, and that you were coming back tonight."

I sighed. "I'll get the door." Bringing the swing to a standstill I walked through the kitchen to the door in the dark. I deactivated the security system, inserted my keys into the deadbolt lock and opened the door.

Standing with a boot on the bottom step, his hands in his pockets, Alan looked like a model for Levi jeans, his pale gold hair silvered by the moon, his face shadowed. I stepped back and he entered the dark kitchen. I hadn't turned on the light. "Pour you some tea?" I asked.

"Thanks."

I didn't meet his eyes, concentrating on my hands moving in the dark. Ice clattered into a glass. There was a faint brightness as I opened the fridge, and then the brighter light of the overhead which Alan switched on. The sound of tea as I poured; our footsteps as we walked back to the porch, my bare feet almost soundless, Alan's boots hollow on the wood floors.

And then he settled into the upholstered deck chair across from the swing, the thin hiss of the cushion's air escaping. I had company, yet I felt more alone than ever. I pushed off with my toe, setting the swing in motion again. Waiting. The scent of whiskey fumes crossed the distance between us, vague as the light, yet just as sharp. I was disappointed, somehow, that he had come to me after drinking.

"I've left messages. And then the phone rang all day. You didn't call me back."

It was an accusation, however politely phrased. I hoped this didn't get ugly. "I haven't been back long," I lied, sipping my tea. And then, because I lied, I felt the need to justify myself. "The phone's out, according to Elwyn. And I haven't checked the machine."

Alan said nothing, his eyes dark in the night. My guilt grew, though I hadn't led him on, had I? I hadn't played the tease. And I really didn't want to deal with this tonight. "I needed a break from driving before I went back out to the car for the cell. I haven't even called Jas to tell her I got back safely," I added truthfully, assuaging my conscience.

Night birds called again. The far-off dog barked. A sliver of the moon moved from behind a tree, lighting the porch. "Were you going to call?" he asked softly. "Ever?" The moonlight lit his face, lighting one side, throwing the other into darkest shadow. He looked sad. And something else. Determined? A determined suitor was something I didn't need. I sighed again and sipped my tea, playing for time. Because I didn't know the answer. Not really.

"We've been playing games long enough. Like the kids dancing at your Nana's house. Hokey Pokey, remember? One foot in, one foot out."

I nodded, mute in the darkness, feeling the moonlight exposing half of my soul to him.

"I want you, Ash, and I think you want me. It's time to quit playing games."

That was an odd way to describe our not-quite-relationship, but I knew what he meant. We had been to Miccah's several times, been together at events. We had embarked on a tentative friendship, questing, exploring one another, curious, half-hearted attempts to move forward. And there was that one kiss. Yet, I had held back, refused to reach for him, keeping secret that most private part of myself, giving him only morsels, exposing only bits and pieces, like the moonlight on our faces bared one half, cloaked the other. I had kept part of myself hidden. I sipped my tea. Alan drained his; set aside his empty glass. The clink of crystal against the concrete was a hollow sound. "Alan?"

"Yes," he finally answered.

"I like you. I do. But . . ." I sipped the last of my tea, lubricating my suddenly dry throat. Took a deep breath. "But I'm not ready. Jack's death is too new. Too fresh."

Abruptly I remembered the sound of earth as clumps thudded down onto Jack's coffin the day I buried him. Barren sounds, dull and vacant, as if the coffin was empty. As if Jack had somehow escaped after they closed the lid and was waiting somewhere close. Watching.

I remembered Alan's kiss, his lips moving on mine, warm. Too soon. It was too soon.

"I'm sorry," I said softly. "I'm not ready. I can't make any promises, Alan. I'm . . . sorry." I put my tea glass down gently in the shadows. The moon was higher, lifting to the edge of the porch roof. It wasn't quite as bright now. The bright half of Alan's face wasn't quite as sharp. Wasn't quite so easy to read. And strangely, he laughed. It was a low sound. Mocking.

I blinked into the dark, frozen, not knowing how to respond to the tone.

He stretched in the chair across from me, his arms over his head, his knuckles cracking. Stretching his arms out to either side, along the chair back and down the sides, he relaxed and laughed again. And the sound of his laughter raised the hair on the back of my neck.

"Well, that's too bad Ash. It would have been easier if you'd fallen for me. Less painful."

"Painful?"

"Ash, you're a bright woman. Quick. Sharp. Intelligent." The tone of his voice was like the tone of his laughter, amused, but with a lilt. Artificial. False. Almost . . . jeering? I was confused, as much by the words as by the shadows that transfigured his face. Light/dark. Silver/black. Good/evil.

"Where is it, Ashlee?" he asked. "You disconnected the listening devices, but before you did, I got enough information to deduce that you had found the evidence. I must have it back. Tonight."

The owl called again. Plaintive. "Who? Whoo? Whooo?" I felt dizzy, as if I had drunk wine, not tea. Alan tilted his head, throwing his face entirely into shadow. His voice dropped. Slow. Menacing. "Where is the original report, Ashlee? And the file, the one you supposedly don't have?" His hands moved up, one in shadow, one in light. Slowly. Toward me. "Where is it? Give it to me or—"

I was up and running before the threat could penetrate, before the words consciously made sense. With my first step, I knocked over my tea, the glass breaking, shattering the night.

"Ash!" *His* voice. For all these weeks. Disguised, but *his*. I could hear it now. *Where is it?* His was the threat. *Alan was Dixon's boss. But Alan wasn't an investor.* I made the doorway and turned right, for the study and Jack's gun cabinet. Remembering the sight of my dogs, cold and stiff, covered with black blood. The attacks by Dixon in the emergency room and the gazebo. Alan. Alan was Stinky Dixon's boss. Alan had done it all.

Behind me, I heard him trip, stumble, and curse, and a fresh tinkle of broken glass. His leg, I remembered. The muscles were still weak from the accident. *I could use that.* Odd thought. Not really real. I spun into the study, fell against the gun cabinet. Empty. "Oh, God." My heart thumped painfully against my chest.

The robbery. They had taken all the guns. *Alan.* Alan had taken all the guns.

All but the holstered 9mm locked in the car's glove box. And the shotgun in the barn.

Alan crashed into the study, sucking on his hand. Blood, black in the moonlight that filtered through the windows, stained his white shirt, smeared his jeans. So neat and starched, the creases precise and black with blood.

My keys. They were still in the back door, dangling from my key ring in the lock where I had left them when I invited Alan in. Without them, I couldn't get to the gun in the car. Our eyes met in the blackness before I turned and ran. Pulled open the outer door and escaped from the office into moonlit brightness that hid nothing. Panting, slipping on wet grass, I ran for the barn.

Shadows and silver light, harsh and deadly. Shadows that should have enchanted and turned the world into a magical place, instead were evil, hiding vicious secrets. Savage and ruthless. Exposing everything.

Hot sweat broke out down my torso. Wet and sticky. The night was silent, now. No owls, no crickets, no whippoorwill, no dogs barking.

Mine were dead or at the vet's. I should have left Big Dog here, Elwyn be damned. The grass was wet with dew, slick beneath my bare feet. A stone bruised my heel as I ran. A small branch, hidden by the shadows pricked, scratching tender skin. I hadn't gone barefoot in years. Irrelevant thought.

I ran for the path, my steps slower than the pounding of my heart. My breath was short, gasping, rough and burning. I found the path from the house to the barn. It was slick with mold and wet. Weeds had grown up between the cracks. Spindly things with colorless flowers that beat against my jeans. Jack always kept them clipped flat. Too long. Jack had been dead too long.

I rounded the curve, dashing into the shadows of the poplars Jack had left as a shield between the house and the barn. Dark, murky bands of blackness. The door to the house banged shut behind me. "Ash!" he bellowed.

I went down. Sliding in the damp. My feet, accustomed to the support of work boots, slid on the sheen of moss lining the slates. My legs went sharply out to the side. I fell. Hard. I heard the bone break, even as I landed. Quick and clean snap. My little toe. Fifth metatarsal, high up in the foot. I rolled through the too-tall grass, biting my lip. Screaming inside. But silent. My breath, so rough and tight, was the only evidence of the break. That was going to hurt.

Extraordinary concerns. Alan was going to kill me. And I was worried about a broken toe. The sound that finally escaped me was half-laughter, half-sob, silent in the night. I pushed to my knees, regained my feet, and limped on.

The door of the barn was secured with a simple block of wood and rope. The lock left undone now that Elwyn was here. The dogs had always been enough warning when a stranger was on the premises. We had never needed to secure the horses. Now I had no dogs. Limping, I pushed the block counterclockwise and shoved on the door. Safety.

The shot took me through the upper thigh. High on the outside. I felt the burning before I heard the report. A single crack, remarkably like the sound of my toe breaking.

The shock of pain drove me forward, into the barn and total blackness. I slammed shut the door. Turned the wooden block. Jamming home the sliver of wood that would hold it in place. For a few minutes. If I was lucky. I leaned my back against the rough wood of the barn wall. My leg was weak. Both numb and aching at once. Burning and icy. The denim of my jeans was wet with blood and dew. At least it was the same leg as the broken toe. I almost laughed again at the spurious thoughts. But the sound that vibrated past my lips was more groan.

I pushed away from the barn wall and took a step toward the tack room. The pain was like lightning. Quivering up my leg. Taking my whole left side in paralyzing heat. Dragging the leg, I reached the tack room door and grabbed at the catch. Felt the lock Wicked had applied only days past. Elwyn had locked this one. "Keys," I whispered. "The keys." I could picture them in the lock, dangling. Hear again the jingle as I closed the door before opening the fridge for tea.

A horse stamped in the darkness. A soft scrape at the door. *Alan.* There was another way in to the tack room and the shotgun hanging on the wall—from the hayloft and the hole in the upstairs floor through which hay and feed could be dropped to the feed troughs below. If I could make it up the ladder. If I could reach the shotgun from above. Or survive the drop into the room.

Horses snorted and moved in the confines of their stalls. Uneasy. Restless. Agitated by the unexpected late night visit. And the scent of gunpowder and blood. My blood. I clung to the latch and lock on the tack room, hoping it would somehow just open. Open sesame. I sobbed. Tasted salt and the metallic flavor of fresh blood. I had bitten my lip. The metal lock grew slick and hot in my hand. Behind me, the barn door rattled. "Ashlee?" It rattled again. Then silence.

And then a thunderous sound as he threw himself at the door. Bands of moonlight widened and vanished and appeared again as the door rattled. "Ash? Damn it, Ash, open this door!" The door rattled again as the bands of light did a little cha-cha. The horses shifted, anxious. "Damn it Ash, I don't want to hurt you."

Liar. The mares snorted. One stamped. Stamped again, signaling displeasure.

I could run. Or take a horse and slip out the back. If I could find a bridle in the blackness, get it over the head of a horse, get it on and get out. Fat chance. For the only time in my life, I regretted my refusal to take riding lessons.

Limping in the blackness, I touched the ladder. Pulled myself up one rung. Another.

Something dripped in the darkness of the barn. A steady drip-drip-drip sound. Distinct above the uneven sound of my breathing and the thudding of my heart and the increasingly frustrated sounds of the man at the door. Dripdripdrip. *My blood,* I realized. Running down my leg. Trickling to the floor of the barn. Taking with it my strength. I pulled up another rung. And another. Only five more left. Or was it six? I had never counted. Jas would have known—and thank God she wasn't here. Not tonight. I sobbed again. Remembered the last sight I had of her, standing on the grassy lawn by the beach house, watching me drive away.

My right leg pushed at the rungs, but the upward motion was all on my arms. A burning in my triceps and deltoids. A weakness, a running pain all over. As if my body were melting like wax. An acid pain. Another rung. Another.

"Ash!" The door banged open behind me. Dull light washed over the dark confines of the barn. The horses called out. Frightened sounds. Wood splintered as one kicked. Mabel. Protective of her foal. Snorting her threats.

I reached the loft. Pulled myself over in the darkness. Using my elbows and my good leg, I pulled myself through loose hay, easing my way behind stacked bales to the illusion of safety. Trying to be quiet. Trying not to scream with pain each time I scraped across the floor.

My fingers found the opening above the tack room. The tools Jimmy Ray used to feed the horses and clean the loft clinked, bumped by my elbow. The barn flooded with light. He had found the switch. But then, he had been here before. When he slaughtered my dogs. Alan and Dixon. "Ash. I know you're up there. I see the blood all over the floor and up the ladder. I guess I hit you, huh?" His voice was soft. Consoling. The soothing tones he had used when we talked about our dead spouses. *Liar.*

"Come on, Ash. You're bleeding. Come on down, sweetheart."

The tack room was faintly lit by filtered light. Saddle supports and softly gleaming leather were directly below the opening. The shotgun hung just above them. I stretched down. *Not even close.* I pulled my body out over the hole and stretched down again. Too low. Too low to reach. A cat, wary and distrustful, slunk beneath the saddles, tail twitching.

I needed to buy myself some time. "I'm not your sweetheart," I gasped. "And yes. Macon found the evidence. But it's too late. Too many people know about it now. About Charles Whitmore's death." I hooked my right foot around a roof support and lowered my body down, scratching on the wall. Straining for the shotgun. Gasping. Trying to ignore the stabbing of one of Jimmy Ray's tools beneath my ribs. Sweat dripped off the end of my nose. Blood pooled beneath me. Feverishly, I weighed my options.

If I lowered myself any further, I would loose my grip, feeble as it was. And if I lowered myself into the tack room feet first, then how would I get back up again? That is, if I survived the drop in the first place. Seconds had passed. Long seconds. What was he doing downstairs?

There was no way out of the tack room. I would have to use the shotgun to blow a hole in the hinges or the latch. Meanwhile, I would be a sitting duck. A good hunter's term. Much easier to hit than a flying duck. I had to keep moving. I pulled myself to the floor of the loft. Pushed at something stabbing my chest. Recognized the baling hook. The wooden handle was still warm from the heat of the loft. Warm and smooth. I levered myself up to a sitting position. Felt the ridge of a box at my back. The box holding the corrective hooves we had used on Annie Oakley.

"Come on, Ashlee. It's never too late. If there's no evidence, there's no crime. So, all I have to do is get the evidence and I'm home free. I'd rather have had it *and* Davenport Hills, but you wouldn't fall in love with me," he said sadly. "It's your fault, Ash. I'll just have to take the evidence and live without you." I struggled to remember what he was talking about. Oh, yes . . . *The canisters. The reports. Charles Whitmore's murder.*

His feet landed on the bottom rung. Bump bump. A soft impact, both feet landing on the same step before continuing to the next. Favoring his bad leg. "You interrupted our search by leaving that message, coming home from work that night. Your fault we were driving too fast. Your fault we crashed and Margie died. And you found my briefcase during the accident. You must have taken it to the hospital. It's the only thing that makes sense. After you had it, the few files I discovered when Margie and I searched Jack's office were missing."

Briefcase? What briefcase? I tried to follow his words, to make sense of them. All I could understand was the bump bump, bump bump, bump bump. Like the slow beating of a heart as he climbed the ladder. His head was just visible, rising above the opening to the loft. And beside his head, the dark shape of a gun barrel held in one hand.

I located the light without really looking at it. Protecting my eyes and the night vision I would need. And I slung the baling hook. It whirred and the barn went dark; tinkling glass and the soft thump of the hook as it landed. A thrill of exhilaration shot through me, twinned with the pain. He cursed into the darkness, his tone as foul as his words.

"Son of a bitch," he growled as he moved in the black barn. "Ash, you've had warnings. If I don't get the evidence back, then I have to be sure no one else has access to it either."

And then I understood what he had said earlier, about the accident being my fault. About my call interrupting his and Margie's search of Jack's office. Alan had been in Jack's office the night of the accident, searching for the evidence in the safe. Evidence he couldn't get at. And I had never put the accident together with the search. I had never let it make sense.

Silence stretched between us. I reached down the wall, using the time I had bought, stretching lower. Lower. Levered my body out over the hole above the tack room and stretched down again, clawing splinters from the wall. Searching for the smooth wood stock or the cool metal of barrel. Nothing. Nothing. I couldn't find it. I couldn't reach it.

"I have no choice, Ash!" His voice was low, coarse. "If you don't give it back, then I have to make sure you can't use it. Do you understand, Ash?"

You'll kill me. I'm not stupid, I thought, as I clawed further down the wall, gasping with the pain of my weight against the gunshot wound. *Just lonely.* The thought came out of nowhere. It was loneliness that had driven me here, to die in a hayloft over Mabel's stall. I sobbed aloud.

"Ah, Ash." The gentleness was back in his voice. "Let me help you. You're bleeding. I can feel it all over the ladder."

A splinter jabbed deep, thrusting up under my nail. I couldn't reach the shotgun. I couldn't. Carefully I pulled myself back up to the floor of the loft. I couldn't risk dropping down into the tack room. The pain in my thigh was spreading now, a damp, moist pain that moved from down my leg and up into my torso. A liquefied agony, burning with each heartbeat.

Bump bump. Bump bump. The sound of hay shuffling. He was in the loft.

If I dropped down into the tack room, I'd have to shoot my way past the lock. Hadn't I thought that once before? And meantime Alan would have every chance to shoot me from the loft. He could find me, even in the dark from the muzzle flash of the shotgun. . . . My two shells against his several.

Unless I could find a weapon other than the shotgun.

The plastic corner of the box storing Annie Oakley's old corrective shoes stabbed again. Alan moved slowly. I reached back, touching the rusted metal snarled together in the bottom. How many? Six pair? Seven? Two years worth. "Ash?"

I answered with a horseshoe, tossed Frisbee fashion. It landed harmlessly on a bale of hay. I tossed another and another, hearing them land with near silence or with a hollow clatter on the loft floor. I never hit him. But it slowed him down. He made no noise during the barrage of shoes. But stayed in one place, probably tucked behind a stack of hay. And the shoes, so few, were gone. I wasn't thinking. I'd have done better to toss the horseshoes at the light and use the baling hook on him. Nothing like hindsight to figure out how to keep myself alive. I dropped back to the straw, throat burning with tears, my cheek on my hand against the floor, my palm resting on wood. Rounded and satiny. *The way a handle felt after years of use.* Following the shape, I searched for the end.

"Ash." He sounded irritated again. Like someone who had just dodged a boxful of horseshoes. I breathed in the dark, hay dust filling my mouth and nostrils. "Come on. I'm gonna' win in the end. We both know that. I told you once that I always win. Always. Remember? We were at the turkey-shoot."

My fingers slid down the handle. Farther down. Touched the shaped metal implement. Traced the tines down to their multiple sharp points. Pitchfork.

"I stood a chance of coming in second, right? Or tied with that redneck?" Alan's voice was cajoling, insulting, his feet moving slowly in the loose hay. If he had been looking up when I threw the baling hook, then he knew where I was.

"That guy, King. He *knew* he was gonna' win, remember sweetheart?"

I lifted myself up and sat in the hay. My fingers gripping, lifting the pitchfork. Turning it.

"But he never came back from a trip to his truck. And I won. That was my doing, Ash. I made sure he wouldn't return to the turkey-shoot." He sounded amused. Infinitely confident.

His voice was closer. I pushed myself to my right knee. And then to my feet, my body bent forward in the dark, fighting for breath. The pain was growing. The burger I ate on the road burbled hot in my stomach, sour and rancid. Shivers gripped me, pulling me into a tight ball. Trying to force me into a fetal position. I fought the contracting muscles, raised myself up higher.

"And you were so happy, remember? That I won? Well, I always win. Always."

I found him, finally, as my eyes adjusted to the night. A pale shadow moving in shadows.

"And I have to win, now, Ash. All those questions you've been asking, all the polite queries from that nigger lawyer of yours, have my partners sweating. They're not happy people right now. Not happy at all."

His partners? Jerel Taylor? Jerel didn't need DavInc. Something in Alan's words fell wrongly on my ears but there was no time to question it.

"So, I have to find the reports and the files and the metal canisters, Ashlee. You can understand that."

The openings in the hayloft floor were lined up exactly. A short row of them. One behind my heel. And another about . . . there. "Your partners . . . Jerel?" I asked, stalling again.

Alan moved closer, searching for me in the night, my clothes blending in the shadows. Closer, a step in line with the opening through which we tossed hay to the horses below. Another. Talking all the while. "No, Ash. Jerel's just my employer. The Beck's are my business partners, have been for years. But you don't need to know all that Ash. You just need to give me the evidence. I know you have it, Ash. I searched the house and your cars and even this stinking barn. I've looked everywhere. And Monica looked again the night we 'robbed' the house. So, it must be in the safe. Good safe crackers are hard to find, did you know that?" he asked conversationally. "Most of them are in jail or working for themselves. And it's practically impossible to open your safe, Ash. That's where it all is, isn't it? In the safe?"

I wavered, the barn floor seeming to tilt beneath me. *My Monica? That Beck?* I gripped the pitchfork handle.

He stepped in line with the hay drop. A dull floating shadow.

I lunged. And fell forward. Falling from my right leg to my left. Shoving the pitchfork before me. Hard.

A soft "Ooaahfnn," sounded, and my own scream as the pain shot up my leg. A savage sizzle of pure agony.

I fell forward to the hay bales. Alan fell back. Pushed by the tines of the fork, low down on his stomach. Piercing. Quick tear of cloth and the almost rubbery tear of flesh beneath. His feet scrabbling on the wood flooring. Hollow thumps. The wrench of the pitchfork jerked from my grip. The exquisite pain as I landed. Burning up and through me like a brand, searing my flesh to the bone.

Screams. The sound of gagging. Mine? His?

And the slow, silent swish of air as he fell. Landed. An echo of dead weight on wood. A dull, reverberating sound. The horses went crazy. Kicking, screaming. Beating against the wooden walls. And the higher scream of pain as one horse injured herself.

I lay there. Lost my supper in the hay. Retched for a while for good measure. My body rested on the bales, a foot or so off the ground.

And when the horses quieted, long minutes later, I eased up. My hand, pushing on the stiff hay, encountered the rounded, cool plastic of Alan's gun butt. He'd dropped it. Clutching at the pitchfork. Trying to throw it off. Or pull it out. I slid the gun into my shirt neckline and it slid to my waistband, warm against my skin. I half-remembered to worry about the safety.

I moved to the hay drop and looked down at Mabel. She was blowing, snorting, pawing at a darker shadow in the shadows of her stall. A gleam of moonlight touched the blond of Alan's hair. He was on the floor of the stall, unmoving and silent.

I made it to the ladder and down to the floor. Made it up the path to the house for the keys and back to the vehicles. There I rested. Cool night breezes had sprung up, soothing the sweat on my body. Chilling me in the humid heat.

The moon had risen high. Still bright. The shadows that had striped the lawn were almost gone. No longer dark slivers of blackness, they were pools beneath the trees, beneath the cars, piled against the house like heaps on the shrubbery. Hunched. Waiting.

Eventually I opened the back of the Jeep and reached inside for the red jump kit of Rescue Squad supplies strapped to the side support. Found, by feel and moonlight, the bandages, tape, scissors and Betadine. Dropped them all down the front of my T-shirt where they jumbled against the waistband of my jeans and the gun.

After a second short rest—during which the shadows began to lengthen again and the owls began to call—I opened the Volvo door and dropped the phone down my shirt front as well.

I was inordinately pleased that I was still thinking well enough to remember the phone. I left the 9mm in the glove box. "See, Jack? I didn't have to use a gun," I whispered. And I laughed, the cackles crazy. I was shocky. Shaking and short winded. I needed help, fast.

The house looked oddly unchanged, normal and unimpressive. The air was still and unmoving, as if I had left it long ago. I limped inside. There was blood in the hallway and smeared along a wall where Alan had braced himself. Cut by broken glass. The blood-red color was drying out to a rusty brown. How long had I been in the barn?

There was no blood in the kitchen. It was bright with the light Alan had switched on when I invited him in.

I fell into the chair. Retching again. Shivering uncontrollably. My fingers were foreign-looking in the sharp light. Thin, as if they baked of moisture. White with blood loss. Gray-tinged with oxygen deprivation. Deeply ground with blood. The night Jack died my hands had looked like this. Interesting thought. Oxygen deprivation. I was in shock. Okay. But what was I supposed to do now? The blankets were in the other room and I knew I couldn't make it. Not now. I rested my head on my arms on the table.

The shakes passed, long minutes later. And as the shivers subsided, the pain also lessened. A long moment of . . . almost . . . peace followed. A moment when my leg ached only intermittently, rhythmically, with the throb of my heart. Between beats was icy ease. I raised my head from the table. Pulled out the hem of my T-shirt. Tugging it slowly from the waistband of my jeans. Collected the jumble of bandages and tape, scissors and phone on my bloody lap. Set them on the table. The sound of them landing on the surface was tinny and keen, my ears picking up the tenor note and missing the bass. I didn't think that was a good sign.

Alan's gun was among the stuff on the table. Which was really stupid. I didn't remember putting it down inside my shirt. It could have gone off. I could have shot myself. Which struck me suddenly as hilarious. I laughed. An agonized sound like a stranger's panicked whine. When it subsided, I looked down.

The bleeding was pretty bad. My jeans were soaked. Both legs. There was a puddle on the floor beneath my chair about the size of a dinner plate. A smaller one at my ankle. My toes were creased with dried blood and traced with fresh. One foot was black with bruising beneath the bright and rusty red.

Up high on my thigh, blood welled, thick and bright. Carefully I applied pressure to the wound and slightly above it. Blood welled out between my fingers. The pain returned with sharp heat, dimming the light in the room. But I didn't have time to pass out. And again I laughed. The crazed sound bounced back from the walls.

I fumbled with the phone. Opened it with hands slick and nearly numb. Dialed 911.

The click as help answered. "Nine-one-one. What is the nature of your emergency?"

"I need . . ." My voice was dry and sticky. I cleared it and tried again. "I need help."

"What's your emergency?"

So precise. So calm and professional. No wasted words. The tone should have restored me. Should have brought all my training to the fore. Instead my hands started shaking again and I wanted to cry. Pain throbbed. Arching up my leg and down. Twisting my calf muscle into tortured knots of pain. "Hello. Can you tell me what your emergency is?"

"I've been shot."

"Can you give me your location?" A man's voice. Henry. Henry Davis. I had helped train him. Good looking kid. Going to college on a tennis scholarship. "I need your location, Ma'am. You're calling from a cell phone and I don't—"

"It's the old Chadwick Farm, Henry. Down to Felix's Texaco." I was whispering, the sound of my breath like a wind in my ears. But I was so accustomed to giving directions I could do it in my sleep. "Right on Mount Zion Church Road and left into Chadwick Acres. Right onto Chadwick Farm Road." I licked my cracked lips. They tasted salty. My tongue was dry. Swollen.

"I've lost about two pints of blood. Maybe three. And you better send the cops, too."

"Ashlee? Is this Ashlee Davenport?" When I didn't answer he asked again "Ash?"

I licked my lips again. "Yeah. Ash. 'ss me."

"Are you at home?"

"Yeah. Home."

"Ash, where on your body are you shot?"

"Left leg. About four inches distal from the hip. I have entrance and exit wounds on the outer portion of . . . maybe the vastis lateralis." A strange calm settled on me. A peculiar comfort derived from the detached terminology of my profession and the familiar voice on the other end of the line. "I have—" I broke off. Focused on a form standing in the doorway. Bleeding. Clothes torn. Faint stench of feces. The face of a dead man, pale, bloodied. Bruised and torn.

Alan wavered, holding the pitchfork in his left hand. He was bloody and trampled. But then he had fallen into Mabel's stall, hadn't he? I stretched my lips up over dry, rough teeth, grinning, though my face felt strange, muscles stiff. Mabel didn't like men. The skin on the left side of Alan's face was gone. Ripped away in a wide swathe as if it had been pounded off. He took a step into the room.

A wash of terror flooded through me. I set the phone down. Gently. Henry's voice was a weak rattle from the tabletop. The terror settled out. Slipped away. I looked at the things on the table. My hand moved from the phone, shaking but careful. I was being very careful tonight, yet I'd managed to get myself shot. A weird crazy sound gurgled in my throat. I picked up the gun. Rested the weight of it on the table.

Blood on my hands made me clumsy and the gun slick. I retched. Swallowed down the taste of bile and acid. A fresh, burning tang, overpowering the taste of old blood and vomit. Everything was moving so slowly. Even the tilting room. Righting itself slowly and tilting again. I was amazed, remotely, that the dishes stayed in place in the cabinets. I blinked.

Alan's eyes glittered, a dull menace. The holes across his lower abdomen were evenly placed, two in the right quadrant. Two in the left. A neat row of them. There was little bleeding. Just the scent of feces to tell me that I had punctured his intestines. Torn something inside. The blood came from his cut hand and his torn face. "Remember, Ash. I never lose."

He came at me. Moving slowly as if he plowed through thick oil. Turning the pitchfork in his hands. So slowly. Stumbling. Slipping in my blood. His feet leaving red smears. The bloody tines lifted toward me. The room tilted again. A faint sensation of falling.

I fired the gun. And though I knew I couldn't have, I seemed to see the round leave the barrel. Travel through the air in slow, slow motion. And enter his body. Just below the sternum. Mid-center.

I hit the floor. The gun went off again. The shot going wild. I landed on my bad leg. The pain in the joint shot out, lightning hot, jagged. Darkness pulled me under. A slow-moving cloud of blackness, like the moon shadows outside. I wondered which would reach me first. The pain or the darkness. Before either claimed me, I saw him fall.

He landed in a long graceful tumble. Bounced slightly on the bloody floor. Settled gently, his eyes on mine.

The pitchfork fell beside him. A silent clatter. The sound buried beneath the gun blasts.

He writhed there, his face inches from mine. Curled into a tight ball. His eyes were bewildered. Confused. And though I couldn't hear the words, I could see his lips. Read their meaning.

"I lost. I . . . I lost."

And as if we were conversing about the weather or the symphony or a new exhibit at the museum, I nodded. My cheek sliding through my blood on the floor tiles. A stately nod. Almost regal. And I watched him die.

CHAPTER EIGHTEEN

I didn't remember passing out. For that matter, I didn't remember coming to. I was just suddenly aware that there were at least a hundred people in my kitchen, all shouting at the top of their lungs, tramping blood and red mud all over my once-clean kitchen floor and generally making a mess of things.

The kitchen was still tilted, the floor and walls rising on one side and falling on the other. Yet, my dishes and pots didn't roll out of the cabinets and shelves and slam to the floor.

My next insight was pain. Waves and waves of pain up my left leg; pain crawling like angry snakes beneath my skin, fangs embedded, poison spreading. I was sure I screamed, yet the sound came out a puny moan. Someone rolled me over. Bret McDermott and Mick Ethridge knelt to either side; Mick applied pressure to my leg, Bret checked my pupils, pulse, respiration.

"Snakes," I whispered. Nausea welled in me like a strong tide. The room seemed to darken and remain that way a moment before slowly growing light again.

Bret smiled down at me. "It's okay, Ashlee. We're here."

The world righted again in a sickening lurch as I remembered. "Alan. . . ."

"He's dead, Ash," Bret said gently.

"No shit, Ashlee. You blew the fu— ah, you blew him away."

I focused on Alan, face down on the floor, a pitchfork beside him. Nana stood over him, shaking her head. "I really liked that boy," she said, sounding confused.

"Dantucket. Course you liked him, you ol' fool. He jist as charmin' as that weasel Tom Hamilton you married oncet. I done tol' you, you ain't never been a decent judge of character. You never be marryin' him the first place if you listen to me."

"Shut up Moses."

"Humph."

I smiled and pushed against the floor with my elbows until Bret got the idea and propped me up. I was weak, but at least the room stayed level, and the urge to vomit faded. *What was Bret doing here?* And then that thought faded too.

Aunt Mosetta was sitting in a chair, wearing fuzzy red slippers and a purple chenille robe. Her hair was up in curlers, the pink foam partially hidden by a turquoise western-style bandanna. Nana was in jeans ripped up the side, her cast bright white against the blood. A plain white cotton nightgown peeked out beneath her sweatshirt and her crutches rested inches from Alan. A sheriff's deputy asked her to wait outside, adding that this was a crime scene. Nana didn't move. She was in her rockslide mode, her face set and hard, determined as the most stubborn mule.

The deputy, who was half Nana's size and looked too young to be allowed out this late, searched for moral support from his fellows. Finding none, he shrugged and moved around her. There were three deputies, four or five Rescue Squad members, two uniformed EMTs bringing in a stretcher and jump kits, and sirens in the distance. "Lovely. Just lovely," I sighed.

Someone called for the coroner. I could hear the voice and the codes being requested from dispatch, but couldn't locate the speaker. The room twirled around me and my stomach heaved threateningly.

Macon and Wicked stood to one side, Wicked with a digital video camera, the little red light steady as he filmed the action. Wicked would upload the footage to a secure link. The police would try to confiscate it if I was charged with a crime, but at least the record would exist.

Charged with a crime. The thought slithered into my mind with a dry, scaly sound.

I had killed a man.

I closed my eyes.

I had invited a guest into my home and then killed him. Mother would be mortified, I thought stupidly. What a dreadful lapse of manners. My nausea increased and subsided, moving through me like ocean waves.

Bret pushed me gently back to the floor and wrapped a tourniquet around my arm. I started shivering.

"Bret McDermott, my granddaughter's cold."

"Yes, ma'am, I know, but—"

"Well, warm up one of those blankets in the microwave and wrap her up in it," Nana said.

"I'll do it," Mick said softly, exchanging a glance with Bret. Family members who interfered with lifesaving activities were the bane of emergency workers everywhere, but no one in his right mind would disagree with my Nana.

A uniformed EMT took his place. "You guys got here quick," he said.

"Heard it on the scanner," Mick said, from somewhere out of sight. "Recognized the address. I just live a couple miles up the road. And Ash is an old buddy, right, Ash?"

Old buddy?

A quick stabbing pain plunged into my left hand. "Ouch!"

"Sorry, Ash."

"BP's eighty over sixty. A little low."

"I usually run one-o-five over seventy," I said. It all seemed so normal, I thought. So medically correct. And only feet away lay Alan Mathison, dead. I had killed him.

"Ash."

I looked up. It was Wicked, without his camera, bending over me. "It wasn't Senator Waldrop," I said, in an instant of clear and coherent thought. "But he said he worked with Monica. So . . . So . . . Jerel Taylor is . . . I mean . . ." I went blank. What had I been saying? My shivering worsened. It was bewildering. The voices rose and dropped, a babble of confusion. Individual words picked out of the chaos around me only made the confusion worse.

". . . thirty eight. . . ."

". . . no exit wound. . . ."

". . . three chambers empty. . . ."

". . . same weapon . . . ?"

The words flowed in an irregular rhythm, rough and uncertain, like a car engine in need of a tune-up. The people moved in similar fashion, jerky and coarse.

"Jerel Taylor?" Wicked asked.

"Jerel?" I repeated. I shook my head, the threads of the conversation coming back to me. "I don't . . . No. Monica. And Alan. He said something about his briefcase. And a file. Ouch!" I yelped again, trying to pull my right hand away. A second IV needle was being inserted there. I had forgotten how badly an eighteen gauge Jelco could hurt. A hot blanket was wrapped around me, the heat a blessing from heaven. I smiled at Mick, feeling the shivers instantly subside.

"A briefcase?" Bret sat down beside me on the kitchen floor. "Oh, Ashlee, it's my fault."

"How's that, Bret?" Wicked squatted beside him, glancing over at Sheriff Gaskin and the cops. They were busily collecting evidence in small plastic and paper bags, ignoring us entirely.

"At the accident last month. At Magnet Hole Creek, you remember?" Bret asked softly.

I watched the men nod. The motions were vaguely sickening. Someone tucked a second hot blanket around me. Precious sensation of heat.

Nana pulled a chair up and sat. Aunt Mosetta was talking to the cops, pointing out a bit of straw they had missed.

Bret took a deep breath, guilt a distinct emotion on his face. Why would Bret be guilty? I wondered. "Alan had a briefcase when we found him," he said. "Ash took it away and pushed it through the mud to us."

"Wait a minute, Bret McDermott. Are you saying that man over there is the same one Ashlee saved?" Nana asked. "Did anyone tell me that?"

"Yes, ma'am. Same guy." Bret took my hand, his eyes on mine. Under ordinary circumstances I didn't think I would like Bret holding my hand. His grip was too intimate and too tight, but his fingers were warm and brought a hint of life to my cold skin, so I said nothing. "The briefcase was open papers inside, files of government papers and permits for Davenport Hills."

"The missing files," Macon said softly, kneeling beside me. I looked like an indolent queen with her lazy sycophants relaxing around her. Someone moved my leg. I gasped and retched as pain spiraled up.

Bret talked through my agony as if he didn't know I was dying right here on my kitchen floor. "There was a Corps of Engineers report about Prosperity Creek. I have it in my car. It was strange finding it there, to say the least. Until you started seeing Alan, and then . . ." Bret's words trickled away. I wanted to roll to one side as nausea bubbled up inside me. I had no idea what Bret was talking about. All I wanted was for them all to go away and let me throw up in peace.

"I'm not following this, son," Nana said. "But I have a feeling that this discussion is for family and not the general public. You other boys step outside for a few minutes and give us some privacy," she ordered, her voice stern.

Yeah. Make them go away so I can be sick in peace.

"Mick, go on, now. Skedaddle. Ashlee'll be fine. Bret here can take care of her, and Wallace is on the way. Don't look at me like that, young man. Do what I say or I'll tell your mother you were disobedient to an elder."

"No shit, Mrs. Hamilton. It's policy that we can't leave a patient."

"You don't want your mouth washed out with soap, you'll *get* like I told you. And take these others with you," Nana snapped. I had a sudden vision of Mick bent over the sink, Nana's hand on the back of his neck and a bar of Ivory in his mouth. Nana would do it, too.

Mick puffed out an irritated breath. One of the EMTs was standing at an angle where I could finally see him. I struggled with his name until it came to me. Dusty Lowell, so named for the dusting of freckles across his skin.

"I need a smoke," he said wryly. "She's stable, I reckon, and some-one should check out our other patient. Bret, you holler if there's a change."

Surprisingly, they left, leaving only family around me. I wondered why they didn't put me on a stretcher first. The floor was cold and hard and my leg was a steady beat of pain like the constant pounding of a bass drum. But then, no one was paying that much attention to me. I was actually incidental to all this. Perhaps I always had been. An inci-dental victim in Jack's life and Jack's problems. Tears started at the corners of my eyes. Fresh waves of nausea rolled over me. I closed my eyes against the pain. Its rhythm was a steady thrum, matching the beat of my heart.

"Now. Start over. And make sense this time," Nana commanded. "Layman's terms, so I can follow."

"The report on top of the file was a Corps of Engineers report on the parcel of property that eventually became Davenport Hills. It said there were numerous watershed problems at Prosperity Creek. And yet I knew Jack had gotten an approval. Nothing made sense." Bret shook his head and squeezed my hand. His Citadel ring cut into my flesh. I tried to pull away, but had no strength against his grip. The pain in my hand helped take my mind off the nausea swirling through me, but did nothing to ease the pain in my leg. "I didn't know why this guy had DavInc's papers, but I didn't like the look of the report, considering the obvious drainage problems at Davenport Hills. I knew Jack, ah . . . walked a thin line in some of his business dealings, and it crossed my mind that, well, that there had been some—"

"You thought Ashlee's husband had broken the law, cheated on the Corps report," Nana said, her voice gruff.

"Yes. I was wrong. I have some contacts in Washington through Senator Waldrop. He made a few calls the day after the accident at Magnet Hole Creek and discovered the truth."

Nana rolled her eyes and muttered under her breath. It sounded something like, "Fools grow without watering."

Macon simply blinked and looked at me again. Senator Waldrop knew about the Corps report the day he came to the house. The day I stuffed cookies into his mouth. He had known I was in some kind of trouble about Davenport Hills even then. He had been trying to be nice.

"There was no problem with the report. A second inspector went over everything. Even came out to Davenport Hills to see about any problems. I guess Jack worked it all out somehow. I've been trying to get the report and the permits back to Ashlee for days, but I can't seem to get any time alone with her."

"The turkey-shoot," I said softly. "That's what you meant at the turkey-shoot when you said something about seeing me."

Bret smiled his professional banker's smile and met my eyes again. The smile changed, becoming almost forlorn. "Well, that too. But then I realized you were *seeing* Alan Mathison and thought you must have known that he had the permits and the report. I knew then that I wasn't doing you a favor to keep them. I've been trying to get them back to you ever since."

He put a heavy emphasis on the word seeing, turning it into dating by his tone. I shook my head, moving slowly to avoid worsening the nausea. "I wasn't dating him," I said.

"But you were having dinner with him at Miccah's, and the reports and the maps were scattered all over the table . . ." His voice trailed off. "You weren't trying to . . . I mean, you weren't—"

"No," I said. "I wasn't." The nausea rolled again, writhing up toward my mouth. I moaned softly in warning and put out a hand.

Someone walked across the kitchen floor, boots clomping. Macon leaned into my line of vision and whispered. "Alan made a pass at you. You said no. And he got violent. Keep it simple until we can talk. Understand?"

"Yes," I said, my voice slurred and my mouth was sickly wet. "But I'd give this left leg for a glass of ice water right now."

"Ashlee, are you ready to give a statement or would you rather wait until a doctor's had a chance to look you over?" Sheriff Gaskins asked from somewhere over my head.

I rolled to the side and vomited all over Bret McDermott's lap. At least he let go of my hand. The relief in my fingers was so great I couldn't even summon up a feeling of shame for ruining his good banker's black suit. "Jeeez Louise," Bret swore.

Nana made a "tisking" sound.

"Ashlee, you've always been more trouble than you're worth. Excuse me, Sheriff, Macon." Wallace nudged his way in beside me, a task much easier now than only moments before when I had made the area around me a less-than-prime location.

He opened his little black bag and pulled out a stethoscope. I had never seen him with the old fashioned doctor's bag, more accustomed to the black briefcase he took to work.

"I'm sick," I managed, as the world roiled around me. "And shot."

"So I see. You guys carry phenergan?" he called out to the EMTs standing in the door, big grins on their faces. "I need a BP, pulse, and let's transport ASAP."

I smiled up at Wallace as the world darkened again around me. I was passing out, but before the darkness took me I said, "My cousin. My hero." The last thing I remembered was the sound of Wallace's laughter. My next memory was the emergency room.

It was a madhouse as usual, with a full code going on in the next room and a drunk shooting victim in the bed next to me, two fingers of one hand blown off by a .45. A flimsy, floral curtain separated us, and though I couldn't see him, I could hear his fluent obscenities. It was the kind of language I had missed in the weeks of my leave of absence. From my vantage point on the stretcher—thank God for stretchers—I could see myriad tiny blood splatters in the weave of the privacy curtain. I could see the water spot in the ceiling panel over my head. It was new, still damp in the center and bowed down like it might fall through and land on me at any moment. Home Sweet Home.

Wallace had given me something for the pain and Dr. Rameris, a surgeon, was sewing something up in my leg. The specifics didn't seem important at the moment. I was bundled in warm blankets on a comfortable stretcher, the pain was a distant reality—all bleary around the edges and indistinct, like a dream monster, forgotten upon waking—and my nausea was eased, deposited all over Bret's lap. All things considered, I felt amazingly content. Until in the hallway, I saw C.C. Gaskin, and heard the sheriff volunteer to go to the morgue with the coroner. My hazy feeling of comfort vanished. Tears leaked from my eyes.

Macon appeared at my bedside. "Ash, are you awake?" my lawyer whispered.

"The sheriff's gone to see Alan, hasn't he?" My mouth had turned dry and sour, and my tongue felt like a moldy hunk of old shoe leather someone had stuffed between my teeth. I wiped my eyes.

"Weird as it seems, I think he's trying to give us some time to talk before he takes your statement. But we don't have long. Do you remember what happened?"

"Yes," I said. I licked my lips and tasted blood. I hoped it was mine. Fresh nausea sloshed through me.

"Good. Listen carefully. Thanks to Stinky Dixon's partial confession, here's what the sheriff thinks happened, and there's enough evidence in Alan's car to confirm if it matches your statement. Alan and Emory Beck had been business partners for years. They were conspiring to gain control of Davenport Hills. Alan was both romancing you and gathering information about the development. When you turned him down, and he had no way of getting his hands on the development, he snapped. Would that be about right?"

There was something wrong with the scenario Macon had just painted, but I couldn't think what it was. It had something to do with the soil samples in Jack's safe. And the man who had died, *Charles Whitmore*. And then the name penetrated.

"Emory. Monica's husband. He killed . . . helped kill Charles Whitmore?"

"Looks like it, Ash."

Emory Beck. Monica Schoenfuss Beck's husband was a murderer. Alan had said the Beck's were his business partners. Monica, who had called and called and sent cards and tried to take me to lunch and actually acted like a friend. Monica, who had been known in high school as Cat Woman. Monica, who had acted as if she had no idea who Alan Mathison was at the symphony so long ago. Who had batted her eyes at him, and drawn attention to her bountiful cleavage, and who had more than likely slept with him if her reputation was even half deserved.

Alan had given himself away the night of the concert, if I had even bothered to consider it. After my attack he had taken me up the back stairs to Monica's bedroom. I hadn't even known that there *were* back stairs until then. Had Monica planned for me to be attacked at the Patron's Party? Had she helped set it up? Or had she been Emory's dupe? I might never know. I wasn't certain I wanted to. I closed my eyes and turned away.

When I opened them again, Sheriff Gaskin was standing beside my bed. He gave a kindly smile as he bent over me. An investigator stood to the side with a less friendly expression on his face. I couldn't remember the investigator's name, but like so many of the details of this long night, it didn't seem important.

It was a frivolous observation, but the sheriff needed to clip his nose hair. It stuck out in long tangled masses from each nostril. I almost told him so, but the specter of my mother appeared in the doorway and my manners snapped back in place. "My baby!" the specter wailed.

"Oh my God," I moaned. "It's real."

My mother nearly knocked over the investigator and shoved the sheriff to the side. Babbling and shrieking, she bent over me, careful not to touch my bloody skin or my bloody clothes and stain her immaculate apparel. I tried to envision this surgically correct, melodramatic woman as the lively, carefree girl described by Reverend Perry. I couldn't.

Mama gave a pretty good imitation of concern until I felt a wrench of pain and moaned, rolling my head over the side of the rails. At that point, she decided to have her case of hysterics elsewhere, someplace where the audience wouldn't smear her new linen suit. As I watched her go, I felt sorry for her, for all the times she had missed out on being a mother over the years. And for the relationship we'd never had. I rolled back and the sheriff moved into my line of sight, his eyes following my mother. Her trim little backside and her long, lean legs did look enticing in the slim linen slacks. Liposuction, no doubt.

"You wanted a statement," I said. My voice was weak and breathy. I had never been given the ice water I asked for. I could envision the tall glass, covered with condensation, the droplets sliding slowly down the side of the glass.

C.C. turned back, his "good cop" expression firmly in place. "If you're up to it, Ashlee."

"You realize my client is heavily sedated, Sheriff, and she may not be entirely lucid nor of sound mind," Macon said. He had come up on the other side and the sheriff jumped. He hadn't known Macon was there. C.C. was trying to pull a fast one and question me outside the presence of my lawyer. Sneaky old bastard. "I will not have her badgered in this condition," Macon said.

Neither lucid nor of sound mind, I thought. That's me. I haven't been lucid or of sound mind since Jack died. I was growing maudlin with the painkillers, and took a deep breath against threatening tears.

"I understand that Mrs. Davenport is in no condition to make a *formal* statement. That can be handled at a later date, tomorrow or the next day at the Law Enforcement Center or at her house whichever is her preference." As the sheriff spoke, the scowling investigator stepped away. It wasn't a good time to play good cop-bad cop. Not in front of a lawyer. "However, there are a few questions I need answered tonight."

Macon watched the investigator step into the hallway, his face troubled, but I could handle C.C. Just like my Nana could. "Connie Carol."

The sheriff's mouth turned down in irritation. Every man has a weakness. C.C.'s female names were his. To C.C., being called Connie Carol was on par with being called a girl, or a pig.

"Connie my friend, I intend to cooperate to the fullest. You want to know why Alan Mathison was at my house tonight, right?" C.C. nodded and pulled out a notebook.

"He kissed me the night of the turkey-shoot." I licked my lips. They were still bloody. And the pain was suddenly no longer a bleary vision hovering at the edges of my mind. Now it was closer, sharper, crisper, as if it moved toward me with steady steps.

"I told him no. I told him I wasn't ready for anything . . . like that. Tonight he came back. Got a little too . . ." I searched for a word that Nana might have used; settled on one my mother might have used instead. "familiar. And when I told him no again, he got angry, started shouting about the business and Davenport Hills." Wasn't that the story Macon wanted me to tell? And it was the truth, as far as I went with it.

The shivers, which had left me on the kitchen floor, were back. Little tremors along my spine, warning signs of the misery to come, like the specter of pain I could feel stirring in my leg. Numbness and pain, mingling in my icy limb. The surgeon stepped into the room, checked the monitor, patted my leg and left. The pat of his hand was a dull half-pain. Why were people always patting me, as if I needed soothing like a skittish filly or a nervous dog?

"I thought he was going to hurt me," I whispered. Again, the truth. What was it Macon hadn't wanted me to tell? "I ran for the office. The gun cabinet. The phone."

I stopped. Elwyn's note said the phones were out. Had that meant the office phones as well? What if I had slammed the office door and turned the little latch? It was scant protection, but it might have bought me the time to dial 911. I shook my head, fighting the return of nausea and tears. "He followed me. I . . . I panicked, ran for the barn. But he shot me." Tears rolled down my face. Would there have been time to use the office phone? Had it worked? Had I killed Alan Mathison when I could have called for help instead?

"I made it up to the loft, but he followed me. He was threatening me. Talking about how he would get what he wanted one way or another."

My words made it sound like Alan wanted sex, or DavInc, or both. What he had wanted was my files, the soil samples. The scrap of letter Macon had hidden away. Yes. That was what Macon didn't want me to say. Not until we had a chance to investigate more on our own.

Tears pooled on my dry lips. Salt and blood merged and melted. *Oh God. What had I done?* I looked up at Macon. I had to know.

"Was the office phone dead too? Could I have called for help?"

"All the lines were dead, Ash, so Wicked could run a complete check. He expected you to stay another night at the beach and come home in the morning. You couldn't have called for help. Wicked's blaming himself for the whole mess. So's Mama Moses." Macon smiled sadly. "I heard her tell him his nickname should be 'damn fool', not Wicked. Can't remember the last time I actually heard her use a four-letter word."

I lifted my hand to wipe my face. The IV taped there held my fingers stiff. Macon reached behind him for tissues and wiped my cheeks, dabbed my upper lip. The tissue came away bloody.

"What happened next, Mrs. Davenport?" C.C. asked.

Mrs. Davenport. Not Ashlee. The sheriff was taking notes, making this official. I needed to blow my nose. I sniffed. The pain was a dull thud in my veins, like the steady beat of a drum in an old Tarzan movie, a warning of danger. "He followed me up the ladder and I used the bailing hook to knock out the light and threw Annie Oakley's corrective shoes at him."

"Annie Oakley?"

"Annie Oakley is one of the horses at the barn. She stepped on something sharp and cut through her sensitive sole, bruising her coffin bone. So she had to wear corrective shoes until the cut and the bruising healed." I looked up at the sheriff. "Horses feet heal slowly, C.C. It took forever, and I had a small collection of shoes to throw, not that they did any good. Alan kept coming. And so I picked up a pitchfork and held it between us. But he kept on coming. I poked him in the abdomen." The words rushed out and stopped. I remembered the feel of steel tines passing through human flesh. Rubbery and soft all at once. Macon patted my cheeks again. My throat was so tight it hurt to speak. I couldn't swallow back the pain. *I killed a man.*

"And I pushed him back away from me. He fell through the hay drop into Mabel's stall. I thought he was dead," I sobbed once and my teeth started chattering.

"Ashlee's had enough, Sheriff. Can't the rest of this wait?"

I took Macon's hand with my taped fingers. The IV line wrapped around his wrist. "Let me finish," I said, through my tears and chattering.

"I found his gun in the dark and made it back to the Volvo. I got the phone and some supplies to bandage my leg." My words were staccato. Fast and fluid as my tears. "I went to the kitchen and called 911." I stopped again, my breath heaving. The ER was silent. I knew everyone within hearing distance was listening. Even the obnoxious drunk on the next stretcher was silent.

"Alan came through the door, carrying the pitchfork. I could see the holes where I'd stabbed him. And Mabel had kicked him pretty badly. He said he'd had enough and was going to kill me. I put down the phone and I shot him. And he's dead." I broke down. The pain in my leg was a livid, living, breathing entity, alive and devouring me whole. Shivers quaked through my body. I squeezed shut my eyes and sank my teeth into my lip. It was sore, and there was actually a tooth shaped hole in it that I could feel with my tongue. When had I bitten it?

"What the hell are you doing to my patient, Sheriff?" Wallace's voice. His timing always had been slow. "Anything you don't have now, you get some other time, some other place. She's too doped to be coherent, or hadn't you noticed? Anything she's said is—"

"Perfectly fine," Macon interrupted. The lopsided smile was in his voice. "She gave a complete statement. Remembered everything. In fact, I think the sheriff here could just type up her statement and get her to sign it like it is."

"Not quite. There is the matter of Emory Beck and his involvement in all this." I could hear the determination in C.C. Gaskin's voice. Like a bulldog with his teeth in a bone.

"I didn't know," I whispered. "I had no idea he was involved. If he wanted to buy the development, he could have just asked. I was thinking about sellin' anyway."

"Out," Wallace said. "Both of you. Out. I don't care who you are, my patient needs rest."

I opened my eyes, surprised to see Wallace pushing Macon with one arm and gesturing to the sheriff with the other. Neither man resisted, preceding my doctor from the room. My hero. I smiled through the tears and the pain.

"Ready for a little more painkiller?"

I nodded. "I don't know what you're giving me, but it's pretty good stuff. I see why people get hooked on it."

"Well enjoy it. It's your last shot."

"Torturer."

"I've been called worse. By you as I recall. Lynnie Bee? Anytime now."

"Got it, Dr. Chadwick," Lynnie Bee said.

"How do you like Macon's plan?" Wallace asked, his voice low, mouth close to my ear.

I opened my eyes, not even aware that I had closed them. "Which plan is that?" I whispered back. Macon was full of plans. Always had been. Like the time with the rock in the big pond. The time he beaned a redneck. I smiled at the memory.

"The plan to get you out of this core soil sample mess. He told Nana about it earlier, in case she had to handle it for you."

Earlier? Had I slept through something? And why would Macon tell Nana? Then I remembered. I had told Macon to talk to Nana in case her investment in Davenport Hills was involved. Lynnie Bee pushed clear fluid through my IV line. Almost before she finished, the mirage that was my demon pain began to fade. "How?" I asked, my voice going dreamy.

"Sell Davenport Hills and DavInc to Senator Waldrop's daughter." Wallace was grinning a smile full of devilment.

I had seen photographs of Elizabeth Anne Waldrop Cummings, an elegant woman, older than I, with upswept silver hair and lots of diamonds. Her husband was a blue blood. His ancestors had come over on the *Mayflower* or the *Santa Maria* or something. Some lineage my mother likely knew by heart. "Why would she want it?" I asked. The pain in my lip where I had bitten through the flesh was gone. My lips were numb, and my words came out slurred and slow.

"She doesn't. But the senator does. When he was in town last, he asked Bret McDermott to make inquiries about the matter. Called him from the dentist's chair from what I gather; something about chocolate chips and a damaged upper plate."

Aunt Mosetta would be pleased to discover that her cookies had helped to save the day. I sighed as the last of my pain floated out the door into the hallway. I knew it hadn't gone far and would return with a vengeance, but for now, I was pain free. I took a deep breath and let it go.

"Bret's been pouring his heart out to Macon and Wicked in the waiting room, between conversations with the sheriff and various police officials and running back to hold your hand. Speaking of which, I understand you did great with the sheriff."

I closed my eyes, blocking out the lights, which had a curious halo of glare around them. I hadn't noticed before that the light hurt my eyes. "What good would selling the company do me?" I asked Macon as Wallace stepped to my left side.

"First off, it would get you back here at the hospital where you belong instead of out tending to golf courses and business meetings," Wallace said. "Your replacement needs written instructions and cue cards to apply a Band-Aid."

"Second," Macon picked up the narrative, "the wetlands rulings have undergone some changes in the last ten years. You turn over the core soil samples and all the paperwork to the senator, and he has it reevaluated by today's standards. A few string pulling sessions later, and his daughter's a landholder. Simple."

I shook my head in self-imposed darkness. "If it was so simple, why didn't Jack do it?"

His voice gentle, Macon said, "Jack could have been waiting for the right moment to have the property reevaluated. Or he could have held onto the evidence and the profits both. I don't know what he was planning."

There were questions I had been dreading all evening, the only questions that really mattered to Jasmine's future. Could I protect my daughter from discovering that her father had been party to a murder? Could I protect our Jazzy Baby? I wanted to keep the truth from her. But what about Charles Whitmore's murderer? I looked from Macon to

Wallace. What truth did I owe the world? What sacrifice to justice? "Did Jack kelp kill Charles Whitmore?" I asked. "Or was he innocent of murder?"

"We don't know. We may never know. But I'll handle it, Ash."

"No. Let me handle it." Wicked's voice from the doorway. Subdued. Angry. I focused on his wicked smile. Wicked Owens knew a secret. "The cops all know Dixon was holding back on them. He knew more than he told." Wicked's voice changed. "He didn't mention Whitmore's murder, but he *did* tell all he knew about Alan Mathison and Emory Beck." There was delight in his voice, a sound like bliss. Wicked was enjoying himself.

"Are you telling me that the sheriff *knew* about Alan and the danger he posed to Ashlee, and yet he did nothing?" Wallace asked, his voice almost as derisive as Wicked's.

"The senior elected law enforcement official of Dawkins County allowed a dangerous man continued freedom, refusing to act quickly enough to protect Ashlee Davenport, a prominent citizen." Wicked placed a hand over his heart as he spoke.

"Oh, my," I murmured, closing my eyes. I was wrapped in a warm drugged space, cocooned all around with Chadwicks. *Family.* "Connie Carol is in trouble now." I remembered a recent fear that had enveloped me. Fear of being alone. Fear of isolation. Fear of the unknown once Jasmine left home for college. Foolish fears. I was a Chadwick; Chadwicks are never alone.

"Exactly," Wicked said. I could almost see his grin, lopsided and mischievous. "And believe me, Nana was pissed."

"Shame on you, Wicked Owens," I said. With my numb lips it came out as "Sham yu, Wick Ow." Wicked laughed. "Wash yu mou out wi' soap."

"Mama Moses already gave me absolution. She said—and I quote—'Wicked, chile, you fix this, you hear? You fix this and it all be fine fo' you. You mess this up and you deal wit' *me.*' So. I can say Nana's pissed with no fear of an oral cavity laundering," Wicked laughed. Wallace and Macon joined in.

"In fact Nana's so pissed, she cornered Sheriff Gaskin and reamed him out from both ends for putting you in danger. In front of God and everybody, including a reporter from the Dawkins Herald, who just happened to be standing there."

I smiled my drugged smile. "How convenient," I murmured. "And isn't it surprising that Wicked just happened to be around."

The men laughed knowingly.

This was my family. The Chadwicks. With them, I would never be alone.

EPILOGUE

It is now weeks later, and I can finally pass through the kitchen without averting my head from the place where Alan lay, dead, a bullet in his heart. I can finally enter the barn and climb into the hayloft without my pulse racing and my breath coming short. I can finally open a newspaper and read the front page without seeing my name and the Beck's prominently displayed in a story titled, SCANDAL. I can finally pick up the pieces and regain my life.

It isn't the life I had planned for myself, when, as a child, I looked to the future, a life with a loving husband and at least four rambunctious children. It isn't the life Jack and I had envisioned for ourselves when we first married, when we were caught in the throes of new passion. It is instead a life forever changed by the death of two men.

Although I have still not found the courage to contact Robyn, my one-time friend and Jack's lover, I have returned to church, and to teaching my Sunday School class of third graders. And I have even returned to prayer and the solace of my Bible, the Bible with an un-marked envelope containing a single strand of Jack's silver hair.

Reverend Perry has visited me. Together, we have walked in the pasture and watched the yearlings play, Big Dog loping his three-legged run before us. We have talked of forgiveness, and of my mother, and of my life on the farm. A life I have begun to plan for, to look forward to.

I am healing, both physically and emotionally. I am finding joy in the rising of the sun and the falling of summer rains and the song of birds outside my window. I have discovered a pleasure in Jack's horses, and a particular attachment to Jack's Resurrection, Mabel's colt. My life, so damaged by the deceit and infidelity of my husband, has found a new resurrection, a new beginning.

Senator Waldrop—or rather the senator's daughter's financial advisor—began negotiations to purchase DavInc and Davenport Hills the day after I shot Alan. Macon and Elizabeth Waldrop Cummings' lawyer are still playing coy with one another about details and specifics of the sale, but I figure it will go through. If so, I will retain silent partner status, but the headaches and worries of DavInc will not be mine. The relief I feel at giving up control is so great that I know there will be no regrets over the decision to sell. DavInc was Jack's love, not mine, and Jack was no longer here to give the company meaning or importance.

The Senator was also heading up a quiet investigation into the death of Charles Whitmore, the investigator who died just days after taking soil samples from Davenport Hills. The soil samples in the safe had been turned over to the senator's handpicked investigator, along with the scrap of letter and a transcript of Stinky Dixon's jailhouse interviews. Stinky himself has disappeared. Considering the length of time since Whitmore died, it would be difficult, if not impossible, to determine if his death was due to natural causes or was murder. With the death of Alan and Jack, it might be impossible to point a finger at the killer.

Macon and Wicked, however, had privately informed me of their conclusion that Alan and Stinky killed the investigator. I would never know how involved Jack had been in the cover-up. Jack's death had ripped away the veneer of gentility with which he had clothed himself. Yet, to the world, and to his daughter, he would always be innocent of murder. I had seen to that.

I am having supper with Nana and Aunt Mosetta tonight, just us three. An evening when Nana and I will talk of crops and the weather and practical things, and Aunt Mosetta will fill me with wonderful food and tales of Chadwick history. They have stood by me, these two strong women, as people talked and the press camped out on my lawn and the story of the widow with a gun made headlines on the evening news. Perhaps it took the horrible events of the last weeks for me to recognize the strength my Nana had proclaimed in me, to discover myself and the person I might someday become.

I don't know where I'll go from this point, I don't know what changes I might make in my life. I only know that the future is a wide-open space filled with possibilities and opportunities, and that nothing I might want to do or be is beyond me. I have a life to live.

Not as part of another person, wife, hostess, partner to a husband, but as myself. Ashlee Davenport. A Chadwick.

The End

About the Author

Under the pen names, Gary Hunter, Gwen Hunter, and Faith Hunter, the author writes action adventure, mysteries, thrillers, fantasy and urban fantasy. She currently has 21 books in print in 26 countries.

Along with eight other writers, Hunter participates in a writing forum called www.magicalwords.net, geared to helping writers of fantasy and other genres.

Hunter was born in Louisiana and was raised all over the south. She fell in love with reading in fifth grade, and loved SiFi, fantasy, thrillers, and gothic mystery, with a secret passion for romance novels. She decided to become a writer in high school, when a teacher told her she had talent. Now, she writes full-time and works in a hospital lab, (for the benefits) tries to keep house, and is a workaholic with a passion for travel, jewelry making, whitewater kayaking, and writing. She and her husband love to travel with their dogs in their RV to rivers all over the Southeast.

For more information please visit:
www.gwenhunter.com
www.faithhunter.net
www.magicalwords.net

CPSIA information can be obtained
at www.ICGtesting.com
Printed in the USA
FSHW011947110419
57186FS